CONTENTS

ACKNOWLEDGEMENTS

The fourteen illustrations by Luke Fildes have been reproduced from a set of the original six parts of *The Mystery of Edwin Drood* owned by Smith College, Northampton, Massachusetts. I am most grateful to the Mortimer Rare Book Room of the William Allen Neilsen Library for permission to reproduce these images. I am also much indebted to Karen V. Kulik, Associate Curator of Rare Books, for the invaluable assistance she extended as I completed the final stage of my work for this edition.

1812   *7 February* Charles John Huffam Dickens born at Portsmouth, where his father is a clerk in the Navy Pay Office. The eldest son in a family of eight, two of whom die in childhood.

1817   Family move to Chatham.

1822   Family move to London.

1824   Dickens's father in Marshalsea Debtors' Prison for three months. Dickens employed in a blacking warehouse, labelling bottles. Attends Wellington House Academy, a private school, 1824–7.

1827   Becomes a solicitor's clerk.

1832   Becomes a parliamentary reporter after mastering shorthand. In love with Maria Beadnell, 1830–33.

1833   First published story, 'A Dinner at Poplar Walk', in the *Monthly Magazine*. Further stories and sketches in this and other periodicals, 1834–5.

1834   Becomes reporter on the *Morning Chronicle*.

1835   Engaged to Catherine Hogarth, daughter of editor of the *Evening Chronicle*.

1836   *Sketches by Boz*, First and Second Series, published. Marries Catherine Hogarth. Meets John Forster, his literary adviser and future biographer.

1837   *The Pickwick Papers* published in one volume (issued in monthly parts, 1836–7). Birth of a son, the first of ten children. Death of Mary Hogarth, Dickens's sister-in-law. Edits *Bentley's Miscellany*, 1837–9.

1838   *Oliver Twist* published in three volumes (serialized monthly in *Bentley's Miscellany*, 1837–9). Visits Yorkshire schools of the Dotheboys type.

1839   *Nicholas Nickleby* published in one volume (issued in monthly parts, 1838–9).

1841   Declines invitation to stand for Parliament. *The Old Curiosity Shop* and *Barnaby Rudge* published in separate volumes after appearing in weekly numbers in *Master Humphrey's Clock*, 1840–41. Public dinner in his honour at Edinburgh.

1842   *January–June* First visit to North America, described in *American Notes*, two volumes.

1843   *December A Christmas Carol* appears.

1844   *Martin Chuzzlewit* published in one volume (issued in monthly parts, 1843–4). Dickens and family leave for Italy, Switzerland and France. Dickens returns to London briefly to read *The Chimes* to friends before its publication in December.

1845   Dickens and family return from Italy. *The Cricket on the Hearth* published at Christmas. Writes autobiographical fragment, ?1845–6, not published until included in Forster's *Life* (three volumes, 1872–4).

1846   Becomes first editor of the *Daily News* but resigns after seventeen issues. *Pictures from Italy* published. Dickens and family in Switzerland and Paris. *The Battle of Life* published at Christmas.

1847   Returns to London. Helps Miss Burdett Coutts to set up, and later to run, a 'Home for Homeless Women'.

1848   *Dombey and Son* published in one volume (issued in monthly parts, 1846–8). Organizes and acts in charity performances of *The Merry Wives of Windsor* and *Every Man in His Humour* in London and elsewhere. *The Haunted Man* published at Christmas.

1850   *Household Words*, a weekly journal 'Conducted by Charles Dickens', begins in March and continues until 1859. Dickens makes a speech at first meeting of Metropolitan Sanitary Association. *David Copperfield* published in one volume (issued in monthly parts, 1849–50).

1851   Death of Dickens's father. Further theatrical activities in aid of the Guild of Literature and Art, including a performance before Queen Victoria. *A Child's History of England* appears at intervals in *Household Words*, published in three volumes (1852, 1853, 1854).

1853   *Bleak House* published in one volume (issued in monthly parts,

1852–3). Dickens gives first public readings (from *A Christmas Carol*).

1854   Visits Preston, Lancashire, to observe industrial unrest. *Hard Times* appears weekly in *Household Words* and is published in book form.

1855   Speech in support of the Administrative Reform Association.

1856   Dickens buys Gad's Hill Place, near Rochester.

1857   *Little Dorrit* published in one volume (issued in monthly parts, 1855–7). Dickens acts in Wilkie Collins's melodrama *The Frozen Deep* and falls in love with the young actress Ellen Ternan. *The Lazy Tour of Two Idle Apprentices*, written jointly with Wilkie Collins about a holiday in Cumberland, appears in *Household Words*.

1858   Publishes *Reprinted Pieces* (articles from *Household Words*). Separation from his wife followed by statement in *Household Words*. Dickens's household now largely run by his sister-in-law Georgina.

1859   *All the Year Round*, a weekly journal again 'Conducted by Charles Dickens', begins. *A Tale of Two Cities*, serialized both in *All the Year Round* and in monthly parts, appears in one volume.

1860   Dickens sells London house and moves family to Gad's Hill.

1861   *Great Expectations* published in three volumes after appearing weekly in *All the Year Round* (1860–61). *The Uncommercial Traveller* (papers from *All the Year Round*) appears; expanded edition, 1868. Further public readings, 1861–3.

1863   Death of Dickens's mother, and of his son Walter (in India). Reconciled with Thackeray, with whom he had quarrelled, shortly before the latter's death. Publishes 'Mrs Lirriper's Lodgings' in Christmas number of *All the Year Round*.

1865   *Our Mutual Friend* published in two volumes (issued in monthly parts, 1864–5). Dickens severely shocked after a train accident when returning from France with Ellen Ternan and her mother.

1866   Begins another series of readings. Takes a house for Ellen at Slough. 'Mugby Junction' appears in Christmas number of *All the Year Round*.

1867   Moves Ellen to Peckham. Second journey to America. Gives readings in Boston, New York, Washington and elsewhere, despite increasing ill-health. 'George Silverman's Explanation' appears in *Atlantic Monthly* (then in *All the Year Round*, 1868).

1868   Returns to England. Readings now include the sensational 'Sikes and Nancy' from *Oliver Twist*; Dickens's health further undermined.

1870   Farewell readings in London. *The Mystery of Edwin Drood* issued in six monthly parts, intended to be completed in twelve. *9 June* Dies, after collapse at Gad's Hill, aged fifty-eight. Buried in Westminster Abbey.

Stephen Wall, 1995

Raymond Chandler's definition of perfection in novels dealing with a puzzling crime deftly explains some of the appeal of Dickens's unfinished *Mystery of Edwin Drood* (April to September 1870). 'The ideal mystery', wrote the creator of Philip Marlowe, 'was one you would read if the end was missing.'[1] Incompleteness in the case of *Edwin Drood* extends well beyond any conventional sense of 'end' to include the work's entire second half. Had Dickens lived to finish his fifteenth novel, he would have completed a work critics would probably rank among his major achievements. In its partial state, the novel exercises for many an even greater allure on account of that which is not there.

The publisher's agreement Dickens signed in August 1869 specified a novel – subsequently called *The Mystery of Edwin Drood* – in twelve monthly parts to begin in April 1870. Of these Dickens lived to contribute six and saw through the press the instalments for April, May and June. Each consisted of thirty-two pages and two illustrations. The remaining material completed before he died on 9 June 1870 followed in three subsequent numbers. These appeared in July, August and September, together with the simultaneous publication of the unfinished work in a single volume on 31 August 1870.

The consequences of this incompleteness strike everyone who has succumbed to the power of *The Mystery of Edwin Drood*. As a composition built around a presumed crime – the murder of a nephew by his uncle – Dickens entices us with a proven fictional formula. Readers naturally expect that murder will out and that justice will be done. But instead of participating in this process, imbrued, like Mr Wopsle in *Great Expectations* (1860–61), 'in blood to the eyebrows' (ch. 18), we face a challenge Dickens did not foresee. How might we offer from the available evidence a plausible answer to the inevitable question: what happened? What clues to the 'mystery' exist? Working from both the text and from other material relevant to the half-finished novel, how might readers turned detective use their intelligence to determine whether or not Edwin Drood is dead? Committed to the rational principle that truth in crime fiction is verifiable, that a sequence of events can be reconstructed to explain what happened, what is the best course of action for those intent on resolving John Jasper's innocence or guilt?

Some comments by Dickens in an essay about London's 'Detective Police' published in 1850 offer an instructive lesson to anyone who ventures answers to these questions. This 'Detective Force', a consequence of the Metropolitan Police Act of 1829, was a small, well-chosen body of men 'engaged in the service of the public' from the mid-1840s onwards. Unlike their distant predecessors, the old Bow Street Runners, whom Pip later ridicules in *Great Expectations* for trying to fit the circumstances of a crime to 'the ideas, instead of trying to extract ideas from the circumstances' (ch. 16), members of this new confederation proceeded differently. Meeting one evening in 1850 with almost 'the whole Detective Force from Scotland Yard' in the office of *Household Words*, Dickens was impressed. Seven in number, the two officers and five sergeants were described as calm and steady. They sat in a 'semi-circle' at a little distance from a round table and faced 'the editorial sofa', occupied by Dickens. 'Every man of them, in a glance, immediately takes an inventory of the furniture and an accurate sketch of the editorial presence.' Careful observers, slow, methodical workers, they were famous 'for pursuing steadily the inductive process', for working from small beginnings until, finally, each bagged his man.[2]

Students of *The Mystery of Edwin Drood* will do well to note Dickens's approval of 'the inductive process'. They are also well advised to follow a similar procedure when they discuss the novel. For to work from 'small beginnings' requires patiently relating evidence from external sources to the incomplete text in an attempt to confirm Dickens's intentions. Testimony from outside the text includes the written and recorded comments of the illustrators who corroborated with Dickens, the words of family members and others close to the novelist, and memoranda and observations by the author himself.

Treated as a whole, moreover, these documents confirm Dickens's intentions as they evolved both in the period prior to the composition of the novel and during the months of writing spent before the publication of the first number in April 1870.

Our inquiry properly begins in the summer of 1869 and extends through the ensuing months of the composition of *The Mystery of Edwin Drood* and its serial publication until Dickens's death the following June. In the interests of precision, however, we must acknowledge that one thread of the work pre-dates its inception and part publication by almost a decade. Accuracy in the case of this dating, one should note, is not absolute. But if we follow Fred Kaplan's dating of entry number 72 in Dickens's *Book of Memoranda*, the earliest idea for the plot of *Edwin Drood* appears to have been conceived 'no earlier than May 1857 and no later than Nov 1860'. The relevant entry reads as follows:

The idea of a story beginning in this; – two people – boy and girl, or very young – going apart from one another, pledged to be married after many years – at the end of the book. The interest to arise out of the tracing of their separate ways, and the impossibility of telling what will be done with *that* impending Fate.[3]

John Forster, Dickens's first biographer, offered a later date for this notion, attributing the origin of what he terms Dickens's 'first fancy for the tale' to the middle of July 1869.[4] Then a month later, citing a letter Dickens addressed to him on 6 August 1869, Forster notes how Dickens laid aside 'the fancy' he had described earlier for 'a very curious and new idea'. Explained Dickens: the idea was not 'communicable . . . (or the interest of the book would be gone), but a very strong one, though difficult to work'.[5] Almost immediately afterwards, Forster learned the main details of the story, either from another letter, which no longer survives, or from Dickens's own lips. What remains therefore we must accept as Forster's summary or paraphrase from an unidentified yet evidently authentic source. In it we see an outline for the novel as definitive as the keel of a ship laid out in a dry dock. In the chapter 'Last Book', Forster provides this account:

The story . . . was to be that of the murder of a nephew by his uncle; the originality of which was to consist in the review of the murderer's career by himself at the close, when its temptations were to be dwelt upon as if, not he the culprit, but some other man, were tempted. The last chapters were to be written in the condemned cell, to which his wickedness, all elaborately elicited from him as if told of another, had brought him. Discovery by the murderer of the utter needlessness of the murder for its object, was to follow hard upon commission of the deed; but all discovery of the murderer was to be baffled till towards the close, when, by means of a gold ring which had resisted the corrosive effects of the lime into which he had thrown the body, not only the person to be murdered was to be identified but the locality of the crime and the man who committed it.[6]

Evidence from other sources corroborates Forster's synopsis of the plot. Of obvious importance are the working notes Dickens devised as a way to track his novels in progress. The Number Plans are incomplete in the case of *Edwin Drood* and terminate abruptly when Dickens died while at work on the sixth instalment. The entries, however, leave little room for doubt as to Dickens's intentions. While recorded solely for personal use and not for publication, they contain such revealing phrases as 'You won't take warning then?', 'Uncle and Nephew. Murder very far off', 'quarrel (Fomented by Jasper)', 'Jasper lays his ground' and 'Lay the ground for the manner of the murder, to come out at last'.[7]

Appended to the sheets of paper Dickens used to record these notes is a separate leaf devoted almost exclusively to titles (see Appendix 2). Dated Friday 20 August 1869, the page records as many as seventeen possibilities. Some of these, as Margaret Cardwell notes, 'show variants in spelling only'.[8] But the projected titles – as with all good titles – reveal an interesting range of attempts to indicate the novel's principal emphasis on a victim while retaining some degree of ambiguity: 'loss', 'Disappearance', 'flight' and 'Mystery' account for the fact that Edwin Drood vanishes from Cloisterham. But none definitively rules him out as would 'Murder', a word Dickens had cautioned against for giving away too much when he advised Robert Lytton, novelist and contributor to *All the Year Round*, to substitute 'Disappearance' in the title originally proposed for his story whose relevance to *Edwin Drood* I shall discuss shortly.[9]

'Dead? Or alive?' puts the novel's enigma most succinctly, an option Dickens also considered but turned down. Another title shifts the primary emphasis from Edwin to his relatives – 'The Mystery in the Drood Family' – while four others, as Cardwell notes, draw attention to Jasper. One simply links him with Edwin – '<u>The Two Kinsmen</u>', while three focus 'the attention on his behaviour through the greater part of the novel: "Sworn to avenge it", "One object in Life", "A Kinsman's Devotion"'. Intriguing though these are they go little further than suggesting the novel's concern with three major characters. These are aptly described by Cardwell as 'a victim, an avenger, and a suspect to be hunted down'.[10] The names of several figures to the far right of the sheet point simply to secondary concerns: the novel's clerical setting and the satire against aggressive philanthropy (see Appendix 2).

George Dolby, Dickens's readings manager from 1866 to 1870, records that the novelist remained 'sorely puzzled' over the seventeen variants until he settled a month later on *The Mystery of Edwin Drood*. The selection of the title merited a celebration, and, according to Dolby, the novelist gave a little dinner, 'a sort of christening party'.[11] From that point on, the work went forward, as Dickens balanced the demands of writing with the need to prepare for his Farewell Readings, a series of twelve to be given in London between January and March 1870. In April we find him labouring away, telling another friend, 'I have been most perseveringly and ding-dong-doggedly at work, making headway but slowly.'[12]

The extant letters from the period preceding the composition of *Edwin Drood* offer little further assistance with our investigation into the novel's principal crime. With the exception of the two passages already cited, the surviving references in Dickens's correspondence allude only briefly to the novel and reveal nothing about its substance. We learn, for example, of the decision to opt for a new, reduced form, a novel in twelve monthly parts rather than the customary twenty. This departure from practice, suggests Robert Patten, appears to owe as much to Dickens's realism about the changing market for the sale of three-deckers following their serialization as it owes to concerns about his health.[13] The contract with Chapman and Hall called for twelve monthly parts with two illustrations to each shilling number. Arrangements for the illustrations followed shortly afterwards (see Appendix 3). Scattered comments to various correspondents in the remaining letters show Dickens settling down to write. On 18 October 1869, in a letter to the actor W. C. Macready, he spoke of going through what he termed 'the preliminary agonies of a new book';[14] but within a week or so he had finished the first number, which he read 'with great spirit' to Forster, and by the end of November had closed in on the second.[15]

Evidence from two other external sources proves more useful than the extant letters. Most significant are the recollections of the novel's two illustrators. Early in 1871, Augustin Daly, an American adapter of Dickens's works for the stage, contacted Charles Dickens, Junior, expressing his hope that the novelist's son might have information that would help Daly produce a dramatic version of the incomplete *Drood* in New York. Daly learned nothing useful from Dickens's eldest son, who maintained that the novel's intended ending 'was as great a mystery to him as to the public at large'.[16] However, subsequent queries by Daly to the novel's two illustrators, Samuel Luke Fildes and Charles Allston Collins, who had married Katherine (Katey) Dickens, the novelist's favourite daughter, in 1860, yielded results. Directed to Collins by Fildes, who replied on 4 May 1871, Daly received information that corroborates Forster's description of the ending in two important ways. First, Dickens's son-in-law gave his view, based on 'some general outlines' for the scheme of the novel communicated to him by Dickens 'at a very early stage in the development of the idea', that 'Edwin Drood *was never to reappear*, he having been murdered by Jasper'. Second, Collins explained his understanding of a portion of the monthly wrapper he had drawn on being engaged by Dickens to illustrate the novel:

It was intended that Jasper himself should urge on the search after Edwin Drood and the pursuit of his murderer, thus endeavoring to direct suspicion from himself, the real murderer. This is indicated in the design, on the right side of the cover, of the figures hurrying up the spiral staircase emblematic of a pursuit. They are led on by Jasper, who points unconsciously to his own figure in the drawing at the head of the title.[17]

Against this explanation we must set assertions from Fildes. Contrary to what Collins says in his letter to Daly, Fildes maintains that Collins 'had not the faintest notion' of what the enigmatic scenes on the cover meant. 'He did them under Dickens's directions, but was told nothing of the story.'[18] Furthermore, Katey Dickens Collins, while supporting Forster's description of the novel's conclusion, concurs on this point. She maintained that her husband knew little of the cover's total design, and she expressed scepticism about his claim to have known the meaning of the scenes he depicted. 'My father, it may be presumed, intended to puzzle his readers by the cover,' a legitimate objective, she thought. For had his meaning been perfectly clear, 'the interest in the book would be gone'.[19]

The conflicting views expressed here, however, do not negate the certainty with which Charles Collins corroborates Forster's version of the novel's conclusion. And Fildes, for all the doubts he expressed about Collins's claim to have known the meaning of the various groups of figures on the monthly cover, in fact, provides evidence to support Jasper's guilt. Taking over the work from Charles Collins, when ill health compelled the latter to retire, Fildes gradually earned Dickens's confidence as he began supplying illustrations for the monthly parts. At work on material for the fourth number, Fildes paused to ask Dickens about the printer's 'rough proof' he had received, which called for an illustration of Jasper wearing 'a neckerchief of such dimensions as to go twice round his neck' when previously he had shown the choirmaster wearing 'a little black tie once round his neck'. The question apparently took Dickens by surprise, compelling him to confide to Fildes that the garment was necessary. After a short silence, and cogitating, Dickens suddenly said: 'Can you keep a secret? . . . I must have the double necktie! It is necessary, for Jasper strangles Edwin Drood with it.'[20]

Testimony from Fildes is significant in one other respect. Although he received from Dickens only sufficient information for him to proceed with one or two plates at a time, one crucial fact emerges from what he knew. In the course of his work he learned that the subject for the last illustration had been determined not long after the first monthly instalment of the novel appeared in April 1870:

I remember well the twenty-fourth and last was decided on, and we were to visit the scene [Maidstone Gaol], where [Dickens] told me he himself had not been since he was a child. Only twelve drawings were made, and six of them after Dickens' death. I was going down to Gad's Hill on the 10th of June, and my luggage was packed ready to go, when I read of his death in the morning paper.[21]

Other sources confirm that the projected final sketch was to feature the condemned cell with Jasper as its occupant. We cannot take anything said by either illustrator as an ironclad guarantee of truth. Their joint testimony, however, on the key issues of Edwin's murder and Jasper's guilt finds support from family members. Katey Dickens Collins, for example, offered some of the most convincing evidence when she argued that 'It was not . . . for the intricate working of his plot alone, that my father cared to write this story.' While she did not mean to imply that the mystery itself 'had no strong hold' on Dickens's imagination, the information he gave Forster

certainly points to the fact that he was quite as deeply fascinated and absorbed in the study of the criminal Jasper, as in the dark and sinister crime that has given the book its title . . . but it was through his wonderful observation of character, and his strange insight into the tragic secrets of the human heart, that he desired his greatest triumph to be achieved.[22]

Less eloquent but to the point is the anecdote told by Dickens's eldest son. Writing in his Introduction to the Macmillan edition of the novel published in 1923, Charles Dickens, Junior, recounts:

It was during the last walk I ever had with him at Gadshill, and our talk, which had been principally concerned with literary matters connected with *All the Year Round*, presently drifting to *Edwin Drood*, my father asked me if I did not think he had let out too much of his story too soon. I assented, and added, 'Of course, Edwin Drood was murdered?' Whereupon he turned upon me with an expression of astonishment at my having asked such an unnecessary question, and said: 'Of course; what else do you suppose?'[23]

To conjecture otherwise is to invite the ingenuity that has bedevilled much of the commentary the novel has generated. Better therefore to consider our final external source – fictional works that apparently influenced *Edwin Drood* – and then turn to the text itself. Viewing the evidence of Dickens's principal borrowings, we might usefully refer to T. S. Eliot's words on the appropriation of sources. In 1920 Eliot had this to say about literary pilfering:

One of the surest of tests is the way in which a poet borrows. Immature poets imitate; mature poets steal; bad poets deface what they take, and good poets make it into something better, or at least something different. The good poet welds his theft into a whole of feeling which is unique, utterly different from that from which it was torn; the bad poet throws it into something which has no cohesion. A good poet will usually borrow from authors remote in time, or alien in language, or diverse in interest.[24]

So far as it is possible to identify borrowings relevant to *Edwin Drood* they seem to have come from writers who were neither remote nor particularly alien in language. They are, however, from authors whose talents fall far below Dickens's, and whose literary accomplishments, with the exception of Wilkie Collins's, lie decently buried. In each of the following instances, Dickens unquestionably knew the material since he published it in *All the Year Round*, the weekly journal he 'Conducted'. Two are slight but deserve mention: 'An Experience', a short story in two parts by Emily Jolly, which appeared on 14 and 21 August 1869, and a longer piece of fiction in five instalments by Robert Lytton (18 September to 16 October 1869) called 'The Disappearance of John Ackland: A True Story'. Both involve murder. In the first a premeditated scheme for revenge is subsequently abandoned; in the second the murder is meticulously planned and executed. Aside from any foul play – whether relinquished or carried out – the case for resemblances between these two works and that of Dickens rests on the tangential issue of the closeness of the killers to their prey. Jolly's intended target is a surgeon nursed back to life by a widow whose frail daughter dies following his failed attempt to cure the child of her lameness. In Lytton's story, the eponymous hero is invited to his friend's plantation in Virginia and then murdered in order to forestall the payment of a long-standing debt. Jolly's widow shares Jasper's hypnotic power, while her touch makes the surgeon shudder; the discovery of Ackland's body, hidden for six years, comes about with the aid of a clairvoyant, who intuits Ackland's death from a letter she reads 'magnetically'. She is prompted to undertake this task by a sharp-eyed jeweller who recognizes a watch the murdered man formerly owned, which is now in the possession of someone else.

More compelling, and more easily sustained, is the case for the resemblances between Dickens's novel and Wilkie Collins's best-selling *The Moonstone*. The two authors were close. Collins, a former protégé turned friend and then partner in fiction, developed steadily under Dickens's eye and won an increasing following in the two journals Dickens edited. The success of *The Moonstone*, which ran serially in *All the Year Round* from 4 January to 8 August 1868, in fact earned permanent recognition and was judged in 1927 by T. S. Eliot 'the first and greatest of English detective novels'.[25]

An inventory of the resemblances between *Edwin Drood* and *The Moonstone* provides enough evidence to suggest substantial influence.[26] Both novels draw on the East to impart an air of exotic mystery; each has an evil character who leads a double life, masking villainy and lust under the cloak of respectability. Passages in both also reveal that their respective authors drew on an incident described in Dr John Elliotson's *Human Physiology* (1840) as the source for asserting that an item misplaced in a state of intoxication could be found when that state was reduplicated, even though the principals retain no conscious memory of the initial act.[27] Are we then to concur with Collins, who differed sharply with Forster's praise of Dickens's novel? In his often-quoted comment on *Drood*, Collins annotated Forster's assessment of the book as follows: 'To my mind it was cruel to compare Dickens in the radiant prime of his genius with Dickens's last laboured effort, the melancholy work of a worn-out brain.'[28]

Critics differ in the importance they attach to the closeness of the two novels. Sue Lonoff, for example, comments that '*Edwin Drood* contains a number of recognizably Collinsian elements'. Maintaining on the one hand that Collins had nothing to teach Dickens, she admits on the other that the two 'may have been in hidden competition'. For despite their close friendship, the older master possibly felt rivalrous and perhaps even resentful of the recognition *The Moonstone* won in the pages of *All the Year Round*.[29]

A fiercer version of competition occurs to Jerome Meckier, who sees novel writing as a form of open combat between master and pupil. For Dickens, writing *Edwin Drood* was a way to retaliate against Collins by creating his version of a taut, sensational novel. For the pupil, outclassed and outranked, the options were limited. Collins's condemnation of *Edwin Drood*, contends Meckier, was 'a last-ditch attempt at self-defense'. Collins delivered his negative verdict, he conjectures, as a beaten man, an author who had been out-manoeuvred, out-thought and out-witted on every fictional front.

Read in the context of Meckier's over-arching thesis, his chapter 'Inimitability Regained: *The Mystery of Edwin Drood*' has much to commend it. The story told in *Hidden Rivalries in Victorian Fiction: Dickens, Realism, & Revaluation* is one of epic proportion. Throughout the nineteenth century, the major novelists engaged in a constant battle in which winners attempted to take all. One could only stay on top, Meckier argues, at the expense of discrediting one's rivals in an unending fight to command the broadest fictional readership. Thus Dickens's transformations of Collins, he contends, 'are never so radical that they cannot be coaxed out of hiding'. Equal to the task, Meckier offers a spirited polemic. His study argues that Dickens managed to surpass and outdo all his rivals, correcting in the course of writing *Edwin Drood* Collins's 'errors' by settling old scores, 'if only through violent fantasies cleverly worked out within the confines of his art'.[30]

Meckier's version of literary Darwinism provides lively reading, but it is to the novel itself we must look for information about the book's central focus. 'It would be a very stupid and inattentive reader', writes Philip Collins, 'who could fail to see that John Jasper is a wicked man, that he has "cause, and will, and strength, and means" to kill Edwin, [and] that he makes careful preparations to do so and to throw suspicion elsewhere.' Some may take exception to Collins's bluntness.

But I find it hard to detect any serious discrepancy between what Collins calls 'the obvious implications' of the story and the accounts of the novel's outline by those individuals close to Dickens whom I have cited. Their testimony provides no help with unanswerable matters such as Datchery's identity and the role the Landlesses would play. Only futile guessing games supply fanciful details about Jasper's family history or the nature of his relationship with the opium woman. We can never know what motive lay behind her decision to follow him to Cloisterham on Christmas Eve, the role of Deputy in Jasper's eventual downfall or the meaning of the scream heard by Durdles almost one year before Drood was murdered. But of the principal matters we can have little doubt. Jasper leads a double life. He hides wicked passions behind a respectable ecclesiastical career. He lusts after his nephew's fiancée, and plots to remove Edwin by making plans for the disposal of his body, while also throwing suspicion for foul play on another party. Two other characters suspect him of murder. Throughout the novel he lives in shadows, 'wholeheartedly, though secretly, the Wicked Man', the last in the line of figures Philip Collins traces from 'Sikes and Rudge to Jonas Chuzzlewit, Slinkton and Bradley Headstone'. This pedigree extends, Collins reminds us, from members of the 'criminal classes' like Bill Sikes and Fagin, to 'the middleclass citizen apparently of the utmost propriety'. Where Jasper differs from his predecessors is in his intelligence, his respectability, his psychological complexity and in the greater ambiguity of his relation to society.[31]

Lacking the second half of the novel, we are in no position to deduce the reasons for Jasper's behaviour. But what the first half successfully conveys is the narrator's unequivocal view that someone like Jasper is 'a horrible wonder apart'. Where people err, including even the 'professed students' of the criminal intellect, is in attempting to reconcile the behaviour of men like Jasper 'with the average intellect of average men' (ch. 20). What baffles Rosa – and presumably others – as she recoils from Jasper's assault in the sun-dial scene is her inability to reconcile what he says on that occasion with her own suspicions. If Jasper had committed the deed, why did he persist in treating his nephew's disappearance as murder? If he really were guilty, would he have admitted that, had the ties between him and his dear boy 'been one silken thread less strong' (ch. 19), he might have swept even him aside in the torrent of his mad love? Could he have feigned the desire for vengeance he expressed in his anxiety to apprehend Edwin's murderer? To Rosa the difficulties inherent in her questions suggest innocence rather than guilt, prompting her to ignore the 'fancy that scarcely dared to hint itself'. 'Am I so wicked in my thoughts', she reflects, 'as to conceive a wickedness that others cannot imagine?' (ch. 20).

To those skilled at reading the human countenance, interpreting Jasper's behaviour in 'the quaint old garden' of the Nuns' House proves less daunting. Dickens narrator, for example, calls attention to Jasper's cunning in making his vehement declaration of love where Rosa can be seen and heard. '"I do not forget how many windows command a view of us", he says glancing towards them . . . "Sit down, and there will be no mighty wonder in your music-master's leaning idly against a pedestal and speaking with you . . . Sit down, my beloved."' True to the posture he adopts, Jasper preserves an 'easy attitude' all the more terrifying given the frightful vehemence of the man as his words build to a climax. '"I love you, love you, love you. If you were to cast me off now – but you will not – you would never be rid of me. No one should come between us. I would pursue you to the death."' But for all his assumed ease, this wicked man fails to control one sign whose significance is not lost on the narrator. Throughout the interview, his violent confession renders his features and hands 'convulsive [and] absolutely diabolical' (ch. 19).

Two analogies exist for Jasper's behaviour in the walled garden of the Nuns' House. The first is fictional and has been noted by others. Readers familiar with 'The Whole Case' Bradley Headstone puts to Lizzie Hexam in *Our Mutual Friend* (1864–5) will recognize similarities. The topographical settings, each emphasizing enclosure, impart a sense of claustrophobia all the more extreme on account of the words of the two suitors. Both speak in equally absolute terms. '"Yes! you are the ruin – the ruin – the ruin – of me,"' confesses Headstone importunately, pacing a 'square court' enclosed by iron rails near the church of St Peter's in the City of London. '"You know what I am going to say. I love you ... I am under the influence of some tremendous attraction which I have resisted in vain, and which overmasters me. You could draw me to fire, you could draw me to water, you could draw me to the gallows,"' he continues, as a prelude to proposing marriage (Book the Second, ch. 15). '"I don't ask for your love; give me yourself and your hatred ... it will be enough for me,"' confesses Jasper in similar extreme terms, before adopting an air of calm and assuring Rosa he will wait '"for some encouragement and hope"' (ch. 19). An equally wild energy characterizes the lovers' gestures, seen particularly in 'the passionate action' of their nervous hands as each vents homicidal threats against his rival. In both cases the young women shrink from the slightest touch, finding their admirers totally repugnant.

The second parallel requires a broader context. To explore it we must turn to Dickens's journalism and to real crimes committed by 'members of the vermin-race', whose scarlet deeds, so widely reported, featured prominently in Victorian public life.[32] This thread of the novel also connects us with something we have noticed already: Dickens's admiration for the detective police. Of particular relevance in the case of Jasper is Dickens's interest in the willingness of good officers to admit the need for caution when judging appearances. Under suspicion, innocence may assume the appearance of guilt. By the same token, clever felons can mislead the unwary. 'Nothing is so common or deceptive as such appearances at first,' Dickens proposed, as he burrowed for information on a series of points related to the art of detection.[33] And, he might have added, if the officers of 'keen observation and quick perception' he assembled one evening rose to the level of William Hogarth, the eighteenth-century painter and engraver whose 'fertility of mind' Dickens most admired, they would employ 'the attentive eyes' that 'saw the manners in the face'.[34]

The prosecution of Dr William Palmer for murder in May 1856 at London's Central Criminal Court offers an instructive instance of guilt masked by an elaborate profession of innocence. Palmer's behaviour during the trial, moreover, was of particular concern to Dickens. For twelve days the accused – a respectable surgeon – faced a parade of hostile witnesses. And for twelve days damaging evidence about the deaths of several family members and one gambling associate, all of whom had been under Palmer's care, failed to upset the calm demeanour he projected. Neither did sharp questions from prominent colleagues about the use of poison, nor medical testimony related to the deadly effects of arsenic, unsettle him. The man in the dock, newspaper readers were told, retained an air of 'tranquillity' and gazed calmly and politely at his accusers as he confronted one witness after another. Asked how he pleaded when charged with murder, Palmer responded in 'a clear, low, but perfectly audible and distinct tone, "Not guilty."' More subjectively, it was reported that 'there are no marks of care' about Palmer's face. The countenance of the prisoner 'is clear and open, the forehead high, the complexion ruddy, and the general impression one would form from his appearance would be favourable rather than otherwise'. Day followed day, eight hours of gruelling testimony at a stretch. Yet throughout Palmer maintained an extraordinary sense of composure. Some sense of the sympathy his innocent demeanour evoked may be inferred from the response to the conclusion of the defence entered by the physician's counsel. Notes *The Times*'s reporter on 22 May, when Mr Serjeant Shea finished his eight-hour summing up: 'There were some slight indications of an attempt to applaud' at the close, 'but they were instantly hushed.'[35]

Interpretative comments like these framing the publication of complete transcripts of each day's proceedings in *The Times* provoked a public response from Dickens. He wrote 'The Demeanour of Murderers' for *Household Words*, he explained to Miss Burdett Coutts, as 'a quiet protest' against the misinformed accounts of Palmer's bearing during the trial by members of the press. Newspaper depictions of the surgeon at the Old Bailey as cool, collected and self-possessed, Dickens thought, 'are harmful to the public at large', and are 'even in themselves, altogether blind and wrong'.[36]

Dickens opens his essay by noting the uniformity of opinion expressed by reporters covering the case. All the accounts of Palmer's behaviour in court that he had read, Dickens states, agree 'in more or less suggesting that there is something admirable, and difficult to reconcile with guilt, in the bearing so elaborately set forth'. For his part, however, Dickens expresses a belief that 'Nature never writes a bad hand', and that her writing, 'as it may be read in the human countenance, is invariably legible, if we come at all trained to the reading of it'. Continuing in words remarkably close to those of the narrator commenting on Rosa's confused state when the possibility crosses her mind that Jasper might have committed the murder, Dickens writes:

Some little weighing and comparing are necessary. It is not enough in turning our eyes on the demon in the Dock, to say that he has fresh color, or a high head, or a bluff manner, or what not, and therefore he does not look like a murderer, and we are surprised and shaken. The physiognomy and conformation of the Poisoner whose trial occasions these remarks, were exactly in accordance with his deeds; and every guilty consciousness he had gone on storing up in his mind, had set its mark upon him.[37]

The challenge to experts, as this passage suggests, is to discern the 'marks' set on a countenance so seemingly at odds with guilt. How does one reconcile Palmer's studied coolness, composure and confidence with the capacity for cruelty and insensibility necessary to any carefully planned murder? For the doctor to have dispatched as many victims as he did, there can be no question in Dickens's mind about the significance of the absence of 'any lingering traces of sensibility' in the man who betrayed his Hippocratic oath by making it his trade 'to be learned in poisons'. 'If I had any natural human feeling for my face to express, do you imagine that those medicines of my prescribing and administering would ever have been taken from my hand?'[38]

The text of the novel offers good reasons to assume that John Jasper has a similar aptitude both for meticulous preparation and for sustained deception. How else are we to explain actions whose cumulative significance attests to the implementation of a carefully laid plan to dispose of a rival? Relevant considerations include Jasper's interest in quicklime, the midnight exploration of the Cathedral crypt and the quarrel he foments between Neville Landless and Edwin Drood.

Dickens contends that 'demons' like Palmer evince studied coolness because they lack any capacity for pity or sentiment. Devoid of 'any natural human feeling', what else do you expect such fiends to express? Yet in one respect such monsters are 'Distinctly *not* quite composed'.

More observant and more perceptive than *The Times*'s reporter, Dickens notes how Palmer was 'very restless' during his trial. 'At one time, he was incessantly pulling on and pulling off his glove; at another time, his hand was constantly passing over and over his face.'[39] Returning to Jasper's interview with Rosa in the garden, we see similar compulsive behaviour uncannily suggestive of Palmer's in the dock.

For all the privacy the walled garden of the Nuns' House affords, its enclosed space is, as we have noted, overlooked by many of the school's own windows. This layout, not unlike the confined court space of the former Old Bailey, encourages rather than inhibits Jasper. But one action links him with evil men like Palmer and offers a glimpse of the agitation his professed calmness belies: the movement of 'his convulsive hands'. Repeatedly, as he lays one wild declaration after another before the terrified Rosa, the narrator notes how each is punctuated by 'an action of the hands, as though he cast down something precious' (ch. 19).

Anticipating an objection to 'some slight ingenuity' in his endeavour to interpret the demeanour of Palmer and his kind, Dickens hastens to assure readers of *Household Words* that he can find parallels by the score to sustain his point. Most telling is the case of John Thurtell, 'one of the murderers best remembered in England', Dickens asserts. His collected and resolute behaviour during his trial 'was exactly that of the Poisoner's'. Granting that the circumstances of Thurtell's guilt were not 'comparable in atrocity' with those of Palmer, Dickens sketches the 'points of strong resemblance' between the two men in terms that curiously anticipate his fictional portrait of the murderous choirmaster of Cloisterham:

Each was born in a fair station, and educated in conformity with it; each murdered a man with whom he had been on terms of intimate association, and for whom he professed a friendship at the time of the murder; both were members of that vermin-race of outer betters and blacklegs [betting brokers and turf swindlers] . . .[40]

Had Dickens lived to finish *The Mystery of Edwin Drood* we could rejoice for several reasons. Students of the novel would have been spared much contentious speculation about Jasper's evident guilt (or innocence) and his nephew's ultimate fate (murdered or alive). They would also have a clearer idea of how the novel relates to tensions that predominate in Dickens's writing. Of these, we can distinguish several running through all his fiction to which this last unfinished novel is no exception. Not unlike John Keats, whose imagination Walter Jackson Bate describes as 'Januslike' in the final year of his writing, Dickens's 'fancy' characteristically looked two ways.[41] On the one hand, we see his mind turned inwards to reverie and dream; on the other, outwards, to the concrete, external world.

Dickens himself provides a succinct introduction to his inward orientation in 'Nurse's Stories'. As one of seventeen essays published originally as part of his 'Uncommercial Traveller' series in *All the Year Round*, it offers interesting autobiographical reflections on the role fiction played in Dickens's life. Throughout his life he maintained a habit developed in childhood of deriving comfort, support and imaginative consolation from fiction. 'There are not many places that I find it more agreeable to revisit when I am in an idle mood', the essay opens, 'than some places to which I have never been.'[42]

This 'idle mood', a pre-condition to accepting the nourishment Dickens thought fiction could and should provide, has a related side which the essay also explores: the ability of story-tellers to force readers into the dark corners of the mind, against their will. Introduced to such fiction by his nurse as a child, a taste for forcing himself to go back to places he was reluctant to visit, and for taking readers with him, forms another of Dickens's characteristic strategies. From 1836 until his death, Dickens did not swerve from writing novels that offered comfort by keeping alive 'fancy' among his readers while simultaneously exploring what Harry Stone calls the 'night side' of his mind.[43]

This dual agenda combines with a further primary element: Dickens's commitment to recording the contours of the everyday world around him. As Walter Bagehot aptly characterized this aspect of Dickens's genius in 1858, his novels 'aim to delineate nearly all that part of our national life which can be delineated . . . The amount of detail which there is in them is something amazing, – to an ordinary writer something incredible.'[44]

All three strands of Dickens's imagination play a significant role in *The Mystery of Edwin Drood*. But they are unequally represented owing to the novel's unfinished state. Had Dickens lived to complete the second half, a counter theme to the oppressive darkness associated with John Jasper would have emerged. Dickens carefully lays the ground for this development in various ways. Take the two pairs of characters destined to play an important role later in the book: Septimus Crisparkle and Lieutenant Tartar, and Rosa Bud and Helena Landless. All four are youthful, energetic and engagingly attractive – the men, one a canon active in the Church, the other a former First Lieutenant in the Royal Navy; the women, two pupils resident at Miss Twinkleton's Seminary for Young Ladies. Each, too, is capable of surprising readers in convincing ways, to employ E. M. Forster's old-fashioned test of a 'round' character.[45]

Their ability to do so is perhaps most evident in the capacity the four show for crossing boundaries and defying readerly expectations. In a telling phrase, the narrator notes how Crisparkle, the man of the Church, occupies a 'Christian beat', on which course he 'polices' in a variety of ways (ch. 2). Vigilant as a tutor and student of language, he corrects Mr Tope's faulty grammar; physically conditioned by daily bouts of shadow-boxing and plunges into the local weir, he scales heights without trouble. He can also perform, if necessary, the task of taking refractory individuals into custody with the skill of 'a Police Expert' (ch. 8). The former naval officer, Crisparkle's junior and friend from school, is equally agile and strong. Yet Tartar, this robust and 'manly' man who has knocked about the world for twelve or fifteen years in the tough conditions to which England's fighting men at sea were subject, has skills in household management equal to those of Esther Summerson in *Bleak House* (1852–3). Tartar has only to touch a spring-laden knob in his neat chambers and 'a dazzling enchanted repast' appears before his guests; on land he tends a flower garden, the envy of even a professional horticulturist (ch. 22). Crisparkle and Tartar, moreover, hold an affection for each other which they express – 'for Englishmen' – in a very un-English way. When they unexpectedly meet after an interval of many years, they look 'joyfully into each other's face' and shake hands 'with great earnestness', demonstrating a warmth of feeling evidently outside the national norm (ch. 21).

Not to be outdone in unconventionality, Rosa Bud and Helena Landless test expectations commonly associated with female characters. The diminutive Rosa – 'pet pupil . . . wonderfully pretty, wonderfully childish, wonderfully whimsical' and of course called Rosebud (ch. 3) – nevertheless acts with convincing authority in the scene when she takes the initiative in dissolving her engagement to Edwin, a pre-arrangement neither party is happy with but is unwilling to challenge until Rosa, belittled by her fiancé as 'Pussy', rises to the occasion (ch. 13). Equally unusual and certainly an imaginative stretch for Dickens is the intrepid Helena Landless. Adept at disguising herself, bravely resistant to pain as a child and evidently in command of telepathic and perhaps mesmeric powers, she represents a figure outside his usual range. Also a departure is the introduction of the intimacy between Rosa and Helena. In an interesting extension of the relationship between Lizzie Hexam and Bella Wilfer in *Our Mutual Friend*, Dickens presents in the novel that followed it a more sustained portrait of two women who see strength and virtue in each other. Friendship between women, as Wendy Jacobson has remarked, represents a topic previously untreated in the Victorian novel.[46]

A prevailing thread in the imagery supports these motifs of change and development, all of which serve as variant antidotes to the novel's initially sombre colours and pervading sense of darkness. While the story opens as both the day and the year wane, with the low sun fiery 'yet cold behind the monastery ruin' (ch. 2), the seasonal background against which the action unfolds prepares for renewal and for a cyclical movement that brings the return of light. Hours before Dickens slipped from consciousness he wrote one of the most beautiful passages in his career. I refer to the description of the brilliant summer morning in Chapter 23, which shines on 'the old city' and imparts a 'surpassing beauty' to its antiquities and ruins. For all the unsettling words about the Cathedral in the opening chapters, the fictional building based on Rochester's cathedral church of St Andrew nevertheless retains a capacity for regeneration. Like the autumn wind that brings darkness in Shelley's 'Ode to the West Wind' (1819), the destroyer is also a preserver, the harbinger of a cycle that moves through death and decay to new life. The brilliant morning subdues the earthy odour of the Cathedral's cold stones. The tombs of centuries grow warm and the 'glorious light' preaches 'the Resurrection and the Life'. This eloquent description clearly serves as the prelude to a movement in the novel that Dickens did not live to write.

The other important component of the novel proves less elusive. I refer to the Dickens who, in Bagehot's memorable phrase, 'describes London like a special correspondent for posterity'.[47] For *The Mystery of Edwin Drood*, like all of Dickens's novels, is packed with news. True to the etymology of the word itself, this novel bristles with information. In a typically Dickensian fashion old news and new news are blended against a telling time slightly out of joint with the now of the narration. If 'animal magnetism', 'Muscular Christianity', misdirected philanthropy and the introduction of rail travel belong to the metropolis of the mid-century, then news about Egypt, the Suez Canal, Governor Eyre and the world abroad belongs to the second half of the nineteenth century. A growing interest in smoking opium rather than taking it orally as laudanum represents another late development.[48]

Characteristically, Dickens the journalist, with an eye for those aspects of England's national life within what Bagehot calls 'the limits which social morality prescribes to social art', brings together all the latest developments, refracted through his cosmological eye, the eye of a superb story-teller.[49]

In these various respects, *The Mystery of Edwin Drood* for all its fragmentary nature partakes in the full range of imaginative expression evident in each of Dickens's finished novels. Smaller in scope than any of the five he published in weekly instalments, diminutive in comparison with the panoramic novels of his maturity, Dickens's last fragment nevertheless carries the signature of his greatest fiction. What an accomplishment, one might exclaim, what wholeness when so much is missing, what totality hinted at and yet unfulfilled. Like the lovers on Keats's Grecian Urn (1819), readers of *The Mystery of Edwin Drood* are for ever panting, for ever drawn to a song whose melodies, though sweet, are never heard in full.

NOTES

1. Raymond Chandler, 'Introduction to "The Simple Art of Murder"' (1950), in *Later Novels and Other Writings* (New York, 1995), p. 1017.

2. 'Detective Police', *Household Words* (27 July 1850), in *Charles Dickens: Selected Journalism, 1850–1870*, ed. David Pascoe (Harmondsworth, 1997), pp. 246–7. Cited in the notes below as *Journalism*.

3. *Charles Dickens' Book of Memoranda*, ed. Fred Kaplan (New York, 1981), p. 97.

4. John Forster, *The Life of Charles Dickens*, 2 vols. (1872–4; London, 1969), 2.365. Cited in the notes below as 'Forster', by volume and page number.

5. *The Letters of Charles Dickens*, ed. Walter Dexter, the Nonesuch Edition, 3 vols. (London, 1938), p. 735. Cited in the notes below as Nonesuch, by volume and page number.

6. Forster, 2.366.

7. Proponents of the theory that Edwin did not die can point to no comparable 'proof' to support their hypothesis. True, Dickens could have changed his plan for the story in the next monthly number. Instances of late revisions include Dickens's decision not to make Edith Dombey Carker's mistress (*Dombey and Son*, 1846–8) and the revised ending of *Great Expectations* (1860–61); in the latter, unlike the original, in which Estella remarries after the death of her husband, she remains a widow in the revised ending when she meets Pip, thereby establishing the eligibility Dickens denied her in the first version. But the champions of Edwin's survival stand on flimsy ground. Some choose fanciful solutions by importing exotic matter wholly extraneous to the existing fragment, thereby turning the novel into a guessing game (see Further Reading, Aylmer, Duffield, Proctor, Walters). Others reduce the text to the evidentiary rules and procedures of a court of law in an attempt to try Jasper and win a verdict (see Further Reading, Ley, Patterson). Recent and more sophisticated arguments for Edwin's survival rest on an analysis of images of rebirth, salvation and resurrection implicit in the novel's undeveloped counter-movement (see Further Reading, Manheim, Parker, Perkins, Sanders, Thomas, Thurley).

8. *The Mystery of Edwin Drood*, the Clarendon Edition, ed. Margaret Cardwell (Oxford, 1972), p. xiv, n. All further references to this edition will appear in the notes below as 'Cardwell'.

9. Nonesuch, 3.740.

10. Cardwell, pp. xiv, xv.

11. George Dolby, *Charles Dickens as I Knew Him: The Story of the Reading Tours . . . 1866–1870* (1885), p. 436.

12. Nonesuch, 3.772.

13. Robert L. Patten, *Charles Dickens and His Publishers* (Oxford, 1978), pp. 315–16.

14. Nonesuch, 3.746.

15. Forster, 2.408.

16. Quoted in Joseph Francis Daly, *The Life of Augustin Daly* (New York, 1917), p. 107.

17. Quoted in ibid., pp. 107–8: Charles Collins, letter of 4 May 1871 to Augustin Daly.

18. David Croal Thomson, *The Life and Works of Luke Fildes, R. A.* (1895), p. 27.

19. Kate Perugini ['Katey' Dickens], '*Edwin Drood*, And the Last Days of Charles Dickens', *Pall Mall Magazine* 37 (June 1906), p. 650.

20. Luke Fildes, letter to *The Times Literary Supplement* 199 (3 November 1905), p. 373.

21. Thomson, *The Life and Works of Luke Fildes*, p. 28.

22. Perugini, '*Edwin Drood*, And the Last Days of Charles Dickens', p. 646.

23. Charles Dickens, Jr, Introduction, *The Mystery of Edwin Drood* (London, 1923), p. xv.

24. T. S. Eliot, 'Philip Massinger', *Selected Essays* (London, 1980), p. 206.

25. Eliot, 'Wilkie Collins and Dickens', *Selected Essays*, p. 464.

26. For an exhaustive (and sometimes over-stretched) discussion of the resemblances between *The Moonstone* and *Edwin Drood*, and of Dickens's attempt to gain the upper hand by 'revaluing' Collins, see Jerome Meckier, *Hidden Rivalries in Victorian Fiction: Dickens, Realism, & Revaluation* (Lexington, KY, 1987), pp. 151–200. See also Sue Lonoff, 'Charles Dickens and Wilkie Collins', *Nineteenth-Century Fiction* 35 (1980), pp. 163–5.

27. See note 12 to Chapter 3.

28. Wilkie Collins, 'Wilkie Collins about Charles Dickens', *Pall Mall Gazette* (20 January 1890), p. 3.

29. Lonoff, 'Charles Dickens and Wilkie Collins', pp. 163, 169.

30. Meckier, *Hidden Rivalries in Victorian Fiction*, pp. 197, 195.

31. Philip Collins, *Dickens and Crime* (London, 1962), pp. 291, 296–7.

32. 'Demeanour of Murderers', *Household Words* (14 June 1856), in *Journalism*, p. 480.

33. 'Detective Police', *Household Words* (27 July and 10 August 1850), in *Journalism*, p. 249.

34. Samuel Johnson's epitaph on Hogarth, quoted by Dickens with 'fervid energy and feeling' one day, as he paused at the set of Hogarth engravings displayed on the stairs at Gad's Hill. See James T. Fields, *In and Out of Doors with Charles Dickens* (Boston, 1876), p. 115.

35. For the coverage of the trial by *The Times*, see the verbatim accounts published on 15, 16, 17, 19, 20, 21, 22, 23, 24, 26, 27 and 28 May 1856. *The Dictionary of National Biography* contains a full entry on William Palmer (1824–56); see also Richard D. Altick, *Victorian Studies in Scarlet* (New York, 1970), pp. 152–9.

36. *The Letters of Charles Dickens*, the Pilgrim Edition, ed. Madeline House, Graham Storey, Kathleen Tillotson et al. (in progress; 10 vols. to date, Oxford, 1965–), 8.128.

37. 'Demeanour of Murderers', in *Journalism*, p. 477.

38. Ibid., p. 478.

39. Ibid.

40. Ibid., p. 480.

41. Walter Jackson Bate, *John Keats* (1963; Cambridge, MA, 1979), p. 125.

42. 'Nurse's Stories', *All the Year Round* (8 September 1860), in *Journalism*, p. 92.

43. Harry Stone, *The Night Side of Dickens: Cannibalism, Passion, Necessity* (Columbus, OH, 1994).

44. Walter Bagehot, 'Charles Dickens', *National Review* (October 1858), in *Dickens: The Critical Heritage*, ed. Philip Collins (London, 1971), pp. 391, 393.

45. E. M. Forster, *Aspects of the Novel*, ed. Oliver Stallybrass, Penguin Modern Classics (Harmondsworth, 2000), ch. 4.

46. Wendy Jacobson, 'Freedom and Friendship: Women in *The Mystery of Edwin Drood*', *Dickens Quarterly* 18 (June 2001), pp. 70–82.

47. Walter Bagehot, 'Charles Dickens', in *The Critical Heritage*, p. 394.

48. See Notes for brief entries on these and other topics and Appendix 5 for opium smoking in Victorian England.

49. Walter Bagehot, 'Charles Dickens', in *The Critical Heritage*, p. 391.

1. REFERENCE WORKS

Butt, John and Kathleen Tillotson, *Dickens at Work* (1957; London, Methuen, 1968).

Cardwell, Margaret (ed.), *The Mystery of Edwin Drood*, The Clarendon Dickens (Oxford, Clarendon Press, 1972): the most thorough textual study of the novel available.

Cohen, Jane R., *Charles Dickens and His Original Illustrators* (Columbus, Ohio State University Press, 1980): incisive commentary on the work of Collins and Fildes.

Collins, Philip (ed.), *Dickens: The Critical Heritage* (London, Routledge and Kegan Paul, 1971): extracts from six contemporary reviews; for a fuller listing of contemporary reactions, see Cox, pp. 193–209.

Cox, Don Richard, *Charles Dickens's 'The Mystery of Edwin Drood': An Annotated Bibliography* (New York, AMS Press, 1998): an indispensable guide through the thickets of *Drood* writing, arranged topically and chronologically.

Dexter, Walter (ed.), *The Letters of Charles Dickens*, vol. 3, 1858–1870, The Nonesuch Dickens (Bloomsbury, Nonesuch Press, 1938).

Forster, John, *The Life of Charles Dickens* (1872–4; London, Dent, 1969).

Jacobson, Wendy S., *The Companion to 'The Mystery of Edwin Drood'* (London, Allen & Unwin, 1986): a comprehensive annotative guide to the novel, keyed to chapters and paragraph openings.

Johnson, Edgar, *Charles Dickens: His Tragedy and Triumph*, 2 vols. (New York, Simon and Schuster, 1952): a balanced modern supplement to John Forster's *Life*.

Kaplan, Fred (ed.), *Charles Dickens' Book of Memoranda* (New York, New York Public Library, 1981).

Schlicke, Paul (ed.), *Oxford Reader's Companion to Dickens* (Oxford, Oxford University Press, 1999): succinct entries on many pertinent topics.

Stone, Harry (ed.), *Dickens' Working Notes for His Novels* (Chicago, University of Chicago Press, 1987).

2. BOOKS, ARTICLES AND ESSAYS

Aylmer, Felix, *The Drood Case* (London, Rupert Hart-Davis, 1964): a leading proponent of Jasper's innocence argued on an inverted reading of the text, which sees hints of his homicidal tendencies as intentionally deceptive.

Baker, Richard M., *The Drood Murder Case: Five Studies in Dickens's Edwin Drood* (Berkeley, University of California Press, 1951): examines influences on the novel and analyses Jasper as the murderer.

Bolton, Philip, 'The Mystery of Edwin Drood', in *Dickens Dramatized* (London, Mansell, 1987), pp. 442–9: chronological listing of dramatic adaptations of the novel.

Cardwell, Margaret, '*The Mystery of Edwin Drood* After-History 1870–1878', Appendix G in Clarendon Dickens (1972), pp. 249–55: attempted continuations and adaptations following Dickens's death in 1870.

Collins, Philip, *Dickens and Crime* (1962; Bloomington, Indiana University Press, 1968), pp. 290–316: argues strenuously against biographical readings of Dickens as Jasper and the proponents of Jasper's dual personality, relating him instead to a tradition of criminals developed since *Oliver Twist*.

Connor, Steven, 'Unfinished Business: The History of Continuations, Conclusions and Solutions', Appendix C in *The Mystery of Edwin Drood*, ed. Steven Connor (London, Dent, 1996), pp. 286–307: informative survey of the efforts of detective-critics to lay to rest the novel's insoluble mysteries.

Connor, Steven, 'Dickens and His Critics', in *The Mystery of Edwin Drood*, ed. Steven Connor, pp. 308–17: a compact narrative of serious critical attention given to the novel, beginning with Edmund Wilson (see below).

Cordery, Gareth, 'The Cathedral as Setting and Symbol in *The Mystery of Edwin Drood*', *Dickens Studies Newsletter* 10 (1979), pp. 97–103: proposes the Cathedral as the dominant symbol, having both negative and positive implications.

Duffield, Howard, 'John Jasper – Strangler', *The Bookman* 70 (1930), pp. 581–8: an influential essay, important for emphasizing that the mystery lay in Jasper's own secret, violent life.

Forsyte, Charles [Mavis and Gordon Philo], *The Decoding of Edwin Drood* (New York, Charles Scribner's, 1980): a comprehensive survey of the 'mystery' issues.

Garfield, Leon, *The Mystery of Edwin Drood* (New York, Pantheon Books, 1980): a predominantly successful conclusion, based on Forster's version of the ending and written in Dickens's style, grafted to the text of the 1875 Charles Dickens Edition of the novel.

Jackson, Henry, *About Edwin Drood* (Cambridge, Cambridge University Press, 1911): an early close reading, arguing for Jasper as the murderer.

[Ley, J. W. T.], *The Trial of John Jasper, Lay Precentor of Cloisterham Cathedral in the County of Kent, for the Murder of Edwin Drood, Engineer. Verbatim Report of the Proceedings from the Shorthand Notes of J. W. T. Ley* (London, Chapman and Hall, 1914): records the proceedings of the 1914 London 'trial' of Jasper.

Manheim, Leonard F., 'Thanatos: The Death Instinct in Dickens' Later Novels', in *Hidden Patterns: Studies in Psychoanalytic Literary Criticism* (New York, Macmillan, 1985), pp. 113–31: suggests Drood survives Jasper's attack. The latter, who believes he has committed the crime, murders Neville to cover his imagined murder.

Parker, David, 'Drood Redux: Mystery and the Art of Fiction', *Dickens Studies Annual* 24 (1996), pp. 185–95: argues that Edwin must live in order for Dickens to complete his 'sentimental education'.

Patterson, John M. (ed.), *Trial of John Jasper for the Murder of Edwin Drood* (Philadelphia, Philadelphia Branch of the Dickens Fellowship, 1914): record of the trial that took place in Philadelphia, 29 April 1914, to raise money for local hospitals.

Perkins, Donald, *Charles Dickens. A New Perspective* (Edinburgh, Floris Books, 1982), pp. 22–3, 104–5: argues for resurrection as an overriding theme in Dickens's fiction and asserts Drood's resurrection as highly probable.

Proctor, Richard A., *Watched by the Dead: A Loving Study of Dickens' Half-Told Tale* (London, W. H. Allen, 1887): an earnest and early proponent of Drood's resurrection.

Robson, W. W., '*The Mystery of Edwin Drood*: The Solution?', *The Times Literary Supplement* (11 November 1983), pp. 1246, 1259: proposes that Dickens's intensely personal involvement with the novel stimulated him to make the unprecedented move of writing himself into the story.

Sanders, Andrew, 'The Mystery of Edwin Drood', in *Charles Dickens: Resurrectionist* (London, Macmillan, 1982), pp. 198–218: reads *Drood* in the context of Dickens's strongly held religious beliefs about salvation and rebirth, themes convincingly present throughout his work.

Sedgwick, Eve Kosofsky, 'Up the Postern Stair: *Edwin Drood* and the Homophobia of Empire', in *Between Men: English Literature and Male Homosocial Desire* (New York, Columbia University Press, 1985), pp. 180–200: reads the novel as the expression of binary tensions within a culture that compartmentalizes male desire and Englishness and non-Englishness.

Thacker, John, *Edwin Drood: Antichrist in the Cathedral* (London, Vision Press, 1980): compare Cordery above; proposes a counter movement in the second half of the novel to the pessimism and death of the first.

Thomas, Marilyn, '*Edwin Drood*: A Bone Yard Awaiting Resurrection', *Dickens Quarterly* 2 (1985), pp. 12–18: argues for the resurrection of Drood by Crisparkle and Datchery, two redemptive figures also intent on bringing the Church and the community back to life.

Thurley, Geoffrey, *The Dickens Myth: Its Genesis and Structure* (New York, St Martin's Press, 1978), pp. 329–50: a mythic-symbolic reading of the novel, presenting Drood as slain and risen god of James G. Frazer's *The Golden Bough*.

Walters, J. Cuming, *The Complete Mystery of Edwin Drood: The History, Continuations, and Solutions (1870–1912)* (London, Chapman and Hall, 1912): the novel's text, together with a chart tabulating the theories of various authors.

Wilson, Edmund, 'Dickens: The Two Scrooges', in *The Wound and the Bow* (Cambridge, MA, 1941), pp. 1–101: assimilates Duffield's argument and presents Jasper as a radically divided personality, whose warring halves he traces to the author.

The contract Dickens signed with publishers Chapman and Hall in late August 1869 specified a novel in twelve monthly parts. Each number, consisting of thirty-two pages and two illustrations, would cost a shilling and would run from April 1870 to March 1871. Of the twelve instalments contracted only six appeared, three during Dickens's lifetime (April to June) and three posthumously (July to September), after his death on 9 June 1870 terminated the story. The following announcement (dated 12 August 1870) appeared in the last published instalment:

All that was left in Manuscript of *Edwin Drood* is contained in the Number now published – the sixth. Its last entire page had not been written two hours when the event occurred which one very touching passage in it (grave and sad but also cheerful and reassuring) might seem almost to have anticipated. The only notes in reference to the story that have since been found concern that portion of it exclusively, which is treated in the earlier Numbers. Beyond the clues therein afforded to its conduct or catastrophe, nothing whatever remains; and it is believed that what the author would himself have most desired is done, in placing before the reader without further notice or suggestion the fragment of *The Mystery of Edwin Drood*.

The published part-divisions were as follows:

I	April 1870	chs. 1–4
II	May 1870	chs. 5–9
III	June 1870	chs. 10–12
IV	July 1870	chs. 13–16
V	August 1870	chs. 17–20
VI	September 1870	chs. 21–23

The end of a monthly part is marked in the text by an asterisk.

Dickens's death almost exactly halfway through the novel created problems for subsequent editors. Two of the remaining parts (four and five) he had read in proof while the sixth, almost complete, existed only in manuscript. Faced with the responsibility of making available as much of the fragment as he could, Dickens's literary executor, John Forster, decided as follows: (1) to restore the excisions Dickens had made in proof (some 150 lines) when he found he had overwritten the August number; (2) to redress the resulting imbalance by splitting the original Chapter 20 ('Divers Flights') in two and modifying the title; (3) to carry over the second part of the divided chapter (with a new title entirely of his devising) into the September (and final) number, thereby bringing it closer to the required thirty-two pages. The changes thus increased the total number of chapters by one and introduced two new chapter titles: 'A Flight' and 'A Recognition'.

This edition combines Forster's solution with the text of the novel prepared for Penguin Books by Arthur J. Cox in 1974. Cox's text is based on a comparison of the manuscript and partial proofs of the novel in the Forster Collection at the Victoria and Albert Museum with the text of the first edition published serially in 1870. I have retained Cox's version of the final chapters based on his reading of the manuscript. But I have not adopted, as he did, Dickens's chapter titles and divisions for the original Chapters 21 and 22. Double quotation marks have been replaced by singles ones, and the full point after 'Mr', 'Mrs', 'Dr' and 'St' has been omitted. Em-rules have been replaced by spaced en-rules.

THE MYSTERY

OF

EDWIN DROOD.

BY

CHARLES DICKENS.

WITH TWELVE ILLUSTRATIONS BY S. L. FILDES,

AND A PORTRAIT.

LONDON:

CHAPMAN AND HALL, 193 PICCADILLY.

1870.

[*The right of Translation is reserved.*]

CONTENTS

LIST OF ILLUSTRATIONS

CHAPTER I

The Dawn[1]

An ancient English Cathedral town? How can the ancient English Cathedral town[2] be here! The well-known massive grey square tower of its old Cathedral? How can that be here! There is no spike of rusty iron in the air, between the eye and it, from any point of the real prospect. What is the spike that intervenes, and who has set it up? Maybe, it is set up by the Sultan's orders[3] for the impaling of a horde of Turkish robbers, one by one. It is so, for cymbals clash, and the Sultan goes by to his palace in long procession. Ten thousand scimitars flash in the sunlight, and thrice ten thousand dancing-girls strew flowers. Then, follow white elephants caparisoned in countless gorgeous colors, and infinite in number and attendants. Still, the Cathedral tower rises in the background, where it cannot be, and still no writhing figure is on the grim spike.[4] Stay! Is the spike so low a thing as the rusty spike on the top of a post of an old bedstead that has tumbled all awry? Some vague period of drowsy laughter must be devoted to the consideration of this possibility.

Shaking from head to foot, the man whose scattered consciousness[5] has thus fantastically pieced itself together, at length rises, supports his trembling frame upon his arms, and looks around. He is in the meanest and closest of small rooms. Through the ragged window-curtain, the light of early day steals in from a miserable court. He lies, dressed, across a large unseemly bed, upon a bedstead that has indeed given way under the weight upon it. Lying, also dressed and also across the bed, not longwise, are a Chinaman, a Lascar,[6] and a haggard woman. The two first are in a sleep or stupor; the last is blowing at a kind of pipe, to kindle it. And as she blows, and shading it with her lean hand, concentrates its red spark of light, it serves in the dim morning as a lamp to show him what he sees of her.

'Another?' says this woman, in a querulous, rattling whisper. 'Have another?'

He looks about him, with his hand to his forehead.

'Ye've smoked as many as five since ye come in at midnight,' the woman goes on, as she chronically complains. 'Poor me, poor me, my head is so bad. Them two come in after ye. Ah, poor me, the business is slack, is slack! Few Chinamen about the Docks, and fewer Lascars, and no ships coming in, these say! Here's another ready for ye, deary. Ye'll remember like a good soul, won't ye, that the market price is dreffle high just now? More nor three shillings and sixpence for a thimbleful! And ye'll remember that nobody but me (and Jack China-man t'other side the court; but he can't do it as well as me) has the true secret of mixing it?[7] Ye'll pay up according, deary, won't ye?'

She blows at the pipe as she speaks, and, occasionally bubbling at it, inhales much of its contents.

'O me, O me, my lungs is weak, my lungs is bad! It's nearly ready for ye, deary. Ah, poor me, poor me, my poor hand shakes like to drop off! I see ye coming-to, and I ses to my poor self, "I'll have another ready for him, and he'll bear in mind the market price of opium, and pay according." O my poor head! I makes my pipes of old penny ink-bottles, ye see, deary – this is one – and I fits in a mouthpiece, this way, and I takes my mixter out of this thimble with this little horn spoon; and so I fills, deary. Ah, my poor nerves! I got Heavens-hard drunk for sixteen year afore I took to this; but this don't hurt me, not to speak of. And it takes away the hunger as well as wittles, deary.'

She hands him the nearly-emptied pipe, and sinks back, turning over on her face.

He rises unsteadily from the bed, lays the pipe upon the hearthstone, draws back the ragged curtain, and looks with repugnance at his three companions. He notices that the woman has opium-smoked herself into a strange likeness of the Chinaman. His form of cheek, eye, and temple, and his color, are repeated in her. Said Chinaman convulsively wrestles with one of his many Gods, or Devils, perhaps, and snarls horribly. The Lascar laughs and dribbles at the mouth. The hostess is still.

In the Court

'What visions can *she* have?' the waking man muses, as he turns her face towards him, and stands looking down at it. 'Visions of many butchers' shops, and public-houses, and much credit? Of an increase of hideous customers, and this horrible bedstead set upright again, and this horrible court swept clean? What can she rise to, under any quantity of opium, higher than that! – Eh?'

He bends down his ear, to listen to her mutterings.

'Unintelligible!'

As he watches the spasmodic shoots and darts that break out of her face and limbs, like fitful lightning out of a dark sky, some contagion in them seizes upon him: insomuch that he has to withdraw himself to a lean arm-chair by the hearth – placed there, perhaps, for such emergencies – and to sit in it, holding tight, until he has got the better of this unclean spirit of imitation.[8]

Then he comes back, pounces on the Chinaman, and, seizing him with both hands by the throat, turns him violently on the bed. The Chinaman clutches the aggressive hands, resists, gasps, and protests.

'What do you say?'

A watchful pause.

'Unintelligible!'

Slowly loosening his grasp as he listens to the incoherent jargon with an attentive frown, he turns to the Lascar and fairly drags him forth upon the floor. As he falls, the Lascar starts into a half-risen attitude, glares with his eyes, lashes about him fiercely with his arms, and draws a phantom knife. It then becomes apparent that the woman has taken possession of his knife, for safety's sake; for, she too starting up, and restraining and expostulating with him, the knife is visible in her dress, not in his, when they drowsily drop back, side by side.

There has been chattering and clattering enough between them, but to no purpose. When any distinct word has been flung into the air, it has had no sense or sequence. Wherefore 'unintelligible!' is again the comment of the watcher, made with some reassured nodding of his head, and a gloomy smile. He then lays certain silver money on the table, finds his hat, gropes his way down the broken stairs, gives a good morning to some rat-ridden doorkeeper, in bed in a black hutch beneath the stairs, and passes out.

*

That same afternoon,[9] the massive grey square tower of an old Cathedral rises before the sight of a jaded traveller. The bells are going for daily vesper service, and he must needs attend it, one would say, from his haste to reach the open Cathedral door. The choir are getting on their sullied white robes, in a hurry, when he arrives among them, gets on his own robe,[10] and falls into the procession filing in to service. Then, the Sacristan locks the iron-barred gates that divide the sanctuary from the chancel, and all of the procession having scuttled into their places, hide their faces; and then the intoned words, 'WHEN THE WICKED MAN –'[11] rise among groins of arches and beams of roof, awakening muttered thunder.

CHAPTER 2

A Dean, and a Chapter Also[1]

Whosoever has observed that sedate and clerical bird, the rook,[2] may perhaps have noticed that when he wings his way homeward towards nightfall,[3] in a sedate and clerical company, two rooks will suddenly detach themselves from the rest, will retrace their flight for some distance, and will there poise and linger; conveying to mere men[4] the fancy that it is of some occult importance to the body politic, that this artful couple should pretend to have renounced connexion with it.

Similarly, service being over in the old Cathedral with the square tower, and the choir scuffling out again, and divers venerable persons of rook-like aspect dispersing, two of these latter retrace their steps, and walk together in the echoing Close.

Not only is the day waning, but the year.[5] The low sun is fiery and yet cold behind the monastery ruin, and the Virginia creeper on the Cathedral wall has showered half its deep-red leaves down on the pavement. There has been rain this afternoon, and a wintry shudder goes among the little pools on the cracked uneven flag-stones, and through the giant elm trees as they shed a gust of tears. Their fallen leaves lie strewn thickly about.[6] Some of these leaves, in a timid rush, seek sanctuary[7] within the low arched Cathedral door; but two men coming out, resist them, and cast them forth[8] again with their feet; this done, one of the two locks the door with a goodly key, and the other flits away with a folio music book.

'Mr Jasper[9] was that, Tope?'[10]

'Yes, Mr Dean.'

'He has stayed late.'

'Yes, Mr Dean. I have stayed for him, your Reverence. He has been took a little poorly.'

'Say "taken," Tope – to the Dean,' the younger rook interposes in a low tone with this touch of correction, as who should say: 'You may offer bad grammar to the laity, or the humbler clergy, not to the Dean.'

Mr Tope, Chief Verger and Showman, and accustomed to be high with excursion parties, declines with a silent loftiness to perceive that any suggestion has been tendered to him.

'And when and how has Mr Jasper been taken – for, as Mr Crisparkle[11] has remarked, it is better to say taken – taken –' repeats the Dean; 'when and how has Mr Jasper been Taken –'

'Taken, sir,' Tope deferentially murmurs.

'– Poorly, Tope?'

'Why, sir, Mr Jasper was that breathed[12] –'

'I wouldn't say "That breathed," Tope,' Mr Crisparkle interposes, with the same touch as before. 'Not English – to the Dean.'

'Breathed to that extent,' the Dean (not unflattered by this indirect homage) condescendingly remarks, 'would be preferable.'

'Mr Jasper's breathing was so remarkably short' – thus discreetly does Mr Tope work his way round the sunken rock – 'when he came in, that it distressed him mightily to get his notes out: which was perhaps the cause of his having a kind of fit on him after a little. His memory grew DAZED.' Mr Tope, with his eyes on the Reverend Mr Crisparkle, shoots this word out, as defying him to improve upon it: 'and a dimness and giddiness crept over him as strange as ever I saw: though he didn't seem to mind it particularly, himself. However, a little time and a little water brought him out of his DAZE.' Mr Tope repeats the word and its emphasis, with the air of saying: 'As I *have* made a success, I'll make it again.'

'And Mr Jasper has gone home quite himself, has he?' asks the Dean.

'Your Reverence, he has gone home quite himself. And I'm glad to see he's having his fire kindled up, for it's chilly after the wet, and the Cathedral had both a damp feel and a damp touch this afternoon, and he was very shivery.'

They all three look towards an old stone gatehouse crossing the Close, with an arched thoroughfare passing beneath it. Through its latticed window, a fire shines out upon the fast-darkening scene, involving in shadow the pendent masses of ivy and creeper covering the building's front. As the deep Cathedral-bell strikes the hour, a ripple of wind goes through these at their distance, like a ripple of the solemn sound that hums through tomb and tower, broken niche and defaced statue, in the pile close at hand.

'Is Mr Jasper's nephew with him?' the Dean asks.

'No, sir,' replies the Verger, 'but expected. There's his own solitary shadow betwixt his two windows – the one looking this way, and the one looking down into the High Street – drawing his own curtains now.'

'Well, well,' says the Dean, with a sprightly air of breaking up the little conference, 'I hope Mr Jasper's heart may not be too much set upon his nephew.[13] Our affections, however laudable, in this transitory world, should never master us; we should guide them, guide them. I find I am not disagreeably reminded of my dinner, by hearing my dinner-bell. Perhaps, Mr Crisparkle, you will, before going home, look in on Jasper?'

'Certainly, Mr Dean. And tell him that you had the kindness to desire to know how he was?'

'Aye; do so, do so. Certainly. Wished to know how he was. By all means. Wished to know how he was.'

With a pleasant air of patronage, the Dean as nearly cocks his quaint hat as a Dean in good spirits may, and directs his comely gaiters towards the ruddy dining-room of the snug old red-brick house where he is at present 'in residence'[14] with Mrs Dean and Miss Dean.

Mr Crisparkle, Minor Canon,[15] fair and rosy, and perpetually pitching himself head-foremost into all the deep running water[16] in the surrounding country; Mr Crisparkle, Minor Canon, early riser, musical, classical, cheerful, kind, good-natured, social, contented, and boy-like; Mr Crisparkle, Minor Canon and good man, lately 'Coach' upon the chief Pagan high roads, but since promoted by a patron (grateful for a well-taught son) to his present Christian beat; betakes himself to the gatehouse, on his way home to his early tea.[17]

'Sorry to hear from Tope that you have not been well, Jasper.'

'Oh, it was nothing, nothing!'

'You look a little worn.'

'Do I? Oh, I don't think so. What is better, I don't feel so. Tope has made too much of it, I suspect. It's his trade to make the most of everything appertaining to the Cathedral, you know.'

'I may tell the Dean – I call expressly from the Dean – that you are all right again?'

The reply, with a slight smile, is: 'Certainly; with my respects and thanks to the Dean.'

'I'm glad to hear that you expect young Drood.'

'I expect the dear fellow every moment.'

'Ah! He will do you more good than a doctor, Jasper.'

'More good than a dozen doctors. For I love him dearly, and I don't love doctors, or doctors' stuff.'[18]

Mr Jasper is a dark man of some six-and-twenty, with thick, lustrous, well-arranged black hair and whisker. He looks older than he is, as dark men often do. His voice is deep and good, his face and figure are good, his manner is a little sombre. His room is a little sombre, and may have had its influence in forming his manner. It is mostly in shadow. Even when the sun shines brilliantly, it seldom touches the grand piano in the recess, or the folio music-books on the stand, or the bookshelves on the wall, or the unfinished picture of a blooming schoolgirl[19] hanging over the chimneypiece; her flowing brown hair tied with a blue riband, and her beauty remarkable for a quite childish, almost babyish, touch of saucy discontent, comically conscious of itself. (There is not the least artistic merit in this picture, which is a mere daub; but it is clear that the painter has made it humorously – one might almost say, revengefully – like the original.)

'We shall miss you, Jasper, at the "Alternate Musical Wednesdays" to-night; but no doubt you are best at home. Good-night. God bless you! "Tell me, shep-herds, te-e-ell me;[20] tell me-e-e, have you seen (have you seen, have you seen, have you seen) my-y-y Flo-o-ora-a pass this way!"' Melodiously good Minor Canon the Reverend Septimus[21] Crisparkle thus delivers himself, in musical rhythm, as he withdraws his amiable face from the doorway and conveys it down stairs.

Sounds of recognition and greeting pass between the Reverend Septimus and somebody else, at the stair-foot. Mr Jasper listens, starts from his chair, and catches a young fellow in his arms, exclaiming:

'My dear Edwin!'[22]

'My dear Jack! So glad to see you!'

'Get off your greatcoat, bright boy, and sit down here in your own corner. Your feet are not wet? Pull your boots off. Do pull your boots off.'

'My dear Jack, I am as dry as a bone. Don't moddley-coddley,[23] there's a good fellow.. I like anything better than being moddley-coddleyed.'

With the check upon him of being unsympathetically restrained in a genial outburst of enthusiasm, Mr Jasper stands still, and looks on intently at the young fellow, divesting himself of his outer coat, hat, gloves, and so forth. Once for all, a look of intentness and intensity[24] – a look of hungry, exacting, watchful, and yet devoted affection – is always, now and ever afterwards, on the Jasper face whenever the Jasper face is addressed in this direction. And whenever it is so addressed, it is never, on this occasion or on any other, dividedly addressed; it is always concentrated.

'Now I am right, and now I'll take my corner, Jack. Any dinner, Jack?'

Mr Jasper opens a door at the upper end of the room, and discloses a small inner room pleasantly lighted and prepared, wherein a comely dame is in the act of setting dishes on table.

'What a jolly old Jack it is!'[25] cries the young fellow, with a clap of his hands. 'Look here, Jack; tell me; whose birthday is it?'

'Not yours, I know,' Mr Jasper answers, pausing to consider.

'Not mine, you know? No; not mine, I know! Pussy's!'[26]

Fixed as the look the young fellow meets is, there is yet in it some strange power of suddenly including the sketch over the chimneypiece.

'Pussy's, Jack! We must drink Many happy returns to her. Come, uncle; take your dutiful and sharp-set nephew in to dinner.'

As the boy (for he is little more) lays a hand on Jasper's shoulder, Jasper cordially and gaily lays a hand on *his* shoulder, and so Marseillaise-wise[27] they go in to dinner.

'And, Lord! Here's Mrs Tope!' cries the boy. 'Lovelier than ever!'

'Never you mind me, Master Edwin,' retorts the Verger's wife; 'I can take care of myself.'

'You can't. You're much too handsome. Give me a kiss, because it's Pussy's birthday.'

'I'd Pussy you, young man, if I was Pussy, as you call her,' Mrs Tope blushingly retorts, after being saluted. 'Your uncle's too much wrapt up in you, that's where it is. He makes so much of you, that it's my opinion you think you've only to call your Pussys by the dozen, to make 'em come.'

'You forget, Mrs Tope,' Mr Jasper interposes, taking his place at table with a genial smile, 'and so do you, Ned, that Uncle and Nephew are words prohibited here by common consent and express agreement. For what we are going to receive His holy name be praised!'

'Done like the Dean! Witness, Edwin Drood! Please to carve, Jack, for I can't.'

This sally ushers in the dinner. Little to the present purpose, or to any purpose, is said, while it is in course of being disposed of. At length the cloth is drawn, and a dish of walnuts and a decanter of rich-colored sherry are placed upon the table.

'I say! Tell me, Jack,' the young fellow then flows on: 'do you really and truly feel as if the mention of our relationship divided us at all? *I* don't.'

'Uncles as a rule, Ned, are so much older than their nephews,' is the reply, 'that I have that feeling instinctively.'

'As a rule? Ah, may-be! But what is a difference in age of half a dozen years or so? And some uncles, in large families, are even younger than their nephews. By George, I wish it was the case with us!'

'Why?'

'Because if it was, I'd take the lead with you, Jack, and be as wise as Begone dull care[28] that turned a young man grey, and begone dull care that turned an old man to clay. – Halloa, Jack! Don't drink.'

'Why not?'

'Asks why not, on Pussy's birthday, and no Happy Returns proposed! Pussy, Jack, and many of 'em! Happy returns, I mean.'

Laying an affectionate and laughing touch on the boy's extended hand, as if it were at once his giddy head and his light heart, Mr Jasper drinks the toast in silence.

'Hip, hip, hip, and nine times nine, and one to finish with, and all that, understood. Hooray, hooray, hooray! And now, Jack, let's have a little talk about Pussy. Two pairs of nut-crackers? Pass me one, and take the other.' Crack. 'How's Pussy getting on, Jack?'

'With her music? Fairly.'

'What a dreadfully conscientious fellow you are, Jack. But *I* know, Lord bless you! Inattentive, isn't she?'

'She can learn anything, if she will.'

'*If* she will! Egad, that's it. But if she won't?'

Crack. On Mr Jasper's part.

'How's she looking, Jack?'

Mr Jasper's concentrated face again includes the portrait[29] as he returns: 'Very like your sketch indeed.'

'I *am* a little proud of it,' says the young fellow, glancing up at the sketch with complacency, and then shutting one eye, and taking a corrected prospect of it over a level bridge of nut-cracker in the air: 'Not badly hit off from memory. But I ought to have caught that expression pretty well, for I have seen it often enough.'

Crack. On Edwin Drood's part.

Crack. On Mr Jasper's part.

'In point of fact,' the former resumes, after some silent dipping among his fragments of walnut with an air of pique, 'I see it whenever I go to see Pussy. If I don't find it on her face, I leave it there. – You know I do, Miss Scornful Pert. Booh!' With a twirl of the nut-crackers at the portrait.

Crack. Crack. Crack. Slowly, on Mr Jasper's part.

Crack. Sharply, on the part of Edwin Drood.

Silence on both sides.

'Have you lost your tongue, Jack?'

'Have you found yours, Ned?'

'No, but really; – isn't it, you know, after all?'

Mr Jasper lifts his dark eyebrows enquiringly.

'Isn't it unsatisfactory to be cut off from choice in such a matter? There, Jack! I tell you! If I could choose, I would choose Pussy from all the pretty girls in the world.'

'But you have not got to choose.'

'That's what I complain of. My dead and gone father and Pussy's dead and gone father must needs marry us together by anticipation.[30] Why the – Devil, I was going to say, if it had been respectful to their memory – couldn't they leave us alone?'

'Tut, tut, dear boy,' Mr Jasper remonstrates, in a tone of gentle deprecation.

'Tut, tut? Yes, Jack, it's all very well for *you*. *You* can take it easily. *Your* life is not laid down to scale, and lined and dotted out for you, like a surveyor's plan. *You* have no uncomfortable suspicion that you are forced upon anybody, nor has anybody an uncomfortable suspicion that she is forced upon you, or that you are forced upon her. *You* can choose for yourself. Life, for *you*, is a plum with the natural bloom on; it hasn't been over-carefully wiped off for *you* –'

'Don't stop, dear fellow. Go on.'

'Can I anyhow have hurt your feelings, Jack?'

'How can you have hurt my feelings?'

'Good Heaven, Jack, you look frightfully ill! There's a strange film come over your eyes.'

Mr Jasper, with a forced smile, stretches out his right hand, as if at once to disarm apprehension and gain time to get better. After a while he says faintly:

'I have been taking opium for a pain[31] – an agony – that sometimes overcomes me. The effects of the medicine steal over me like a blight or a cloud, and pass. You see them in the act of passing; they will be gone directly. Look away from me. They will go all the sooner.'

With a scared face, the younger man complies, by casting his eyes downward at the ashes on the hearth. Not relaxing his own gaze at the fire, but rather strengthening it with a fierce, firm grip upon his elbow-chair, the elder sits for a few moments rigid, and then, with thick drops standing on his forehead, and a sharp catch of his breath, becomes as he was before. On his so subsiding in his chair, his nephew gently and assiduously tends him while he quite recovers. When Jasper is restored, he lays a tender hand upon his nephew's shoulder, and, in a tone of voice less troubled than the purport of his words – indeed with something of raillery or banter in it – thus addresses him:

'There is said to be a hidden skeleton in every house; but you thought there was none in mine, dear Ned.'

'Upon my life, Jack, I did think so. However, when I come to consider that even in Pussy's house – if she had one – and in mine – if I had one –'

'You were going to say (but that I interrupted you in spite of myself) what a quiet life mine is. No whirl and uproar around me, no distracting commerce or calculation, no risk, no change of place, myself devoted to the art I pursue, my business my pleasure.'

'I really was going to say something of the kind, Jack; but you see, you, speaking of yourself, almost necessarily leave out much that I should have put in. For instance: I should have put in the foreground your being so much respected as Lay Precentor, or Lay Clerk,[32] or whatever you call it, of this Cathedral; your enjoying the reputation of having done such wonders with the choir; your choosing your society, and holding such an independent position in this queer old place; your gift of teaching (why, even Pussy, who don't like being taught, says there never was such a Master as you are!); and your connexion.'

'Yes; I saw what you were tending to. I hate it.'

'Hate it, Jack?' (Much bewildered.)

'I hate it. The cramped monotony of my existence grinds me away[33] by the grain. How does our service sound to you?'

'Beautiful! Quite celestial!'

'It often sounds to me quite devilish.[34] I am so weary of it. The echoes of my own voice among the arches seem to mock me with my daily drudging round. No wretched monk who droned his life away in that gloomy place, before me, can have been more tired of it than I am. He could take for relief (and did take) to carving demons out of the stalls and seats and desks. What shall I do? Must I take to carving them out of my heart?'

'I thought you had so exactly found your niche in life, Jack,' Edwin Drood returns, astonished, bending forward in his chair to lay a sympathetic hand on Jasper's knee, and looking at him with an anxious face.

'I know you thought so. They all think so.'

'Well; I suppose they do,' says Edwin, meditating aloud. 'Pussy thinks so.'

'When did she tell you that?'

'The last time I was here. You remember when. Three months ago.'

'How did she phrase it?'

'Oh! She only said that she had become your pupil, and that you were made for your vocation.'

The younger man glances at the portrait. The elder sees it in him.

'Anyhow, my dear Ned,' Jasper resumes, as he shakes his head with a grave cheerfulness: 'I must subdue myself to my vocation: which is much the same thing outwardly. It's too late to find another now. This is a confidence between us.'

'It shall be sacredly preserved, Jack.'

'I have reposed it in you, because –'

'I feel it, I assure you. Because we are fast friends, and because you love and trust me, as I love and trust you. Both hands, Jack.'

As each stands looking into the other's eyes, and as the uncle holds the nephew's hands, the uncle thus proceeds:

'You know now, don't you, that even a poor monotonous chorister and grinder of music – in his niche – may be troubled with some stray sort of ambition, aspiration, restlessness, dissatisfaction, what shall we call it?'

'Yes, dear Jack.'

'And you will remember?'

'My dear Jack, I only ask you, am I likely to forget what you have said with so much feeling?'

'Take it as a warning, then.'

In the act of having his hands released, and of moving a step back,

Edwin pauses for an instant to consider the application of these last words. The instant over, he says, sensibly touched:

'I am afraid I am but a shallow, surface kind of fellow, Jack, and that my headpiece is none of the best. But I needn't say I am young; and perhaps I shall not grow worse as I grow older. At all events, I hope I have something impressible within me, which feels – deeply feels – the disinterestedness of your painfully laying your inner self bare, as a warning to me.'

Mr Jasper's steadiness of face and figure becomes so marvellous that his breathing seems to have stopped.

'I couldn't fail to notice, Jack, that it cost you a great effort, and that you were very much moved, and very unlike your usual self. Of course I knew that you were extremely fond of me, but I really was not prepared for your, as I may say, sacrificing yourself to me, in that way.'

Mr Jasper, becoming a breathing man again without the smallest stage of transition between the two extreme states, lifts his shoulders, laughs, and waves his right arm.

'No; don't put the sentiment away, Jack; please don't; for I am very much in earnest. I have no doubt that that unhealthy state of mind which you have so powerfully described is attended with some real suffering, and is hard to bear. But let me reassure you, Jack, as to the chances of its overcoming Me. I don't think I am in the way of it. In some few months less than another year, you know, I shall carry Pussy off from school as Mrs Edwin Drood. I shall then go engineering into the East,[35] and Pussy with me. And although we have our little tiffs now, arising out of a certain unavoidable flatness that attends our love-making, owing to its end being all settled beforehand, still I have no doubt of our getting on capitally then, when it's done and can't be helped. In short, Jack, to go back to the old song I was freely quoting at dinner (and who knows old songs better than you!), my wife shall dance and I will sing, so merrily pass the day. Of Pussy's being beautiful there cannot be a doubt; – and when you are good besides, Little Miss Impudence,' once more apostrophizing the portrait, 'I'll burn your comic likeness and paint your music-master another.'

Mr Jasper, with his hand to his chin, and with an expression of musing benevolence on his face, has attentively watched every animated look and gesture attending the delivery of these words. He remains in that attitude after they are spoken, as if in a kind of fascination attendant on his strong interest in the youthful spirit that he loves so well. Then, he says with a quiet smile:

'You won't be warned, then?'

'No, Jack.'

'You can't be warned, then?'

'No, Jack, not by you. Besides that I don't really consider myself in danger, I don't like your putting yourself in that position.'

'Shall we go and walk in the churchyard?'

'By all means. You won't mind my slipping out of it for half a moment to the Nuns' House, and leaving a parcel there? Only gloves for Pussy;[36] as many pairs of gloves as she is years old to-day. Rather poetical, Jack?'

Mr Jasper, still in the same attitude, murmurs: ' "Nothing half so sweet in life,"[37] Ned!'

'Here's the parcel in my greatcoat pocket. They must be presented to-night, or the poetry is gone. It's against regulations for me to call at night, but not to leave a packet. I am ready, Jack!'

Mr Jasper dissolves his attitude, and they go out together.

CHAPTER 3

The Nuns' House

For sufficient reasons which this narrative will itself unfold as it advances, a fictitious name must be bestowed upon the old Cathedral town. Let it stand in these pages as Cloisterham.[1] It was once possibly known to the Druids by another name, and certainly to the Romans by another, and to the Saxons by another, and to the Normans by another; and a name more or less in the course of many centuries can be of little moment to its dusty chronicles.

An ancient city, Cloisterham, and no meet dwelling-place for any one with hankerings after the noisy world. A monotonous, silent city, deriving an earthy flavor throughout, from its Cathedral crypt, and so abounding in vestiges of monastic graves, that the Cloisterham children grow small salad in the dust[2] of abbots and abbesses, and make dirt-pies of nuns and friars; while every ploughman in its outlying fields renders to once puissant Lord Treasurers, Archbishops, Bishops, and such-like, the attention which the Ogre in the story-book desired to render to his unbidden visitor, and grinds their bones to make his bread.[3]

A drowsy city, Cloisterham, whose inhabitants seem to suppose, with an inconsistency more strange than rare, that all its changes lie behind it, and that there are no more to come. A queer moral to derive from antiquity, yet older than any traceable antiquity. So silent are the streets of Cloisterham (though prone to echo on the smallest provocation), that of a summer-day the sunblinds of its shops scarce dare to flap in the south wind; while the sun-browned tramps,[4] who pass along and stare, quicken their limp a little, that they may the sooner get beyond the confines of its oppressive respectability. This is a feat not difficult of achievement, seeing that the streets of Cloisterham city are little more than one narrow street by which you get into it and get out of it: the rest being mostly disappointing yards with pumps in them and no thoroughfare – exception made of the Cathedral-close, and a paved Quaker settlement,[5] in color and general conformation very like a Quakeress's bonnet, up in a shady corner.

In a word, a city of another and a bygone time is Cloisterham, with its hoarse Cathedral-bell, its hoarse rooks hovering about the Cathedral tower, its hoarser and less distinct rooks in the stalls far beneath. Fragments of old wall, saint's chapel, chapter-house, convent and monastery, have got incongruously or obstructively built into many of its houses and gardens, much as kindred jumbled notions have become incorporated into many of its citizens' minds. All things in it are of the past. Even its single pawnbroker takes in no pledges, nor has he for a long time, but offers vainly an unredeemed stock for sale, of which the costlier articles are dim and pale old watches apparently in a slow perspiration, tarnished sugar-tongs with ineffectual legs, and odd volumes of dismal books. The most abundant and the most agreeable evidences of progressing life in Cloisterham are the evidences of vegetable life in its many gardens; even its drooping and despondent little theatre has its poor strip of garden, receiving the foul fiend, when he ducks from its stage into the infernal regions, among scarlet beans or oyster-shells, according to the season of the year.

In the midst of Cloisterham stands the Nuns' House; a venerable brick edifice, whose present appellation is doubtless derived from the legend of its conventual uses. On the trim gate enclosing its old courtyard is a resplendent brass plate flashing forth the legend: 'Seminary for Young Ladies.[6] Miss Twinkleton.'[7] The house-front is so old and worn, and the brass plate is so shining and staring, that the general result has reminded imaginative strangers of a battered old beau with a large modern eye-glass stuck in his blind eye.[8]

Whether the nuns of yore, being of a submissive rather than a stiff-necked generation,[9] habitually bent their contemplative heads to avoid collision with the beams in the low ceilings of the many chambers of their House; whether they sat in its long low windows, telling their beads for their mortification instead of making necklaces of them for their adornment; whether they were ever walled up alive[10] in odd angles and jutting gables of the building for having some ineradicable leaven of busy mother Nature in them which has kept the fermenting world alive ever since; these may be matters of interest to its haunting ghosts (if any), but constitute no item in Miss Twinkleton's half-yearly accounts. They are neither of Miss Twinkleton's inclusive regulars, nor of her extras. The lady who undertakes the poetical department of the establishment at so much (or so little) a quarter has no pieces in her list of recitals bearing on such unprofitable questions.

As, in some cases of drunkenness, and in others of animal magnetism, there are two states of consciousness which never clash,[11] but each of which pursues its separate course as though it were continuous instead of broken (thus, if I hide my watch when I am drunk, I must be drunk again before I can remember where[12]), so Miss Twinkleton has two distinct and separate phases of being. Every night, the moment the young ladies have retired to rest, does Miss Twinkleton smarten up her curls a little, brighten up her eyes a little, and become a sprightly Miss Twinkleton whom the young ladies have never seen. Every night, at the same hour, does Miss Twinkleton resume the topics of the previous night, comprehending the tenderer scandal of Cloisterham, of which she has no knowledge whatever by day, and references to a certain season at Tunbridge Wells[13] (airily called by Miss Twinkleton in this state of her existence 'The Wells'), notably the season wherein a certain finished gentleman[14] (compassionately called by Miss Twinkleton, in this state of her existence, 'Foolish Mr Porters') revealed a homage of the heart, whereof Miss Twinkleton, in her scholastic state of existence, is as ignorant as a granite pillar. Miss Twinkleton's companion in both states of existence, and equally adaptable to either, is one Mrs Tisher: a deferential widow with a weak back, a chronic sigh, and a suppressed voice, who looks after the young ladies' wardrobes, and leads them to infer that she has seen better days.[15] Perhaps this is the reason why it is an article of faith with the servants, handed down from race to race, that the departed Tisher was a hairdresser.

The pet pupil of the Nuns' House is Miss Rosa Bud, of course called Rosebud; wonderfully pretty, wonderfully childish, wonderfully whimsical. An awkward interest (awkward because romantic) attaches to Miss Bud in the minds of the young ladies, on account of its being known to them that a husband has been chosen for her by will and bequest, and that her guardian is bound down to bestow her on that husband when he comes of age. Miss Twinkleton, in her seminarial state of existence, has combated the romantic aspect of this destiny by affecting to shake her head over it behind Miss Bud's dimpled shoulders, and to brood on the unhappy lot of that doomed little victim. But with no better effect – possibly some unfelt touch of foolish Mr Porters has undermined the endeavour – than to evoke from the young ladies an unanimous bedchamber cry of 'Oh! what a pretending old thing Miss Twinkleton is, my dear!'

The Nuns' House is never in such a state of flutter as when this allotted husband calls to see little Rosebud. (It is unanimously understood by the young ladies that he is lawfully entitled to this privilege, and that if Miss Twinkleton disputed it she would be instantly taken up and transported.[16]) When his ring at the gate bell is expected, or takes place, every young lady who can, under any pretence, look out of window, looks out of window: while every young lady who is 'practising,' practises out of time; and the French class becomes so demoralized that the Mark goes round[17] as briskly as the bottle at a convivial party in the last century.

On the afternoon of the day next after the dinner of two at the Gate House, the bell is rung with the usual fluttering results.

'Mr Edwin Drood to see Miss Rosa.'

This is the announcement of the parlor-maid in chief. Miss Twinkleton, with an exemplary air of melancholy on her, turns to the sacrifice, and says: 'You may go down, my dear.' Miss Bud goes down, followed by all eyes.

Mr Edwin Drood is waiting in Miss Twinkleton's own parlor: a dainty room, with nothing more directly scholastic in it than a terrestrial and a celestial globe. These expressive machines imply (to parents and guardians) that even when Miss Twinkleton retires into the bosom of privacy, duty may at any moment compel her to become a sort of Wandering Jewess,[18] scouring the earth and soaring through the skies in search of knowledge for her pupils.

The last new maid, who has never seen the young gentleman Miss Rosa is engaged to, and who is making his acquaintance between the hinges of the open door, left open for the purpose, stumbles guiltily down the kitchen stairs, as a charming little apparition, with its face concealed by a little silk apron thrown over its head, glides into the parlor.

'Oh! It *is* so ridiculous!' says the apparition, stopping and shrinking. 'Don't, Eddy!'

'Don't what, Rosa?'

'Don't come any nearer, please. It *is* so absurd.'

'What is absurd, Rosa?'

'The whole thing is. It *is* so absurd to be an engaged orphan; and it *is* so absurd to have the girls and the servants scuttling about after one, like mice in the wainscot;[19] and it *is* so absurd to be called upon!'

The apparition appears to have a thumb in the corner of its mouth while making this complaint.

'You give me an affectionate reception, Pussy, I must say.'

'Well, I will in a minute, Eddy, but I can't just yet. How are you?' (very shortly.)

'I am unable to reply that I am much the better for seeing you, Pussy, inasmuch as I see nothing of you.'

This second remonstrance brings a dark bright pouting eye out from a corner of the apron; but it swiftly becomes invisible again, as the apparition exclaims: 'Oh! Good Gracious, you have had half your hair cut off!'

'I should have done better to have had my head cut off, I think,' says Edwin, rumpling the hair in question, with a fierce glance at the looking-glass, and giving an impatient stamp. 'Shall I go?'

'No; you needn't go just yet, Eddy. The girls would all be asking questions why you went.'

'Once for all, Rosa, will you uncover that ridiculous little head of yours and give me a welcome?'

The apron is pulled off the childish head, as its wearer replies: 'You're very welcome, Eddy. There! I'm sure that's nice. Shake hands. No, I can't kiss you, because I've got an acidulated drop in my mouth.'

'Are you at all glad to see me, Pussy?'

'Oh, yes, I'm dreadfully glad. – Go and sit down. – Miss Twinkleton.'

It is the custom of that excellent lady, when these visits occur, to appear every three minutes, either in her own person or in that of Mrs Tisher, and lay an offering on the shrine of Propriety by affecting to look for some desiderated article. On the present occasion, Miss Twinkleton, gracefully gliding in and out, says, in passing: 'How do you do, Mr Drood? Very glad indeed to have the pleasure. Pray excuse me. Tweezers. Thank you!'

'I got the gloves last evening, Eddy, and I like them very much. They are beauties.'

'Well, that's something,' the affianced replies, half grumbling. 'The smallest encouragement thankfully received. And how did you pass your birthday, Pussy?'[20]

'Delightfully! Everybody gave me a present. And we had a feast. And we had a ball at night.'

'A feast and a ball, eh? These occasions seem to go off tolerably well without me, Pussy.'

'De-lightfully!' cries Rosa, in a quite spontaneous manner, and without the least pretence of reserve.

'Hah! And what was the feast?'

'Tarts, oranges, jellies, and shrimps.'

'Any partners at the ball?'

'We danced with one another, of course, sir. But some of the girls made game to be their brothers. It *was* so droll!'

'Did anybody make game to be –'

'To be you? Oh dear yes!' cries Rosa, laughing with great enjoyment. 'That was the first thing done.'

'I hope she did it pretty well,' says Edwin, rather doubtfully.

'Oh! It was excellent! – I wouldn't dance with you, you know.'

Edwin scarcely seems to see the force of this; begs to know if he may take the liberty to ask why?

'Because I was so tired of you,' returns Rosa. But she quickly adds, and pleadingly too, seeing displeasure in his face: 'Dear Eddy, you were just as tired of me, you know.'

'Did I say so, Rosa?'

'Say so! Do you ever say so? No, you only showed it. Oh, she did it so well!' cries Rosa, in a sudden ecstasy with her counterfeit betrothed.

'It strikes me that she must be a devilish impudent girl,' says Edwin Drood. 'And so, Pussy, you have passed your last birthday in this old house.'

'Ah, yes!' Rosa clasps her hands, looks down with a sigh, and shakes her head.

'You seem to be sorry, Rosa.'

'I am sorry for the poor old place. Somehow, I feel as if it would miss me, when I am gone so far away, so young.'

'Perhaps we had better stop short, Rosa?'

She looks up at him with a swift bright look; next moment shakes her head, sighs, and looks down again.

'That is to say, is it, Pussy, that we are both resigned?'

She nods her head again, and after a short silence, quaintly bursts out with: 'You know we must be married, and married from here, Eddy, or the poor girls will be so dreadfully disappointed!'

For the moment there is more of compassion, both for her and for himself, in her affianced husband's face, than there is of love. He checks the look, and asks: 'Shall I take you out for a walk, Rosa dear?'

Rosa dear does not seem at all clear on this point, until her face, which has been comically reflective, brightens. 'Oh, yes, Eddy; let us go for a walk! And I tell you what we'll do. You shall pretend that you are engaged to somebody else, and I'll pretend that I am not engaged to anybody, and then we shan't quarrel.'

'Do you think that will prevent our falling out, Rosa?'

'I know it will. Hush! Pretend to look out of window. – Mrs Tisher!'

Through a fortuitous concourse of accidents, the matronly Tisher heaves in sight, says, in rustling through the room like the legendary ghost of a Dowager[21] in silken skirts: 'I hope I see Mr Drood well; though I needn't ask, if I may judge from his complexion? I trust I disturb no one; but there *was* a paper-knife – Oh, thank you, I am sure!' and disappears with her prize.

'One other thing you must do, Eddy, to oblige me,' says Rosebud. 'The moment we get into the street, you must put me outside, and keep close to the house yourself – squeeze and graze yourself against it.'

'By all means, Rosa, if you wish it. Might I ask why?'

'Oh! because I don't want the girls to see you.'

'It's a fine day; but would you like me to carry an umbrella up?'

'Don't be foolish, sir. You haven't got polished leather boots on,' pouting, with one shoulder raised.

'Perhaps that might escape the notice of the girls, even if they did see me,' remarks Edwin, looking down at his boots with a sudden distaste for them.

'Nothing escapes their notice, sir. And then I know what would happen. Some of them would begin reflecting on me by saying (for *they* are free) that they never will on any account engage themselves to lovers without polished leather boots. Hark! Miss Twinkleton. I'll ask for leave.'

That discreet lady being indeed heard without, enquiring of nobody in a blandly conversational tone as she advances: 'Eh? Indeed! Are you quite sure you saw my mother-of-pearl button-holder on the work-table in my room?' is at once solicited for walking leave, and graciously accords it. And soon the young couple go out of the Nuns'

House, taking all precautions against the discovery of the so vitally defective boots of Mr Edwin Drood: precautions, let us hope, effective for the peace of Mrs Edwin Drood that is to be.

'Which way shall we take, Rosa?'

Rosa replies: 'I want to go to the Lumps-of-Delight shop.'

'To the –?'

'A Turkish sweetmeat, sir. My gracious me, don't you understand anything? Call yourself an Engineer, and not know *that*?'

'Why, how should I know it, Rosa?'

'Because I am very fond of them. But oh! I forgot what we are to pretend. No, you needn't know anything about them; never mind.'

So he is gloomily borne off to the Lumps-of-Delight shop, where Rosa makes her purchase, and, after offering some to him (which he rather indignantly declines), begins to partake of it with great zest: previously taking off and rolling up a pair of little pink gloves, like rose-leaves, and occasionally putting her little pink fingers to her rosy lips, to cleanse them from the Dust of Delight that comes off the Lumps.

'Now, be a good-tempered Eddy, and pretend. And so you are engaged?'

'And so I am engaged.'

'Is she nice?'

'Charming.'

'Tall?'

'Immensely tall!' (Rosa being short.)

'Must be gawky, I should think,' is Rosa's quiet commentary.

'I beg your pardon; not at all,' contradiction rising in him. 'What is termed a fine woman; a splendid woman.'

'Big nose, no doubt,' is the quiet commentary again.

'Not a little one, certainly,' is the quick reply. (Rosa's being a little one.)

'Long pale nose, with a red knob in the middle, *I* know the sort of nose,' says Rosa, with a satisfied nod, and tranquilly enjoying the Lumps.

'You *don't* know the sort of nose, Rosa,' with some warmth; 'because it's nothing of the kind.'

'Not a pale nose, Eddy?'

'No.' Determined not to assent.

'A red nose? Oh! I don't like red noses. However, to be sure, she can always powder it.'

'She would scorn to powder it,' says Edwin, becoming heated.

'Would she? What a stupid thing she must be! Is she stupid in everything?'

'No. In nothing.'

After a pause, in which the whimsically wicked face has not been unobservant of him, Rosa says:

'And this most sensible of creatures likes the idea of being carried off to Egypt; does she, Eddy?'

'Yes. She takes a sensible interest in triumphs of engineering skill: especially when they are to change the whole condition of an undeveloped country.'

'Lor!' says Rosa, shrugging her shoulders, with a little laugh of wonder.

'Do you object,' Edwin enquires, with a majestic turn of his eyes downward upon the fairy figure: 'do you object, Rosa, to her feeling that interest?'

'Object? My dear Eddy! But really. Doesn't she hate boilers and things?'

'I can answer for her not being so idiotic as to hate Boilers,' he returns with angry emphasis; 'though I cannot answer for her views about Things; really not understanding what Things are meant.'

'But don't she hate Arabs, and Turks, and Fellahs, and people?'

'Certainly not.' Very firmly.

'At least, she *must* hate the Pyramids? Come, Eddy?'

'Why should she be such a little – tall, I mean – Goose, as to hate the Pyramids, Rosa?'

'Ah! you should hear Miss Twinkleton,'[22] often nodding her head, and much enjoying the Lumps, 'bore about them, and then you wouldn't ask. Tiresome old burying-grounds! Isises, and Ibises, and Cheopses,[23] and Pharaohses; who cares about them? And then there was Belzoni or somebody, dragged out by the legs, half choked with bats and dust.[24] All the girls say serve him right, and hope it hurt him, and wish he had been quite choked.'

The two youthful figures, side by side, but not now arm-in-arm, wander discontentedly about the old Close; and each sometimes stops and slowly imprints a deeper footstep in the fallen leaves.

'Well!' says Edwin, after a lengthy silence. 'According to custom. We can't get on, Rosa.'

Rosa tosses her head, and says she don't want to get on.

'That's a pretty sentiment, Rosa, considering.'

'Considering what?'

'If I say what, you'll go wrong again.'

'*You*'ll go wrong, you mean, Eddy. Don't be ungenerous.'

'Ungenerous! I like that!'

'Then I *don't* like that, and so I tell you plainly,' Rosa pouts.

'Now, Rosa, I put it to you. Who disparaged my profession, my destination –'

'You are not going to be buried in the Pyramids, I hope?' she interrupts, arching her delicate eyebrows. 'You never said you were. If you are, why haven't you mentioned it to me? I can't find out your plans by instinct.'

'Now, Rosa; you know very well what I mean, my dear.'

'Well then, why did you begin with your detestable red-nosed Giantesses? And she would, she would, she would, she would, she WOULD powder it!' cries Rosa, in a little burst of comical contradictory spleen.

'Somehow or other, I never can come right in these discussions,' says Edwin, sighing and becoming resigned.

'How is it possible, sir, that you ever can come right when you're always wrong? And as to Belzoni, I suppose he's dead; – I'm sure I hope he is – and how can his legs or his chokes concern you?'

'It is nearly time for your return, Rosa. We have not had a very happy walk, have we?'

'A happy walk? A detestably unhappy walk, sir. If I go upstairs the moment I get in and cry till I can't take my dancing-lesson, you are responsible, mind!'

'Let us be friends, Rosa.'

'Ah!' cries Rosa, shaking her head and bursting into real tears. 'I wish we *could* be friends! It's because we can't be friends, that we try one another so. I am a young little thing, Eddy, to have an old heartache; but I really, really have, sometimes. Don't be angry. I know you have one yourself, too often. We should both of us have done better, if What is to be had been left What might have been. I am quite a serious little thing now, and not teasing you. Let each of us forbear, this one time, on our own account, and on the other's!'

Disarmed by this glimpse of a woman's nature in the spoilt child, though for an instant disposed to resent it as seeming to involve the enforced infliction of himself upon her, Edwin Drood stands watching her as she childishly cries and sobs, with both hands to the handkerchief at her eyes, and then – she becoming more composed, and indeed beginning in her young inconstancy to laugh at herself for having been so moved – leads her to a seat hard by, under the elm trees.

'One clear word of understanding, Pussy dear. I am not clever out of my own line – now I come to think of it, I don't know that I am particularly clever in it – but I want to do right. There is not – there may be – I really don't see my way to what I want to say, but I must say it before we part – there is not any other young –'

'Oh no, Eddy! It's generous of you to ask me; but no, no, no!'

They have come very near to the Cathedral windows, and at this moment the organ and the choir sound out sublimely. As they sit listening to the solemn swell, the confidence of last night rises in young Edwin Drood's mind, and he thinks how unlike this music is to that discordance.

'I fancy I can distinguish Jack's voice,' is his remark in a low tone in connexion with the train of thought.

'Take me back at once, please,' urges his Affianced, quickly laying her light hand upon his wrist. 'They will all be coming out directly; let us get away. Oh, what a resounding chord! But don't let us stop to listen to it; let us get away!'

Her hurry is over, as soon as they have passed out of the Close. They go, arm-in-arm now, gravely and deliberately enough, along the old High Street, to the Nuns' House. At the gate, the street being within sight empty, Edwin bends down his face to Rosebud's.

She remonstrates, laughing, and is a childish schoolgirl again.

'Eddy, no! I'm too stickey to be kissed. But give me your hand, and I'll blow a kiss into that.'

33

Under the trees

He does so. She breathes a light breath into it and asks, retaining it and looking into it:

'Now say, what do you see?'

'See, Rosa?'

'Why, I thought you Egyptian boys could look into a hand and see all sorts of phantoms?[25] Can't you see a happy Future?'

For certain, neither of them sees a happy Present, as the gate opens and closes, and one goes in and the other goes away.

CHAPTER 4

Mr Sapsea[1]

Accepting the jackass as the type of self-sufficient stupidity and conceit – a custom, perhaps, like some few other customs, more conventional than fair – then the purest Jackass in Cloisterham is Mr Thomas Sapsea, Auctioneer.

Mr Sapsea 'dresses at' the Dean;[2] has been bowed to for the Dean, in mistake; has even been spoken to in the street as My Lord, under the impression that he was the Bishop come down unexpectedly, without his chaplain. Mr Sapsea is very proud of this, and of his voice, and of his style. He has even (in selling landed property) tried the experiment of slightly intoning in his pulpit, to make himself more like what he takes to be the genuine ecclesiastical article. So, in ending a Sale by Public Auction, Mr Sapsea finishes off with an air of bestowing a benediction on the assembled brokers, which leaves the real Dean – a modest and worthy gentleman – far behind.

Mr Sapsea has many admirers; indeed, the proposition is carried by a large local majority, even including non-believers in his wisdom, that he is a credit to Cloisterham. He possesses the great qualities of being portentous and dull, and of having a roll in his speech, and another roll in his gait; not to mention a certain gravely flowing action with his hands, as if he were presently going to Confirm the individual

35

with whom he holds discourse. Much nearer sixty years of age than fifty, with a flowing outline of stomach, and horizontal creases in his waistcoat; reputed to be rich; voting at elections in the strictly respectable interest; morally satisfied that nothing but he himself has grown since he was a baby; how can dunder-headed Mr Sapsea be otherwise than a credit to Cloisterham, and society?

Mr Sapsea's premises are in the High Street, over against the Nuns' House. They are of about the period of the Nuns' House, irregularly modernized here and there, as steadily deteriorating generations found, more and more, that they preferred air and light to Fever and the Plague.[3] Over the doorway is a wooden effigy, about half life-size, representing Mr Sapsea's father, in a curly wig and toga, in the act of selling. The chastity of the idea, and the natural appearance of the little finger, hammer, and pulpit, have been much admired.

Mr Sapsea sits in his dull ground-floor sitting-room, giving first on his paved back yard, and then on his railed-off garden. Mr Sapsea has a bottle of port wine on a table before the fire – the fire is an early luxury, but pleasant on the cool, chilly autumn evening – and is characteristically attended by his portrait, his eight-day clock,[4] and his weather-glass. Characteristically, because he would uphold himself against mankind, his weather-glass against weather, and his clock against time.

By Mr Sapsea's side on the table are a writing-desk and writing materials. Glancing at a scrap of manuscript, Mr Sapsea reads it to himself with a lofty air, and then, slowly pacing the room with his thumbs in the arm-holes of his waistcoat, repeats it from memory: so internally, though with much dignity, that the word 'Ethelinda'[5] is alone audible.

There are three clean wineglasses in a tray on the table. His serving-maid entering, and announcing 'Mr Jasper is come, sir,' Mr Sapsea waves 'Admit him' and draws two wineglasses from the rank, as being claimed.

'Glad to see you, sir. I congratulate myself on having the honor of receiving you here for the first time.' Mr Sapsea does the honors of his house in this wise.

'You are very good. The honor is mine and the self-congratulation is mine.'

'You are pleased to say so, sir. But I do assure you that it is a satisfaction to me to receive you in my humble home. And that is what I would not say to everybody.' Ineffable loftiness on Mr Sapsea's part accompanies these words, as leaving the sentence to be understood: 'You will not easily believe that your society can be a satisfaction to a man like myself; nevertheless, it is.'

'I have for some time desired to know you, Mr Sapsea.'

'And I, sir, have long known you by reputation as a man of taste. Let me fill your glass. I will give you, sir,' says Mr Sapsea, filling his own:

> 'When the French come over,
> May we meet them at Dover!'[6]

This was a patriotic toast in Mr Sapsea's infancy, and he is therefore fully convinced of its being appropriate to any subsequent era.

'You can scarcely be ignorant, Mr Sapsea,' observes Jasper, watching the auctioneer with a smile as the latter stretches out his legs before the fire, 'that you know the world.'

'Well, sir,' is the chuckling reply, 'I think I know something of it; something of it.'

'Your reputation for that knowledge has always interested and surprised me, and made me wish to know you. For, Cloisterham is a little place. Cooped up in it myself, I know nothing beyond it, and feel it to be a very little place.'

'If I have not gone to foreign countries, young man,' Mr Sapsea begins, and then stops: – 'You will excuse my calling you young man, Mr Jasper? You are much my junior.'

'By all means.'

'If I have not gone to foreign countries, young man, foreign countries have come to me.[7] They have come to me in the way of business, and I have improved upon my opportunities. Put it that I take an inventory, or make a catalogue. I see a French clock.[8] I never saw him before, in my life, but I instantly lay my finger on him and say "Paris!" I see some cups and saucers of Chinese make, equally strangers to me personally: I put my finger on them, then and there, and I say "Pekin, Nankin, and Canton." It is the same with Japan, with Egypt, and with bamboo and sandal-wood⁹ from the East Indies; I put my finger on them all. I have put my finger on the North Pole before now, and said, "Spear of Esquimaux make, for half a pint of pale sherry!"'

'Really? A very remarkable way, Mr Sapsea, of acquiring a knowledge of men and things.'

'I mention it, sir,' Mr Sapsea rejoins, with unspeakable complacency, 'because, as I say, it don't do to boast of what you are; but show how you came to be it, and then you prove it.'

'Most interesting. We were to speak of the late Mrs Sapsea.'

'We were, sir.' Mr Sapsea fills both glasses, and takes the decanter into safe keeping again. 'Before I consult your opinion as a man of taste on this little trifle' – holding it up – 'which is *but* a trifle, and still has required some thought, sir, some little fever of the brow, I ought perhaps to describe the character of the late Mrs Sapsea, now dead three quarters of a year.'¹⁰

Mr Jasper, in the act of yawning behind his wineglass, puts down that screen and calls up a look of interest. It is a little impaired in its expressiveness by his having a shut-up gape still to dispose of, with watering eyes.

'Half a dozen years ago, or so,' Mr Sapsea proceeds, 'when I had enlarged my mind up to – I will not say to what it now is, for that might seem to aim at too much, but up to the pitch of wanting another mind to be absorbed in it – I cast my eye about me for a nuptial partner. Because, as I say, it is not good for man to be alone.'¹¹

Mr Jasper appears to commit this original idea to memory.

'Miss Brobity¹² at that time kept, I will not call it the rival establishment to the establishment at the Nuns' House opposite, but I will call it the other parallel establishment down town. The world did have it that she showed a passion for attending my sales, when they took place on half-holidays, or in vacation time. The world did put it about, that she admired my style. The world did notice that as time flowed by, my style became traceable in the dictation-exercises of Miss Brobity's pupils.¹³ Young man, a whisper even sprang up in obscure malignity, that one ignorant and besotted Churl (a parent) so committed himself as to object to it by name. But I do not believe this. For is it likely that any human creature in his right senses would so lay himself open to be pointed at, by what I call the finger of scorn?'[14]

Mr Jasper shakes his head. Not in the least likely. Mr Sapsea, in a grandiloquent state of absence of mind, seems to refill his visitor's glass, which is full already; and does really refill his own, which is empty.

'Miss Brobity's Being, young man, was deeply imbued with homage to Mind. She revered Mind, when launched, or, as I say, precipitated, on an extensive knowledge of the world. When I made my proposal, she did me the honor to be so overshadowed with a species of Awe, as to be able to articulate only the two words, "O Thou!" – meaning myself. Her limpid blue eyes were fixed upon me, her semi-transparent hands were clasped together, pallor overspread her aquiline features, and, though encouraged to proceed, she never did proceed a word further. I disposed of the parallel establishment, by private contract, and we became as nearly one as could be expected under the circumstances. But she never could, and she never did, find a phrase satisfactory to her perhaps-too-favorable estimate of my intellect. To the very last (feeble action of liver), she addressed me in the same unfinished terms.'

Mr Jasper has closed his eyes as the auctioneer has deepened his voice. He now abruptly opens them, and says, in unison with the deepened voice 'Ah!' – rather as if stopping himself on the extreme verge of adding – 'men!'

'I have been since,' says Mr Sapsea, with his legs stretched out, and solemnly enjoying himself with the wine and the fire, 'what you behold me; I have been since a solitary mourner; I have been since, as I say, wasting my evening conversation on the desert air.[15] I will not say that I have reproached myself; but there have been times when I have asked myself the question: What if her husband had been nearer on a level with her? If she had not had to look up quite so high, what might the stimulating action have been upon the liver?'

Mr Jasper says, with an appearance of having fallen into dreadfully low spirits, that he 'supposes it was to be.'

'We can only suppose so, sir,' Mr Sapsea coincides. 'As I say, Man proposes, Heaven disposes.[16] It may or may not be putting the same thought in another form; but that is the way I put it.'

Mr Jasper murmurs assent.

'And now, Mr Jasper,' resumes the auctioneer, producing his scrap of manuscript, 'Mrs Sapsea's monument having had full time to settle and dry, let me take your opinion, as a man of taste, on the inscription I have (as I before remarked, not without some little fever of the brow) drawn out for it. Take it in your own hand. The setting out of the lines requires to be followed with the eye, as well as the contents with the mind.'

Mr Jasper complying, sees and reads as follows:

ETHELINDA,
Reverential Wife of
MR THOMAS SAPSEA,
AUCTIONEER, VALUER, ESTATE AGENT, &c.,
OF THIS CITY.
Whose Knowledge of the World,
Though somewhat extensive,
Never brought him acquainted with
A SPIRIT
More capable of
LOOKING UP TO HIM.
STRANGER PAUSE
And ask thyself the Question,
CANST THOU DO LIKEWISE?
If Not,
WITH A BLUSH RETIRE.[17]

Mr Sapsea having risen and stationed himself with his back to the fire, for the purpose of observing the effect of these lines on the countenance of a man of taste, consequently has his face towards the door, when his serving-maid, again appearing, announces, 'Durdles[18] is come, sir!' He promptly draws forth and fills the third wineglass, as being now claimed, and replies, 'Show Durdles in.'

'Admirable!' quoth Mr Jasper, handing back the paper.

'You approve, sir?'

'Impossible not to approve. Striking, characteristic, and complete.'

The auctioneer inclines his head, as one accepting his due and giving a receipt; and invites the entering Durdles to take off that glass of wine (handing the same), for it will warm him.

Durdles is a stonemason; chiefly in the gravestone, tomb, and monument way, and wholly of their color from head to foot. No man is better known in Cloisterham. He is the chartered libertine of the place.[19] Fame trumpets him a wonderful workman – which, for aught that anybody knows, he may be (as he never works); and a wonderful sot[20] – which everybody knows he is. With the Cathedral crypt he is better acquainted than any living authority; it may even be than any dead one. It is said that the intimacy of this acquaintance began in his habitually resorting to that secret place, to lock out the Cloisterham boy-populace, and sleep off the fumes of liquor: he having ready access to the Cathedral, as contractor for rough repairs. Be this as it may, he does know much about it, and, in the demolition of impedimental fragments of wall, buttress, and pavement, has seen strange sights. He often speaks of himself in the third person; perhaps being a little misty as to his own identity when he narrates; perhaps impartially adopting the Cloisterham nomenclature in reference to a character of acknowledged distinction. Thus he will say, touching his strange sights: 'Durdles come upon the old chap,' in reference to a buried magnate of ancient time and high degree, 'by striking right into the coffin with his pick. The old chap gave Durdles a look with his open eyes, as much as to say "Is your name Durdles? Why, my man, I've been waiting for you a Devil of a time!" And then he turned to powder.'[21] With a two-foot rule always in his pocket, and a mason's hammer all but always in his hand, Durdles goes continually sounding and tapping[22] all about and about the Cathedral; and whenever he says to Tope: 'Tope, here's another old 'un in here!' Tope announces it to the Dean as an established discovery.

In a suit of coarse flannel with horn buttons, a yellow neckerchief with draggled ends, an old hat more russet-colored than black, and laced boots of the hue of his stony calling, Durdles leads a hazy, gipsy sort of life, carrying his dinner about with him in a small bundle, and sitting on all manner of tombstones to dine. This dinner of Durdles's has become quite a Cloisterham institution: not only because of his never appearing in public without it, but because of its having been, on certain renowned occasions, taken into custody along with Durdles (as drunk and incapable), and exhibited before the Bench of Justices at the Town Hall. These occasions, however, have been few and far apart: Durdles being as seldom drunk as sober. For the rest, he is an old bachelor, and he lives in a little antiquated hole of a house that was never finished: supposed to be built, so far, of stones stolen from the city wall. To this abode there is an approach, ankle-deep in stone chips, resembling a petrified grove of tombstones, urns, draperies, and broken columns, in all stages of sculpture. Herein, two journeymen incessantly chip, while other two journeymen, who face each other, incessantly saw stone; dipping as regularly in and out of their sheltering sentry-boxes, as if they were mechanical figures emblematical of Time and Death.[23]

To Durdles, when he has consumed his glass of port, Mr Sapsea entrusts that precious effort of his Muse. Durdles unfeelingly takes out his two-foot rule, and measures the lines calmly, alloying them with stone-grit.

'This is for the monument, is it, Mr Sapsea?'

'The Inscription. Yes.' Mr Sapsea waits for its effect on a common mind.

'It'll come in to a eighth of a inch,' says Durdles. 'Your servant, Mr Jasper. Hope I see you well.'

'How are you, Durdles?'

'I've got a touch of the Tombatism on me, Mr Jasper, but that I must expect.'

'You mean the Rheumatism,' says Sapsea, in a sharp tone. (He is nettled by having his composition so mechanically received.)

'No, I don't. I mean, Mr Sapsea, the Tombatism. It's another sort from Rheumatism. Mr Jasper knows what Durdles means. You get among them Tombs afore it's well light on a winter morning, and keep on, as the Catechism says, a walking in the same all the days of your life,[24] and *you*'ll know what Durdles means.'

'It is a bitter cold place,' Mr Jasper assents, with an antipathetic shiver.

'And if it's bitter cold for you, up in the chancel, with a lot of live breath smoking out about you, what the bitterness is to Durdles, down in the crypt among the earthy damps there, and the dead breath of the old 'uns,' returns that individual, 'Durdles leaves you to judge. − Is this to be put in hand at once, Mr Sapsea?'

Mr Sapsea, with an Author's anxiety to rush into publication, replies that it cannot be out of hand too soon.

'You had better let me have the key, then,' says Durdles.

'Why, man, it is not to be put inside the monument!'

'Durdles knows where it's to be put, Mr Sapsea; no man better. Ask 'ere a man in Cloisterham whether Durdles knows his work.'

Mr Sapsea rises, takes a key from a drawer, unlocks an iron safe let into the wall, and takes from it another key.

'When Durdles puts a touch or a finish upon his work, no matter where, inside or outside, Durdles likes to look at his work all round, and see that his work is a doing him credit,' Durdles explains, doggedly.

The key proffered him by the bereaved widower being a large one, he slips his two-foot rule into a side pocket of his flannel trousers made for it, and deliberately opens his flannel coat, and opens the mouth of a large breast-pocket within it before taking the key to place in that repository.

'Why, Durdles!' exclaims Jasper, looking on amused. 'You are undermined with pockets!'

'And I carries weight in 'em too, Mr Jasper. Feel those;' producing two other large keys.

'Hand me Mr Sapsea's likewise. Surely this is the heaviest of the three.'

'You'll find 'em much of a muchness, I expect,' says Durdles. 'They all belong to monuments. They all open Durdles's work. Durdles keeps the keys of his work mostly. Not that they're much used.'

'By the bye,' it comes into Jasper's mind to say, as he idly examines the keys;[25] 'I have been going to ask you, many a day, and have always forgotten. You know they sometimes call you Stony Durdles, don't you?'

'Cloisterham knows me as Durdles, Mr Jasper.'

'I am aware of that, of course. But the boys sometimes −'

'Oh! If you mind them young Imps of boys −' Durdles gruffly interrupts.

'I don't mind them, any more than you do. But there was a discussion the other day among the Choir, whether Stony stood for Tony;' clinking one key against another.

('Take care of the wards, Mr Jasper.')

'Or whether Stony stood for Stephen;' clinking with a change of keys.

('You can't make a pitch-pipe of 'em, Mr Jasper.')

'Or whether the name comes from your trade. How stands the fact?'

Mr Jasper weighs the three keys in his hand, lifts his head from his idly stooping attitude over the fire, and delivers the keys to Durdles with an ingenuous and friendly face.

But the stony one is a gruff one likewise, and that hazy state of his is always an uncertain state, highly conscious of its dignity, and prone to take offence. He drops his two keys back into his pocket one by one, and buttons them up; he takes his dinner-bundle from the chair-back on which he hung it when he came in; he distributes the weight he carries, by tying the third key up in it, as though he were an Ostrich, and liked to dine off cold iron;[26] and he gets out of the room, deigning no word of answer.[27]

Mr Sapsea then proposes a hit at backgammon, which, seasoned with his own improving conversation, and terminating in a supper of cold roast beef and salad, beguiles the golden evening until pretty late. Mr Sapsea's wisdom being, in its delivery to mortals, rather of the diffuse than the epigrammatic order, is by no means expended even then; but his visitor intimates that he will come back for more of the precious commodity on future occasions, and Mr Sapsea lets him off for the present, to ponder on the instalment he carries away.

*

CHAPTER 5

Mr Durdles and Friend[1]

John Jasper, on his way home through the Close,[2] is brought to a standstill by the spectacle of Stony Durdles, dinner-bundle and all, leaning his back against the iron railing of the burial-ground enclosing it from the old cloister-arches; and a hideous small boy in rags flinging stones at him as a well-defined mark in the moonlight. Sometimes the stones hit him, and sometimes they miss him, but Durdles seems indifferent to either fortune. The hideous small boy, on the contrary, whenever he hits Durdles, blows a whistle of triumph through a jagged gap, convenient for the purpose, in the front of his mouth, where half his teeth are wanting; and whenever he misses him, yelps out 'Mulled agin!'[3] and tries to atone for the failure by taking a more correct and vicious aim.

'What are you doing to the man?' demands Jasper, stepping out into the moonlight from the shade.

'Making a cock-shy[4] of him,' replies the hideous small boy.

'Give me those stones in your hand.'

'Yes, I'll give 'em you down your throat, if you come a-ketching hold of me,' says the small boy, shaking himself loose, and backing. 'I'll smash your eye, if you don't look out!'

'Baby-Devil that you are, what has the man done to you?'

'He won't go home.'

'What is that to you?'

'He gives me a 'apenny to pelt him home if I ketches him out too late,' says the boy. And then chants, like a little savage, half stumbling and half dancing[5] among the rags and laces of his dilapidated boots:

> 'Widdy widdy wen![6]
> I – ket – ches – Im – out – ar – ter – ten,
> Widdy widdy wy!
> Then – E – don't – go – then – I – shy –
> Widdy Widdy Wake-cock warning!'

– with a comprehensive sweep on the last word, and one more delivery at Durdles.

This would seem to be a poetical note of preparation,[7] agreed upon, as a caution to Durdles to stand clear if he can, or to betake himself homeward.

John Jasper invites the boy with a beck of his head to follow him (feeling it hopeless to drag him, or coax him) and crosses to the iron railing where the Stony (and stoned) One is profoundly meditating.

'Do you know this thing, this child?'[8] asks Jasper, at a loss for a word that will define this thing.

'Deputy,' said Durdles, with a nod.

'Is that its – his – name?'

'Deputy,' assents Durdles.

'I'm man-servant up at the Travellers' Twopenny[9] in Gas Works Garding,'[10] this thing explains. 'All us man-servants at Travellers' Lodgings is named Deputy.[11] When we're chock full and the Travellers is all a-bed I come out for my 'elth.' Then withdrawing into the road, and taking aim, he resumes:

> 'Widdy widdy wen!
> I – ket – ches – Im – out – ar – ter—'

'Hold your hand,' cries Jasper, 'and don't throw while I stand so near him, or I'll kill you! Come, Durdles; let me walk home with you to-night. Shall I carry your bundle?'

'Not on any account,' replies Durdles, adjusting it. 'Durdles was making his reflections here when you come up, sir, surrounded by his works, like a poplar Author. – Your own brother-in-law;'[12] introducing a sarcophagus within the railing, white and cold in the moonlight. 'Mrs Sapsea;' introducing the monument of that devoted wife.[13] 'Late Incumbent;' introducing the Reverend Gentleman's broken column. 'Departed Assessed Taxes;' introducing a vase and towel, standing on what might represent the cake of soap.[14] 'Former pastrycook and muffin-maker, much respected;' introducing gravestone. 'All safe and sound here, sir, and all Durdles's work! Of the common folk that is merely bundled up in turf and brambles,[15] the less said, the better. A poor lot, soon forgot.'

'This creature, Deputy, is behind us,' says Jasper, looking back. 'Is he to follow us?'

The relations between Durdles and Deputy are of a capricious kind; for, on Durdles's turning himself about with the slow gravity of beery soddenness, Deputy makes a pretty wide circuit into the road and stands on the defensive.

'You never cried Widdy Warning before you begun to-night,' says Durdles, unexpectedly reminded of, or imagining, an injury.

'Yer lie, I did,' says Deputy, in his only form of polite contradiction.

'Own brother, sir,' observes Durdles, turning himself about again, and as unexpectedly forgetting his offence as he had recalled or conceived it; 'own brother to Peter the Wild Boy!¹⁶ But I gave him an object in life.'

'At which he takes aim?' Mr Jasper suggests.

'That's it, sir,' returns Durdles, quite satisfied; 'at which he takes aim. I took him in hand and gave him an object. What was he before? A destroyer. What work did he do? Nothing but destruction. What did he earn by it? Short terms in Cloisterham Jail. Not a person, not a piece of property, not a winder, not a horse, nor a dog, nor a cat, nor a bird, nor a fowl, nor a pig, but what he stoned, for want of an enlightened object. I put that enlightened object before him, and now he can turn his honest halfpenny by the three penn'orth a week.'

'I wonder he has no competitors.'

'He has plenty, Mr Jasper, but he stones 'em all away. Now, I don't know what this scheme of mine comes to,' pursues Durdles, considering about it with the same sodden gravity; 'I don't know what you may precisely call it. It ain't a sort of a – scheme of a – National Education?'¹⁷

'I should say not,' replies Jasper.

'*I* should say not,' assents Durdles; 'then we won't try to give it a name.'

'He still keeps behind us,' repeats Jasper, looking over his shoulder; 'is he to follow us?'

'We can't help going round by the Travellers' Twopenny, if we go the short way, which is the back way,' Durdles answers, 'and we'll drop him there.'

So they go on; Deputy, as a rear rank of one, taking open order,[18] and invading the silence of the hour and place by stoning every wall, post, pillar, and other inanimate object, by the deserted way.

'Is there anything new down in the crypt, Durdles?' asks John Jasper.

'Anything old, I think you mean,' growls Durdles. 'It ain't a spot for novelty.'

'Any new discovery on your part, I meant.'

'There's a old 'un under the seventh pillar on the left as you go down the broken steps of the little underground chapel as formerly was; I make him out (so fur as I've made him out yet) to be one of them old 'uns with a crook. To judge from the size of the passages in the walls, and of the steps and doors, by which they come and went, them crooks must have been a good deal in the way of the old 'uns! Two on 'em meeting promiscuous must have hitched one another by the mitre, pretty often, I should say.'

Without any endeavour to correct the literality of this opinion, Jasper surveys his companion – covered from head to foot with old mortar, lime, and stone grit – as though he, Jasper, were getting imbued with a romantic interest in his weird life.

'Yours is a curious existence.'

Without furnishing the least clue to the question, whether he receives this as a compliment or as quite the reverse, Durdles gruffly answers: 'Yours is another.'

'Well! Inasmuch as my lot is cast in the same old earthy, chilly, never-changing place. Yes. But there is much more mystery and interest in your connexion with the Cathedral than in mine.[19] Indeed, I am beginning to have some idea of asking you to take me on as a sort of student, or free 'prentice, under you, and to let me go about with you sometimes, and see some of these odd nooks in which you pass your days.'

The Stony One replies, in a general way, All right. Everybody knows where to find Durdles, when he's wanted. Which, if not strictly true, is approximately so, if taken to express that Durdles may always be found in a state of vagabondage somewhere.

'What I dwell upon most,' says Jasper, pursuing his subject of romantic interest, 'is the remarkable accuracy with which you would seem to find out where people are buried. – What is the matter? That bundle is in your way; let me hold it.'

Durdles has stopped and backed a little (Deputy, attentive to all his movements, immediately skirmishing into the road), and was looking about for some ledge or corner to place his bundle on, when thus relieved of it.

'Just you give me my hammer out of that,' says Durdles, 'and I'll show you.'

Clink, clink. And his hammer is handed him.

'Now, lookee here. You pitch your note, don't you, Mr Jasper?'

'Yes.'

'So I sound for mine. I take my hammer, and I tap.' (Here he strikes the pavement, and the attentive Deputy skirmishes at a rather wider range, as supposing that his head may be in requisition.) 'I tap, tap, tap. Solid! I go on tapping. Solid still! Tap again. Holloa! Hollow! Tap again, persevering. Solid in hollow! Tap, tap, tap, to try it better. Solid in hollow; and inside solid, hollow again! There you are! Old 'un crumbled away in stone coffin, in vault!'

'Astonishing!'

'I have even done this,' says Durdles, drawing out his two-foot rule (Deputy meanwhile skirmishing nearer, as suspecting that Treasure may be about to be discovered, which may somehow lead to his own enrichment, and the delicious treat of the discoverers being hanged by the neck, on his evidence, until they are dead[20]). 'Say that hammer of mine's a wall – my work. Two; four; and two is six,' measuring on the pavement. 'Six foot inside that wall is Mrs Sapsea.'

'Not really Mrs Sapsea?'

'Say Mrs Sapsea.[21] Her wall's thicker, but say Mrs Sapsea. Durdles taps that wall represented by that hammer, and says, after good sounding: "Something betwixt us!" Sure enough, some rubbish has been left in that same six foot space by Durdles's men!'

Jasper opines that such accuracy 'is a gift.'

'I wouldn't have it as a gift,' returns Durdles, by no means receiving the observation in good part. 'I worked it out for myself. Durdles comes by *his* knowledge through grubbing deep for it, and having it up by the roots when it don't want to come. – Halloa you Deputy!'

'Widdy!' is Deputy's shrill response, standing off again.

'Catch that ha'penny. And don't let me see any more of you to-night, after we come to the Travellers' Twopenny.'

'Warning!' returns Deputy, having caught the halfpenny, and appearing by this mystic word to express his assent to the arrangement.

They have but to cross what was once the vineyard, belonging to what was once the Monastery, to come into the narrow back lane wherein stands the crazy wooden house of two low stories currently known as the Travellers' Twopenny: – a house all warped and distorted, like the morals of the travellers, with scant remains of a lattice-work porch over the door, and also of a rustic fence before its stamped-out garden; by reason of the travellers being so bound to the premises by a tender sentiment (or so fond of having a fire by the roadside in the course of the day), that they can never be persuaded or threatened into departure, without violently possessing themselves of some wooden forget-me-not, and bearing it off.

The semblance of an inn is attempted to be given to this wretched place by fragments of conventional red curtaining in the windows, which rags are made muddily transparent in the night-season by feeble lights of rush or cotton dip[22] burning dully in the close air of the inside. As Durdles and Jasper come near,[23] they are addressed by an inscribed paper lantern over the door, setting forth the purport of the house. They are also addressed by some half-dozen other hideous small boys – whether twopenny lodgers or followers or hangers-on of such, who knows! – who, as if attracted by some carrion-scent of Deputy in the air, start into the moonlight, as vultures might gather in the desert, and instantly fall to stoning him and one another.

'Stop, you young brutes,' cries Jasper, angrily, 'and let us go by!'

This remonstrance being received with yells and flying stones, according to a custom of late years comfortably established among the police regulations of our English communities, where Christians are stoned on all sides, as if the days of Saint Stephen were revived,[24] Durdles remarks of the young savages, with some point, that 'they haven't got an object,' and leads the way down the lane.

At the corner of the lane, Jasper, hotly enraged, checks his companion and looks back. All is silent. Next moment, a stone coming rattling at his hat, and a distant yell of 'Wake-cock! Warning!' followed by a crow, as from some infernally-hatched Chanticleer, apprising him under whose victorious fire he stands, he turns the corner into safety, and takes Durdles home: Durdles stumbling among the litter of his stony yard as if he were going to turn head foremost into one of the unfinished tombs.

John Jasper returns by another way to his Gate House, and entering softly with his key, finds his fire still burning. He takes from a locked press a peculiar-looking pipe, which he fills – but not with tobacco – and, having adjusted the contents of the bowl, very carefully, with a little instrument, ascends an inner staircase of only a few steps, leading to two rooms. One of these is his own sleeping chamber: the other is his nephew's. There is a light in each.

His nephew lies asleep, calm and untroubled. John Jasper stands looking down upon him,[25] his unlighted pipe in his hand, for some time, with a fixed and deep attention. Then, hushing his footsteps, he passes to his own room, lights his pipe, and delivers himself to the Spectres it invokes at midnight.

CHAPTER 6

Philanthropy in Minor Canon Corner

The Reverend Septimus Crisparkle (Septimus, because six little brother Crisparkles before him went out, one by one, as they were born, like six weak little rushlights, as they were lighted), having broken the thin morning ice near Cloisterham Weir with his amiable head, much to the invigoration of his frame, was now assisting his circulation by boxing at a looking-glass with great science and prowess. A fresh and healthy portrait the looking-glass presented of the Reverend Septimus, feinting and dodging with the utmost artfulness, and hitting out from the shoulder with the utmost straightness, while his radiant features teemed with innocence, and soft-hearted benevolence beamed from his boxing-gloves.[1]

It was scarcely breakfast time yet, for Mrs Crisparkle – mother, not wife, of the Reverend Septimus – was only just down, and waiting for the urn. Indeed, the Reverend Septimus left off at this very moment to take the pretty old lady's entering face between his boxing-gloves and kiss it. Having done so with tenderness, the Reverend Septimus turned to again, countering with his left, and putting in his right, in a tremendous manner.

'I say, every morning of my life, that you'll do it at last, Sept,' remarked the old lady, looking on; 'and so you will.'

'Do what, Ma dear?'

'Break the pier-glass, or burst a blood-vessel.'

'Neither, please God, Ma dear. Here's wind,[2] Ma. Look at this!'

In a concluding round of great severity, the Reverend Septimus administered and escaped all sorts of punishment, and wound up by getting the old lady's cap into Chancery[3] – such is the technical term used in scientific circles by the learned in the Noble Art – with a lightness of touch that hardly stirred the lightest lavender or cherry riband on it. Magnanimously releasing the defeated, just in time to get his gloves into a drawer and feign to be looking out of window in a contemplative state of mind when a servant entered, the Reverend Septimus then gave place to the urn and other preparations for breakfast. These completed, and the two alone again, it was pleasant to see (or would have been, if there had been any one to see it, which there never was), the old lady standing to say the Lord's Prayer[4] aloud, and her son, Minor Canon nevertheless, standing with bent head to hear it, he being within five years of forty: much as he had stood to hear the same words from the same lips when he was within five months of four.

What is prettier than an old lady – except a young lady – when her eyes are bright, when her figure is trim and compact, when her face is cheerful and calm, when her dress is as the dress of a china shepherdess: so dainty in its colors,[5] so individually assorted to herself, so neatly moulded on her? Nothing is prettier, thought the good Minor Canon frequently, when taking his seat at table opposite his long-widowed mother. Her thought at such times may be condensed into the two words that oftenest did duty together in all her conversations: 'My Sept!'

They were a good pair to sit breakfasting together in Minor Canon Corner, Cloisterham. For, Minor Canon Corner was a quiet place in the shadow of the Cathedral, which the cawing of the rooks, the echoing footsteps of rare passers, the sound of the Cathedral bell, or the roll of the Cathedral organ, seemed to render more quiet than absolute silence. Swaggering fighting men[6] had had their centuries of ramping and raving about Minor Canon Corner, and beaten serfs had had their centuries of drudging and dying there, and powerful monks had had their centuries of being sometimes useful and sometimes harmful there, and behold they were all gone out of Minor Canon Corner, and so much the better. Perhaps one of the highest uses of their ever having been there, was, that there might be left behind, that blessed air of tranquillity which pervaded Minor Canon Corner, and that serenely romantic state of the mind – productive for the most part of pity and forbearance – which is engendered by a sorrowful story that is all told, or a pathetic play that is played out.[7]

Red-brick walls harmoniously toned down in color by time, strong-rooted ivy, latticed windows, panelled rooms, big oaken beams in little places, and stone-walled gardens where annual fruit yet ripened upon monkish trees were the principal surroundings of pretty old Mrs Crisparkle and the Reverend Septimus as they sat at breakfast.

'And what, Ma dear,' enquired the Minor Canon, giving proof of a wholesome and vigorous appetite, 'does the letter say?'

The pretty old lady, after reading it, had just laid it down upon the breakfast-cloth. She handed it over to her son.

Now, the old lady was exceedingly proud of her bright eyes being so clear that she could read writing without spectacles. Her son was also so proud of the circumstance, and so dutifully bent on her deriving the utmost possible gratification from it, that he had invented the pretence that he himself could *not* read writing without spectacles. Therefore he now assumed a pair, of grave and prodigious proportions, which not only seriously inconvenienced his nose and his breakfast, but seriously impeded his perusal of the letter. For, he had the eyes of a microscope and a telescope combined, when they were unassisted.

'It's from Mr Honeythunder, of course,' said the old lady, folding her arms.

'Of course,' assented her son. He then lamely read on:

> '"Haven of Philanthropy,[8]
> '"Chief Offices, London, Wednesday.

'"DEAR MADAM,

'"I write in the –"'; In the what's this? What does he write in?'

'In the chair,' said the old lady.

The Reverend Septimus took off his spectacles, that he might see her face, as he exclaimed:

'Why, what should he write in?'

'Bless me, bless me, Sept,' returned the old lady, 'you don't see the context! Give it back to me, my dear.'

Glad to get his spectacles off (for they always made his eyes water), her son obeyed: murmuring that his sight for reading manuscript got worse and worse daily.

'"I write,"' his mother went on, reading very perspicuously and precisely, '"from the chair, to which I shall probably be confined for some hours."'

Septimus looked at the row of chairs against the wall, with a half-protesting and half-appealing countenance.

'"We have,"' the old lady read on with a little extra emphasis, '"a meeting of our Convened Chief Composite Committee of Central and District Philanthropists, at our Head Haven as above; and it is their unanimous pleasure that I take the chair."'

Septimus breathed more freely, and muttered: 'Oh! If he comes to *that*, let him.'

'"Not to lose a day's post, I take the opportunity of a long report being read, denouncing a public miscreant –"'

'It is a most extraordinary thing,' interposed the gentle Minor Canon, laying down his knife and fork to rub his ear in a vexed manner, 'that these Philanthropists are always denouncing somebody. And it is another most extraordinary thing that they are always so violently flush of miscreants!'

' "Denouncing a public miscreant!" ' – the old lady resumed, ' "to get our little affair of business off my mind. I have spoken with my two wards, Neville and Helena Landless,[9] on the subject of their defective education, and they give in to the plan proposed; as I should have taken good care they did, whether they liked it or not."

'And it is another most extraordinary thing,' remarked the Minor Canon in the same tone as before, 'that these Philanthropists are so given to seizing their fellow-creatures by the scruff of the neck, and (as one may say) bumping them into the paths of peace.[10] – I beg your pardon, Ma dear, for interrupting.'

' "Therefore, dear Madam, you will please prepare your son, the Rev. Mr Septimus, to expect Neville as an inmate to be read with, on Monday next. On the same day Helena will accompany him to Cloisterham, to take up her quarters at the Nuns' House, the establishment recommended by yourself and son jointly. Please likewise to prepare for her reception and tuition there. The terms in both cases are understood to be exactly as stated to me in writing by yourself, when I opened a correspondence with you on this subject, after the honor of being introduced to you at your sister's house in town here. With compliments to the Rev. Mr Septimus, I am, Dear Madam, Your affectionate brother (In Philanthropy),[11] LUKE HONEYTHUNDER." '

'Well, Ma,' said Septimus, after a little more rubbing of his ear, 'we must try it. There can be no doubt that we have room for an inmate, and that I have time to bestow upon him, and inclination too. I must confess to feeling rather glad that he is not Mr Honeythunder himself. Though that seems wretchedly prejudiced – does it not? – for I never saw him. Is he a large man, Ma?'

'I should call him a large man, my dear,' the old lady replied after some hesitation, 'but that his voice is so much larger.'[12]

'Than himself?'

'Than anybody.'

'Hah!' said Septimus. And finished his breakfast as if the flavor of the Superior Family Souchong,[13] and also of the ham and toast and eggs, were a little on the wane.

Mrs Crisparkle's sister, another piece of Dresden china, and matching her so neatly that they would have made a delightful pair of ornaments for the two ends of any capacious old-fashioned chimney-piece, and by right should never have been seen apart, was the childless wife of a clergyman holding Corporation preferment in London City.[14] Mr Honeythunder in his public character of Professor of Philanthropy had come to know Mrs Crisparkle during the last re-matching of the china ornaments (in other words during her last annual visit to her sister), after a public occasion of a philanthropic nature, when certain devoted orphans of tender years had been glutted with plum buns,[15] and plump bumptiousness. These were all the antecedents known in Minor Canon Corner of the coming pupils.

'I am sure you will agree with me, Ma,' said Mr Crisparkle, after thinking the matter over, 'that the first thing to be done, is, to put these young people as much at their ease as possible. There is nothing disinterested in the notion, because we cannot be at our ease with them unless they are at their ease with us. Now, Jasper's nephew is down here at present; and like takes to like, and youth takes to youth. He is a cordial young fellow, and we will have him to meet the brother and sister at dinner. That's three. We can't think of asking him, without asking Jasper. That's four. Add Miss Twinkleton and the fairy bride that is to be,[16] and that's six. Add our two selves, and that's eight. Would eight at a friendly dinner at all put you out, Ma?'

'Nine would, Sept,' returned the old lady, visibly nervous.

'My dear Ma, I particularize eight.'

'The exact size of the table and the room, my dear.'

So it was settled that way; and when Mr Crisparkle called with his mother upon Miss Twinkleton, to arrange for the reception of Miss Helena Landless at the Nuns' House, the two other invitations having reference to that establishment were proffered and accepted. Miss Twinkleton did, indeed, glance at the globes, as regretting that they were not formed to be taken out into society; but became reconciled to leaving them behind. Instructions were then despatched to the Philanthropist for the departure and arrival, in good time for dinner, of Mr Neville and Miss Helena; and stock for soup became fragrant in the air of Minor Canon Corner.

In those days there was no railway to Cloisterham, and Mr Sapsea said there never would be. Mr Sapsea said more; he said there never should be. And yet, marvellous to consider, it has come to pass, in these days, that Express Trains don't think Cloisterham worth stopping at, but yell and whirl through it on their larger errands, casting the dust off their wheels as a testimony against its insignificance. Some remote fragment of Main Line to somewhere else, there was, which was going to ruin the Money Market if it failed, and Church and State if it succeeded,[17] and (of course), the Constitution, whether or no; but even that had already so unsettled Cloisterham traffic, that the traffic, deserting the high road, came sneaking in from an unprecedented part of the country by a back stable-way, for many years labelled at the corner: 'Beware of the Dog.'

To this ignominious avenue of approach, Mr Crisparkle repaired, awaiting the arrival of a short squat omnibus,[18] with a disproportionate heap of luggage on the roof – like a little Elephant with infinitely too much Castle[19] – which was then the daily service between Cloisterham and external mankind. As this vehicle lumbered up, Mr Crisparkle could hardly see anything else of it for a large outside passenger seated on the box,[20] with his elbows squared, and his hands on his knees, compressing the driver into a most uncomfortably small compass, and glowering about him with a strongly marked face.

'Is this Cloisterham?' demanded the passenger, in a tremendous voice.

'It is,' replied the driver, rubbing himself as if he ached, after throwing the reins to the ostler. 'And I never was so glad to see it.'

'Tell your master to make his box seat wider, then,' returned the passenger. 'Your master is morally bound – and ought to be legally, under ruinous penalties – to provide for the comfort of his fellow-man.'

The driver instituted, with the palms of his hands, a superficial perquisition into the state of his skeleton; which seemed to make him anxious.

'Have I sat upon you?' asked the passenger.

'You have,' said the driver, as if he didn't like it at all.

'Take that card, my friend.'

'I think I won't deprive you on it,' returned the driver, casting his eyes over it with no great favor, without taking it. 'What's the good of it to me?'

'Be a Member of that Society,' said the passenger.

'What shall I get by it?' asked the driver.

'Brotherhood,' returned the passenger, in a ferocious voice.

'Thankee,' said the driver, very deliberately, as he got down; 'my mother was contented with myself, and so am I. I don't want no brothers.'

'But you must have them,' replied the passenger, also descending, 'whether you like it or not. I am your brother.'

'I say!' expostulated the driver, becoming more chafed in temper; 'not too fur! The worm *will*, when – '²¹

But here Mr Crisparkle interposed, remonstrating aside, in a friendly voice: 'Joe, Joe, Joe! don't forget yourself, Joe, my good fellow!' and then, when Joe peaceably touched his hat, accosting the passenger with: 'Mr Honeythunder?'

'That is my name, sir.'

'My name is Crisparkle.'

'Reverend Mr Septimus? Glad to see you, sir. Neville and Helena are inside. Having a little succumbed of late, under the pressure of my public labors, I thought I would take a mouthful of fresh air, and come down with them, and return at night. So you are the Reverend Mr Septimus, are you?' surveying him on the whole with disappointment, and twisting a double eye-glass by its ribbon, as if he were roasting it; but not otherwise using it. 'Hah! I expected to see you older, sir.'

'I hope you will,' was the good-humored reply.

'Eh?' demanded Mr Honeythunder.

'Only a poor little joke. Not worth repeating.'

'Joke? Aye; I never see a joke,' Mr Honeythunder frowningly retorted. 'A joke is wasted upon me, sir. Where are they? Helena and Neville, come here! Mr Crisparkle has come down to meet you.'

An unusually handsome lithe young fellow, and an unusually handsome lithe girl; much alike; both very dark, and very rich in color; she of almost the gipsy type; something untamed about them both; a certain air upon them of hunter and huntress; yet withal a certain air of being the objects of the chase, rather than the followers. Slender, supple, quick of eye and limb; half shy, half defiant; fierce of look; an indefinable kind of pause coming and going on their whole expression, both of face and form, which might be equally likened to the pause before a crouch, or a bound. The rough mental notes made in the first five minutes by Mr Crisparkle would have read thus, *verbatim*.

He invited Mr Honeythunder to dinner, with a troubled mind (for the discomfiture of the dear old china shepherdess lay heavy on it), and gave his arm to Helena Landless. Both she and her brother, as they walked all together through the ancient streets, took great delight in what he pointed out of the Cathedral and the Monastery-ruin, and wondered – so his notes ran on – much as if they were beautiful barbaric captives brought from some wild tropical dominion. Mr Honeythunder walked in the middle of the road, shouldering the natives out of his way, and loudly developing a scheme he had, for making a raid on all the unemployed persons in the United Kingdom, laying them every one by the heels in jail, and forcing them, on pain of prompt extermination, to become philanthropists.

Then they came to Minor Canon Corner.[22] Mrs Crisparkle had need of her own share of philanthropy when she beheld this very large and very loud excrescence[23] on the little party. Always something in the nature of a Boil upon the face of society, Mr Honeythunder expanded into an inflammatory Wen in Minor Canon Corner. Though it was not literally true, as was facetiously charged against him by public unbelievers, that he called aloud to his fellow-creatures: 'Curse your souls and bodies, come here and be blessed!' still his philanthropy was of that gunpowderous sort that the difference between it and animosity was hard to determine. You were to abolish military force, but you were first to bring all commanding officers who had done their duty, to trial by court martial[24] for that offence, and shoot them. You were to abolish war, but were to make converts by making war upon them, and charging them with loving war as the apple of their eye. You were to have no capital punishment, but were first to sweep off the face of the earth all legislators, jurists, and judges, who were of the contrary opinion. You were to have universal concord, and were to get it by eliminating all the people who wouldn't, or conscientiously couldn't, be concordant. You were to love your brother as yourself,[25] but after an indefinite interval of maligning him (very much as if you hated him), and calling him all manner of names. Above all things, you were to do nothing in private, or on your own account. You were to go to the offices of the Haven of Philanthropy, and put your name down as a Member and a Professing Philanthropist. Then, you were to pay up your subscription, get your card of membership and your riband and medal, and were evermore to live upon a platform,[26] and evermore to say what Mr Honeythunder said, and what the Treasurer said, and what the sub-Treasurer said, and what the Committee said, and what the sub-Committee said, and what the Secretary said, and what the Vice Secretary said. And this was usually said in the unanimously carried resolution under hand and seal, to the effect: 'That this assembled Body of Professing Philanthropists views, with indignant scorn and contempt, not unmixed with utter detestation and loathing abhorrence,' – in short, the baseness of all those who do not belong to it, and pledges itself to make as many obnoxious statements as possible about them, without being at all particular as to facts.

The dinner was a most doleful breakdown. The philanthropist deranged the symmetry of the table, sat himself in the way of the waiting, blocked up the thoroughfare, and drove Mr Tope (who assisted the parlor-maid) to the verge of distraction by passing plates and dishes on, over his own head. Nobody could talk to anybody, because he held forth to everybody at once, as if the company had no individual existence, but were a Meeting. He impounded the Reverend Mr Septimus, as an official personage to be addressed, or kind of human peg to hang his oratorical hat on, and fell into the exasperating habit, common among such orators, of impersonating him as a wicked and weak opponent. Thus, he would ask: 'And will you, sir, now stultify yourself by telling me' – and so forth, when the innocent man had not opened his lips, nor meant to open them. Or he would say: 'Now see, sir, to what a position you are reduced. I will leave you no escape. After exhausting all the resources of fraud and falsehood, during years upon years; after exhibiting a combination of dastardly meanness with ensanguined daring, such as the world has not often witnessed; you have now the hypocrisy to bend the knee before the most degraded of mankind, and to sue and whine and howl for mercy!' Whereat the unfortunate Minor Canon would look, in part indignant and in part perplexed: while his worthy mother sat bridling, with tears in her eyes, and the remainder of the party lapsed into a sort of gelatinous state, in which there was no flavor or solidity, and very little resistance.

But the gush of philanthropy that burst forth when the departure of Mr Honeythunder began to impend, must have been highly gratifying to the feelings of that distinguished man. His coffee was produced, by the special activity of Mr Tope, a full hour before he wanted it. Mr Crisparkle sat with his watch in his hand, for about the same period, lest he should overstay his time. The four young people were unanimous in believing that the Cathedral clock struck three-quarters, when it actually struck but one. Miss Twinkleton estimated the distance to the omnibus at five-and-twenty minutes' walk, when it was really five. The affectionate kindness of the whole circle hustled him into his great-coat, and shoved him out into the moonlight, as if he were a fugitive traitor with whom they sympathized, and a troop of horse were at the back door. Mr Crisparkle and his new charge, who took him to the omnibus, were so fervent in their apprehensions of his catching cold, that they shut him up in it instantly and left him, with still half an hour to spare.

CHAPTER 7

More Confidences than One

'I know very little of that gentleman, sir,' said Neville to the Minor Canon as they turned back.

'You know very little of your guardian?' the Minor Canon repeated.

'Almost nothing.'

'How came he –'

'To *be* my guardian? I'll tell you, sir. I suppose you know that we come (my sister and I) from Ceylon?'[1]

'Indeed, no.'

'I wonder at that. We lived with a stepfather there. Our mother died there, when we were little children. We have had a wretched existence. She made him our guardian, and he was a miserly wretch who grudged us food to eat, and clothes to wear. At his death, he passed us over to this man; for no better reason that I know of, than his being a friend or connexion of his, whose name was always in print and catching his attention.'

'That was lately, I suppose?'

'Quite lately, sir. This stepfather of ours was a cruel brute as well as a grinding one. It was well he died when he did, or I might have killed him.'

Mr Crisparkle stopped short in the moonlight and looked at his hopeful pupil in consternation.

'I surprise you, sir?' he said, with a quick change to a submissive manner.

'You shock me; unspeakably shock me.'

The pupil hung his head for a little while, as they walked on, and then said: 'You never saw him beat your sister. I have seen him beat mine, more than once or twice, and I never forgot it.'

'Nothing,' said Mr Crisparkle, 'not even a beloved and beautiful sister's tears under dastardly ill-usage;' he became less severe, in spite of himself, as his indignation rose; 'could justify those horrible expressions that you used.'

'I am sorry I used them, and especially to you, sir. I beg to recall them. But permit me to set you right on one point. You spoke of my sister's tears. My sister would have let him tear her to pieces, before she would have let him believe that he could make her shed a tear.'

Mr Crisparkle reviewed those mental notes of his, and was neither at all surprised to hear it, nor at all disposed to question it.

'Perhaps you will think it strange, sir,' – this was said in a hesitating voice – 'that I should so soon ask you to allow me to confide in you, and to have the kindness to hear a word or two from me in my defence?'

'Defence?' Mr Crisparkle repeated. 'You are not on your defence, Mr Neville.'

'I think I am, sir. At least I know I should be, if you were better acquainted with my character.'

'Well, Mr Neville,' was the rejoinder. 'What if you leave me to find it out?'

'Since it is your pleasure, sir,' answered the young man, with a quick change in his manner to sullen disappointment: 'since it is your pleasure to check me in my impulse, I must submit.'

There was that in the tone of this short speech which made the conscientious man to whom it was addressed uneasy. It hinted to him that he might, without meaning it, turn aside a trustfulness beneficial to a mis-shapen young mind and perhaps to his own power of directing and improving it. They were within sight of the lights in his windows, and he stopped.

'Let us turn back and take a turn or two up and down, Mr Neville, or you may not have time to finish what you wish to say to me. You are hasty in thinking that I mean to check you. Quite the contrary. I invite your confidence.'

'You have invited it, sir, without knowing it, ever since I came here. I say "ever since," as if I had been here a week! The truth is, we came here (my sister and I) to quarrel with you, and affront you, and break away again.'

'Really?' said Mr Crisparkle, at a dead loss for anything else to say.

'You see, we could not know what you were beforehand, sir; could we?'

'Clearly not,' said Mr Crisparkle.

'And having liked no one else with whom we have ever been brought into contact, we had made up our minds not to like you.'

'Really?' said Mr Crisparkle again.

'But we do like you, sir, and we see an unmistakable difference between your house and your reception of us, and anything else we have ever known. This – and my happening to be alone with you – and everything around us seeming so quiet and peaceful after Mr Honeythunder's departure – and Cloisterham being so old and grave and beautiful, with the moon shining on it – these things inclined me to open my heart.'

'I quite understand, Mr Neville. And it is salutary to listen to such influences.'

'In describing my own imperfections, sir, I must ask you not to suppose that I am describing my sister's. She has come out of the disadvantages of our miserable life, as much better than I am, as that Cathedral tower is higher than those chimneys.'

Mr Crisparkle in his own breast was not so sure of this.

'I have had, sir, from my earliest remembrance, to suppress a deadly and bitter hatred. This has made me secret and revengeful. I have been always tyrannically held down by the strong hand. This has driven me, in my weakness, to the resource of being false and mean. I have been stinted of education, liberty, money, dress, the very necessaries of life, the commonest pleasures of childhood, the commonest possessions of youth. This has caused me to be utterly wanting in I don't know what emotions, or remembrances, or good instincts – I have not even a name for the thing, you see! – that you have had to work upon in other young men to whom you have been accustomed.'

'This is evidently true. But this is not encouraging,' thought Mr Crisparkle as they turned again.

'And to finish with, sir: I have been brought up among abject and servile dependants, of an inferior race,[2] and I may easily have contracted some affinity with them. Sometimes, I don't know but that it may be a drop of what is tigerish in their blood.'

'As in the case of that remark just now,' thought Mr Crisparkle.

'In a last word of reference to my sister, sir (we are twin children), you ought to know, to her honor, that nothing in our misery ever subdued her, though it often cowed me. When we ran away from it (we ran away four times in six years, to be soon brought back and cruelly punished), the flight was always of her planning and leading. Each time she dressed as a boy,[3] and showed the daring of a man. I take it we were seven years old when we first decamped; but I remember, when I lost the pocket-knife with which she was to have cut her hair short, how desperately she tried to tear it out, or bite it off. I have nothing further to say, sir, except that I hope you will bear with me and make allowance for me.'

'Of that, Mr Neville, you may be sure,' returned the Minor Canon. 'I don't preach more than I can help, and I will not repay your confidence with a sermon. But I entreat you to bear in mind, very seriously and steadily, that if I am to do you any good, it can only be with your own assistance; and that you can only render that, efficiently, by seeking aid from Heaven.'

'I will try to do my part, sir.'

'And, Mr Neville, I will try to do mine. Here is my hand on it. May God bless our endeavours!'

They were now standing at his house-door, and a cheerful sound of voices and laughter was heard within.

'We will take one more turn before going in,' said Mr Crisparkle, 'for I want to ask you a question. When you said you were in a changed mind concerning me, you spoke, not only for yourself, but for your sister too?'

'Undoubtedly I did, sir.'

'Excuse me, Mr Neville, but I think you have had no opportunity of communicating with your sister, since I met you. Mr Honeythunder was very eloquent; but perhaps I may venture to say, without ill-nature, that he rather monopolized the occasion. May you not have answered for your sister without sufficient warrant?'

Neville shook his head with a proud smile.

'You don't know, sir, yet, what a complete understanding can exist between my sister and me,[4] though no spoken word – perhaps hardly as much as a look – may have passed between us. She not only feels as I have described, but she very well knows that I am taking this opportunity of speaking to you, both for her and for myself.'

Mr Crisparkle looked in his face, with some incredulity; but his face expressed such absolute and firm conviction of the truth of what he said, that Mr Crisparkle looked at the pavement, and mused, until they came to his door again.

'I will ask for one more turn, sir, this time,' said the young man, with a rather heightened color rising in his face. 'But for Mr Honeythunder's – I think you called it eloquence, sir?' (somewhat slyly).

'I – yes, I called it eloquence,' said Mr Crisparkle.

'But for Mr Honeythunder's eloquence, I might have had no need to ask you what I am going to ask you. This Mr Edwin Drood, sir: I think that's the name?'

'Quite correct,' said Mr Crisparkle. 'D-r-double o-d.'

'Does he – or did he – read with you, sir?'

'Never, Mr Neville. He comes here visiting his relation, Mr Jasper.'

'Is Miss Bud his relation too, sir?'

('Now, why should he ask that, with sudden superciliousness!' thought Mr Crisparkle.) Then he explained, aloud, what he knew of the little story of their betrothal.

'Oh! *That's* it, is it?' said the young man. 'I understand his air of proprietorship now!'

This was said so evidently to himself, or to anybody rather than Mr Crisparkle, that the latter instinctively felt as if to notice it would be almost tantamount to noticing a passage in a letter which he had read by chance over the writer's shoulder. A moment afterwards they re-entered the house.

Mr Jasper was seated at the piano as they came into his drawing-room, and was accompanying Miss Rosebud while she sang. It was a consequence of his playing the accompaniment without notes, and of her being a heedless little creature very apt to go wrong, that he followed her lips most attentively,[5] with his eyes as well as hands; carefully and softly hinting the key-note from time to time. Standing with an arm drawn round her, but with a face far more intent on Mr Jasper than on her singing, stood Helena, between whom and her brother an instantaneous recognition passed, in which Mr Crisparkle saw, or thought he saw, the understanding that had been spoken of, flash out. Mr Neville then took his admiring station, leaning against the piano, opposite the singer; Mr Crisparkle sat down by the china shepherdess; Edwin Drood gallantly furled and unfurled Miss Twinkleton's fan; and that lady passively claimed that sort of exhibitor's proprietorship in the accomplishment on view, which Mr Tope, the Verger, daily claimed in the Cathedral service.

The song went on. It was a sorrowful strain of parting, and the fresh young voice was very plaintive and tender. As Jasper watched the pretty lips, and ever and again hinted the one note, as though it were a low whisper from himself, the voice became less steady, until all at once the singer broke into a burst of tears, and shrieked out, with her hands over her eyes: 'I can't bear this! I am frightened! Take me away!'

At the piano

With one swift turn of her lithe figure, Helena laid the little beauty on a sofa, as if she had never caught her up. Then, on one knee beside her, and with one hand upon her rosy mouth, while with the other she appealed to all the rest, Helena said to them: 'It's nothing; it's all over; don't speak to her for one minute, and she is well!'

Jasper's hands had, in the same instant, lifted themselves from the keys, and were now poised above them, as though he waited to resume. In that attitude he yet sat quiet: not even looking round, when all the rest had changed their places and were reassuring one another.

'Pussy's not used to an audience; that's the fact,' said Edwin Drood. 'She got nervous, and couldn't hold out. Besides, Jack, you are such a conscientious master, and require so much, that I believe you make her afraid of you. No wonder.'

'No wonder,' repeated Helena.

'There, Jack, you hear! You would be afraid of him, under similar circumstances, wouldn't you, Miss Landless?'

'Not under any circumstances,' returned Helena.

Jasper brought down his hands, looked over his shoulder, and begged to thank Miss Landless for her vindication of his character. Then he fell to dumbly playing, without striking the notes, while his little pupil was taken to an open window for air, and was otherwise petted and restored. When she was brought back, his place was empty. 'Jack's gone, Pussy,' Edwin told her. 'I am more than half afraid he didn't like to be charged with being the Monster who had frightened you.' But she answered never a word, and shivered, as if they had made her a little too cold.

Miss Twinkleton now opining that indeed these were late hours, Mrs Crisparkle, for finding ourselves outside the walls of the Nuns' House, and that we who undertook the formation of the future wives and mothers of England[6] (the last words in a lower voice, as requiring to be communicated in confidence) were really bound (voice coming up again) to set a better example than one of rakish habits, wrappers were put in requisition, and the two young cavaliers volunteered to see the ladies home. It was soon done, and the gate of the Nuns' House closed upon them.

The boarders had retired, and only Mrs Tisher in solitary vigil awaited the new pupil. Her bedroom being within Rosa's, very little introduction or explanation was necessary, before she was placed in charge of her new friend, and left for the night.

'This is a blessed relief, my dear,' said Helena. 'I have been dreading all day, that I should be brought to bay at this time.'

'There are not many of us,' returned Rosa, 'and we are good-natured girls; at least the others are; I can answer for them.'

'I can answer for you,' laughed Helena, searching the lovely little face with her dark fiery eyes, and tenderly caressing the small figure. 'You will be a friend to me, won't you?'

'I hope so. But the idea of my being a friend to you seems too absurd, though.'

'Why?'

'Oh! I am such a mite of a thing, and you are so womanly and handsome. You seem to have resolution and power enough to crush me. I shrink into nothing by the side of your presence even.'

'I am a neglected creature, my dear, unacquainted with all accomplishments, sensitively conscious that I have everything to learn, and deeply ashamed to own my ignorance.'

'And yet you acknowledge everything to me!' said Rosa.

'My pretty one, can I help it? There is a fascination in you.'

'Oh! Is there though?' pouted Rosa, half in jest and half in earnest. 'What a pity Master Eddy doesn't feel it more!'

Of course her relations towards that young gentleman had been already imparted, in Minor Canon Corner.

'Why, surely he must love you with all his heart!' cried Helena, with an earnestness that threatened to blaze into ferocity if he didn't.

'Eh? Oh, well, I suppose he does,' said Rosa, pouting again; 'I am sure I have no right to say he doesn't. Perhaps it's my fault. Perhaps I am not as nice to him as I ought to be. I don't think I am. But it *is* so ridiculous!'

Helena's eyes demanded what was.

'*We* are,' said Rosa, answering as if she had spoken. 'We are such a ridiculous couple. And we are always quarrelling.'

'Why?'

'Because we both know we are ridiculous, my dear!' Rosa gave that answer as if it were the most conclusive answer in the world.

Helena's masterful look was intent upon her face for a few moments, and then she impulsively put out both her hands and said:

'You will be my friend and help me?'

'Indeed, my dear, I will,' replied Rosa, in a tone of affectionate childishness that went straight and true to her heart; 'I will be as good a friend as such a mite of a thing can be to such a noble creature as you. And be a friend to me, please; for I don't understand myself: and I want a friend who can understand me, very much indeed.'

Helena Landless kissed her, and retaining both her hands, said:

'Who is Mr Jasper?'

Rosa turned aside her head in answering: 'Eddy's uncle, and my music-master.'

'You do not love him?'

'Ugh!' She put her hands up to her face, and shook with fear or horror.

'You know that he loves you?'

'Oh, don't, don't, don't!' cried Rosa, dropping on her knees, and clinging to her new resource. 'Don't tell me of it! He terrifies me. He haunts my thoughts, like a dreadful ghost. I feel that I am never safe from him. I feel as if he could pass in through the wall[7] when he is spoken of.' She actually did look round, as if she dreaded to see him standing in the shadow behind her.

'Try to tell me more about it, darling.'

'Yes, I will, I will. Because you are so strong. But hold me the while, and stay with me afterwards.'

'My child! You speak as if he had threatened you in some dark way.'

'He has never spoken to me about – that. Never.'

'What has he done?'

'He has made a slave of me with his looks. He has forced me to understand him, without his saying a word; and he has forced me to keep silence, without his uttering a threat. When I play, he never moves his eyes from my hands. When I sing, he never moves his eyes from my lips. When he corrects me, and strikes a note, or a chord, or plays a passage, he himself is in the sounds, whispering that he pursues me as a lover, and commanding me to keep his secret. I avoid his eyes, but he forces me to see them without looking at them. Even when a glaze comes over them (which is sometimes the case), and he seems to wander away into a frightful sort of dream in which he threatens most, he obliges me to know it, and to know that he is sitting close at my side, more terrible to me then than ever.'

'What is this imagined threatening, pretty one? What is threatened?'

'I don't know. I have never even dared to think or wonder what it is.'

'And was this all, to-night?'

'This was all; except that to-night when he watched my lips so closely as I was singing, besides feeling terrified I felt ashamed and passionately hurt. It was as if he kissed me, and I couldn't bear it, but cried out. You must never breathe this to any one. Eddy is devoted to him. But you said to-night that you would not be afraid of him, under any circumstances, and that gives me – who am so much afraid of him – courage to tell only you. Hold me! Stay with me! I am too frightened to be left by myself.'

The lustrous gipsy-face drooped over the clinging arms and bosom, and the wild black hair fell down protectingly over the childish form. There was a slumbering gleam of fire in the intense dark eyes, though they were then softened with compassion and admiration. Let whomsoever it most concerned look well to it!

CHAPTER 8

Daggers Drawn

The two young men, having seen the damsels, their charges, enter the courtyard of the Nuns' House, and finding themselves coldly stared at by the brazen door-plate, as if the battered old beau with the glass in his eye were insolent, look at one another, look along the perspective of the moonlit street, and slowly walk away together.

'Do you stay here long, Mr Drood?' says Neville.

'Not this time,' is the careless answer. 'I leave for London again, to-morrow. But I shall be here, off and on, until next Midsummer; then I shall take my leave of Cloisterham, and England too; for many a long day, I expect.'

'Are you going abroad?'

'Going to wake up Egypt a little,'[1] is the condescending answer.

'Are you reading?'

'Reading!' repeats Edwin Drood, with a touch of contempt. 'No. Doing, working, engineering. My small patrimony was left a part of the capital of the Firm I am with, by my father, a former partner; and I am a charge upon the Firm until I come of age; and then I step into my modest share in the concern. Jack – you met him at dinner – is, until then, my guardian and trustee.'

'I heard from Mr Crisparkle of your other good fortune.'

'What do you mean by my other good fortune?'

Neville has made his remark in a watchfully advancing, and yet furtive and shy manner, very expressive of that peculiar air already noticed, of being at once hunter and hunted. Edwin has made his retort with an abruptness not at all polite. They stop and interchange a rather heated look.

'I hope,' says Neville, 'there is no offence, Mr Drood, in my innocently referring to your betrothal?'

'By George!' cries Edwin, leading on again at a somewhat quicker pace. 'Everybody in this chattering old Cloisterham refers to it. I wonder no Public House has been set up, with my portrait for the sign of The Betrothed's Head. Or Pussy's portrait. One or the other.'

'I am not accountable for Mr Crisparkle's mentioning the matter to me, quite openly,' Neville begins.

'No; that's true; you are not,' Edwin Drood assents.

'But,' resumes Neville, 'I am accountable for mentioning it to you. And I did so, on the supposition that you could not fail to be highly proud of it.'

Now, there are these two curious touches of human nature working the secret springs of this dialogue. Neville Landless is already enough impressed by Little Rosebud, to feel indignant that Edwin Drood (far below her) should hold his prize so lightly. Edwin Drood is already enough impressed by Helena, to feel indignant that Helena's brother (far below her) should dispose of him so coolly, and put him out of the way so entirely.

However, the last remark had better be answered. So, says Edwin:

'I don't know, Mr Neville' (adopting that mode of address from Mr Crisparkle), 'that what people are proudest of, they usually talk most about; I don't know either, that what they are proudest of, they most like other people to talk about. But I live a busy life, and I speak under correction by you readers, who ought to know everything, and I dare say do.'

By this time they have both become savage; Mr Neville out in the open; Edwin Drood under the transparent cover of a popular tune, and a stop now and then to pretend to admire picturesque effects in the moonlight before him.

'It does not seem to me very civil in you,' remarks Neville, at length, 'to reflect upon a stranger who comes here, not having had your advantages, to try to make up for lost time. But, to be sure, *I* was not brought up in "busy life," and my ideas of civility were formed among Heathens.'[2]

'Perhaps, the best civility, whatever kind of people we are brought up among,' retorts Edwin Drood, 'is to mind our own business. If you will set me that example, I promise to follow it.'

'Do you know that you take a great deal too much upon yourself,' is the angry rejoinder; 'and that in the part of the world I come from, you would be called to account for it?'

'By whom, for instance?' asks Edwin Drood, coming to a halt, and surveying the other with a look of disdain.

But, here a startling right hand is laid on Edwin's shoulder, and Jasper stands between them. For it would seem that he, too, has strolled round by the Nuns' House, and has come up behind them on the shadowy side of the road.

'Ned, Ned, Ned!' he says. 'We must have no more of this. I don't like this. I have overheard high words between you two. Remember, my dear boy, you are almost in the position of host to-night. You belong, as it were, to the place, and in a manner represent it towards a stranger. Mr Neville is a stranger, and you should respect the obligations of hospitality. And, Mr Neville:' laying his left hand on the inner shoulder of that young gentleman, and thus walking on between them, hand to shoulder on either side: 'you will pardon me; but I appeal to you to govern your temper too. Now, what is amiss? But why ask! Let there be nothing amiss, and the question is superfluous. We are all three on a good understanding, are we not?'

After a silent struggle between the two young men who shall speak last, Edwin Drood strikes in with: 'So far as I am concerned, Jack, there is no anger in me.'

'Nor in me,' says Neville Landless, though not so freely; or perhaps so carelessly. 'But if Mr Drood knew all that lies behind me, far away from here, he might know better how it is that sharp-edged words have sharp edges to wound me.'

'Perhaps,' says Jasper, in a smoothing manner, 'we had better not qualify our good understanding. We had better not say anything having the appearance of a remonstrance or condition; it might not seem generous. Frankly and freely, you see there is no anger in Ned. Frankly and freely, there is no anger in you, Mr Neville?'

'None at all, Mr Jasper.' Still, not quite so frankly or so freely; or, be it said once again, not quite so carelessly perhaps.

'All over then! Now, my bachelor Gate House is a few yards from here, and the heater is on the fire, and the wine and glasses are on the table, and it is not a stone's throw from Minor Canon Corner. Ned, you are up and away to-morrow. We will carry Mr Neville in with us, to take a stirrup-cup.'

'With all my heart, Jack.'

'And with all mine, Mr Jasper.' Neville feels it impossible to say less, but would rather not go. He has an impression upon him that he has lost hold of his temper; feels that Edwin Drood's coolness, so far from being infectious, makes him red hot.

Mr Jasper, still walking in the centre, hand to shoulder on either side, beautifully turns the Refrain of a drinking-song, and they all go to his rooms. There, the first object visible, when he adds the light of a lamp to that of the fire, is the portrait over the chimneypiece. It is not an object calculated to improve the understanding between the two young men, as rather awkwardly reviving the subject of their difference. Accordingly, they both glance at it consciously, but say nothing. Jasper, however (who would appear from his conduct to have gained but an imperfect clue to the cause of their late high words), directly calls attention to it.

'You recognize that picture, Mr Neville?' shading the lamp to throw the light upon it.

'I recognize it, but it is far from flattering the original.'

'Oh, you are hard upon it! It was done by Ned, who made me a present of it.'

'I am sorry for that, Mr Drood,' Neville apologizes, with a real intention to apologize; 'if I had known I was in the artist's presence –'

'Oh, a joke, sir, a mere joke,' Edwin cuts in, with a provoking yawn. 'A little humoring of Pussy's points! I'm going to paint her gravely, one of these days, if she's good.'

The air of leisurely patronage and indifference with which this is said, as the speaker throws himself back in a chair and clasps his hands at the back of his head, as a rest for it, is very exasperating to the excitable and excited Neville. Jasper looks observantly from the one to the other, slightly smiles, and turns his back to mix a jug of mulled wine at the fire.[3] It seems to require much mixing and compounding.

'I suppose, Mr Neville,' says Edwin, quick to resent the indignant protest against himself in the face of young Landless, which is fully as visible as the portrait, or the fire, or the lamp: 'I suppose that if you painted the picture of your lady love –'

'I can't paint,' is the hasty interruption.

'That's your misfortune, and not your fault. You would if you could. But if you could, I suppose you would make her (no matter what she was in reality) Juno, Minerva, Diana, and Venus,[4] all in one. Eh?'

'I have no lady love, and I can't say.'

'If I were to try my hand,' says Edwin, with a boyish boastfulness getting up in him, 'on a portrait of Miss Landless – in earnest, mind you; in earnest – you should see what I could do!'

'My sister's consent to sit for it being first got, I suppose? As it never will be got, I am afraid I shall never see what you can do. I must bear the loss.'

Jasper turns round from the fire, fills a large goblet glass for Neville, fills a large goblet glass for Edwin, and hands each his own; then fills for himself, saying:

'Come, Mr Neville, we are to drink to my Nephew, Ned. As it is his foot that is in the stirrup – metaphorically – our stirrup-cup is to be devoted to him. Ned, my dearest fellow, my love!'

Jasper sets the example of nearly emptying his glass, and Neville follows it. Edwin Drood says, 'Thank you both very much,' and follows the double example.

'Look at him!' cries Jasper, stretching out his hand admiringly and tenderly, though rallyingly too. 'See where he lounges so easily, Mr Neville! The world is all before him where to choose.[5] A life of stirring work and interest, a life of change and excitement, a life of domestic ease and love! Look at him!'

Edwin Drood's face has become quickly and remarkably flushed by the wine; so has the face of Neville Landless. Edwin still sits thrown back in his chair, making that rest of clasped hands for his head.

'See how little he heeds it all!' Jasper proceeds in a bantering vein. 'It hardly is worth his while to pluck the golden fruit that hangs ripe on the tree[6] for him. And yet consider the contrast, Mr Neville. You and I have no prospect of stirring work and interest, or of change and excitement, or of domestic ease and love. You and I have no prospect (unless you are more fortunate than I am, which may easily be), but the tedious, unchanging round of this dull place.'

'Upon my soul, Jack,' says Edwin, complacently, 'I feel quite apologetic for having my way smoothed as you describe. But you

On dangerous ground

know what I know, Jack, and it may not be so very easy as it seems, after all. May it, Pussy?' To the portrait, with a snap of his thumb and finger. 'We have got to hit it off yet; haven't we, Pussy? You know what I mean, Jack.'

His speech has become thick and indistinct. Jasper, quiet and self-possessed, looks to Neville, as expecting his answer or comment. When Neville speaks, *his* speech is also thick and indistinct.

'It might have been better for Mr Drood to have known some hardships,' he says, defiantly.

'Pray,' retorts Edwin, turning merely his eyes in that direction, 'pray why might it have been better for Mr Drood to have known some hardships?'

'Aye,' Jasper assents with an air of interest; 'let us know why?'

'Because they might have made him more sensible,' says Neville, 'of good fortune that is not by any means necessarily the result of his own merits.'

Mr Jasper quickly looks to his nephew for his rejoinder.

'Have *you* known hardships, may I ask?' says Edwin Drood, sitting upright.

Mr Jasper quickly looks to the other for his retort.

'I have.'

'And what have they made *you* sensible of?'

Mr Jasper's play of eyes between the two holds good throughout the dialogue, to the end.

'I have told you once before to-night.'

'You have done nothing of the sort.'

'I tell you I have. That you take a great deal too much upon yourself.'

'You added something else to that, if I remember?'

'Yes, I did say something else.'

'Say it again.'

'I said that in the part of the world I come from, you would be called to account for it.'

'Only there?' cries Edwin Drood, with a contemptuous laugh. 'A long way off, I believe? Yes; I see! That part of the world is at a safe distance.'

'Say here, then,' rejoins the other, rising in a fury. 'Say anywhere! Your vanity is intolerable, your conceit is beyond endurance, you talk as if you were some rare and precious prize, instead of a common boaster. You are a common fellow, and a common boaster.'

'Pooh, pooh,' says Edwin Drood, equally furious, but more collected; 'how should you know? You may know a black common fellow, or a black common boaster, when you see him (and no doubt you have a large acquaintance that way); but you are no judge of white men.'

This insulting allusion to his dark skin[7] infuriates Neville to that violent degree, that he flings the dregs of his wine at Edwin Drood, and is in the act of flinging the goblet after it, when his arm is caught in the nick of time by Jasper.

'Ned, my dear fellow!' he cries in a loud voice; 'I entreat you, I command you, to be still!' There has been a rush of all the three, and a clattering of glasses and overturning of chairs. 'Mr Neville, for shame! Give this glass to me. Open your hand, sir. I WILL have it!'

But Neville throws him off, and pauses for an instant, in a raging passion, with the goblet yet in his uplifted hand. Then, he dashes it down under the grate, with such force that the broken splinters fly out again in a shower; and he leaves the house.

When he first emerges into the night air, nothing around him is still or steady; nothing around him shows like what it is; he only knows that he stands with a bare head in the midst of a blood-red whirl, waiting to be struggled with, and to struggle to the death.[8]

But, nothing happening, and the moon looking down upon him as if he were dead after a fit of wrath, he holds his steam-hammer beating head and heart,[9] and staggers away. Then, he becomes half conscious of having heard himself bolted and barred out, like a dangerous animal; and thinks what shall he do?

Some wildly passionate ideas of the river dissolve under the spell of the moonlight on the Cathedral and the graves, and the remembrance of his sister, and the thought of what he owes to the good man who has but that very day won his confidence and given him his pledge. He repairs to Minor Canon Corner, and knocks softly at the door.

It is Mr Crisparkle's custom to sit up last of the early household, very softly touching his piano and practising his favorite parts in concerted vocal music. The south wind that goes where it lists,[10] by way of Minor Canon Corner on a still night, is not more subdued than Mr Crisparkle at such times, regardful of the slumbers of the china shepherdess.

His knock is immediately answered by Mr Crisparkle himself. When he opens the door, candle in hand, his cheerful face falls, and disappointed amazement is in it.

'Mr Neville! In this disorder! Where have you been?'

'I have been to Mr Jasper's, sir. With his nephew.'

'Come in.'

The Minor Canon props him by the elbow with a strong hand (in a strictly scientific manner, worthy of his morning trainings), and turns him into his own little book-room, and shuts the door.

'I have begun ill, sir. I have begun dreadfully ill.'

'Too true. You are not sober, Mr Neville.'

'I am afraid I am not, sir, though I can satisfy you at another time that I have had very little indeed to drink, and that it overcame me in the strangest and most sudden manner.'

'Mr Neville, Mr Neville,' says the Minor Canon, shaking his head with a sorrowful smile; 'I have heard that said before.'

'I think – my mind is much confused, but I think – it is equally true of Mr Jasper's nephew, sir.'

'Very likely,' is the dry rejoinder.

'We quarrelled, sir. He insulted me most grossly. He had heated that tigerish blood I told you of to-day, before then.'

'Mr Neville,' rejoins the Minor Canon, mildly, but firmly: 'I request you not to speak to me with that clenched right hand. Unclench it, if you please.'

'He goaded me, sir,' pursues the young man, instantly obeying, 'beyond my power of endurance. I cannot say whether or no he meant it at first, but he did it. He certainly meant it at last. In short, sir,' with an irrepressible outburst, 'in the passion into which he lashed me, I would have cut him down if I could, and I tried to do it.'

'You have clenched that hand again,' is Mr Crisparkle's quiet commentary.

'I beg your pardon, sir.'

'You know your room, for I showed it to you before dinner; but I will accompany you to it once more. Your arm, if you please. Softly, for the house is all a-bed.'

Scooping his hand into the same scientific elbow-rest as before, and backing it up with the inert strength of his arm, as skilfully as a Police Expert, and with an apparent repose quite unattainable by Novices, Mr Crisparkle conducts his pupil to the pleasant and orderly old room prepared for him. Arrived there, the young man throws himself into a chair, and, flinging his arms upon his reading-table, rests his head upon them with an air of wretched self-reproach.

The gentle Minor Canon has had it in his thoughts to leave the room, without a word. But, looking round at the door, and seeing this dejected figure, he turns back to it, touches it with a mild hand, and says 'Good night!' A sob is his only acknowledgment. He might have had many a worse; perhaps, could have had few better.

Another soft knock at the outer door attracts his attention as he goes down stairs. He opens it to Mr Jasper, holding in his hand the pupil's hat.

'We have had an awful scene with him,' says Jasper, in a low voice.

'Has it been so bad as that?'

'Murderous!'

Mr Crisparkle remonstrates: 'No, no, no. Do not use such strong words.'

'He might have laid my dear boy dead at my feet. It is no fault of his, that he did not. But that I was, through the mercy of God, swift and strong with him, he would have cut him down on my hearth.'

The phrase smites home. 'Ah!' thinks Mr Crisparkle. 'His own words!'

'Seeing what I have seen to-night, and hearing what I have heard,' adds Jasper, with great earnestness, 'I shall never know peace of mind when there is danger of those two coming together with no one else to interfere. It was horrible. There is something of the tiger in his dark blood.'

'Ah!' thinks Mr Crisparkle. 'So he said!'

'You, my dear sir,' pursues Jasper, taking his hand, 'even you, have accepted a dangerous charge.'[11]

'You need have no fear for me, Jasper,' returns Mr Crisparkle, with a quiet smile. 'I have none for myself.'

'I have none for myself,' returns Jasper, with an emphasis on the last pronoun, 'because I am not, nor am I in the way of being, the object of his hostility. But you may be, and my dear boy has been. Good night!'

Mr Crisparkle goes in, with the hat that has so easily, so almost imperceptibly, acquired the right to be hung up in his hall; hangs it up; and goes thoughtfully to bed.

CHAPTER 9

Birds in the Bush[1]

Rosa, having no relation that she knew of in the world, had, from the seventh year of her age, known no home but the Nuns' House, and no mother but Miss Twinkleton. Her remembrance of her own mother was of a pretty little creature like herself (not much older than herself, it seemed to her), who had been brought home in her father's arms, drowned. The fatal accident had happened at a party of pleasure. Every fold and color in the pretty summer dress, and even the long wet hair, with scattered petals of ruined flowers still clinging to it,[2] as the dead young figure, in its sad, sad beauty lay upon the bed, were fixed indelibly in Rosa's recollection. So were the wild despair and the subsequent bowed-down grief of her poor young father, who died brokenhearted on the first anniversary of that hard day.

The betrothal of Rosa grew out of the soothing of his year of mental distress by his fast friend and old college companion, Drood: who likewise had been left a widower in his youth. But he, too, went the silent road into which all earthly pilgrimages merge, some sooner, and some later; and thus the young couple had come to be as they were.

The atmosphere of pity surrounding the little orphan girl when she first came to Cloisterham, had never cleared away. It had taken brighter hues as she grew older, happier, prettier; now it had been golden, now roseate, and now azure; but it had always adorned her with some soft light of its own. The general desire to console and caress her, had caused her to be treated in the beginning as a child much younger than her years; the same desire had caused her to be still petted when she was a child no longer. Who should be her favorite, who should anticipate this or that small present, or do her this or that small service; who should take her home for the holidays; who should write to her the oftenest when they were separated, and whom she would most rejoice to see again when they were reunited; even these gentle rivalries were not without their slight dashes of bitterness in the Nuns' House. Well for the poor Nuns in their day, if they hid no harder strife under their veils and rosaries!

Thus Rosa had grown to be an amiable, giddy, wilful, winning little creature; spoilt, in the sense of counting upon kindness from all around her; but not in the sense of repaying it with indifference. Possessing an exhaustless well of affection in her nature, its sparkling waters had freshened and brightened the Nuns' House for years, and yet its depths had never yet been moved: what might betide when that came to pass; what developing changes might fall upon the heedless head, and light heart then; remained to be seen.

By what means the news that there had been a quarrel between the two young men over-night, involving even some kind of onslaught by Mr Neville upon Edwin Drood, got into Miss Twinkleton's establishment[3] before breakfast, it is impossible to say. Whether it was brought in by the birds of the air, or came blowing in with the very air itself, when the casement windows were set open; whether the baker brought it kneaded into the bread, or the milkman delivered it as part of the adulteration of his milk;[4] or the housemaids, beating the dust out of their mats against the gateposts, received it in exchange deposited on the mats by the town atmosphere; certain it is that the news permeated every gable of the old building before Miss Twinkleton was down, and that Miss Twinkleton herself received it through Mrs Tisher, while yet in the act of dressing; or (as she might have expressed the phrase to a parent or guardian of a mythological turn) of sacrificing to the Graces.[5]

Miss Landless's brother had thrown a bottle at Mr Edwin Drood.

Miss Landless's brother had thrown a knife at Mr Edwin Drood.

A knife became suggestive of a fork, and Miss Landless's brother had thrown a fork at Mr Edwin Drood.

As in the governing precedent of Peter Piper,[6] alleged to have picked the peck of pickled pepper, it was held physically desirable to have evidence of the existence of the peck of pickled pepper which Peter Piper was alleged to have picked: so, in this case, it was held psychologically important to know Why Miss Landless's brother threw a bottle, knife, or fork – or bottle, knife, *and* fork – for the cook had been given to understand it was all three – at Mr Edwin Drood?

Well, then. Miss Landless's brother had said he admired Miss Bud. Mr Edwin Drood had said to Miss Landless's brother that he had no business to admire Miss Bud. Miss Landless's brother had then 'up'd' (this was the cook's exact information) with the bottle, knife, fork, and decanter (the decanter now coolly flying at everybody's head, without the least introduction), and thrown them all at Mr Edwin Drood.

Poor little Rosa put a forefinger into each of her ears when these rumors began to circulate, and retired into a corner, beseeching not to be told any more; but Miss Landless, begging permission of Miss Twinkleton to go and speak with her brother, and pretty plainly showing that she would take it if it were not given, struck out the more definite course of going to Mr Crisparkle's for accurate intelligence.

When she came back (being first closeted with Miss Twinkleton, in order that anything objectionable in her tidings might be retained by that discreet filter), she imparted to Rosa only, what had taken place; dwelling with a flushed cheek on the provocation her brother had received, but almost limiting it to that last gross affront as crowning 'some other words between them,' and, out of consideration for her new friend, passing lightly over the fact that the other words had originated in her lover's taking things in general so very easily. To Rosa direct, she brought a petition from her brother that she would forgive him; and, having delivered it with sisterly earnestness, made an end of the subject.

It was reserved for Miss Twinkleton to tone down the public mind of the Nuns' House. That lady, therefore, entering in a stately manner what plebeians might have called the school-room, but what, in the patrician language of the head of the Nuns' House, was euphuistically, not to say round-aboutedly, denominated 'the apartment allotted to study,' and saying with a forensic air, 'Ladies!' all rose. Mrs Tisher at the same time grouped herself behind her chief, as representing Queen Elizabeth's first historical female friend at Tilbury Fort.[7] Miss Twinkleton then proceeded to remark that Rumor, Ladies, had been represented by the bard of Avon – needless were it to mention the immortal SHAKESPEARE, also called the Swan of his native river,[8] not improbably with some reference to the ancient superstition that that bird of graceful plumage (Miss Jennings will please stand upright) sang sweetly on the approach of death, for which we have no ornithological authority, – Rumor, Ladies, had been represented by that bard –[9] hem! –

'who drew
The celebrated Jew,'[10]

as painted full of tongues. Rumor in Cloisterham (Miss Ferdinand will honor me with her attention) was no exception to the great limner's portrait of Rumor elsewhere.[11] A slight *fracas* between two young gentlemen occurring last night within a hundred miles of these peaceful walls (Miss Ferdinand, being apparently incorrigible, will have the kindness to write out this evening, in the original language, the first four fables of our vivacious neighbour, Monsieur La Fontaine[12]) had been very grossly exaggerated by Rumor's voice. In the first alarm and anxiety arising from our sympathy with a sweet young friend, not wholly to be dissociated from one of the gladiators in the bloodless arena in question (the impropriety of Miss Reynolds's appearing to stab herself in the band with a pin, is far too obvious, and too glaringly unlady-like, to be pointed out), we descended from our maiden elevation to discuss this uncongenial and this unfit theme. Responsible enquiries having assured us that it was but one of those 'airy nothings'[13] pointed at by the Poet (whose name and date of birth[14] Miss Giggles will supply within half an hour), we would now discard the subject, and concentrate our minds upon the grateful labors of the day.

But the subject so survived all day, nevertheless, that Miss Ferdinand got into new trouble by surreptitiously clapping on a paper moustache[15] at dinner-time, and going through the motions of aiming a water-bottle at Miss Giggles, who drew a table-spoon in defence.

Now, Rosa thought of this unlucky quarrel a great deal, and thought of it with an uncomfortable feeling that she was involved in it, as cause, or consequence, or what not, through being in a false position altogether as to her marriage engagement. Never free from such uneasiness when she was with her affianced husband, it was not likely that she would be free from it when they were apart. To-day, too, she was cast in upon herself, and deprived of the relief of talking freely with her new friend, because the quarrel had been with Helena's brother, and Helena undisguisedly avoided the subject as a delicate and difficult one to herself. At this critical time, of all times, Rosa's guardian was announced as having come to see her.

Mr Grewgious had been well selected for his trust, as a man of incorruptible integrity, but certainly for no other appropriate quality discernible on the surface. He was an arid, sandy man, who, if he had been put into a grinding-mill, looked as if he would have ground immediately into high-dried snuff. He had a scanty flat crop of hair, in color and consistency like some very mangy yellow fur tippet; it was so unlike hair, that it must have been a wig, but for the stupendous improbability of anybody's voluntarily sporting such a head. The little play of feature that his face presented, was cut deep into it, in a few hard curves that made it more like work; and he had certain notches in his forehead, which looked as though Nature had been about to touch them into sensibility or refinement, when she had impatiently thrown away the chisel, and said: 'I really cannot be worried to finish off this man; let him go as he is.'

With too great length of throat at his upper end, and too much ankle-bone and heel at his lower; with an awkward and hesitating manner; with a shambling walk, and with what is called a near sight[16] – which perhaps prevented his observing how much white cotton stocking he displayed to the public eye, in contrast with his black suit – Mr Grewgious still had some strange capacity in him of making on the whole an agreeable impression.

Mr Grewgious was discovered by his ward, much discomfited by being in Miss Twinkleton's company in Miss Twinkleton's own sacred room. Dim forebodings of being examined in something, and not coming well out of it, seemed to oppress the poor gentleman when found in these circumstances.

'My dear, how do you do? I am glad to see you. My dear, how much improved you are. Permit me to hand you a chair, my dear.'

Miss Twinkleton rose at her little writing-table, saying, with general sweetness, as to the polite Universe: 'Will you permit me to retire?'

'By no means, madam, on my account. I beg that you will not move.'

'I must entreat permission to *move*,' returned Miss Twinkleton, repeating the word with a charming grace; 'but I will not withdraw, since you are so obliging. If I wheel my desk to this corner window, shall I be in the way?'

'Madam! In the way!'

'You are very kind. Rosa, my dear, you will be under no restraint, I am sure.'

Here Mr Grewgious, left by the fire with Rosa, said again: 'My dear, how do you do? I am glad to see you, my dear.' And having waited for her to sit down, sat down himself.

'My visits,' said Mr Grewgious, 'are, like those of the angels[17] – not that I compare myself to an angel.'

'No, sir,' said Rosa.

'Not by any means,' assented Mr Grewgious. 'I merely refer to my visits, which are few and far between. The angels are, we know very well, upstairs.'

Miss Twinkleton looked round with a kind of stiff stare.

'I refer, my dear,' said Mr Grewgious, laying his hand on Rosa's, as the possibility thrilled through his frame of his otherwise seeming to take the awful liberty of calling Miss Twinkleton my dear; 'I refer to the other young ladies.'

Miss Twinkleton resumed her writing.

Mr Grewgious, with a sense of not having managed his opening point quite as neatly as he might have desired, smoothed his head from back to front as if he had just dived, and were pressing the water out – this smoothing action, however superfluous, was habitual with him – and took a pocket-book from his coat-pocket, and a stump of black-lead pencil from his waistcoat pocket.

'I made,' he said, turning the leaves: 'I made a guiding memorandum or so – as I usually do, for I have no conversational powers whatever – to which I will, with your permission, my dear, refer. "Well and happy." Truly. You are well and happy, my dear? You look so.'

'Yes, indeed, sir,' answered Rosa.

'For which,' said Mr Grewgious, with a bend of his head towards the corner window, 'our warmest acknowledgments are due, and I am sure are rendered, to the maternal kindness and the constant care and consideration of the lady whom I have now the honor to see before me.'

This point, again, made but a lame departure from Mr Grewgious, and never got to its destination; for, Miss Twinkleton, feeling that the courtesies required her to be by this time quite outside the conversation, was biting the end of her pen, and looking upward, as waiting for the descent of an idea from any member of the Celestial Nine[18] who might have one to spare.

Mr Grewgious smoothed his smooth head again, and then made another reference to his pocket-book; lining out 'well and happy' as disposed of.

' "Pounds, shillings, and pence" '[19] is my next note. A dry subject for a young lady, but an important subject too. Life is pounds, shillings, and pence. Death is –' A sudden recollection of the death of her two parents seemed to stop him, and he said in a softer tone, and evidently inserting the negative as an after-thought: 'Death is *not* pounds, shillings, and pence.'

His voice was as hard and dry as himself, and Fancy might have ground it straight, like himself, into high-dried snuff. And yet, through the very limited means of expression that he possessed, he seemed to express kindness. If Nature had but finished him off, kindness might have been recognizable in his face at this moment. But if the notches in his forehead wouldn't fuse together, and if his face would work and couldn't play, what could he do, poor man!

'"Pounds, shillings, and pence." You find your allowance always sufficient for your wants, my dear?'

Rosa wanted for nothing, and therefore it was ample.

'And you are not in debt?'

Rosa laughed at the idea of being in debt. It seemed, to her inexperience, a comical vagary of the imagination. Mr Grewgious stretched his near sight to be sure that this was her view of the case. 'Ah!' he said, as comment, with a furtive glance towards Miss Twinkleton, and lining out 'pounds, shillings, and pence': 'I spoke of having got among the angels! So I did!'

Rosa felt what his next memorandum would prove to be, and was blushing and folding a crease in her dress with one embarrassed hand, long before he found it.

'"Marriage." Hem!' Mr Grewgious carried his smoothing hand down over his eyes and nose, and even chin, before drawing his chair a little nearer, and speaking a little more confidentially: 'I now touch, my dear, upon the point that is the direct cause of my troubling you with the present visit. Otherwise, being a particularly Angular man, I should not have intruded here. I am the last man to intrude into a sphere for which I am so entirely unfitted. I feel, on these premises, as if I was a bear – with the cramp – in a youthful Cotillon.'[20]

His ungainliness gave him enough of the air of his simile to set Rosa off laughing heartily.

'It strikes you in the same light,' said Mr Grewgious, with perfect calmness. 'Just so. To return to my memorandum. Mr Edwin has been to and fro here, as was arranged. You have mentioned that, in your quarterly letters to me. And you like him, and he likes you.'

'I *like* him very much, sir,' rejoined Rosa.

'So I said, my dear,' returned her guardian, for whose ear the timid emphasis was much too fine. 'Good. And you correspond.'

'We write to one another,' said Rosa, pouting, as she recalled their epistolary differences.

'Such is the meaning that I attach to the word "correspond" in this application, my dear,' said Mr Grewgious. 'Good. All goes well, time works on, and at this next Christmas-time it will become necessary, as a matter of form, to give the exemplary lady in the corner window, to whom we are so much indebted, business notice of your departure in the ensuing half-year. Your relations with her are far more than business relations, no doubt; but a residue of business remains in them, and business is business ever. I am a particularly Angular man,' proceeded Mr Grewgious, as if it suddenly occurred to him to mention it, 'and I am not used to give anything away. If, for these two reasons, some competent Proxy would give *you* away, I should take it very kindly.'

Rosa intimated, with her eyes on the ground, that she thought a substitute might be found, if required.

'Surely, surely,' said Mr Grewgious. 'For instance, the gentleman who teaches Dancing here – he would know how to do it with graceful propriety. He would advance and retire in a manner satisfactory to the feelings of the officiating clergyman, and of yourself, and the bridegroom, and all parties concerned. I am – I am a particularly Angular man,' said Mr Grewgious, as if he had made up his mind to screw it out at last: 'and should only blunder.'

Rosa sat still and silent. Perhaps her mind had not quite got so far as the ceremony yet, but was lagging on the way there.

'Memorandum. "Will." Now, my dear,' said Mr Grewgious, refer-ring to his notes, disposing of 'marriage' with his pencil, and taking a paper from his pocket: 'although I have before possessed you with the contents of your father's will, I think it right at this time to leave a certified copy of it in your hands. And although Mr Edwin is also aware of its contents, I think it right at this time likewise to place a certified copy of it in Mr Jasper's hands –'

'Not in his own!' asked Rosa, looking up quickly. 'Cannot the copy go to Eddy himself?'

'Why, yes, my dear, if you particularly wish it; but I spoke of Mr Jasper as being his trustee.'

'I do particularly wish it, if you please,' said Rosa, hurriedly and earnestly; 'I don't like Mr Jasper to come between us, in any way.'

'It is natural, I suppose,' said Mr Grewgious, 'that your young husband should be all in all. Yes. You observe that I say, I suppose.

The fact is, I am a particularly Unnatural man, and I don't know from my own knowledge.'

Rosa looked at him with some wonder.

'I mean,' he explained, 'that young ways were never my ways. I was the only offspring of parents far advanced in life, and I half believe I was born advanced in life myself.[21] No personality is intended towards the name you will so soon change, when I remark that while the general growth of people seem to have come into existence, buds, I seem to have come into existence a chip. I was a chip – and a very dry one – when I first became aware of myself. Respecting the other certified copy, your wish shall be complied with. Respecting your inheritance, I think you know all. It is an annuity of two hundred and fifty pounds. The savings upon that annuity, and some other items to your credit, all duly carried to account, with vouchers, will place you in possession of a lump-sum of money, rather exceeding Seventeen Hundred Pounds. I am empowered to advance the cost of your preparations for your marriage out of that fund. All is told.'

'Will you please tell me,' said Rosa, taking the paper with a prettily knitted brow, but not opening it: 'whether I am right in what I am going to say? I can understand what you tell me, so very much better than what I read in law-writings. My poor papa and Eddy's father made their agreement together, as very dear and firm and fast friends, in order that we, too, might be very dear and firm and fast friends after them?'

'Just so.'

'For the lasting good of both of us, and the lasting happiness of both of us?'

'Just so.'

'That we might be to one another even much more than they had been to one another?'

'Just so.'

'It was not bound upon Eddy, and it was not bound upon me, by any forfeit, in case –'

'Don't be agitated, my dear. In the case that it brings tears into your affectionate eyes even to picture to yourself – in the case of your not marrying one another – no, no forfeiture on either side. You would then have been my ward until you were of age. No worse would have befallen you. Bad enough perhaps!'

'And Eddy?'

'He would have come into his partnership derived from his father, and into its arrears to his credit (if any), on attaining his majority, just as now.'

Rosa, with her perplexed face and knitted brow, bit the corner of her attested copy, as she sat with her head on one side, looking abstractedly on the floor, and smoothing it with her foot.

'In short,' said Mr Grewgious, 'this betrothal is a wish, a sentiment, a friendly project, tenderly expressed on both sides. That it was strongly felt, and that there was a lively hope that it would prosper, there can be no doubt. When you were both children, you began to be accustomed to it, and it *has* prospered. But circumstances alter cases; and I made this visit to-day, partly, indeed principally, to discharge myself of the duty of telling you, my dear, that two young people can only be betrothed in marriage (except as a matter of convenience, and therefore mockery and misery) of their own free will, their own attachment, and their own assurance (it may or it may not prove a mistaken one, but we must take our chance of that), that they are suited to each other and will make each other happy. Is it to be supposed, for example, that if either of your fathers were living now, and had any mistrust on that subject, his mind would not be changed by the change of circumstances involved in the change of your years? Untenable, unreasonable, inconclusive, and preposterous!'

Mr Grewgious said all this, as if he were reading it aloud; or, still more, as if he were repeating a lesson. So expressionless of any approach to spontaneity were his face and manner.

'I have now, my dear,' he added, blurring out 'Will' with his pencil, 'discharged myself of what is doubtless a formal duty in this case, but still a duty in such a case. Memorandum, "Wishes:" My dear, is there any wish of yours that I can further?'

Rosa shook her head, with an almost plaintive air of hesitation in want of help.

'Is there any instruction that I can take from you with reference to your affairs?'

'I – I should like to settle them with Eddy first, if you please,' said Rosa, plaiting the crease in her dress.

'Surely. Surely,' returned Mr Grewgious. 'You two should be of one mind in all things. Is the young gentleman expected shortly?'

'He has gone away only this morning. He will be back at Christmas.'

'Nothing could happen better. You will, on his return at Christmas, arrange all matters of detail with him; you will then communicate with me; and I will discharge myself (as a mere business acquittance) of my business responsibilities towards the accomplished lady in the corner window. They will accrue at that season.' Blurring pencil once again. 'Memorandum. "Leave." Yes. I will now, my dear, take my leave.'

'Could I,' said Rosa, rising, as he jerked out of his chair in his ungainly way: 'could I ask you, most kindly to come to me at Christmas, if I had anything particular to say to you?'

'Why, certainly, certainly,' he rejoined; apparently – if such a word can be used of one who had no apparent lights or shadows about him – complimented by the question. 'As a particularly Angular man, I do not fit smoothly into the social circle, and consequently I have no other engagement at Christmas-time than to partake, on the twenty-fifth, of a boiled turkey and celery sauce with a – with a particularly Angular clerk I have the good fortune to possess, whose father, being a Norfolk farmer,[22] sends him up (the turkey up), as a present to me, from the neighbourhood of Norwich. I should be quite proud of your wishing to see me, my dear. As a professional Receiver of rents, so very few people *do* wish to see me, that the novelty would be bracing.'

For his ready acquiescence, the grateful Rosa put her hands upon his shoulders, stood on tiptoe, and instantly kissed him.

'Lord bless me!' cried Mr Grewgious. 'Thank you, my dear! The honor is almost equal to the pleasure. Miss Twinkleton, Madam, I have had a most satisfactory conversation with my ward, and I will now release you from the incumbrance of my presence.'

'Nay, sir,' rejoined Miss Twinkleton, rising with a gracious condescension: 'say not incumbrance. Not so, by any means. I cannot permit you to say so.'

'Thank you, Madam. I have read in the newspapers,' said Mr Grewgious, stammering a little, 'that when a distinguished visitor (not that I am one: far from it) goes to a school (not that this is one: far from it), he asks for a holiday, or some sort of grace.[23] It being now the afternoon in the – College – of which you are the eminent head, the young ladies might gain nothing, except in name, by having the rest of the day allowed them. But if there is any young lady at all under a cloud, might I solicit – ?'

'Ah, Mr Grewgious, Mr Grewgious!' cried Miss Twinkleton, with a chastely-rallying forefinger. 'Oh, you gentlemen, you gentlemen! Fie for shame, that you are so hard upon us poor maligned disciplinarians of our sex, for your sakes! But as Miss Ferdinand is at present weighed down by an incubus' – Miss Twinkleton might have said a pen-and-ink-ubus[24] of writing out Monsieur La Fontaine – 'go to her, Rosa my dear, and tell her the penalty is remitted, in deference to the intercession of your guardian, Mr Grewgious.'

Miss Twinkleton here achieved a curtsey, suggestive of marvels happening to her respective legs, and which she came out of nobly, three yards behind her starting-point.

As he held it incumbent upon him to call on Mr Jasper before leaving Cloisterham, Mr Grewgious went to the Gate House, and climbed its postern stair. But Mr Jasper's door being closed, and presenting on a slip of paper the word 'Cathedral,' the fact of its being service-time was borne into the mind of Mr Grewgious. So he descended the stair again, and, crossing the Close, paused at the great western folding-door of the Cathedral, which stood open on the fine and bright, though short-lived, afternoon, for the airing of the place.

'Dear me,' said Mr Grewgious, peeping in, 'it's like looking down the throat of Old Time.'

Old Time heaved a mouldy sigh from tomb and arch and vault; and gloomy shadows began to deepen in corners; and damps began to rise from green patches of stone; and jewels, cast upon the pavement of the nave from stained glass by the declining sun, began to perish. Within the grill-gate of the chancel, up the steps surmounted loomingly by the fast darkening organ, white robes could be dimly seen, and one feeble voice, rising and falling in a cracked monotonous mutter, could at intervals be faintly heard. In the free outer air, the river, the green pastures, and the brown arable lands, the teeming hills and dales, were reddened by the sunset: while the distant little windows in windmills and farm homesteads, shone, patches of bright beaten gold. In the Cathedral, all became grey, murky, and sepulchral, and the cracked monotonous mutter went on like a dying voice, until the organ and the choir burst forth, and drowned it in a sea of music. Then the sea fell, and the dying voice made another feeble effort, and then the sea rose high, and beat its life out, and lashed the roof, and surged among the arches, and pierced the heights of the great tower; and then the sea was dry, and all was still.

Mr Grewgious had by that time walked to the chancel-steps, where he met the living waters coming out.[25]

'Nothing is the matter?' Thus Jasper accosted him, rather quickly. 'You have not been sent for?'

'Not at all, not at all. I came down of my own accord.[26] I have been to my pretty ward's, and am now homeward bound again.'[27]

'You found her thriving?'

'Blooming indeed. Most blooming. I merely came to tell her, seriously, what a betrothal by deceased parents is.'

'And what is it – according to your judgment?'

Mr Grewgious noticed the whiteness of the lips that asked the question, and put it down to the chilling account of the Cathedral.

'I merely came to tell her that it could not be considered binding, against any such reason for its dissolution as a want of affection, or want of disposition to carry it into effect, on the side of either party.'

'May I ask, had you any especial reason for telling her that?'

Mr Grewgious answered somewhat sharply: 'The especial reason of doing my duty, sir. Simply that.' Then he added: 'Come, Mr Jasper; I know your affection for your nephew, and that you are quick to feel on his behalf. I assure you that this implies not the least doubt of, or disrespect to, your nephew.'[28]

'You could not,' returned Jasper, with a friendly pressure of his arm, as they walked on side by side, 'speak more handsomely.'

Mr Grewgious pulled off his hat to smooth his head, and, having smoothed it, nodded it contentedly, and put his hat on again.

'I will wager,' said Jasper, smiling – his lips were still so white that he was conscious of it, and bit and moistened them while speaking: 'I will wager that she hinted no wish to be released from Ned.'

'And you will win your wager, if you do,' retorted Mr Grewgious. 'We should allow some margin for little maidenly delicacies in a young motherless creature, under such circumstances, I suppose; it is not in my line; what do you think?'

'There can be no doubt of it.'

'I am glad you say so. Because,' proceeded Mr Grewgious, who had all this time very knowingly felt his way round to action on his remembrance of what she had said of Jasper himself: 'because she seems to have some little delicate instinct that all preliminary arrangements had best be made between Mr Edwin Drood and herself, don't you see? She don't want us, don't you know?'

Jasper touched himself on the breast, and said, somewhat indistinctly: 'You mean me.'

Mr Grewgious touched himself on the breast, and said: 'I mean us.[29] Therefore, let them have their little discussions and councils together, when Mr Edwin Drood comes back here at Christmas, and then you and I will step in, and put the final touches to the business.'

'So, you settled with her that you would come back at Christmas?' observed Jasper.[30] 'I see! Mr Grewgious, as you quite fairly said just now, there is such an exceptional attachment between my nephew and me, that I am more sensitive for the dear, fortunate, happy, happy fellow than for myself. But it is only right that the young lady should be considered, as you have pointed out, and that I should accept my cue from you. I accept it. I understand that at Christmas they will complete their preparations for May, and that their marriage will be put in final train by themselves, and that nothing will remain for us but to put ourselves in train also, and have everything ready for our formal release from our trusts, on Edwin's birthday.'

'That is my understanding,' assented Mr Grewgious, as they shook hands to part. 'God bless them both!'

'God save them both!' cried Jasper.

'I said, bless them,' remarked the former, looking back over his shoulder.

'I said, save them,' returned the latter. 'Is there any difference?'

*

CHAPTER 10

Smoothing the Way

It has been often enough remarked[1] that women have a curious power of divining the characters of men, which would seem to be innate and instinctive; seeing that it is arrived at through no patient process of reasoning, that it can give no satisfactory or sufficient account of itself, and that it pronounces in the most confident manner even against accumulated observation on the part of the other sex. But it has not been quite so often remarked that this power (fallible, like every other human attribute) is for the most part absolutely incapable of self-revision; and that when it has delivered an adverse opinion which by all human lights is subsequently proved to have failed, it is undistinguishable from prejudice, in respect of its determination not to be corrected. Nay, the very possibility of contradiction or disproof, however remote, communicates to this feminine judgment from the first, in nine cases out of ten, the weakness attendant on the testimony of an interested witness: so personally and strongly does the fair diviner connect herself with her divination.

'Now, don't you think, Ma dear,' said the Minor Canon to his mother one day as she sat at her knitting in his little book-room, 'that you are rather hard on Mr Neville?'

'No, I do *not*, Sept,' returned the old lady.

'Let us discuss it, Ma.'

'I have no objection to discuss it, Sept. I trust, my dear, I am always open to discussion.' There was a vibration in the old lady's cap, as though she internally added: 'and I should like to see the discussion that would change *my* mind!'

'Very good, Ma,' said her conciliatory son. 'There is nothing like being open to discussion.'

'I hope not, my dear,' returned the old lady, evidently shut to it.

'Well! Mr Neville, on that unfortunate occasion, commits himself under provocation.'

'And under mulled wine,' added the old lady.

'I must admit the wine. Though I believe the two young men were much alike in that regard.'

'I don't!' said the old lady.

'Why not, Ma?'

'Because I *don't*,' said the old lady. 'Still, I am quite open to discussion.'

'But, my dear Ma, I cannot see how we are to discuss, if you take that line.'

'Blame Mr Neville for it, Sept, and not me,' said the old lady, with stately severity.

'My dear Ma! Why Mr Neville?'

'Because,' said Mrs Crisparkle, retiring on first principles, 'he came home intoxicated, and did great discredit to this house, and showed great disrespect to this family.'

'That is not to be denied, Ma. He was then, and he is now, very sorry for it.'

'But for Mr Jasper's well-bred consideration in coming up to me, next day, after service, in the Nave itself, with his gown still on, and expressing his hope that I had not been greatly alarmed or had my rest violently broken, I believe I might never had heard of that disgraceful transaction,' said the old lady.

'To be candid, Ma, I think I should have kept it from you if I could: though I had not decidedly made up my mind. I was following Jasper out, to confer with him on the subject, and to consider the expediency of his and my jointly hushing the thing up on all accounts, when I found him speaking to you. Then it was too late.'

'Too late, indeed, Sept. He was still as pale as gentlemanly ashes at what had taken place in his rooms over-night.'

'If I *had* kept it from you, Ma, you may be sure it would have been for your peace and quiet, and for the good of the young men, and in my best discharge of my duty according to my lights.'

The old lady immediately walked across the room and kissed him; saying, 'Of course, my dear Sept, I am sure of that.'

'However, it became the town-talk,' said Mr Crisparkle, rubbing his ear, as his mother resumed her seat, and her knitting, 'and passed out of my power.'

'And I said then, Sept,' returned the old lady, 'that I thought ill of Mr Neville. And I say now, that I think ill of Mr Neville. And I said then, and I say now, that I hope Mr Neville may come to good, but I don't believe he will.' Here the cap vibrated again, considerably.

'I am sorry to hear you say so, Ma –'

'I am sorry to say so, my dear,' interposed the old lady, knitting on firmly, 'but I can't help it.'

'– For,' pursued the Minor Canon, 'it is undeniable that Mr Neville is exceedingly industrious and attentive, and that he improves apace, and that he has – I hope I may say – an attachment to me.'

'There is no merit in the last article, my dear,' said the old lady, quickly; 'and if he says there is, I think the worse of him for the boast.'

'But, my dear Ma, he never said there was.'

'Perhaps not,' returned the old lady; 'still, I don't see that it greatly signifies.'

There was no impatience in the pleasant look with which Mr Crisparkle contemplated the pretty old piece of china as it knitted; but there was, certainly, a humorous sense of its not being a piece of china to argue with very closely.

'Besides, Sept. Ask yourself what he would be without his sister. You know what an influence she has over him; you know what a capacity she has; you know that whatever he reads with you, he reads with her. Give her her fair share of your praise, and how much do you leave for him?'

At these words Mr Crisparkle fell into a little reverie, in which he thought of several things. He thought of the times he had seen the brother and sister together in deep converse over one of his own old college books; now, in the rimy mornings, when he made those sharpening pilgrimages to Cloisterham Weir; now, in the sombre evenings, when he faced the wind at sunset, having climbed his favorite outlook, a beetling fragment of monastery ruin; and the two studious figures passed below him along the margin of the river, in which the town fires and lights already shone, making the landscape bleaker. He thought how the consciousness had stolen upon him that in teaching one, he was teaching two; and how he had almost insensibly adapted his explanations to both minds – that with which his own was daily in contact, and that which he only approached through it. He thought of the gossip that had reached him from the Nuns' House, to the effect that Helena, whom he had mistrusted as so proud and fierce, submitted herself to the fairy-bride (as he called her), and learnt from her what she knew. He thought of the picturesque alliance between those two, externally so very different. He thought – perhaps most of all – could it be that these things were yet but so many weeks old, and had become an integral part of his life?

As, whenever the Reverend Septimus fell a-musing, his good mother took it to be an infallible sign that he 'wanted support,' the blooming old lady made all haste to the dining-room closet, to produce from it the support embodied in a glass of Constantia[2] and a home-made biscuit. It was a most wonderful closet, worthy of Cloisterham and of Minor Canon Corner. Above it, a portrait of Handel in a flowing wig[3] beamed down at the spectator, with a knowing air of being up to the contents of the closet, and a musical air of intending to combine all its harmonies in one delicious fugue. No common closet with a vulgar door on hinges, openable all at once, and leaving nothing to be disclosed by degrees, this rare closet had a lock in mid-air, where two perpendicular slides met: the one falling down, and the other pushing up. The upper slide, on being pulled down (leaving the lower a double mystery), revealed deep shelves of pickle-jars, jam-pots, tin canisters, spice boxes, and agreeably outlandish vessels of blue and white, the luscious lodgings of preserved tamarinds and ginger. Every benevolent inhabitant of this retreat had his name inscribed upon his stomach. The pickles, in a uniform of rich brown double-breasted buttoned coat, and yellow or sombre drab continuations, announced their portly forms, in printed capitals, as Walnut, Gherkin, Onion, Cabbage, Cauliflower, Mixed, and other members of that noble family. The jams, as being of a less masculine temperament, and as wearing curl-papers, announced themselves in feminine calligraphy, like a soft whisper, to be Raspberry, Gooseberry, Apricot, Plum, Damson, Apple, and Peach. The scene closing on these charmers, and the lower slide ascending, oranges were revealed, attended by a mighty japanned sugar-box, to temper their acerbity if unripe. Home-made biscuits waited at the Court of these Powers, accompanied by a goodly fragment of plum-cake, and various slender ladies' fingers, to be dipped into sweet wine and kissed. Lowest of all, a compact leaden vault enshrined the sweet wine and a stock of cordials: whence issued whispers of Seville Orange, Lemon, Almond, and Caraway-seed. There was a crowning air upon this closet of closets, of having been for ages hummed through by the Cathedral bell and organ, until those venerable bees had made sublimated honey of everything in store; and it was always observed that every dipper among the shelves (deep, as has been noticed, and swallowing up head, shoulders, and elbows) came forth again mellow-faced, and seeming to have undergone a saccharine transfiguration.

The Reverend Septimus yielded himself up quite as willing a victim to a nauseous medicinal herb-closet, also presided over by the china shepherdess, as to this glorious cupboard. To what amazing infusions of gentian, peppermint, gilliflower, sage, parsley, thyme, rue, rose-mary, and dandelion, did his courageous stomach submit itself! In what wonderful wrappers, enclosing layers of dried leaves, would he swathe his rosy and contented face, if his mother suspected him of a toothache! What botanical blotches would he cheerfully stick upon his cheek, or forehead, if the dear old lady convicted him of an impercept-ible pimple there! Into this herbaceous penitentiary, situated on an upper staircase-landing: a low and narrow whitewashed cell, where bunches of dried leaves hung from rusty hooks in the ceiling, and were spread out upon shelves, in company with portentous bottles: would the Reverend Septimus submissively be led, like the highly-popular lamb who has so long and unresistingly been led to the slaughter,[4] and there would he, *un*like that lamb, bore nobody but himself. Not even doing that much, so that the old lady were busy and pleased, he would quietly swallow what was given him, merely taking a corrective dip of hands and face into the great bowl of dried rose-leaves, and into the other great bowl of dried lavender, and then would go out, as confident in the sweetening powers of Cloisterham Weir and a wholesome mind, as Lady Macbeth was hopeless of those of all the seas that roll.[5]

In the present instance the good Minor Canon took his glass of

Constantia with an excellent grace, and, so supported to his mother's satisfaction, applied himself to the remaining duties of the day. In their orderly and punctual progress they brought round Vesper Service and twilight. The Cathedral being very cold, he set off for a brisk trot after service; the trot to end in a charge at his favorite fragment of ruin, which was to be carried by storm, without a pause for breath.

He carried it in a masterly manner, and, not breathed[6] even then, stood looking down upon the river. The river at Cloisterham is sufficiently near the sea to throw up oftentimes a quantity of seaweed. An unusual quantity had come in with the last tide, and this, and the confusion of the water, and the restless dipping and flapping of the noisy gulls, and an angry light out seaward beyond the brown-sailed barges that were turning black, foreshadowed a stormy night. In his mind he was contrasting the wild and noisy sea with the quiet harbor of Minor Canon Corner, when Helena and Neville Landless passed below him. He had had the two together in his thoughts all day, and at once climbed down to speak to them together. The footing was rough in an uncertain light for any tread save that of a good climber; but the Minor Canon was as good a climber as most men, and stood beside them before many good climbers would have been half-way down.

'A wild evening, Miss Landless! Do you not find your usual walk with your brother too exposed and cold for the time of year? Or at all events, when the sun is down, and the weather is driving in from the sea?'

Helena thought not. It was their favorite walk. It was very retired.

'It is very retired,' assented Mr Crisparkle, laying hold of his opportunity straightway, and walking on with them. 'It is a place of all others where one can speak without interruption, as I wish to do. Mr Neville, I believe you tell your sister everything that passes between us?'

'Everything, sir.'

'Consequently,' said Mr Crisparkle, 'your sister is aware that I have repeatedly urged you to make some kind of apology for that

Mr Crisparkle is overpaid

unfortunate occurrence which befell, on the night of your arrival here.'

In saying it he looked to her, and not to him; therefore it was she, and not he, who replied:

'Yes.'

'I call it unfortunate, Miss Helena,' resumed Mr Crisparkle, 'forasmuch as it certainly has engendered a prejudice against Neville. There is a notion about, that he is a dangerously passionate fellow, of an uncontrollable and furious temper: he is really avoided as such.'

'I have no doubt he is, poor fellow,' said Helena, with a look of proud compassion at her brother, expressing a deep sense of his being ungenerously treated. 'I should be quite sure of it, from your saying so; but what you tell me is confirmed by suppressed hints and references that I meet with every day.'

'Now,' Mr Crisparkle again resumed, in a tone of mild though firm persuasion, 'is not this to be regretted, and ought it not to be amended? These are early days of Neville's in Cloisterham, and I have no fear of his outliving such a prejudice, and proving himself to have been misunderstood. But how much wiser to take action at once, than to trust to uncertain time! Besides; apart from its being politic, it is right. For there can be no question that Neville was wrong.'

'He was provoked,' Helena submitted.

'He was the assailant,' Mr Crisparkle submitted.

They walked on in silence, until Helena raised her eyes to the Minor Canon's face, and said, almost reproachfully: 'Oh, Mr Crisparkle, would you have Neville throw himself at young Drood's feet, or at Mr Jasper's, who maligns him every day! In your heart you cannot mean it. From your heart you could not do it, if his case were yours.'

'I have represented to Mr Crisparkle, Helena,' said Neville, with a glance of deference towards his tutor, 'that if I could do it from my heart, I would. But I cannot, and I revolt from the pretence. You forget, however, that to put the case to Mr Crisparkle as his own, is to suppose Mr Crisparkle to have done what I did.'

'I ask his pardon,' said Helena.

'You see,' remarked Mr Crisparkle, again laying hold of his opportunity, though with a moderate and delicate touch, 'you both instinctively acknowledge that Neville did wrong! Then why stop short, and not otherwise acknowledge it?'

'Is there no difference,' asked Helena, with a little faltering in her manner, 'between submission to a generous spirit, and submission to a base or trivial one?'

Before the worthy Minor Canon was quite ready with his argument in reference to this nice distinction, Neville struck in:

'Help me to clear myself with Mr Crisparkle, Helena. Help me to convince him that I cannot be the first to make concessions without mockery and falsehood. My nature must be changed before I can do so, and it is not changed. I am sensible of inexpressible affront, and deliberate aggravation of inexpressible affront, and I am angry. The plain truth is, I am still as angry when I recall that night as I was that night.'

'Neville,' hinted the Minor Canon, with a steady countenance, 'you have repeated that former action of your hands, which I so much dislike.'

'I am sorry for it, sir, but it was involuntary. I confessed that I was still as angry.'

'And I confess,' said Mr Crisparkle, 'that I hoped for better things.'

'I am sorry to disappoint you, sir, but it would be far worse to deceive you, and I should deceive you grossly if I pretended that you had softened me in this respect. The time may come when your powerful influence will do even that with the difficult pupil whose antecedents you know; but it has not come yet. Is this so, and in spite of my struggles against myself, Helena?'

She, whose dark eyes were watching the effect of what he said on Mr Crisparkle's face, replied – to Mr Crisparkle; not to him: 'It is so.' After a short pause, she answered the slightest look of enquiry conceivable, in her brother's eyes, with as slight an affirmative bend of her own head; and he went on:

'I have never yet had the courage to say to you, sir, what in full openness I ought to have said when you first talked with me on this subject. It is not easy to say, and I have been withheld by a fear of its seeming ridiculous, which is very strong upon me down to this last moment, and might, but for my sister, prevent my being quite open with you even now. – I admire Miss Bud, sir, so very much, that I cannot bear her being treated with conceit or indifference; and even if I did not feel that I had an injury against young Drood on my own account, I should feel that I had an injury against him on hers.'

Mr Crisparkle, in utter amazement, looked at Helena for corroboration, and met in her expressive face full corroboration, and a plea for advice.

'The young lady of whom you speak is, as you know, Mr Neville, shortly to be married,' said Mr Crisparkle, gravely; 'therefore your admiration, if it be of that special nature which you seem to indicate, is outrageously misplaced. Moreover, it is monstrous that you should take upon yourself to be the young lady's champion against her chosen husband. Besides, you have seen them only once. The young lady has become your sister's friend; and I wonder that your sister, even on her behalf, has not checked you in this irrational and culpable fancy.'

'She has tried, sir, but uselessly. Husband or no husband, that fellow is incapable of the feeling with which I am inspired towards the beautiful young creature whom he treats like a doll. I say he is as incapable of it, as he is unworthy of her. I say she is sacrificed in being bestowed upon him. I say that I love her, and despise and hate him!' This with a face so flushed, and a gesture so violent, that his sister crossed to his side, and caught his arm, remonstrating, 'Neville, Neville!'

Thus recalled to himself, he quickly became sensible of having lost the guard he had set upon his passionate tendency, and covered his face with his hand, as one repentant, and wretched.

Mr Crisparkle, watching him attentively, and at the same time meditating how to proceed, walked on for some paces in silence. Then he spoke:

'Mr Neville, Mr Neville, I am sorely grieved to see in you more traces of a character as sullen, angry, and wild, as the night now closing in. They are of too serious an aspect to leave me the resource of treating the infatuation you have disclosed, as undeserving serious consideration. I give it very serious consideration, and I speak to you accordingly. This feud between you and young Drood must not go on. I cannot permit it to go on, any longer, knowing what I now know from you, and you living under my roof. Whatever prejudiced and unauthorized constructions your blind and envious wrath may put upon his character, it is a frank, good-natured character. I know I can trust to it for that. Now, pray observe what I am about to say. On reflection, and on your sister's representation, I am willing to admit that, in making peace with young Drood, you have a right to be met half way. I will engage that you shall be, and even that young Drood shall make the first advance. This condition fulfilled, you will pledge me the honor of a Christian gentleman that the quarrel is for ever at an end on your side. What may be in your heart when you give him your hand, can only be known to the Searcher of all hearts;[7] but it will never go well with you, if there be any treachery there. So far, as to that; next as to what I must again speak of as your infatuation. I understand it to have been confided to me, and to be known to no other person save your sister and yourself. Do I understand aright?'

Helena answered in a low voice: 'It is only known to us three who are here together.'

'It is not at all known to the young lady, your friend?'

'On my soul, no!'

'I require you, then, to give me your similar and solemn pledge, Mr Neville, that it shall remain the secret it is, and that you will take no other action whatsoever upon it than endeavouring (and that most earnestly) to erase it from your mind. I will not tell you that it will soon pass; I will not tell you that it is the fancy of the moment; I will not tell you that such caprices have their rise and fall among the young and ardent every hour; I will leave you undisturbed in the belief that it has few parallels or none, that it will abide with you a long time, and that it will be very difficult to conquer. So much the more weight shall I attach to the pledge I require from you, when it is unreservedly given.'

The young man twice or thrice essayed to speak, but failed.

'Let me leave you with your sister, whom it is time you took home,' said Mr Crisparkle. 'You will find me alone in my room by-and-bye.'

'Pray do not leave us yet,' Helena implored him. 'Another minute.'

'I should not,' said Neville, pressing his hand upon his face, 'have needed so much as another minute, if you had been less patient with me, Mr Crisparkle, less considerate of me, and less unpretendingly good and true. Oh, if in my childhood I had known such a guide!'

'Follow your guide now, Neville,' murmured Helena, 'and follow him to Heaven!'

There was that in her tone which broke the good Minor Canon's voice, or it would have repudiated her exaltation of him. As it was, he laid a finger on his lips, and looked towards her brother.

'To say that I give both pledges, Mr Crisparkle, out of my innermost heart, and to say that there is no treachery in it, is to say nothing!' Thus Neville, greatly moved, 'I beg your forgiveness for my miserable lapse into a burst of passion.'

'Not mine, Neville, not mine. You know with whom forgiveness lies, as the highest attribute conceivable. Miss Helena, you and your brother were twin children. You came into this world with the same dispositions, and you passed your younger days together surrounded by the same adverse circumstances. What you have overcome in yourself, can you not overcome in him? You see the rock that lies in his course. Who but you can keep him clear of it?'

'Who but you, sir?' replied Helena. 'What is my influence, or my weak wisdom, compared with yours!'

'You have the wisdom of Love,' returned the Minor Canon, 'and it was the highest wisdom ever known upon this earth, remember. As to mine – but the less said of that commonplace commodity the better. Good night!'

She took the hand he offered her, and gratefully and almost reverently raised it to her lips.

'Tut!' said the Minor Canon, softly, 'I am much overpaid!' And turned away.

Retracing his steps towards the Cathedral Close, he tried, as he went along in the dark, to think out the best means of bringing to pass what he had promised to effect, and what must somehow be done. 'I shall probably be asked to marry them,' he reflected, 'and I would they were married and gone! But this presses first.' He debated principally, whether he should write to young Drood, or whether he should speak to Jasper. The consciousness of being popular with the whole Cathedral establishment inclined him to the latter course, and the well-timed sight of the lighted Gate House decided him to take it. 'I will strike while the iron is hot,' he said, 'and see him now.'

Jasper was lying asleep on a couch before the fire, when, having ascended the postern-stair, and received no answer to his knock at the door, Mr Crisparkle gently turned the handle and looked in. Long afterwards he had cause to remember how Jasper sprang from the couch in a delirious state between sleeping and waking, crying out: 'What is the matter? Who did it?'[8]

'It is only I, Jasper. I am sorry to have disturbed you.'

The glare of his eyes settled down into a look of recognition, and he moved a chair or two, to make a way to the fireside.

'I was dreaming at a great rate,[9] and am glad to be disturbed from an indigestive after-dinner sleep. Not to mention that you are always welcome.'

'Thank you. I am not confident,' returned Mr Crisparkle as he sat himself down in the easy chair placed for him, 'that my subject will at first sight be quite as welcome as myself; but I am a minister of peace, and I pursue my subject in the interests of peace. In a word, Jasper, I want to establish peace between these two young fellows.'

A very perplexed expression took hold of Mr Jasper's face; a very perplexing expression too, for Mr Crisparkle could make nothing of it.

'How?' was Jasper's enquiry, in a low and slow voice, after a silence.

'For the "How" I come to you. I want to ask you to do me the great favor and service of interposing with your nephew (I have already interposed with Mr Neville), and getting him to write you a short note, in his lively way, saying that he is willing to shake hands. I know what a good-natured fellow he is, and what influence you have with him. And without in the least defending Mr Neville, we must all admit that he was bitterly stung.'

Jasper turned that perplexed face towards the fire. Mr Crisparkle continuing to observe it, found it even more perplexing than before, inasmuch as it seemed to denote (which could hardly be) some close internal calculation.

'I know that you are not prepossessed in Mr Neville's favor,' the Minor Canon was going on, when Jasper stopped him:

'You have cause to say so. I am not, indeed.'

'Undoubtedly, and I admit his lamentable violence of temper, though I hope he and I will get the better of it between us. But I have exacted a very solemn promise from him as to his future demeanour towards your nephew, if you do kindly interpose; and I am sure he will keep it.'

'You are always responsible and trustworthy, Mr Crisparkle. Do you really feel sure that you can answer for him so confidently?'

'I do.'

The perplexed and perplexing look vanished.

'Then you relieve my mind of a great dread, and a heavy weight,' said Jasper; 'I will do it.'

Mr Crisparkle, delighted by the swiftness and completeness of his success, acknowledged it in the handsomest terms.

'I will do it,' repeated Jasper, 'for the comfort of having your guarantee against my vague and unformed fears. You will laugh – but do you keep a Diary?'

'A line for a day; not more.'

'A line for a day would be quite as much as my uneventful life would need, Heaven knows,' said Jasper, taking a book from a desk; 'but that my Diary is, in fact, a Diary of Ned's life too. You will laugh at this entry; you will guess when it was made:

'Past midnight. – After what I have just now seen, I have a morbid dread upon me of some horrible consequences resulting to my dear boy, that I cannot reason with or in any way contend against. All my efforts are vain. The demoniacal passion of this Neville Landless, his strength in his fury, and his savage rage for the destruction of its object, appal me. So profound is the impression, that twice since have I gone into my dear boy's room, to assure myself of his sleeping safely, and not lying dead in his blood.

'Here is another entry next morning:

'Ned up and away. Light-hearted and unsuspicious as ever. He laughed when I cautioned him, and said he was as good a man as Neville Landless any day. I told him that might be, but he was not as bad a man. He continued to make light of it, but I travelled with him as far as I could, and left him most unwillingly. I am unable to shake off these dark intangible presentiments of evil – if feelings founded upon staring facts are to be so called.

'Again and again,' said Jasper, in conclusion, twirling the leaves of the book before putting it by, 'I have relapsed into these moods, as other entries show. But I have now your assurance at my back, and shall put it in my book, and make it an antidote to my black humors.'

'Such an antidote, I hope,' returned Mr Crisparkle, 'as will induce you before long to consign the black humors to the flames. I ought to be the last to find any fault with you this evening, when you have met my wishes so freely; but I must say, Jasper, that your devotion to your nephew has made you exaggerative here.'

'You are my witness,' said Jasper, shrugging his shoulders, 'what my state of mind honestly was, that night, before I sat down to write, and in what words I expressed it. You remember objecting to a word I used, as being too strong? It was a stronger word than any in my Diary.'

'Well, well. Try the antidote,' rejoined Mr Crisparkle, 'and may it give you a brighter and better view of the case! We will discuss it no more now. I have to thank you for myself, and I thank you sincerely.'

'You shall find,' said Jasper, as they shook hands, 'that I will not do the thing you wish me to do, by halves. I will take care that Ned, giving way at all, shall give way thoroughly.'

On the third day after this conversation, he called on Mr Crisparkle with the following letter:

MY DEAR JACK,

I am touched by your account of your interview with Mr Crisparkle, whom I much respect and esteem. At once I openly say that I forgot myself on that occasion quite as much as Mr Landless did, and that I wish that byegone to be a byegone, and all to be right again.

Look here, dear old boy. Ask Mr Landless to dinner on Christmas Eve (the better the day the better the deed), and let there be only we three, and let us shake hands all round there and then, and say no more about it.

My Dear Jack,

Ever your most affectionate,

EDWIN DROOD

P.S. – Love to Miss Pussy at the next music lesson.

'You expect Mr Neville, then?' said Mr Crisparkle.

'I count upon his coming,' said Mr Jasper.

CHAPTER II

A Picture and a Ring [1]

Behind the most ancient part of Holborn, London, where certain gabled houses some centuries of age still stand looking on the public way, as if disconsolately looking for the Old Bourne[2] that has long run dry, is a little nook composed of two irregular quadrangles, called Staple Inn.[3] It is one of those nooks, the turning into which out of the clashing street, imparts to the relieved pedestrian the sensation of having put cotton in his ears,[4] and velvet soles on his boots. It is one of those nooks where a few smoky sparrows twitter in smoky trees,[5] as though they called to one another, 'Let us play at country,' and where a few feet of garden mould and a few yards of gravel enable them to do that refreshing violence to their tiny under-standings. Moreover, it is one of those nooks which are legal nooks; and it contains a little Hall, with a little lantern in its roof:[6] to what obstructive purposes devoted, and at whose expense, this history knoweth not.

In the days when Cloisterham took offence at the existence of a railroad afar off, as menacing that sensitive Constitution, the property of us Britons, the odd fortune of which sacred institution it is to be in exactly equal degrees croaked about, trembled for, and boasted of, whatever happens to anything, anywhere in the world: in those days no neighbouring architecture of lofty proportions had arisen[7] to overshadow Staple Inn. The westering sun bestowed bright glances on it, and the south-west wind blew into it unimpeded.

Neither wind nor sun, however, favored Staple Inn, one December afternoon towards six o'clock, when it was filled with fog, and candles shed murky and blurred rays through the windows of all its thenoccupied sets of chambers; notably, from a set of chambers in a corner house in the little inner quadrangle, presenting in black and white over its ugly portal the mysterious inscription:[8]

P

J   T

1747.

In which set of chambers, never having troubled his head about the inscription, unless to bethink himself at odd times on glancing up at it, that haply it might mean Perhaps John Thomas, or Perhaps Joe Tyler, sat Mr Grewgious writing by his fire.

Who could have told, by looking at Mr Grewgious, whether he had ever known ambition or disappointment? He had been bred to the Bar,[9] and had laid himself out for chamber practice; to draw deeds; 'convey the wise it call,' as Pistol says.[10] But Conveyancing and he had made such a very indifferent marriage of it that they had separated by consent – if there can be said to be separation where there has never been coming together.

No. Coy Conveyancing would not come to Mr Grewgious. She was wooed, not won, and they went their several ways. But an Arbitration being blown towards him by some unaccountable wind,[11] and he gaining great credit in it as one indefatigable in seeking out right and doing right, a pretty fat Receivership was next blown into his pocket by a wind more traceable to its source. So, by chance, he had found his niche. Receiver and Agent now, to two rich estates, and deputing their legal business, in an amount worth having, to a firm of solicitors on the floor below, he had snuffed out his ambition (supposing him to have ever lighted it) and had settled down with his snuffers for the rest of his life under the dry vine and fig-tree[12] of P. J. T., who planted in seventeen-forty-seven.

Many accounts and account-books, many files of correspondence, and several strong boxes, garnished Mr Grewgious's room. They can scarcely be represented as having lumbered it, so conscientious and precise was their orderly arrangement. The apprehension of dying suddenly, and leaving one fact or one figure with any incompleteness or obscurity attaching to it, would have stretched Mr Grewgious stone dead any day. The largest fidelity to a trust was the life-blood of the man. There are sorts of life-blood that course more quickly, more gaily, more attractively; but there is no better sort in circulation.

There was no luxury in his room. Even its comforts were limited to its being dry and warm, and having a snug though faded fireside. What may be called its private life was confined to the hearth, and an easy chair, and an old-fashioned occasional round table that was brought out upon the rug after business hours, from a corner where it elsewise remained turned up like a shining mahogany shield. Behind it, when standing thus on the defensive, was a closet, usually containing something good to drink. An outer room was the clerk's room; Mr Grewgious's sleeping-room was across the common stair; and he held some not empty cellarage at the bottom of the common stair. Three hundred days in the year, at least, he crossed over to the hotel in Furnival's Inn[13] for his dinner, and after dinner crossed back again, to make the most of these simplicities until it should become broad business day once more, with P. J. T., date seventeen-forty-seven.

As Mr Grewgious sat and wrote by his fire that afternoon, so did the clerk of Mr Grewgious sit and write by *his* fire. A pale, puffy-faced, dark-haired person of thirty, with big dark eyes that wholly wanted lustre, and a dissatisfied doughy complexion, that seemed to ask to be sent to the baker's, this attendant was a mysterious being, possessed of some strange power over Mr Grewgious. As though he had been called into existence, like a fabulous Familiar,[14] by a magic spell which had failed when required to dismiss him, he stuck tight to Mr Grewgious's stool, although Mr Grewgious's comfort and convenience would manifestly have been advanced by dispossessing him. A gloomy person with tangled locks, and a general air of having been reared under the shadow of that baleful tree of Java which has given shelter to more lies[15] than the whole botanical kingdom, Mr Grewgious, nevertheless, treated him with unaccountable consideration.

'Now, Bazzard,'[16] said Mr Grewgious, on the entrance of his clerk: looking up from his papers as he arranged them for the night: 'what is in the wind besides fog?'

'Mr Drood,' said Bazzard.

'What of him?'

'Has called,' said Bazzard.

'You might have shown him in.'

'I am doing it,' said Bazzard.

The visitor came in accordingly.

'Dear me!' said Mr Grewgious, looking round his pair of office candles. 'I thought you had called and merely left your name, and gone. How do you do, Mr Edwin? Dear me, you're choking!'

'It's this fog,' returned Edwin; 'and it makes my eyes smart,[17] like Cayenne pepper.'

'Is it really so bad as that? Pray undo your wrappers. It's fortunate I have so good a fire; but Mr Bazzard has taken care of me.'

'No I haven't,' said Mr Bazzard at the door.

'Ah! Then it follows that I must have taken care of myself without observing it,' said Mr Grewgious. 'Pray be seated in my chair. No. I beg! Coming out of such an atmosphere, in *my* chair.'

Edwin took the easy chair in the corner; and the fog he had brought in with him, and the fog he took off with his great-coat and neck-shawl, was speedily licked up by the eager fire.

'I look,' said Edwin, smiling, 'as if I had come to stop.'

' – By-the-bye,' cried Mr Grewgious; 'excuse my interrupting you; do stop. The fog may clear in an hour or two. We can have dinner in from just across Holborn. You had better take your Cayenne pepper here than outside; pray stop and dine.'

'You are very kind,' said Edwin, glancing about him, as though attracted by the notion of a new and relishing sort of gipsy-party.

'Not at all,' said Mr Grewgious; '*you* are very kind to join issue with a bachelor in chambers, and take pot-luck. And I'll ask,' said Mr Grewgious, dropping his voice, and speaking with a twinkling eye, as if inspired with a bright thought: 'I'll ask Bazzard. He mightn't like it else. Bazzard!'

Bazzard reappeared.

'Dine presently with Mr Drood and me.'

'If I am ordered to dine, of course I will, sir,' was the gloomy answer.

'Save the man!' cried Mr Grewgious. 'You're not ordered; you're invited.'

'Thank you, sir,' said Bazzard; 'in that case I don't care if I do.'

'That's arranged. And perhaps you wouldn't mind,' said Mr Grewgious, 'stepping over to the hotel in Furnival's, and asking them to send in materials for laying the cloth. For dinner we'll have a tureen of the hottest and strongest soup available, and we'll have the best made-dish that can be recommended, and we'll have a joint (such as a haunch of mutton), and we'll have a goose, or a turkey, or any little stuffed thing of that sort that may happen to be in the bill of fare – in short, we'll have whatever there is on hand.'

These liberal directions Mr Grewgious issued with his usual air of reading an inventory, or repeating a lesson, or doing anything else by rote. Bazzard, after drawing out the round table, withdrew to execute them.

'I was a little delicate, you see,' said Mr Grewgious, in a lower tone, after his clerk's departure, 'about employing him in the foraging or commissariat department. Because he mightn't like it.'

'He seems to have his own way, sir,' remarked Edwin.

'His own way?' returned Mr Grewgious. 'Oh, dear no! Poor fellow, you quite mistake him. If he had his own way, he wouldn't be here.'

'I wonder where he would be!' Edwin thought. But he only thought it, because Mr Grewgious came and stood himself with his back to the other corner of the fire, and his shoulder-blades against the chimneypiece, and collected his skirts[18] for easy conversation.

'I take it, without having the gift of prophecy, that you have done me the favor of looking in to mention that you are going down yonder – where I can tell you, you are expected – and to offer to execute any little commission from me to my charming ward, and perhaps to sharpen me up a bit in any proceedings? Eh, Mr Edwin?'

'I called, sir, before going down, as an act of attention.'

'Of attention!' said Mr Grewgious. 'Ah! of course, not of impatience?'

'Impatience, sir?'

Mr Grewgious had meant to be arch – not that he in the remotest degree expressed that meaning – and had brought himself into scarcely supportable proximity with the fire, as if to burn the fullest effect of his archness into himself, as other subtle impressions are burnt into hard metals. But his archness suddenly flying before the composed face and manner of his visitor, and only the fire remaining, he started and rubbed himself.

'I have lately been down yonder,' said Mr Grewgious, rearranging his skirts; 'and that was what I referred to, when I said I could tell you you are expected.'

'Indeed, sir! Yes; I knew that Pussy was looking out for me.'

'Do you keep a cat down there?' asked Mr Grewgious.

Edwin colored a little, as he explained: 'I call Rosa Pussy.'

'Oh, really,' said Mr Grewgious, smoothing down his head; 'that's very affable.'

Edwin glanced at his face, uncertain whether or no he seriously objected to the appellation. But Edwin might as well have glanced at the face of a clock.

'A pet name, sir,' he explained again.

'Umps,' said Mr Grewgious, with a nod. But with such an extraordinary compromise between an unqualified assent and a qualified dissent, that his visitor was much disconcerted.

'Did P Rosa –' Edwin began, by way of recovering himself.

'P Rosa?' repeated Mr Grewgious.

'I was going to say Pussy, and changed my mind; – did she tell you anything about the Landlesses?'

'No,' said Mr Grewgious. 'What is the Landlesses? An estate? A villa? A farm?'

'A brother and sister. The sister is at the Nuns' House, and has become a great friend of P—'

'P Rosa's,' Mr Grewgious struck in, with a fixed face.

'She is a strikingly handsome girl, sir, and I thought she might have been described to you, or presented to you, perhaps?'

'Neither,' said Mr Grewgious. 'But here is Bazzard.'

Bazzard returned, accompanied by two waiters – an immoveable waiter, and a flying waiter; and the three brought in with them as much fog as gave a new roar to the fire. The flying waiter, who had brought everything on his shoulders, laid the cloth with amazing rapidity and dexterity; while the immoveable waiter, who had brought nothing, found fault with him. The flying waiter then highly polished all the glasses he had brought, and the immoveable waiter looked through them. The flying waiter then flew across Holborn for the soup, and flew back again, and then took another flight for the made-dish, and flew back again, and then took another flight for the joint and poultry, and flew back again, and between whiles took supplementary flights for a great variety of articles, as it was discovered from time to time that the immoveable waiter had forgotten them all. But let the flying waiter cleave the air as he might, he was always reproached on his return by the immoveable waiter for bringing fog with him, and being out of breath. At the conclusion of the repast, by which time the flying waiter was severely blown, the immoveable waiter gathered up the tablecloth under his arm with a grand air, and having sternly (not to say with indignation) looked on at the flying waiter while he set clean glasses round, directed a valedictory glance towards Mr Grewgious, conveying: 'Let it be clearly understood between us that the reward is mine, and that Nil is the claim of this slave,' and pushed the flying waiter before him out of the room.

It was like a highly finished miniature painting representing My Lords of the Circumlocutional Department,[19] Commandership-in-Chief of any sort, Government. It was quite an edifying little picture to be hung on the line in the National Gallery.[20]

As the fog had been the proximate cause of this sumptuous repast, so the fog served for its general sauce. To hear the outdoor clerks sneezing, wheezing, and beating their feet on the gravel was a zest far surpassing Doctor Kitchener's.[21] To bid, with a shiver, the unfortunate flying waiter shut the door before he had opened it, was a condiment of a profounder flavor than Harvey.[22] And here let it be noticed, parenthetically, that the leg of this young man, in its application to the door, evinced the finest sense of touch: always preceding himself and tray (with something of an angling air about it), by some seconds: and always lingering after he and the tray had disappeared, like Macbeth's leg when accompanying him off the stage[23] with reluctance to the assassination of Duncan.

The host had gone below to the cellar, and had brought up bottles of ruby, straw-colored, and golden drinks, which had ripened long ago in lands where no fogs are, and had since lain slumbering in the shade. Sparkling and tingling after so long a nap, they pushed at their corks to help the corkscrew (like prisoners helping rioters to force their gates), and danced out gaily. If P. J. T. in seventeen-forty-seven, or in any other year of his period, drank such wines – then, for a certainty P. J. T. was Pretty Jolly Too.

Externally, Mr Grewgious showed no signs of being mellowed by these glowing vintages. Instead of his drinking them, they might have been poured over him in his high-dried snuff form, and run to waste, for any lights and shades they caused to flicker over his face. Neither was his manner influenced. But, in his wooden way, he had observant eyes for Edwin; and when, at the end of dinner, he motioned Edwin back to his own easy chair in the fireside corner, and Edwin luxuriously sank into it after very brief remonstrance, Mr Grewgious, as he turned his seat round towards the fire too, and smoothed his head and face, might have been seen looking at his visitor between his smoothing fingers.

'Bazzard!' said Mr Grewgious, suddenly turning to him.

'I follow you, sir,' returned Bazzard; who had done his work of consuming meat and drink in a workmanlike manner, though mostly in speechlessness.

'I drink to you, Bazzard; Mr Edwin, success to Mr Bazzard!'

'Success to Mr Bazzard!' echoed Edwin, with a totally unfounded appearance of enthusiasm, and with the unspoken addition: – 'What in, I wonder!'

'And May!' pursued Mr Grewgious – 'I am not at liberty to be definite – May! – my conversational powers are so very limited that I know I shall not come well out of this – May! – it ought to be put imaginatively, but I have no imagination – May! – the thorn of anxiety[24] is as near the mark as I am likely to get – May it come out at last!'

Mr Bazzard, with a frowning smile at the fire, put a hand into his tangled locks, as if the thorn of anxiety were there; then into his waistcoat, as if it were there; then into his pockets, as if it were there. In all these movements he was closely followed by the eyes of Edwin, as if that young gentleman expected to see the thorn in action. It was not produced, however, and Mr Bazzard merely said: 'I follow you, sir, and I thank you.'

'I am going,' said Mr Grewgious, jingling his glass on the table with one hand, and bending aside under cover of the other, to whisper to Edwin, 'to drink to my ward. But I put Bazzard first. He mightn't like it else.'

This was said with a mysterious wink; or what would have been a wink, if, in Mr Grewgious's hands, it could have been quick enough. So Edwin winked responsively, without the least idea what he meant by doing so.

'And now,' said Mr Grewgious, 'I devote a bumper to the fair and fascinating Miss Rosa. Bazzard, the fair and fascinating Miss Rosa!'

'I follow you, sir,' said Bazzard, 'and I pledge you!'

'And so do I!' said Edwin.

'Lord bless me!' cried Mr Grewgious, breaking the blank silence which of course ensued: though why these pauses *should* come upon us when we have performed any small social rite, not directly inducive of self-examination or mental despondency, who can tell! 'I am a particularly Angular man, and yet I fancy (if I may use the word, not having a morsel of fancy), that I could draw a picture of a true lover's state of mind, to-night.'

'Let us follow you, sir,' said Bazzard, 'and have the picture.'

'Mr Edwin will correct it where it's wrong,' resumed Mr Grewgious, 'and will throw in a few touches from the life. I dare say it is wrong in many particulars, and wants many touches from the life, for I was born a Chip, and have neither soft sympathies nor soft experiences. Well! I hazard the guess that the true lover's mind is completely permeated by the beloved object of his affections. I hazard the guess that her dear name is precious to him, cannot be heard or repeated without emotion, and is preserved sacred. If he has any distinguishing appellation of fondness for her, it is reserved for her, and is not for common ears. A name that it would be a privilege to call her by, being alone with her own bright self, it would be a liberty, a coldness, an insensibility, almost a breach of good faith, to flaunt elsewhere.'

It was wonderful to see Mr Grewgious sitting bolt upright, with his hands on his knees, continuously chopping this discourse out of himself: much as a charity boy with a very good memory might get his catechism said:[25] and evincing no correspondent emotion whatever, unless in a certain occasional little tingling perceptible at the end of his nose.

'My picture,' Mr Grewgious proceeded, 'goes on to represent (under correction from you, Mr Edwin) the true lover as ever impatient to be in the presence or vicinity of the beloved object of his affections; as caring very little for his ease in any other society; and as constantly seeking that. If I was to say seeking that, as a bird seeks its nest, I should make an ass of myself, because that would trench upon what I understand to be poetry; and I am so far from trenching upon poetry at any time, that I never, to my knowledge, got within ten thousand miles of it. And I am besides totally unacquainted with the habits of birds, except the birds of Staple Inn, who seek their nests on ledges, and in gutter-pipes and chimneypots, not constructed for them by the beneficent hand of Nature. I beg, therefore, to be understood as foregoing the bird's-nest. But my picture does represent the true lover as having no existence separable from that of the beloved object of his affections, and as living at once a double life and a halved life. And if I do not clearly express what I mean by that, it is either for the reason that having no conversational powers, I cannot express what I mean, or that having no meaning, I do not mean what I fail to express. Which, to the best of my belief, is not the case.'

Edwin had turned red and turned white, as certain points of this picture came into the light. He now sat looking at the fire, and bit his lip.

'The speculations of an Angular man,' resumed Mr Grewgious, still sitting and speaking exactly as before, 'are probably erroneous on so globular a topic. But I figure to myself (subject, as before, to Mr Edwin's correction), that there can be no coolness, no lassitude, no doubt, no indifference, no half fire and half smoke state of mind, in a real lover. Pray am I at all near the mark in my picture?'

As abrupt in his conclusion as in his commencement and progress, he jerked this enquiry at Edwin, and stopped when one might have supposed him in the middle of his oration.

'I should say, sir,' stammered Edwin, 'as you refer the question to me –'

'Yes,' said Mr Grewgious, 'I refer it to you, as an authority.'

'I should say, then, sir,' Edwin went on, embarrassed, 'that the picture you have drawn is generally correct; but I submit that perhaps you may be rather hard upon the unlucky lover.'

'Likely so,' assented Mr Grewgious, 'likely so. I am a hard man in the grain.'

'He may not show,' said Edwin, 'all he feels; or he may not –'

There he stopped so long, to find the rest of his sentence, that Mr Grewgious rendered his difficulty a thousand times the greater, by unexpectedly striking in with:

'No, to be sure; he *may* not!'

After that, they all sat silent; the silence of Mr Bazzard being occasioned by slumber.

'His responsibility is very great, though,' said Mr Grewgious at length, with his eyes on the fire.

Edwin nodded assent, with *his* eyes on the fire.

'And let him be sure that he trifles with no one,' said Mr Grewgious; 'neither with himself, nor with any other.'

Edwin bit his lip again, and still sat looking at the fire.

'He must not make a plaything of a treasure. Woe betide him if he does! Let him take that well to heart,' said Mr Grewgious.

Though he said these things in short sentences, much as the supposititious charity boy just now referred to might have repeated a verse or two from the Book of Proverbs,[26] there was something dreamy (for so literal a man) in the way in which he now shook his right forefinger at the live coals in the grate, and again fell silent.

But not for long. As he sat upright and stiff in his chair, he suddenly rapped his knees, like the carved image of some queer Joss[27] or other coming out of its reverie, and said: 'We must finish this bottle, Mr

Edwin. Let me help you. I'll help Bazzard too, though he *is* asleep. He mightn't like it else.'

He helped them both, and helped himself, and drained his glass, and stood it bottom upward on the table, as though he had just caught a bluebottle in it.

'And now, Mr Edwin,' he proceeded, wiping his mouth and hands upon his handkerchief: 'to a little piece of business. You received from me, the other day, a certified copy of Miss Rosa's father's will. You knew its contents before, but you received it from me as a matter of business. I should have sent it to Mr Jasper, but for Miss Rosa's wishing it to come straight to you, in preference. You received it?'

'Quite safely, sir.'

'You should have acknowledged its receipt,' said Mr Grewgious, 'business being business all the world over. However, you did not.'

'I meant to have acknowledged it when I first came in this evening, sir.'

'Not a business-like acknowledgment,' returned Mr Grewgious; 'however, let that pass. Now, in that document you have observed a few words of kindly allusion to its being left to me to discharge a little trust, confided to me in conversation, at such time as I in my discretion may think best.'

'Yes, sir.'

'Mr Edwin, it came into my mind just now, when I was looking at the fire, that I could, in my discretion, acquit myself of that trust at no better time than the present. Favor me with your attention, half a minute.'

He took a bunch of keys from his pocket, singled out by the candle-light the key he wanted, and then, with a candle in his hand, went to a bureau or escritoire, unlocked it, touched the spring of a little secret drawer, and took from it an ordinary ring-case made for a single ring. With this in his hand, he returned to his chair. As he held it up for the young man to see, his hand trembled.

'Mr Edwin, this rose of diamonds and rubies delicately set in gold, was a ring belonging to Miss Rosa's mother. It was removed from her dead hand, in my presence, with such distracted grief as I hope it may never be my lot to contemplate again. Hard man as I am, I am not hard enough for that. See how bright these stones shine!' opening the case. 'And yet the eyes that were so much brighter, and that so often looked upon them with a light and a proud heart, have been ashes among ashes, and dust among dust,[28] some years! If I had any imagination (which it is needless to say I have not), I might imagine that the lasting beauty of these stones was almost cruel.'

He closed the case again as he spoke.

'This ring was given to the young lady who was drowned so early in her beautiful and happy career, by her husband, when they first plighted their faith to one another. It was he who removed it from her unconscious hand, and it was he who, when his death drew very near, placed it in mine. The trust in which I received it, was, that, you and Miss Rosa growing to manhood and womanhood, and your betrothal prospering and coming to maturity, I should give it to you to place upon her finger. Failing those desired results, it was to remain in my possession.'

Some trouble was in the young man's face, and some indecision was in the action of his hand, as Mr Grewgious, looking steadfastly at him, gave him the ring.

'Your placing it on her finger,' said Mr Grewgious, 'will be the solemn seal upon your strict fidelity to the living and the dead. You are going to her, to make the last irrevocable preparations for your marriage. Take it with you.'

The young man took the little case, and placed it in his breast.

'If anything should be amiss, if anything should be even slightly wrong, between you; if you should have any secret consciousness that you are committing yourself to this step for no higher reason than because you have long been accustomed to look forward to it; then,' said Mr Grewgious, 'I charge you once more, by the living and by the dead, to bring that ring back to me!'

Here Bazzard awoke himself by his own snoring; and, as is usual in such cases, sat apoplectically staring at vacancy, as defying vacancy to accuse him of having been asleep.

'Bazzard!' said Mr Grewgious, harder than ever.

'I follow you, sir,' said Bazzard, 'and I have been following you.'

'In discharge of a trust, I have handed Mr Edwin Drood a ring of diamonds and rubies. You see?'

Edwin reproduced the little case, and opened it; and Bazzard looked into it.

'I follow you both, sir,' returned Bazzard, 'and I witness the transaction.'

Evidently anxious to get away and be alone, Edwin Drood now resumed his outer clothing, muttering something about time and appointments. The fog was reported no clearer (by the flying waiter, who alighted from a speculative flight in the coffee interest), but he went out into it; and Bazzard, after his manner, 'followed' him.

Mr Grewgious, left alone, walked softly and slowly to and fro, for an hour and more. He was restless to-night, and seemed dispirited.

'I hope I have done right,' he said. 'The appeal to him seemed necessary. It was hard to lose the ring, and yet it must have gone from me very soon.'

He closed the empty little drawer with a sigh, and shut and locked the escritoire, and came back to the solitary fireside.

'Her ring,' he went on. 'Will it come back to me? My mind hangs about her ring very uneasily to-night. But that is explainable. I have had it so long, and I have prized it so much! I wonder –'

He was in a wondering mood as well as a restless; for, though he checked himself at that point, and took another walk, he resumed his wondering when he sat down again.

'I wonder (for the ten thousandth time, and what a weak fool I, for what can it signify now!) whether he confided the charge of their orphan child to me, because he knew – Good God, how like her mother she has become!

'I wonder whether he ever so much as suspected that some one doted on her, at a hopeless, speechless distance, when he struck in and won her. I wonder whether it ever crept into his mind who that unfortunate some one was!

'I wonder whether I shall sleep to-night! At all events, I will shut out the world with the bedclothes, and try.'

Mr Grewgious crossed the staircase to his raw and foggy bedroom, and was soon ready for bed. Dimly catching sight of his face in the misty looking-glass, he held his candle to it for a moment.

'A likely some one, *you*, to come into anybody's thoughts in such an aspect!' he exclaimed. 'There, there! there! Get to bed, poor man, and cease to jabber!'

With that, he extinguished his light, pulled up the bedclothes around him, and with another sigh shut out the world. And yet there are such unexplored romantic nooks in the unlikeliest men, that even old tinderous and touch-woody P. J. T. Possibly Jabbered Thus, at some odd times, in or about seventeen-forty-seven.

CHAPTER 12

A Night with Durdles

When Mr Sapsea has nothing better to do, towards evening, and finds the contemplation of his own profundity becoming a little monotonous in spite of the vastness of the subject, he often takes an airing in the Cathedral Close and thereabout. He likes to pass the churchyard with a swelling air of proprietorship, and to encourage in his breast a sort of benignant-landlord feeling, in that he has been bountiful towards that meritorious tenant, Mrs Sapsea, and has publicly given her a prize. He likes to see a stray face or two looking in through the railings, and perhaps reading his inscription. Should he meet a stranger coming from the churchyard with a quick step, he is morally convinced that the stranger is 'with a blush retiring,' as monumentally directed.

Mr Sapsea's importance has received enhancement, for he has become Mayor of Cloisterham. Without mayors, and many of them, it cannot be disputed that the whole framework of society[1] – Mr Sapsea is confident that he invented that forcible figure – would fall to pieces. Mayors have been knighted for 'going up' with addresses:[2] explosive machines intrepidly discharging shot and shell into the English Grammar. Mr Sapsea may 'go up' with an address. Rise, Sir Thomas Sapsea! Of such is the salt of the earth.[3]

Mr Sapsea has improved the acquaintance of Mr Jasper, since their first meeting to partake of port, epitaph, backgammon, beef, and salad. Mr Sapsea has been received at the Gate House with kindred hospitality; and on that occasion Mr Jasper seated himself at the piano, and sang to him, tickling his ears – figuratively, long enough to present a considerable area for tickling. What Mr Sapsea likes in that young man is, that he is always ready to profit by the wisdom of his elders, and that he is sound, sir, at the core. In proof of which, he sang to Mr Sapsea that evening no kickshaw ditties, favorites with national enemies, but gave him the genuine George the Third home-brewed;[4] exhorting him (as 'my brave boys') to reduce to a smashed condition all other islands but this island, and all continents, peninsulas, isthmuses, promontories, and other geographical forms of land[5] soever, besides sweeping the seas in all directions. In short, he rendered it pretty clear that Providence made a distinct mistake in originating so small a nation of hearts of oak, and so many other verminous peoples.

Mr Sapsea, walking slowly this moist evening near the churchyard with his hands behind him, on the look out for a blushing and retiring stranger, turns a corner, and comes instead into the goodly presence of the Dean, conversing with the Verger and Mr Jasper. Mr Sapsea makes his obeisance, and is instantly stricken far more ecclesiastical than any Archbishop of York, or Canterbury.[6]

'You are evidently going to write a book about us, Mr Jasper,' quoth the Dean; 'to write a book about us. Well! We are very ancient, and we ought to make a good book. We are not so richly endowed in possessions as in age; but perhaps you will put *that* in your book, among other things, and call attention to our wrongs.'

Mr Tope, as in duty bound, is greatly entertained by this.

'I really have no intention at all, sir,' replies Jasper, 'of turning author, or archæologist. It is but a whim of mine. And even for my whim, Mr Sapsea here is more accountable than I am.'

'How so, Mr Mayor?' says the Dean, with a nod of good-natured recognition of his Fetch.[7] 'How is that, Mr Mayor?'

'I am not aware,' Mr Sapsea remarks, looking about him for information, 'to what the Very Reverend the Dean does me the honor of referring.' And then falls to studying his original in minute points of detail.

'Durdles,' Mr Tope hints.

'Aye!' the Dean echoes; 'Durdles, Durdles!'

'The truth is, sir,' explains Jasper, 'that my curiosity in the man was first really stimulated by Mr Sapsea. Mr Sapsea's knowledge of mankind, and power of drawing out whatever is recluse or odd around him, first led to my bestowing a second thought upon the man: though of course I had met him constantly about. You would not be surprised by this, Mr Dean, if you had seen Mr Sapsea deal with him in his own parlor, as I did.'

'Oh!' cries Sapsea, picking up the ball thrown to him with ineffable complacency and pomposity; 'yes, yes. The Very Reverend the Dean refers to that? Yes. I happened to bring Durdles and Mr Jasper together. I regard Durdles as a Character.'

'A character, Mr Sapsea, that with a few skilful touches you turn inside out,' says Jasper.

'Nay, not quite that,' returns the lumbering auctioneer. 'I may have a little influence over him, perhaps; and a little insight into his character, perhaps. The Very Reverend the Dean will please to bear in mind that I have seen the world.' Here Mr Sapsea gets a little behind the Dean, to inspect his coat-buttons.

'Well!' says the Dean, looking about him to see what has become of his copyist: 'I hope, Mr Mayor, you will use your study and knowledge of Durdles to the good purpose of exhorting him not to break our worthy and respected Choir Master's neck; we cannot afford it; his head and voice are much too valuable to us.'

Mr Tope is again highly entertained, and, having fallen into respectful convulsions of laughter, subsides into a deferential murmur, importing that surely any gentleman would deem it a pleasure and an honor to have his neck broken, in return for such a compliment from such a source.

'I will take it upon myself, sir,' observes Sapsea, loftily, 'to answer for Mr Jasper's neck. I will tell Durdles to be careful of it. He will mind what *I* say. How is it at present endangered?' he enquires, looking about him with magnificent patronage.

'Only by my making a moonlight expedition with Durdles among the tombs, vaults, towers, and ruins,' returns Jasper. 'You remember suggesting, when you brought us together, that, as a lover of the picturesque,[8] it might be worth my while?'

'*I* remember!' replies the auctioneer. And the solemn idiot really believes that he does remember.

'Profiting by your hint,' pursues Jasper, 'I have had some day-rambles with the extraordinary old fellow, and we are to make a moonlight hole-and-corner exploration to-night.'

'And here he is,' says the Dean.

Durdles, with his dinner-bundle in his hand, is indeed beheld slouching towards them. Slouching nearer, and perceiving the Dean, he pulls off his hat, and is slouching away with it under his arm, when Mr Sapsea stops him.

'Mind you take care of my friend,' is the injunction Mr Sapsea lays upon him.

'What friend o' yourn is dead?' asks Durdles. 'No orders has come in for any friend o' yourn.'

'I mean my live friend, there.'

'Oh! Him?' says Durdles. 'He can take care of himself, can Mister Jarsper.'

'But do you take care of him too,' says Sapsea.

Whom Durdles (there being command in his tone) surlily surveys from head to foot.

'With submission to his Reverence the Dean, if you'll mind what concerns you, Mr Sapsea, Durdles he'll mind what concerns him.'

'You're out of temper,' says Mr Sapsea, winking to the company to observe how smoothly he will manage him. 'My friend concerns me, and Mr Jasper is my friend. And you are my friend.'

'Don't you get into a bad habit of boasting,' retorts Durdles, with a grave cautionary nod. 'It'll grow upon you.'[9]

'You are out of temper,' says Sapsea again; reddening, but again winking to the company.

'I own to it,' returns Durdles; 'I don't like liberties.'

Mr Sapsea winks a third wink to the company, as who should say: 'I think you will agree with me that I have settled *his* business;' and stalks out of the controversy.

Durdles then gives the Dean a good evening, and adding, as he

Durdles cautions Mr Sapsea against boasting

puts his hat on, 'You'll find me at home, Mister Jarsper, as agreed, when you want me; I'm a going home to clean myself,' soon slouches out of sight. This going home to clean himself is one of the man's incomprehensible compromises with inexorable facts; he, and his hat, and his boots, and his clothes, never showing any trace of cleaning, but being uniformly in one condition of dust and grit.

The lamplighter now dotting the quiet Close with specks of light, and running at a great rate up and down his little ladder with that object – his little ladder under the sacred shadow of whose inconvenience generations had grown up, and which all Cloisterham would have stood aghast at the idea of abolishing[10] – the Dean withdraws to his dinner, Mr Tope to his tea, and Mr Jasper to his piano. There, with no light but that of the fire, he sits chanting choir-music in a low and beautiful voice, for two or three hours; in short, until it has been for some time dark, and the moon is about to rise.

Then he closes his piano softly, softly changes his coat for a pea-jacket with a goodly wicker-cased bottle in its largest pocket, and, putting on a low-crowned flap-brimmed hat, goes softly out. Why does he move so softly to-night? No outward reason is apparent for it. Can there be any sympathetic reason crouching darkly within him?

Repairing to Durdles's unfinished house, or hole in the city wall, and seeing a light within it, he softly picks his course among the gravestones, monuments, and stony lumber of the yard, already touched here and there, sidewise, by the rising moon. The two journeymen have left their two great saws sticking in their blocks of stone; and two skeleton journeymen out of the Dance of Death[11] might be grinning in the shadow of their sheltering sentry-boxes, about to slash away at cutting out the gravestones of the next two people destined to die in Cloisterham. Likely enough, the two think little of that now, being alive, and perhaps merry. Curious, to make a guess at the two; – or say at one of the two!

'Ho! Durdles!'

The light moves, and he appears with it at the door. He would seem to have been 'cleaning himself' with the aid of a bottle, jug, and tumbler; for no other cleansing instruments are visible in the bare brick room with rafters overhead and no plastered ceiling, into which he shows his visitor.

'Are you ready?'

'I am ready, Mister Jarsper. Let the old uns come out if they dare, when we go among their tombs. My spirits is ready for 'em.'

'Do you mean animal spirits, or ardent?'[12]

'The one's the t'other,' answers Durdles, 'and I mean 'em both.'

He takes a lantern from a hook, puts a match or two in his pocket wherewith to light it, should there be need, and they go out together, dinner-bundle and all.

Surely an unaccountable sort of expedition![13] That Durdles himself, who is always prowling among old graves and ruins, like a Ghoule – that he should be stealing forth to climb, and dive, and wander without an object, is nothing extraordinary; but that the Choir Master or any one else should hold it worth his while to be with him, and to study moonlight effects in such company, is another affair. Surely an unaccountable sort of expedition, therefore!

''Ware that there mound by the yard-gate, Mister Jarsper.'

'I see it. What is it?'

'Lime.'

Mr Jasper stops, and waits for him to come up, for he lags behind. 'What you call quick-lime?'[14]

'Aye!' says Durdles; 'quick enough to eat your boots. With a little handy stirring, quick enough to eat your bones.'

They go on, presently passing the red windows of the Travellers' Twopenny, and emerging into the clear moonlight of the Monks' Vineyard. This crossed, they come to Minor Canon Corner: of which the greater part lies in shadow until the moon shall rise higher in the sky.

The sound of a closing house-door strikes their ears, and two men come out. These are Mr Crisparkle and Neville. Jasper, with a strange and sudden smile upon his face, lays the palm of his hand upon the breast of Durdles, stopping him where he stands.

At that end of Minor Canon Corner the shadow is profound in the existing state of the light: at that end, too, there is a piece of old dwarf wall, breast high, the only remaining boundary of what was once a garden, but is now the thoroughfare. Jasper and Durdles would have turned this wall in another instant; but, stopping so short, stand behind it.

'Those two are only sauntering,' Jasper whispers; 'they will go out into the moonlight soon. Let us keep quiet here, or they will detain us, or want to join us, or what not.'

Durdles nods assent, and falls to munching some fragments from his bundle. Jasper folds his arms upon the top of the wall, and, with his chin resting on them, watches. He takes no note whatever of the Minor Canon, but watches Neville, as though his eye were at the trigger of a loaded rifle, and he had covered him, and were going to fire. A sense of destructive power is so expressed in his face, that even Durdles pauses in his munching, and looks at him, with an unmunched something in his cheek.

Meanwhile Mr Crisparkle and Neville walk to and fro, quietly talking together. What they say cannot be heard consecutively; but Mr Jasper has already distinguished his own name more than once.

'This is the first day of the week,' Mr Crisparkle can be distinctly heard to observe, as they turn back; 'and the last day of the week is Christmas Eve.'

'You may be certain of me, sir.'

The echoes were favorable at those points, but as the two approach, the sound of their talking becomes confused again. The word 'confidence,' shattered by the echoes, but still capable of being pieced together, is uttered by Mr Crisparkle. As they draw still nearer, this fragment of a reply is heard: 'Not deserved yet, but shall be, sir.' As they turn away again, Jasper again hears his own name, in connexion with the words from Mr Crisparkle: 'Remember that I said I answered for you confidently.' Then the sound of their talk becomes confused again; they halting for a little while, and some earnest action on the part of Neville succeeding. When they move once more, Mr Crisparkle is seen to look up at the sky, and to point before him. They then slowly disappear; passing out into the moonlight at the opposite end of the Corner.

It is not until they are gone that Mr Jasper moves. But then he turns to Durdles, and bursts into a fit of laughter. Durdles, who still has that suspended something in his cheek, and who sees nothing to laugh at, stares at him until Mr Jasper lays his face down on his arms to have his laugh out. Then Durdles bolts the something, as if desperately resigning himself to indigestion.

Among those secluded nooks there is very little stir or movement after dark. There is little enough in the high-tide of the day, but there is next to none at night. Besides that the cheerfully frequented High Street lies nearly parallel to the spot (the old Cathedral rising between the two), and is the natural channel in which the Cloisterham traffic flows, a certain awful hush pervades the ancient pile, the cloisters, and the churchyard, after dark, which not many people care to encounter. Ask the first hundred citizens of Cloisterham, met at random in the streets at noon, if they believed in Ghosts, they would tell you no; but put them to choose at night between these eerie Precincts and the thoroughfare of shops, and you would find that ninety-nine declared for the longer round and the more frequented way. The cause of this is not to be found in any local superstition that attaches to the Precincts – albeit a mysterious lady, with a child in her arms and a rope dangling from her neck, has been seen flitting about there by sundry witnesses as intangible as herself – but it is to be sought in the innate shrinking of dust with the breath of life in it from dust out of which the breath of life has passed; also, in the widely diffused, and almost as widely unacknowledged, reflection: 'If the dead do, under any circumstances, become visible to the living, these are such likely surroundings for the purpose that I, the living, will get out of them as soon as I can.'

Hence, when Mr Jasper and Durdles pause to glance around them, before descending into the crypt by a small side door, of which the latter has a key, the whole expanse of moonlight in their view is utterly deserted. One might fancy that the tide of life was stemmed by Mr Jasper's own Gate House. The murmur of the tide is heard beyond; but no wave passes the archway, over which his lamp burns red behind his curtain, as if the building were a Lighthouse.

They enter, locking themselves in, descend the rugged steps, and are down in the crypt. The lantern is not wanted, for the moonlight strikes in at the groined windows, bare of glass, the broken frames for which cast patterns on the ground. The heavy pillars which support the roof engender masses of black shade, but between them there are lanes of light. Up and down these lanes they walk, Durdles discoursing of the 'old uns' he yet counts on disinterring, and slapping a wall, in which he considers 'a whole family on 'em' to be stoned and earthed up, just as if he were a familiar friend of the family. The taciturnity of Durdles is for the time overcome by Mr Jasper's wicker bottle, which circulates freely; – in the sense, that is to say, that its contents enter freely into Mr Durdles's circulation, while Mr Jasper only rinses his mouth once, and casts forth the rinsing.

They are to ascend the great Tower. On the steps by which they rise to the Cathedral, Durdles pauses for new store of breath. The steps are very dark, but out of the darkness they can see the lanes of light they have traversed. Durdles seats himself upon a step. Mr Jasper seats himself upon another. The odor from the wicker bottle (which has somehow passed into Durdles's keeping) soon intimates that the cork has been taken out; but this is not ascertainable through the sense of sight, since neither can descry the other. And yet, in talking, they turn to one another, as though their faces could commune together.

'This is good stuff, Mister Jarsper!'

'It is very good stuff, I hope. I bought it on purpose.'

'They don't show, you see, the old uns don't, Mister Jarsper!'

'It would be a more confused world than it is, if they could.'

'Well, it *would* lead towards a mixing of things,' Durdles acquiesces: pausing on the remark, as if the idea of ghosts had not previously presented itself to him in a merely inconvenient light, domestically, or chronologically. 'But do you think there may be Ghosts of other things, though not of men and women?'

'What things? Flower-beds and watering-pots? Horses and harness?'

'No. Sounds.'

'What sounds?'

'Cries.'

'What cries do you mean? Chairs to mend?'[15]

'No. I mean screeches. Now, I'll tell you, Mister Jarsper. Wait a bit till I put the bottle right.' Here the cork is evidently taken out again, and replaced again. 'There! *Now* it's right! This time last year, only a few days later,[16] I happened to have been doing what was correct by the season, in the way of giving it the welcome it had a right to expect, when them town-boys set on me at their worst. At length I gave 'em the slip, and turned in here. And here I fell asleep. And what woke me? The ghost of a cry. The ghost of one terrific shriek, which shriek was followed by the ghost of the howl of a dog: a long dismal woeful howl, such as a dog gives when a person's dead. That was *my* last Christmas Eve.'

'What do you mean?' is the very abrupt, and, one might say, fierce retort.

'I mean that I made enquiries everywhere about, and that no living ears but mine heard either that cry or that howl. So I say they was both ghosts; though why they came to me, I've never made out.'

'I thought you were another kind of man,' says Jasper, scornfully.

'So I thought, myself,' answers Durdles with his usual composure; 'and yet I was pricked out for it.'

Jasper had risen suddenly, when he asked him what he meant, and he now says, 'Come; we shall freeze here; lead the way.'

Durdles complies, not over-steadily; opens the door at the top of the steps with the key he has already used; and so emerges on the Cathedral level, in a passage at the side of the chancel. Here, the moonlight is so very bright again that the colors of the nearest stained-glass window are thrown upon their faces. The appearance of the unconscious Durdles, holding the door open for his companion to follow, as if from the grave, is ghastly enough, with a purple band across his face, and a yellow splash upon his brow; but he bears the close scrutiny of his companion in an insensible way, although it is prolonged while the latter fumbles among his pockets for a key confided to him that will open an iron gate, so to enable them to pass to the staircase of the great tower.

'That and the bottle are enough for you to carry,' he says, giving it to Durdles; 'hand your bundle to me; I am younger and longer-winded than you.' Durdles hesitates for a moment between bundle and bottle;

but gives the preference to the bottle as being by far the better company, and consigns the dry weight to his fellow-explorer.

Then they go up the winding staircase of the great tower, toilsomely, turning and turning, and lowering their heads to avoid the stairs above, or the rough stone pivot around which they twist. Durdles has lighted his lantern, by drawing from the cold hard wall a spark of that mysterious fire which lurks in everything, and, guided by this speck, they clamber up among the cobwebs and the dust. Their way lies through strange places. Twice or thrice they emerge into level low-arched galleries, whence they can look down into the moonlit nave; and where Durdles, waving his lantern, shows the dim angels' heads upon the corbels of the roof, seeming to watch their progress. Anon, they turn into narrower and steeper staircases, and the night air begins to blow upon them, and the chirp of some startled jackdaw or frightened rook precedes the heavy beating of wings in a confined space, and the beating down of dust and straws upon their heads. At last, leaving their light behind a stair – for it blows fresh up here – they look down on Cloisterham, fair to see in the moonlight: its ruined habitations and sanctuaries of the dead, at the tower's base: its moss-softened red-tiled roofs and red-brick houses of the living, clustered beyond: its river winding down from the mist on the horizon, as though that were its source, and already heaving with a restless knowledge of its approach towards the sea.

Once again, an unaccountable expedition this! Jasper (always moving softly with no visible reason) contemplates the scene, and especially that stillest part of it which the Cathedral overshadows. But he contemplates Durdles quite as curiously, and Durdles is by times conscious of his watchful eyes.

Only by times, because Durdles is growing drowsy. As aëronauts lighten the load they carry,[17] when they wish to rise, similarly Durdles has lightened the wicker bottle in coming up. Snatches of sleep surprise him on his legs, and stop him in his talk. A mild fit of calenture[18] seizes him, in which he deems that the ground, so far below, is on a level with the tower, and would as lief walk off the tower into the air as not. Such is his state when they begin to come down. And as aëronauts make themselves heavier when they wish to descend, similarly Durdles charges himself with more liquid from the wicker bottle, that he may come down the better.

The iron gate attained and locked – but not before Durdles has tumbled twice, and cut an eyebrow open once – they descend into the crypt again, with the intent of issuing forth as they entered. But, while returning among those lanes of light, Durdles becomes so very uncertain, both of foot and speech, that he half drops, half throws himself down, by one of the heavy pillars, scarcely less heavy than itself, and indistinctly appeals to his companion for forty winks of a second each.

'If you will have it so, or must have it so,' replies Jasper, 'I'll not leave you here. Take them, while I walk to and fro.'

Durdles is asleep at once; and in his sleep he dreams a dream.

It is not much of a dream, considering the vast extent of the domains of dreamland, and their wonderful productions; it is only remarkable for being unusually restless, and unusually real. He dreams of lying there, asleep, and yet counting his companion's footsteps as he walks to and fro. He dreams that the footsteps die away into distance of time and of space, and that something touches him, and that something falls from his hand. Then something clinks and gropes about, and he dreams that he is alone for so long a time, that the lanes of light take new directions as the moon advances in her course. From succeeding unconsciousness he passes into a dream of slow uneasiness from cold; and painfully awakes to a perception of the lanes of light – really changed, much as he had dreamed – and Jasper walking among them, beating his hands and feet.

'Holloa!' Durdles cries out, unmeaningly alarmed.

'Awake at last?' says Jasper, coming up to him. 'Do you know that your forties have stretched into thousands?'

'No.'

'They have though.'

'What's the time?'

'Hark! The bells are going in the Tower!'

They strike four quarters, and then the great bell strikes.

'Two!' cries Durdles, scrambling up; 'why didn't you try to wake me, Mister Jarsper?'

'I did. I might as well have tried to wake the dead: – your own family of dead, up in the corner there.'

'Did you touch me?'

'Touch you? Yes. Shook you.'

As Durdles recalls that touching something in his dream, he looks down on the pavement, and sees the key of the crypt door lying close to where he himself lay.

'I dropped you, did I?' he says, picking it up, and recalling that part of his dream. As he gathers himself again into an upright position, or into a position as nearly upright as he ever maintains, he is again conscious of being watched by his companion.

'Well?' says Jasper, smiling. 'Are you quite ready? Pray don't hurry.'

'Let me get my bundle right, Mister Jarsper, and I'm with you.'

As he ties it afresh, he is once more conscious that he is very narrowly observed.

'What do you suspect me of, Mister Jarsper?' he asks, with drunken displeasure. 'Let them as has any suspicions of Durdles, name 'em.'

'I've no suspicions of you, my good Mr Durdles; but I have suspicions that my bottle was filled with something stiffer than either of us supposed. And I also have suspicions,' Jasper adds, taking it from the pavement and turning it bottom upward, 'that it's empty.'

Durdles condescends to laugh at this. Continuing to chuckle when his laugh is over, as though remonstrant with himself on his drinking powers, he rolls to the door and unlocks it. They both pass out, and Durdles relocks it, and pockets his key.

'A thousand thanks for a curious and interesting night,' says Jasper, giving him his hand; 'you can make your own way home?'

'I should think so!' answers Durdles. 'If you was to offer Durdles the affront to show him his way home, he wouldn't go home.

> 'Durdles wouldn't go home till morning;[19]
> And then Durdles wouldn't go home,

Durdles wouldn't.' This, with the utmost defiance.

'Good-night, then.'

'Good-night, Mister Jarsper.'

Each is turning his own way, when a sharp whistle rends the silence, and the jargon is yelped out:

> 'Widdy widdy wen!
> I – ket – ches – Im – out – ar – ter – ten.
> Widdy widdy wy!
> Then – E – don't – go – then – I – shy –
> Widdy Widdy Wake-cock warning!'

Instantly afterwards, a rapid fire of stones rattles at the Cathedral wall, and the hideous small boy is beheld opposite, dancing in the moonlight.

'What! Is that baby-devil on the watch there!' cries Jasper in a fury: so quickly roused, and so violent, that he seems an older devil himself. 'I shall shed the blood of that Impish wretch! I know I shall do it!' Regardless of the fire, though it hits him more than once, he rushes at Deputy, collars him, and tries to bring him across. But Deputy is not to be so easily brought across. With a diabolical insight into the strongest part of his position, he is no sooner taken by the throat than he curls up his legs, forces his assailant to hang him, as it were, and gurgles in his throat, and screws his body, and twists, as already undergoing the first agonies of strangulation. There is nothing for it but to drop him. He instantly gets himself together, backs over to Durdles, and cries to his assailant, gnashing the great gap in front of his mouth with rage and malice:

'I'll blind yer, s'elp me! I'll stone yer eyes out, s'elp me! If I don't have yer eyesight, bellows me!'[20] At the same time dodging behind Durdles, and snarling at Jasper, now from this side of him, and now from that: prepared, if pounced upon, to dart away in all manner of curvilinear directions, and, if run down after all, to grovel in the dust, the cry: 'Now, hit me when I'm down! Do it!'

'Don't hurt the boy, Mister Jarsper,' urges Durdles, shielding him. 'Recollect yourself.'

'He followed us to-night, when we first came here!'

'Yer lie, I didn't!' replies Deputy, in his one form of polite contradiction.

'He has been prowling near us ever since!'

'Yer lie, I haven't,' returns Deputy. 'I'd only just come out for my 'elth when I see you two a coming out of the Kinfreederel. If –

'I – ket – ches – Im – out – ar – ter – ten,'

(with the usual rhythm and dance, though dodging behind Durdles), 'it ain't *my* fault, is it?'

'Take him home, then,' retorts Jasper, ferociously, though with a strong check upon himself, 'and let my eyes be rid of the sight of you!'

Deputy, with another sharp whistle, at once expressing his relief, and his commencement of a milder stoning of Mr Durdles, begins stoning that respectable gentleman home, as if he were a reluctant ox. Mr Jasper goes to his Gate House, brooding. And thus, as everything comes to an end,[21] the unaccountable expedition comes to an end – for the time.

*

CHAPTER 13

Both at their Best

Miss Twinkleton's establishment was about to undergo a serene hush. The Christmas recess was at hand. What had once, and at no remote period, been called, even by the erudite Miss Twinkleton herself, 'the half'; but what was now called, as being more elegant, and more chastely collegiate, 'the term';[1] would expire to-morrow. A noticeable relaxation of discipline had for some few days pervaded the Nuns' House. Club suppers had occurred in the bedrooms, and dressed tongue had been carved with a pair of scissors, and handed round with the curling-tongs. Portions of marmalade had likewise been distributed on a service of plates constructed of curlpaper; and cowslip wine[2] had been quaffed from the small squat measuring glass in which little

Rickitts (a junior of weakly constitution) took her steel drops daily.[3] The housemaids had been bribed with various fragments of riband, and sundry pairs of shoes more or less down at heel, to make no mention of crumbs in the beds; the airiest costumes had been worn on these festive occasions; and the daring Miss Ferdinand had even surprised the company with a sprightly solo on the comb-and-curlpaper, until suffocated in her own pillow by two flowing-haired executioners.[4]

Nor were these the only tokens of dispersal. Boxes appeared in the bedrooms (where they were capital at other times), and a surprising amount of packing took place, out of all proportion to the amount packed. Largesse, in the form of odds and ends of cold cream and pomatum, and also of hairpins, was freely distributed among the attendants. On charges of inviolable secresy, confidences were interchanged respecting golden youth of England expected to call, 'at home,'[5] on the first opportunity. Miss Giggles (deficient in sentiment) did indeed profess that she, for her part, acknowledged such homage by making faces at the golden youth; but this young lady was outvoted by an immense majority.

On the last night before a recess, it was always expressly made a point of honor that nobody should go to sleep, and that Ghosts should be encouraged by all possible means. This compact invariably broke down, and all the young ladies went to sleep very soon, and got up very early.

The concluding ceremony came off at twelve o'clock on the day of departure; when Miss Twinkleton, supported by Mrs Tisher, held a Drawing-Room in her own apartment[6] (the globes already covered with brown holland), where glasses of white wine, and plates of cut pound-cake were discovered on the table. Miss Twinkleton then said, Ladies, another revolving year[7] had brought us round to that festive period at which the first feelings of our nature bounded in our – Miss Twinkleton was annually going to add 'bosoms,' but annually stopped on the brink of that expression, and substituted 'hearts.' Hearts; our hearts. Hem! Again a revolving year, ladies, had brought us to a pause in our studies – let us hope our greatly advanced studies – and, like the mariner in his bark, the warrior in his tent, the captive in his dungeon, and the traveller in his various conveyances, we yearned for home. Did we say, on such an occasion, in the opening words of Mr Addison's impressive tragedy:[8]

> 'The dawn is overcast, the morning lowers,
> And heavily in clouds brings on the day,
> The great, th' important day——?'

Not so. From horizon to zenith all was *couleur de rose*,[9] for all was redolent of our relations and friends. Might *we* find *them* prospering as *we* expected; might *they* find *us* prospering as *they* expected! Ladies, we would now, with our love to one another, wish one another good-bye, and happiness, until we met again. And when the time should come for our resumption of those pursuits which (here a general depression set in all round), pursuits which, pursuits which; – then let us ever remember what was said by the Spartan General, in words too trite for repetition, at the battle it were superfluous to specify.[10]

The handmaidens of the establishment, in their best caps, then handed the trays, and the young ladies sipped and crumbled, and the bespoken coaches began to choke the street. Then, leave-taking was not long about, and Miss Twinkleton, in saluting each young lady's cheek, confided to her an exceedingly neat letter, addressed to her next friend at law,[11] 'with Miss Twinkleton's best compliments' in the corner. This missive she handed with an air as if it had not the least connexion with the bill,[12] but were something in the nature of a delicate and joyful surprise.

So many times had Rosa seen such dispersals, and so very little did she know of any other Home, that she was contented to remain where she was, and was even better contented than ever before, having her latest friend with her. And yet her latest friendship had a blank place in it of which she could not fail to be sensible. Helena Landless, having been a party to her brother's revelation about Rosa, and having entered into that compact of silence with Mr Crisparkle, shrank from any allusion to Edwin Drood's name. Why she so avoided it, was mysterious to Rosa, but she perfectly perceived the fact. But for the fact, she might have relieved her own little perplexed heart of some of its doubts and hesitations, by taking Helena into her confidence. As it was, she had no such vent: she could only ponder on her own difficulties, and wonder more and more why this avoidance of Edwin's name should last, now that she knew – for so much Helena had told her – that a good understanding was to be re-established between the two young men, when Edwin came down.

It would have made a pretty picture, so many pretty girls kissing Rosa in the cold porch of the Nuns' House, and that sunny little creature peeping out of it (unconscious of sly faces carved on spout and gable peeping at her),[13] and waving farewells to the departing coaches, as if she represented the spirit of rosy youth abiding in the place to keep it bright and warm in its desertion. The hoarse High Street became musical with the cry, in various silvery voices, 'Good-bye, Rosebud, Darling!' and the effigy of Mr Sapsea's father[14] over the opposite doorway seemed to say to mankind: 'Gentlemen, favor me with your attention to this charming little last lot left behind, and bid with a spirit worthy of the occasion!' Then the staid street, so unwontedly sparkling, youthful, and fresh for a few rippling moments, ran dry, and Cloisterham was itself again.

If Rosebud in her bower[15] now waited Edwin Drood's coming with an uneasy heart, Edwin for his part was uneasy too. With far less force of purpose in his composition than the childish beauty, crowned by acclamation fairy queen of Miss Twinkleton's establishment, he had a conscience, and Mr Grewgious had pricked it. That gentleman's steady convictions of what was right and what was wrong in such a case as his, were neither to be frowned aside nor laughed aside. They would not be moved. But for the dinner in Staple Inn, and but for the ring he carried in the breast-pocket of his coat, he would have drifted into their wedding-day without another pause for real thought, loosely trusting that all would go well, left alone. But that serious putting him on his truth to the living and the dead had brought him to a check. He must either give the ring to Rosa, or he must take it back. Once put into this narrowed way of action, it was curious that he began to consider Rosa's claims upon him more unselfishly than he had ever considered them before, and began to be less sure of himself than he had ever been in all his easy-going days.

'Good-bye, Rosebud, Darling!'

'I will be guided by what she says, and by how we get on,' was his decision, walking from the Gate House to the Nuns' House. 'Whatever comes of it, I will bear his words in mind, and try to be true to the living and the dead.'

Rosa was dressed for walking. She expected him. It was a bright frosty day, and Miss Twinkleton had already graciously sanctioned fresh air. Thus they got out together before it became necessary for either Miss Twinkleton, or the Deputy High Priest, Mrs Tisher, to lay even so much as one of those usual offerings on the shrine of Propriety.

'My dear Eddy,' said Rosa, when they had turned out of the High Street, and had got among the quiet walks in the neighbourhood of the Cathedral and the river: 'I want to say something very serious to you. I have been thinking about it for a long, long time.'

'I want to be serious with you too, Rosa dear. I mean to be serious and earnest.'

'Thank you, Eddy. And you will not think me unkind because I begin, will you? You will not think I speak for myself only, because I speak first? That would not be generous, would it? And I know you are generous!'

He said, 'I hope I am not ungenerous to you, Rosa.' He called her Pussy no more. Never again.

'And there is no fear,' pursued Rosa, 'of our quarrelling, is there? Because, Eddy,' clasping her hand on his arm, 'we have so much reason to be very lenient to each other!'

'We will be, Rosa.'

'That's a dear good boy! Eddy, let us be courageous. Let us change to brother and sister from this day forth.'

'Never be husband and wife?'

'Never!'

Neither spoke again for a little while. But after that pause he said, with some effort:

'Of course I know that this has been in both our minds, Rosa, and of course I am in honor bound to confess freely that it does not originate with you.'

'No, nor with you, dear,' she returned, with pathetic earnestness. 'It has sprung up between us. You are not truly happy in our engagement; I am not truly happy in it. Oh, I am so sorry, so sorry!' And there she broke into tears.

'I am deeply sorry too, Rosa! Deeply sorry for you.'

'And I for you, poor boy! And I for you!'

This pure young feeling, this gentle and forbearing feeling of each towards the other, brought with it its reward in a softening light that seemed to shine on their position. The relations between them did not look wilful, or capricious, or a failure, in such a light; they became elevated into something more self-denying, honorable, affectionate, and true.

'If we knew yesterday,' said Rosa, as she dried her eyes, 'and we did know yesterday, and on many, many yesterdays, that we were far from right together in those relations which were not of our own choosing, what better could we do to-day than change them? It is natural that we should be sorry, and you see how sorry we both are; but how much better to be sorry now than then?'

'When, Rosa?'

'When it would be too late. And then we should be angry, besides.'

Another silence fell upon them.

'And you know,' said Rosa, innocently, 'you couldn't like me then; and you can always like me now, for I shall not be a drag upon you, or a worry to you. And I can always like you now, and your sister will not tease or trifle with you. I often did when I was not your sister, and I beg your pardon for it.'

'Don't let us come to that, Rosa; or I shall want more pardoning than I like to think of.'

'No, indeed, Eddy; you are too hard, my generous boy, upon yourself. Let us sit down, brother, on these ruins, and let me tell you how it was with us. I think I know, for I have considered about it very much since you were here, last time. You liked me, didn't you? You thought I was a nice little thing?'

'Everybody thinks that, Rosa.'

'Do they?' She knitted her brow musingly for a moment, and then flashed out with the bright little induction: 'Well; but say they do.

Surely it was not enough that you should think of me only as other people did; now, was it?'

The point was not to be got over. It was not enough.

'And that is just what I mean; that is just how it was with us,' said Rosa. 'You liked me very well, and you had grown used to me, and had grown used to the idea of our being married. You accepted the situation as an inevitable kind of thing, didn't you? It was to be, you thought, and why discuss or dispute it?'

It was new and strange to him to have himself presented to himself so clearly, in a glass of her holding up. He had always patronized her, in his superiority to her share of woman's wit. Was that but another instance of something radically amiss in the terms on which they had been gliding towards a life-long bondage?

'All this that I say of you, is true of me as well, Eddy. Unless it was, I might not be bold enough to say it. Only, the difference between us was, that by little and little there crept into my mind a habit of thinking about it, instead of dismissing it. My life is not so busy as yours, you see, and I have not so many things to think of. So I thought about it very much, and I cried about it very much too (though that was not your fault, poor boy); when all at once my guardian came down, to prepare for my leaving the Nuns' House. I tried to hint to him that I was not quite settled in my mind, but I hesitated and failed, and he didn't understand me. But he is a good, good man. And he put before me so kindly, and yet so strongly, how seriously we ought to consider, in our circumstances, that I resolved to speak to you the next moment we were alone and grave. And if I seemed to come to it easily just now, because I came to it all at once, don't think it was so really, Eddy, for Oh, it was very, very hard, and Oh, I am very, very sorry!'

Her full heart broke into tears again. He put his arm about her waist, and they walked by the river side together.

'Your guardian has spoken to me too, Rosa dear. I saw him before I left London.' His right hand was in his breast, seeking the ring; but he checked it, as he thought: 'If I am to take it back why should I tell her of it?'

'And that made you more serious about it, didn't it, Eddy? And if

I had not spoken to you, as I have, you would have spoken to me? I hope you can tell me so? I don't like it to be *all* my doing, though it *is* so much better for us.'

'Yes, I should have spoken; I should have put everything before you; I came intending to do it. But I never could have spoken to you as you have spoken to me, Rosa.'

'Don't say you mean so coldly or unkindly, Eddy, please if you can help it.'

'I mean so sensibly and delicately, so wisely and affectionately.'

'That's my dear brother!' She kissed his hand in a little rapture. 'The dear girls will be dreadfully disappointed,' added Rosa, laughing, with the dew-drops glistening in her bright eyes. 'They have looked forward to it so, poor pets!'

'Ah! But I fear it will be a worse disappointment to Jack,' said Edwin Drood, with a start. 'I never thought of Jack!'

Her swift and intent look at him as he said the words could no more be recalled than a flash of lightning can. But it appeared as though she would have instantly recalled it, if she could; for she looked down, confused, and breathed quickly.

'You don't doubt its being a blow to Jack, Rosa?'

She merely replied, and that evasively and hurriedly: Why should she? She had not thought about it. He seemed, to her, to have so little to do with it.

'My dear child! Can you suppose that any one so wrapped up in another – Mrs Tope's expression: not mine – as Jack is in me, could fail to be struck all of a heap by such a sudden and complete change in my life? I say sudden, because it will be sudden to *him*, you know.'

She nodded twice or thrice, and her lips parted as if she would have assented. But she uttered no sound, and her breathing was no slower.

'How shall I tell Jack?' said Edwin, ruminating. If he had been less occupied with the thought, he must have seen her singular emotion. 'I never thought of Jack. It must be broken to him, before the town crier knows it. I dine with the dear fellow to-morrow and next day – Christmas Eve and Christmas Day – but it would never do to spoil his feast days. He always worries about me, and moddley-coddleys in the merest trifles. The news is sure to overset him. How on earth shall this be broken to Jack!'

'He must be told, I suppose?' said Rosa.

'My dear Rosa! Who ought to be in our confidence, if not Jack?'

'My guardian promised to come down, if I should write and ask him. I am going to do so. Would you like to leave it to him?'

'A bright idea!' cried Edwin. 'The other trustee. Nothing more natural. He comes down, he goes to Jack, he relates what we have agreed upon, and he states our case better than we could. He has already spoken feelingly to you, he has already spoken feelingly to me, and he'll put the whole thing feelingly to Jack. That's it! I am not a coward, Rosa, but to tell you a secret, I am a little afraid of Jack.'

'No, no! You are not afraid of him?' cried Rosa, turning white and clasping her hands.

'Why, sister Rosa, sister Rosa, what do you see from the turret?'[16] said Edwin, rallying her. 'My dear girl!'

'You frightened me.'

'Most unintentionally, but I am as sorry as if I had meant to do it. Could you possibly suppose for a moment, from any loose way of speaking of mine, that I was literally afraid of the dear fond fellow? What I mean is, that he is subject to a kind of paroxysm, or fit – I saw him in it once – and I don't know but that so great a surprise, coming upon him direct from me whom he is so wrapped up in, might bring it on perhaps. Which – and this is the secret I was going to tell you – is another reason for your guardian's making the communication. He is so steady, precise, and exact, that he will talk Jack's thoughts into shape, in no time: whereas with me Jack is always impulsive and hurried, and, I may say, almost womanish.'

Rosa seemed convinced. Perhaps from her own very different point of view of 'Jack,' she felt comforted and protected by the interposition of Mr Grewgious between herself and him.

And now, Edwin Drood's right hand closed again upon the ring in its little case, and again was checked by the consideration: 'It is certain, now, that I am to give it back to him; then why should I tell her of it?' That pretty sympathetic nature which could be so sorry for him in the blight of their childish hopes of happiness together, and could so quietly find itself alone in a new world to weave fresh wreaths of such flowers as it might prove to bear, the old world's flowers being withered, would be grieved by those sorrowful jewels; and to what purpose? Why should it be? They were but a sign of broken joys and baseless projects; in their very beauty they were (as the unlikeliest of men had said) almost a cruel satire on the loves, hopes, plans, of humanity, which are able to forecast nothing, and are so much brittle dust. Let them be. He would restore them to her guardian when he came down; he in his turn would restore them to the cabinet from which he had unwillingly taken them; and there, like old letters or old vows, or other records of old aspirations come to nothing, they would be disregarded, until, being valuable, they were sold into circulation again, to repeat their former round.

Let them be. Let them lie unspoken of, in his breast. However distinctly or indistinctly he entertained these thoughts, he arrived at the conclusion, Let them be. Among the mighty store of wonderful chains that are for ever forging, day and night, in the vast iron-works of time and circumstance, there was one chain forged in the moment of that small conclusion,[17] riveted to the foundations of heaven and earth, and gifted with invincible force to hold and drag.

They walked on by the river. They began to speak of their separate plans. He would quicken his departure from England, and she would remain where she was, at least as long as Helena remained. The poor dear girls should have their disappointment broken to them gently, and, as the first preliminary, Miss Twinkleton should be confided in by Rosa, even in advance of the reappearance of Mr Grewgious. It should be made clear in all quarters that she and Edwin were the best of friends. There had never been so serene an understanding between them since they were first affianced. And yet there was one reservation on each side; on hers, that she intended through her guardian to withdraw herself immediately from the tuition of her music-master; on his, that he did already entertain some wandering speculations whether it might ever come to pass that he would know more of Miss Landless.

The bright frosty day declined as they walked and spoke together. The sun dipped in the river far behind them, and the old city lay red before them, as their walk drew to a close. The moaning water cast its seaweed duskily at their feet, when they turned to leave its margin; and the rooks hovered above them with hoarse cries, darker splashes in the darkening air.

'I will prepare Jack for my flitting soon,' said Edwin, in a low voice, 'and I will but see your guardian when he comes, and then go before they speak together. It will be better done without my being by. Don't you think so?'

'Yes.'

'We know we have done right, Rosa?'

'Yes.'

'We know we are better so, even now?'

'And shall be far, far better so, by-and-bye.'

Still, there was that lingering tenderness in their hearts towards the old positions they were relinquishing, that they prolonged their parting. When they came among the elm trees by the Cathedral, where they had last sat together, they stopped, as by consent, and Rosa raised her face to his, as she had never raised it in the old days; – for they were old already.

'God bless you, dear! Good-bye!'

'God bless you, dear! Good-bye!'

They kissed each other, fervently.

'Now, please take me home, Eddy, and let me be by myself.'

'Don't look round, Rosa,' he cautioned her, as he drew her arm through his, and led her away. 'Didn't you see Jack?'

'No! Where?'

'Under the trees. He saw us, as we took leave of each other. Poor fellow! he little thinks we have parted. This will be a blow to him, I am much afraid!'

She hurried on, without resting, and hurried on until they had passed under the Gate House into the street; once there, she asked:

'Has he followed us? You can look without seeming to. Is he behind?'

'No. Yes! he is! He has just passed out under the gateway. The dear sympathetic old fellow likes to keep us in sight. I am afraid he will be bitterly disappointed!'

She pulled hurriedly at the handle of the hoarse old bell, and the gate soon opened. Before going in, she gave him one last wide wondering look, as if she would have asked him with imploring emphasis: 'Oh! don't you understand?' And out of that look he vanished from her view.[18]

CHAPTER 14

When Shall These Three Meet Again?[1]

Christmas Eve in Cloisterham. A few strange faces in the streets; a few other faces, half strange and half familiar, once the faces of Cloisterham children, now the faces of men and women who come back from the outer world at long intervals to find the city wonderfully shrunken in size,[2] as if it had not washed by any means well in the meanwhile. To these, the striking of the Cathedral clock, and the cawing of the rooks from the Cathedral tower, are like voices of their nursery time. To such as these, it has happened in their dying hours afar off, that they have imagined their chamber floor to be strewn with the autumnal leaves[3] fallen from the elm trees in the Close: so have the rustling sounds and fresh scents of their earliest impressions revived when the circle of their lives was very nearly traced, and the beginning and the end were drawing close together.

Seasonable tokens are about. Red berries shine here and there in the lattices of Minor Canon Corner; Mr and Mrs Tope are daintily sticking sprigs of holly into the carvings and sconces of the Cathedral stalls, as if they were sticking them into the coat-buttonholes of the Dean and Chapter. Lavish profusion is in the shops: particularly in the articles of currants, raisins, spices, candied peel, and moist sugar. An unusual air of gallantry and dissipation is abroad; evinced in an immense bunch of mistletoe hanging in the greengrocer's shop doorway, and a poor little Twelfth Cake,[4] culminating in the figure of a Harlequin – such a very poor little Twelfth Cake, that one would rather call it a Twenty-Fourth Cake, or a Forty-Eighth Cake – to be raffled for at the pastry-cook's, terms one shilling per member. Public amusements are not wanting. The Wax-Work which made so deep an impression on the reflective mind of the Emperor of China[5] is to be seen by particular desire during Christmas Week only, on the premises of the bankrupt livery-stable keeper up the lane; and a new grand comic Christmas pantomime[6] is to be produced at the Theatre: the latter heralded by the portrait of Signor Jacksonini[7] the clown, saying 'How do you do to-morrow?' quite as large as life, and almost as miserably. In short, Cloisterham is up and doing: though from this description the High School and Miss Twinkleton's are to be excluded. From the former establishment, the scholars have gone home, every one of them in love with one of Miss Twinkleton's young ladies (who knows nothing about it); and only the handmaidens flutter occasionally in the windows of the latter. It is noticed, by-and-bye, that these damsels become, within the limits of decorum, more skittish when thus entrusted with the concrete representation of their sex, than when dividing the representation with Miss Twinkleton's young ladies.

Three are to meet at the Gate House to-night. How does each one of the three get through the day?

Neville Landless, though absolved from his books for the time by Mr Crisparkle – whose fresh nature is by no means insensible to the charms of a holiday – reads and writes in his quiet room, with a concentrated air, until it is two hours past noon. He then sets himself to clearing his table, to arranging his books, and to tearing up and burning his stray papers. He makes a clean sweep of all untidy accumulations, puts all his drawers in order, and leaves no note or scrap of paper undestroyed, save such memoranda as bear directly on his studies. This done, he turns to his wardrobe, selects a few articles of ordinary wear – among them, change of stout shoes and socks for walking – and packs these in a knapsack. This knapsack is new, and he bought it in the High Street yesterday. He also purchased, at the same time and at the same place, a heavy walking stick: strong in the handle for the grip of the hand, and iron-shod. He tries this, swings it, poises it, and lays it by, with the knapsack, on a window-seat. By this time his arrangements are complete.

He dresses for going out, and is in the act of going – indeed has left his room, and has met the Minor Canon on the staircase, coming out of his bedroom upon the same story – when he turns back again for his walking-stick, thinking he will carry it now. Mr Crisparkle, who has paused on the staircase, sees it in his hand on his immediately reappearing, takes it from him, and asks him with a smile how he chooses a stick?

'Really I don't know that I understand the subject,' he answers. 'I chose it for its weight.'

'Much too heavy, Neville; *much* too heavy.'

'To rest upon in a long walk, sir?'

'Rest upon?' repeats Mr Crisparkle, throwing himself into pedestrian form. 'You don't rest upon it; you merely balance with it.'

'I shall know better, with practice, sir. I have not lived in a walking country, you know.'

'True,' says Mr Crisparkle. 'Get into a little training, and we will have a few score miles together. I should leave you nowhere now.[8] Do you come back before dinner?'[9]

'I think not, as we dine early.'

Mr Crisparkle gives him a bright nod and a cheerful good-bye: expressing (not without intention) absolute confidence and ease.

Neville repairs to the Nuns' House, and requests that Miss Landless may be informed that her brother is there, by appointment. He waits at the gate, not even crossing the threshold; for he is on his parole not to put himself in Rosa's way.

His sister is at least as mindful of the obligation they have taken on themselves as he can be, and loses not a moment in joining him. They meet affectionately, avoid lingering there, and walk towards the upper inland country.

'I am not going to tread upon forbidden ground, Helena,' says Neville, when they have walked some distance and are turning; 'you will understand in another moment that I cannot help referring to – what shall I say? – my infatuation.'

'Had you not better avoid it, Neville? You know that I can hear nothing.'

'You can hear, my dear, what Mr Crisparkle has heard, and heard with approval.'

'Yes; I can hear so much.'

'Well, it is this. I am not only unsettled and unhappy myself, but I am conscious of unsettling and interfering with other people. How do I know that, but for my unfortunate presence, you, and – and – the rest of that former party, our engaging guardian excepted, might be dining cheerfully in Minor Canon Corner to-morrow? Indeed it probably would be so. I can see too well that I am not high in the old lady's opinion, and it is easy to understand what an irksome clog I must be upon the hospitalities of her orderly house – especially at this time of year – when I must be kept asunder from this person, and there is such a reason for my not being brought into contact with that person, and an unfavorable reputation has preceded me with such another person, and so on. I have put this very gently to Mr Crisparkle, for you know his self-denying ways; but still I have put it. What I have laid much greater stress upon at the same time is, that I am engaged in a miserable struggle with myself, and that a little change and absence may enable me to come through it the better. So, the weather being bright and hard, I am going on a walking expedition, and intend taking myself out of everybody's way (my own included, I hope) to-morrow morning.'

'When to come back?'

'In a fortnight.'

'And going quite alone?'

'I am much better without company, even if there were any one but you to bear me company, my dear Helena.'

'Mr Crisparkle entirely agrees, you say?'

'Entirely. I am not sure but that at first he was inclined to think it rather a moody scheme, and one that might do a brooding mind harm. But we took a moonlight walk, last Monday night, to talk it over at leisure, and I represented the case to him as it really is. I showed him that I do want to conquer myself, and that, this evening well got over, it is surely better that I should be away from here just now, than here.

I could hardly help meeting certain people walking together here, and that could do no good, and is certainly not the way to forget. A fortnight hence, that chance will probably be over, for the time; and when it again arises for the last time, why, I can again go away. Further, I really do feel hopeful of bracing exercise and wholesome fatigue. You know that Mr Crisparkle allows such things their full weight in the preservation of his own sound mind in his own sound body,[10] and that his just spirit is not likely to maintain one set of natural laws for himself and another for me. He yielded to my view of the matter, when convinced that I was honestly in earnest, and so, with his full consent, I start to-morrow morning. Early enough to be not only out of the streets, but out of hearing of the bells, when the good people go to church.'

Helena thinks it over, and thinks well of it. Mr Crisparkle doing so, she would do so; but she does originally, out of her own mind, think well of it, as a healthy project, denoting a sincere endeavor, and an active attempt at self-correction. She is inclined to pity him, poor fellow, for going away solitary on the great Christmas festival; but she feels it much more to the purpose to encourage him. And she does encourage him.

He will write to her?

He will write to her every alternate day, and tell her all his adventures.

Does he send clothes on, in advance of him?

'My dear Helena, no. Travel like a pilgrim, with wallet and staff. My wallet – or my knapsack – is packed, and ready for strapping on; and here is my staff!'

He hands it to her; she makes the same remark as Mr Crisparkle, that it is very heavy; and gives it back to him, asking what wood it is? Iron-wood.

Up to this point he has been extremely cheerful. Perhaps the having to carry his case with her, and therefore to present it in its brightest aspect, has roused his spirits. Perhaps the having done so with success is followed by a revulsion. As the day closes in, and the city lights begin to spring up before them, he grows depressed.

'I wish I were not going to this dinner, Helena.'

'Dear Neville, is it worth while to care much about it? Think how soon it will be over.'

'How soon it will be over!' he repeats, gloomily. 'Yes. But I don't like it.'

There may be a moment's awkwardness, she cheeringly represents to him, but it can only last a moment. He is quite sure of himself.

'I wish I felt as sure of everything else, as I feel of myself,' he answers her.

'How strangely you speak, dear! What do you mean?'

'Helena, I don't know. I only know that I don't like it. What a strange dead weight there is in the air!'

She calls his attention to those copperous clouds beyond the river, and says that the wind is rising. He scarcely speaks again, until he takes leave of her, at the gate of the Nuns' House. She does not immediately enter, when they have parted, but remains looking after him along the street. Twice he passes the Gate House, reluctant to enter. At length, the Cathedral clock chiming one quarter, with a rapid turn he hurries in.

And so *he* goes up the postern stair.

Edwin Drood passes a solitary day. Something of deeper moment than he had thought has gone out of his life; and in the silence of his own chamber he wept for it last night. Though the image of Miss Landless still hovers in the background of his mind, the pretty little affectionate creature, so much firmer and wiser than he had supposed, occupies its stronghold. It is with some misgivings of his own unworthiness that he thinks of her, and of what they might have been to one another, if he had been more in earnest some time ago; if he had set a higher value on her; if, instead of accepting his lot in life as an inheritance of course, he had studied the right way to its appreciation and enhancement. And still, for all this, and though there is a sharp heartache in all this, the vanity and caprice of youth sustain that handsome figure of Miss Landless in the background of his mind.

That was a curious look of Rosa's when they parted at the gate. Did it mean that she saw below the surface of his thoughts, and down into their twilight depths? Scarcely that, for it was a look of astonished and keen enquiry. He decides that he cannot understand it, though it was remarkably expressive.

As he only waits for Mr Grewgious now, and will depart immediately after having seen him, he takes a sauntering leave of the ancient city and its neighbourhood. He recalls the time when Rosa and he walked here or there, mere children, full of the dignity of being engaged. Poor children! he thinks, with a pitying sadness.

Finding that his watch has stopped, he turns into the jeweller's shop, to have it wound and set. The jeweller is knowing on the subject of a bracelet, which he begs leave to submit, in a general and quite aimless way. It would suit (he considers) a young bride to perfection; especially if of a rather diminutive style of beauty. Finding the bracelet but coldly looked at, the jeweller invites attention to a tray of rings for gentlemen; here is a style of ring, now, he remarks — a very chaste signet — which gentlemen are much given to purchasing, when changing their condition. A ring of a very responsible appearance. With the date of their wedding-day engraved inside, several gentlemen have preferred it to any other kind of memento.

The rings are as coldly viewed as the bracelet. Edwin tells the tempter that he wears no jewellery but his watch and chain, which were his father's; and his shirt-pin.

'That I was aware of,' is the jeweller's reply, 'for Mr Jasper dropped in for a watch-glass the other day, and, in fact, I showed these articles to him, remarking that if he *should* wish to make a present to a gentleman relative, on any particular occasion — But he said with a smile that he had an inventory in his mind of all the jewellery his gentleman relative ever wore; namely, his watch and chain, and shirt-pin.' Still (the jeweller considers) that might not apply to all times, though applying to the present time. 'Twenty minutes past two, Mr Drood, I set your watch at. Let me recommend you not to let it run down, sir.'

Edwin takes his watch, puts it on, and goes out, thinking: 'Dear old Jack! If I were to make an extra crease in my neck-cloth, he would think it worth noticing!'

He strolls about and about, to pass the time until the dinner hour. It somehow happens that Cloisterham seems reproachful to him to-day;

has fault to find with him, as if he had not used it well; but is far more pensive with him than angry. His wonted carelessness is replaced by a wistful looking at, and dwelling upon, all the old landmarks. He will soon be far away, and may never see them again, he thinks. Poor youth! Poor youth![11]

As dusk draws on, he paces the Monks' Vineyard. He has walked to and fro, full half an hour by the Cathedral chimes, and it has closed in dark, before he becomes quite aware of a woman crouching on the ground near a wicket gate in a corner. The gate commands a cross bye-path, little used in the gloaming; and the figure must have been there all the time, though he has but gradually and lately made it out.

He strikes into that path, and walks up to the wicket. By the light of a lamp near it, he sees that the woman is of a haggard appearance, and that her weazen chin is resting on her hands, and that her eyes are staring – with an unwinking, blind sort of stedfastness – before her.

Always kindly, but moved to be unusually kind this evening, and having bestowed kind words on most of the children and aged people he has met, he at once bends down, and speaks to this woman.

'Are you ill?'

'No, deary,' she answers, without looking at him, and with no departure from her strange blind stare.

'Are you blind?'

'No, deary.'

'Are you lost, homeless, faint? What is the matter, that you stay here in the cold so long, without moving?'

By slow and stiff efforts, she appears to contract her vision until it can rest upon him; and then a curious film passes over her, and she begins to shake.

He straightens himself, recoils a step, and looks down at her in a dread amazement; for he seems to know her.

'Good Heaven!' he thinks, next moment. 'Like Jack that night!'

As he looks down at her, she looks up at him, and whimpers: 'My lungs is weakly; my lungs is dreffle bad. Poor me, poor me, my cough is rattling dry!' And coughs in confirmation, horribly.

'Where do you come from?'

'Come from London, deary.'[12] (Her cough still rending her.)

'Where are you going to?'

'Back to London, deary. I came here, looking for a needle in a haystack, and I ain't found it. Look'ee, deary; give me three and sixpence, and don't you be afeard for me. I'll get back to London then, and trouble no one. I'm in a business. — Ah, me! It's slack, it's slack, and times is very bad! — but I can make a shift to live by it.'

'Do you eat opium?'

'Smokes it,' she replies with difficulty, still racked by her cough. 'Give me three and sixpence, and I'll lay it out well, and get back. If you don't give me three and sixpence, don't give me a brass farden. And if you do give me three and sixpence, deary, I'll tell you something.'

He counts the money from his pocket, and puts it in her hand. She instantly clutches it tight, and rises to her feet with a croaking laugh of satisfaction.

'Bless ye! Hark'ee, dear genl'mn. What's your Chris'en name?'

'Edwin.'

'Edwin, Edwin, Edwin,' she repeats, trailing off into a drowsy repetition of the word; and then asks suddenly: 'Is the short of that name Eddy?'

'It is sometimes called so,' he replies, with the color starting to his face.

'Don't sweethearts call it so?' she asks, pondering.

'How should I know!'

'Haven't you a sweetheart, upon your soul?'

'None.'

She is moving away, with another 'Bless ye, and thank'ee, deary!' when he adds: 'You were to tell me something; you may as well do so.'

'So I was, so I was. Well, then. Whisper. You be thankful that your name ain't Ned.'

He looks at her, quite steadily, as he asks: 'Why?'

'Because it's a bad name to have just now.'

'How a bad name?'

'A threatened name. A dangerous name.'

'The proverb says that threatened men live long,'[13] he tells her, lightly.

'Then Ned — so threatened is he, wherever he may be while I am a talking to you, deary — should live to all eternity!' replies the woman.

She has leaned forward, to say it in his ear, with her forefinger shaking before his eyes, and now huddles herself together, and with another 'Bless ye, and thank'ee!' goes away in the direction of the Travellers' Lodging House.

This is not an inspiriting close to a dull day. Alone, in a sequestered place, surrounded by vestiges of old time and decay, it rather has a tendency to call a shudder into being. He makes for the better lighted streets, and resolves as he walks on to say nothing of this to-night, but to mention it to Jack (who alone calls him Ned) as an odd coincidence, to-morrow; of course only as a coincidence, and not as anything better worth remembering.

Still, it holds to him, as many things much better worth remembering never did. He has another mile or so, to linger out before the dinner-hour; and, when he walks over the bridge and by the river, the woman's words are in the rising wind, in the angry sky, in the troubled water, in the flickering lights. There is some solemn echo of them even in the Cathedral chime, which strikes a sudden surprise to his heart as he turns in under the archway of the Gate House.

And so *he* goes up the postern stair.

John Jasper passes a more agreeable and cheerful day than either of his guests. Having no music-lessons to give in the holiday season, his time is his own, but for the Cathedral services. He is early among the shopkeepers, ordering little table luxuries that his nephew likes. His nephew will not be with him long, he tells his provision-dealers, and so must be petted and made much of. While out on his hospitable preparations, he looks in on Mr Sapsea; and mentions that dear Ned, and that inflammable young spark of Mr Crisparkle's, are to dine at the Gate House to-day, and make up their difference. Mr Sapsea is by no means friendly towards the inflammable young spark. He says that his complexion is 'Un-English.'[14] And when Mr Sapsea has once declared anything to be Un-English, he considers that thing everlastingly sunk in the bottomless pit.[15]

John Jasper is truly sorry to hear Mr Sapsea speak thus, for he knows right well that Mr Sapsea never speaks without a meaning, and that he has a subtle trick of being right. Mr Sapsea (by a very remarkable coincidence) is of exactly that opinion.

Mr Jasper is in beautiful voice this day. In the pathetic supplication to have his heart inclined to keep this law,[16] he quite astonishes his fellows by his melodious power. He has never sung difficult music with such skill and harmony, as in this day's Anthem. His nervous temperament is occasionally prone to take difficult music a little too quickly; to-day, his time is perfect.

These results are probably attained through a grand composure of the spirits. The mere mechanism of his throat is a little tender, for he wears, both with his singing-robe and with his ordinary dress, a large black scarf of strong close-woven silk,[17] slung loosely round his neck. But his composure is so noticeable, that Mr Crisparkle speaks of it as they come out from Vespers.

'I must thank you, Jasper, for the pleasure with which I have heard you to-day. Beautiful! Delightful! You could not have so outdone yourself, I hope, without being wonderfully well.'

'I *am* wonderfully well.'

'Nothing unequal,' says the Minor Canon, with a smooth motion of his hand: 'nothing unsteady, nothing forced, nothing avoided; all thoroughly done in a masterly manner, with perfect self-command.'

'Thank you. I hope so, if it is not too much to say.'

'One would think, Jasper, you had been trying a new medicine for that occasional indisposition of yours.'

'No, really? That's well observed; for I have.'

'Then stick to it, my good fellow,' says Mr Crisparkle, clapping him on the shoulder with friendly encouragement, 'stick to it.'

'I will.'

'I congratulate you,' Mr Crisparkle pursues, as they come out of the Cathedral, 'on all accounts.'

'Thank you again. I will walk round to the Corner with you, if you don't object; I have plenty of time before my company come; and I want to say a word to you, which I think you will not be displeased to hear.'

'What is it?'

'Well. We were speaking, the other evening, of my black humors.'

Mr Crisparkle's face falls, and he shakes his head deploringly.

'I said, you know, that I should make you an antidote to those black humors; and you said you hoped I would consign them to the flames.'

'And I still hope so, Jasper.'

'With the best reason in the world! I mean to burn this year's Diary at the year's end.'

'Because you—?' Mr Crisparkle brightens greatly as he thus begins.

'You anticipate me. Because I feel that I have been out of sorts, gloomy, bilious, brain-oppressed, whatever it may be. You said I had been exaggerative. So I have.'

Mr Crisparkle's brightened face brightens still more.

'I couldn't see it then, because I *was* out of sorts; but I am in a healthier state now, and I acknowledge it with genuine pleasure. I made a great deal of a very little; that's the fact.'

'It does me good,' cries Mr Crisparkle, 'to hear you say it!'

'A man leading a monotonous life,' Jasper proceeds, 'and getting his nerves, or his stomach, out of order, dwells upon an idea until it loses its proportions. That was my case with the idea in question. So I shall burn the evidence of my case, when the book is full, and begin the next volume with a clearer vision.'

'This is better,' says Mr Crisparkle, stopping at the steps of his door to shake hands, 'than I could have hoped.'

'Why, naturally,' returns Jasper. 'You had but little reason to hope that I should become more like yourself. You are always training yourself to be, mind and body, as clear as crystal, and you always are, and never change; whereas I am a muddy, solitary, moping weed. However, I have got over that mope. Shall I wait, while you ask if Mr Neville has left for my place? If not, he and I may walk round together.'

'I think,' says Mr Crisparkle, opening the entrance door with his key, 'that he left some time ago; at least I know he left, and I think he has not come back. But I'll enquire. You won't come in?'

'My company wait,' says Jasper, with a smile.

The Minor Canon disappears, and in a few moments returns. As he thought, Mr Neville has not come back; indeed, as he remembers now, Mr Neville said he would probably go straight to the Gate House.

'Bad manners in a host!' says Jasper. 'My company will be there before me! What will you bet that I don't find my company embracing?'

'I will bet – or I would, if I ever did bet,' returns Mr Crisparkle, 'that your company will have a gay entertainer this evening.'

Jasper nods, and laughs Good Night!

He retraces his steps to the Cathedral door, and turns down past it to the Gate House. He sings, in a low voice and with delicate expression, as he walks along. It still seems as if a false note were not within his power to-night, and as if nothing could hurry or retard him. Arriving thus under the arched entrance of his dwelling, he pauses for an instant in the shelter to pull off that great black scarf, and hang it in a loop upon his arm. For that brief time, his face is knitted and stern. But it immediately clears, as he resumes his singing, and his way.

And so *he* goes up the postern stair.

The red light burns steadily all the evening in the lighthouse on the margin of the tide of busy life. Softened sounds and hum of traffic pass it and flow on irregularly into the lonely Precincts; but very little else goes by, save violent rushes of wind. It comes on to blow a boisterous gale.

The Precincts are never particularly well lighted; but the strong blasts of wind blowing out many of the lamps (in some instances shattering the frames too, and bringing the glass rattling to the ground), they are unusually dark to-night. The darkness is augmented and confused, by flying dust from the earth, dry twigs from the trees, and great ragged fragments from the rooks' nests up in the tower. The trees themselves so toss and creak, as this tangible part of the darkness madly whirls about, that they seem in peril of being torn out of the earth: while ever and again a crack, and a rushing fall, denote that some large branch has yielded to the storm.

No such power of wind has blown for many a winter-night. Chimneys topple in the streets,[18] and people hold to posts and corners, and to one another, to keep themselves upon their feet. The violent rushes abate not, but increase in frequency and fury until at midnight, when the streets are empty, the storm goes thundering along them, rattling at all the latches, and tearing at all the shutters, as if warning the people to get up and fly with it, rather than have the roofs brought down upon their brains.

Still, the red light burns steadily. Nothing is steady but the red light.

All through the night the wind blows, and abates not. But early in the morning, when there is barely enough light in the east to dim the stars, it begins to lull. From that time, with occasional wild charges, like a wounded monster dying, it drops and sinks; and at full daylight it is dead.

It is then seen that the hands of the Cathedral clock are torn off; that lead from the roof has been stripped away, rolled up, and blown into the Close; and that some stones have been displaced upon the summit of the great tower. Christmas morning though it be, it is necessary to send up workmen, to ascertain the extent of the damage done. These, led by Durdles, go aloft; while Mr Tope and a crowd of early idlers gather down in Minor Canon Corner, shading their eyes and watching for their appearance up there.

This cluster is suddenly broken and put aside by the hands of Mr Jasper; all the gazing eyes are brought down to the earth by his loudly enquiring of Mr Crisparkle, at an open window:

'Where is my nephew?'

'He has not been here. Is he not with you?'

'No. He went down to the river last night, with Mr Neville, to look at the storm, and has not been back. Call Mr Neville!'

'He left this morning, early.'

'Left this morning, early? Let me in, let me in!'

There is no more looking up at the tower, now. All the assembled eyes are turned on Mr Jasper, white, half-dressed, panting, and clinging to the rail before the Minor Canon's house.

CHAPTER 15

Impeached

Neville Landless had started so early and walked at so good a pace, that when the church bells began to ring in Cloisterham for morning service, he was eight miles away. As he wanted his breakfast by that time, having set forth on a crust of bread, he stopped at the next road-side tavern to refresh.

Visitors in want of breakfast – unless they were horses or cattle, for which class of guests there was preparation enough in the way of water-trough and hay – were so unusual at the sign of The Tilted Wagon,[1] that it took a long time to get the wagon into the track of tea and toast and bacon. Neville, in the interval, sitting in a sanded parlor, wondering in how long a time after he had gone, the sneezy fire of damp fagots would begin to make somebody else warm.

Indeed, The Tilted Wagon, as a cool establishment on the top of a hill, where the ground before the door was puddled with damp hoofs and trodden straw; where a scolding landlady slapped a moist baby (with one red sock on and one wanting) in the bar; where the cheese was cast aground upon a shelf, in company with a mouldy tablecloth and a green-handled knife, in a sort of cast-iron canoe; where the pale-faced bread shed tears of crumb over its ship-wreck in another canoe; where the family linen, half washed and half dried, led a public life of lying about; where everything to drink was drunk out of mugs, and everything else was suggestive of a rhyme to mugs; The Tilted Wagon, all these things considered, hardly kept its painted promise of providing good entertainment for Man and Beast. However, Man, in the present case, was not critical, but took what entertainment he could get, and went on again after a longer rest than he needed.

He stopped at some quarter of a mile from the house, hesitating whether to pursue the road, or to follow a cart-track between two high hedgerows, which led across the slope of a breezy heath, and evidently struck into the road again by-and-bye. He decided in favor of this latter track, and pursued it with some toil; the rise being steep, and the way worn into deep ruts.

He was laboring along, when he became aware of some other pedestrians behind him. As they were coming up at a faster pace than his, he stood aside, against one of the high banks, to let them pass. But their manner was very curious. Only four of them passed. Other four slackened speed, and loitered as intending to follow him when he should go on. The remainder of the party (half a dozen perhaps) turned, and went back at a great rate.

He looked at the four behind him, and he looked at the four before him. They all returned his look. He resumed his way. The four in advance went on, constantly looking back; the four in the rear came closing up.

When they all ranged out from the narrow track upon the open slope of the heath, and this order was maintained, let him diverge as he would to either side, there was no longer room to doubt that he was beset by these fellows. He stopped, as a last test; and they all stopped.

'Why do you attend upon me in this way?' he asked the whole body. 'Are you a pack of thieves?'

'Don't answer him,' said one of the number; he did not see which. 'Better be quiet.'

'Better be quiet?' repeated Neville. 'Who said so?'

Nobody replied.

'It's good advice, whichever of you skulkers gave it,' he went on angrily. 'I will not submit to be penned in between four men there, and four men there. I wish to pass, and I mean to pass, those four in front.'

They were all standing still: himself included.

'If eight men, or four men, or two men, set upon one,'[2] he proceeded, growing more enraged, 'the one has no chance but to set his mark upon some of them.[3] And by the Lord I'll do it, if I am interrupted any further!'

Shouldering his heavy stick, and quickening his pace, he shot on to pass the four ahead. The largest and strongest man of the number changed swiftly to the side on which he came up, and dexterously closed with him and went down with him; but not before the heavy stick had descended smartly.

'Let him be!' said this man in a suppressed voice, as they struggled together on the grass. 'Fair play! His is the build of a girl to mine, and he's got a weight strapped to his back besides. Let him alone. I'll manage him.'

After a little rolling about, in a close scuffle which caused the faces of both to be besmeared with blood, the man took his knee from Neville's chest, and rose, saying: 'There! Now take him arm-in-arm, any two of you!'

It was immediately done.

'As to our being a pack of thieves, Mr Landless,' said the man, as he spat out some blood, and wiped more from his face: 'you know better than that, at midday. We wouldn't have touched you, if you hadn't forced us. We're going to take you round to the high road, anyhow, and you'll find help enough against thieves there, if you want it. Wipe his face somebody; see how it's a-trickling down him!'

When his face was cleansed, Neville recognized in the speaker, Joe, driver of the Cloisterham omnibus, whom he had seen but once, and that on the day of his arrival.

'And what I recommend you for the present, is, don't talk, Mr Landless. You'll find a friend waiting for you, at the high road – gone ahead by the other way when we split into two parties – and you had much better say nothing till you come up with him. Bring that stick along, somebody else, and let's be moving!'

Utterly bewildered, Neville stared around him and said not a word. Walking between his two conductors, who held his arms in theirs, he went on, as in a dream: until they came again into the high road, and into the midst of a little group of people. The men who had turned back were among the group; and its central figures were Mr Jasper and Mr Crisparkle. Neville's conductors took him up to the Minor Canon, and there released him, as an act of deference to that gentleman.

'What is all this, sir? What is the matter? I feel as if I had lost my senses!' cried Neville, the group closing in around him.

'Where is my nephew?' asked Mr Jasper, wildly.

'Where is your nephew?' repeated Neville. 'Why do you ask me?'[4]

'I ask you,' retorted Jasper, 'because you were the last person in his company, and he is not to be found.'

'Not to be found!' cried Neville, aghast.

'Stay, stay,' said Mr Crisparkle. 'Permit me, Jasper. Mr Neville, you are confounded; collect your thoughts; it is of great importance that you should collect your thoughts; attend to me.'

'I will try, sir, but I seem mad.'

'You left Mr Jasper's last night, with Edwin Drood?'

'Yes.'

'At what hour?'

'Was it at twelve o'clock?' asked Neville, with his hand to his confused head, and appealing to Jasper.

'Quite right,' said Mr Crisparkle; 'the hour Mr Jasper has already named to me. You went down to the river together?'

'Undoubtedly. To see the action of the wind there.'

'What followed? How long did you stay there?'

'About ten minutes; I should say not more. We then walked together to your house, and he took leave of me at the door.'

'Did he say that he was going down to the river again?'

'No. He said that he was going straight back.'

The bystanders looked at one another, and at Mr Crisparkle. To whom Mr Jasper, who had been intensely watching Neville, said: in a low distinct suspicious voice: 'What are those stains upon his dress?'

All eyes were turned towards the blood upon his clothes.

'And here are the same stains upon this stick!' said Jasper taking it from the hand of the man who held it. 'I know the stick to be his, and he carried it last night. What does this mean?'

'In the name of God, say what it means, Neville!' urged Mr Crisparkle.

'That man and I,' said Neville, pointing out his late adversary, 'had a struggle for the stick just now, and you may see the same marks on him, sir. What was I to suppose, when I found myself molested by eight people? Could I dream of the true reason when they would give me none at all?'

They admitted that they had thought it discreet to be silent, and that the struggle had taken place. And yet the very men who had seen it, looked darkly at the smears which the bright cold air had already dried.

'We must return, Neville,' said Mr Crisparkle; 'of course you will be glad to come back to clear yourself?'

'Of course, sir.'

'Mr Landless will walk at my side,' the Minor Canon continued, looking around him. 'Come, Neville!'

They set forth on the walk back; and the others, with one exception, straggled after them at various distances. Jasper walked on the other side of Neville, and never quitted that position. He was silent, while Mr Crisparkle more than once repeated his former questions, and while Neville repeated his former answers; also, while they both hazarded some explanatory conjectures. He was obstinately silent, because Mr Crisparkle's manner directly appealed to him to take some part in the discussion, and no appeal would move his fixed face. When they drew near to the city, and it was suggested by the Minor Canon that they might do well in calling on the Mayor at once, he assented with a stern nod; but he spake no word until they stood in Mr Sapsea's parlor.

Mr Sapsea being informed by Mr Crisparkle of the circumstances under which they desired to make a voluntary statement before him, Mr Jasper broke silence by declaring that he placed his whole reliance, humanly speaking, on Mr Sapsea's penetration. There was no conceivable reason why his nephew should have suddenly absconded, unless Mr Sapsea could suggest one, and then he would defer. There was no intelligible likelihood of his having returned to the river, and been accidentally drowned in the dark, unless it should appear likely to Mr Sapsea, and then again he would defer. He washed his hands as clean as he could[5] of all horrible suspicions, unless it should appear to Mr Sapsea that some such were inseparable from his last companion before his disappearance (not on good terms with previously), and then, once more, he would defer. His own state of mind, he being distracted with doubts, and laboring under dismal apprehensions, was not to be safely trusted; but Mr Sapsea's was.

Mr Sapsea expressed his opinion that the case had a dark look; in short (and here his eyes rested full on Neville's countenance), an

Un-English complexion. Having made this grand point, he wandered into a denser haze and maze of nonsense than even a mayor might have been expected to disport himself in, and came out of it with the brilliant discovery that to take the life of a fellow-creature was to take something that didn't belong to you. He wavered whether or no he should at once issue his warrant for the committal of Neville Landless to jail, under circumstances of grave suspicion; and he might have gone so far as to do it but for the indignant protest of the Minor Canon: who undertook for the young man's remaining in his own house, and being produced by his own hands, whenever demanded. Mr Jasper then understood Mr Sapsea to suggest that the river should be dragged, that its banks should be rigidly examined, that particulars of the disappearance should be sent to all outlying places and to London, and that placards and advertisements should be widely circulated imploring Edwin Drood, if for any unknown reason he had withdrawn himself from his uncle's home and society, to take pity on that loving kinsman's sore bereavement and distress, and somehow inform him that he was yet alive. Mr Sapsea was perfectly understood, for this was exactly his meaning (though he had said nothing about it); and measures were taken towards all these ends immediately.

It would be difficult to determine which was the more oppressed with horror and amazement: Neville Landless, or John Jasper. But that Jasper's position forced him to be active, while Neville's forced him to be passive, there would have been nothing to choose between them. Each was bowed down and broken.

With the earliest light of the next morning, men were at work upon the river, and other men – most of whom volunteered for the service – were examining the banks. All the live-long day the search went on; upon the river, with barge and pole, and drag and net; upon the muddy and rushy shore, with jack-boot, hatchet, spade, rope, dogs, and all imaginable appliances. Even at night, the river was specked with lanterns, and lurid with fires; far-off creeks, into which the tide washed as it changed, had their knots of watchers, listening to the lapping of the stream, and looking out for any burden it might bear; remote shingly causeways near the sea, and lonely points off which there was a race of water, had their unwonted flaring cressets and rough-coated figures when the next day dawned; but no trace of Edwin Drood revisited the light of the sun.

All that day, again, the search went on. Now, in barge and boat; and now ashore among the osiers, or tramping amidst mud and stakes and jagged stones in low-lying places, where solitary watermarks and signals of strange shapes showed like spectres, John Jasper worked and toiled. But to no purpose; for still no trace of Edwin Drood revisited the light of the sun.

Setting his watches for that night again, so that vigilant eyes should be kept on every change of tide, he went home exhausted. Unkempt and disordered, bedaubed with mud that had dried upon him, and with much of his clothing torn to rags, he had but just dropped into his easy chair, when Mr Grewgious stood before him.

'This is strange news,' said Mr Grewgious.

'Strange and fearful news.'

Jasper had merely lifted up his heavy eyes to say it, and now dropped them again as he drooped, worn out, over one side of his easy chair.

Mr Grewgious smoothed his head and face, and stood looking at the fire.

'How is your ward?' asked Jasper, after a time, in a faint, fatigued voice.

'Poor little thing! You may imagine her condition.'

'Have you seen his sister?' enquired Jasper, as before.

'Whose?'

The curtness of the counter-question, and the cool slow manner in which, as he put it, Mr Grewgious moved his eyes from the fire to his companion's face, might at any other time have been exasperating. In his depression and exhaustion, Jasper merely opened his eyes to say: 'The suspected young man's.'

'Do you suspect him?' asked Mr Grewgious.

'I don't know what to think. I cannot make up my mind.'

'Nor I,' said Mr Grewgious. 'But as you spoke of him as the suspected young man, I thought you *had* made up your mind. – I have just left Miss Landless.'

'What is her state?'

'Defiance of all suspicion, and unbounded faith in her brother.'

'Poor thing!'

'However,' pursued Mr Grewgious, 'it is not of her that I came to speak. It is of my ward. I have a communication to make that will surprise you. At least, it has surprised me.'

Jasper, with a groaning sigh, turned wearily in his chair.

'Shall I put it off till to-morrow?' said Mr Grewgious. 'Mind! I warn you, that I think it will surprise you!'

More attention and concentration came into John Jasper's eyes as they caught sight of Mr Grewgious smoothing his head again, and again looking at the fire; but now, with a compressed and determined mouth.

'What is it?' demanded Jasper, becoming upright in his chair.

'To be sure,' said Mr Grewgious, provokingly slowly and internally, as he kept his eyes on the fire: 'I might have known it sooner; she gave me the opening; but I am such an exceedingly Angular man, that it never occurred to me; I took all for granted.'

'What is it?' demanded Jasper, once more.

Mr Grewgious, alternately opening and shutting the palms of his hands as he warmed them at the fire, and looking fixedly at him sideways, and never changing either his action or his look in all that followed, went on to reply.

'This young couple, the lost youth and Miss Rosa, my ward, though so long betrothed, and so long recognizing their betrothal, and so near being married —'

Mr Grewgious saw a staring white face, and two quivering white lips, in the easy chair, and saw two muddy hands gripping its sides. But for the hands, he might have thought he had never seen the face.

'— This young couple came gradually to the discovery (made on both sides pretty equally, I think), that they would be happier and better, both in their present and their future lives, as affectionate friends, or say rather as brother and sister, than as husband and wife.'

Mr Grewgious saw a lead-colored face in the easy chair, and on its surface dreadful starting drops or bubbles, as if of steel.

'This young couple formed at length the healthy resolution of interchanging their discoveries, openly, sensibly, and tenderly. They

Mr Grewgious has his suspicions

met for that purpose. After some innocent and generous talk, they agreed to dissolve their existing, and their intended, relations, for ever and ever.'

Mr Grewgious saw a ghastly figure rise, open-mouthed, from the easy chair, and lift its outspread hands towards its head.

'One of this young couple, and that one your nephew, fearful, however, that in the tenderness of your affection for him you would be bitterly disappointed by so wide a departure from his projected life, forbore to tell you the secret, for a few days, and left it to be disclosed by me, when I should come down to speak to you, and he would be gone. I speak to you, and he IS gone.'

Mr Grewgious saw the ghastly figure throw back its head, clutch its hair with its hands, and turn with a writhing action from him.

'I have now said all I have to say: except that this young couple parted, firmly, though not without tears and sorrow, on the evening when you last saw them together.'

Mr Grewgious heard a terrible shriek, and saw no ghastly figure, sitting or standing; saw nothing but a heap of torn and miry clothes upon the floor.[6]

Not changing his action even then, he opened and shut the palms of his hands as he warmed them, and looked down at it.

CHAPTER 16

Devoted[1]

When John Jasper recovered from his fit or swoon, he found himself being tended by Mr and Mrs Tope, whom his visitor had summoned for the purpose. His visitor, wooden of aspect, sat stiffly in a chair, with his hands upon his knees, watching his recovery.

'There! You've come to, nicely now, sir,' said the tearful Mrs Tope; 'you were thoroughly worn out, and no wonder!'

'A man,' said Mr Grewgious, with his usual air of repeating a lesson, 'cannot have his rest broken, and his mind cruelly tormented, and his body overtaxed by fatigue, without being thoroughly worn out.'

'I fear I have alarmed you?' Jasper apologized faintly, when he was helped into his easy chair.

'Not at all, I thank you,' answered Mr Grewgious.

'You are too considerate.'

'Not at all, I thank you,' answered Mr Grewgious again.

'You must take some wine, sir,' said Mrs Tope, 'and the jelly that I had ready for you, and that you wouldn't put your lips to at noon, though I warned you what would come of it, you know, and you not breakfasted; and you must have a wing of the roast fowl that has been put back twenty times if it's been put back once. It shall all be on table in five minutes, and this good gentleman belike will stop and see you take it.'

This good gentleman replied with a snort, which might mean yes, or no, or anything, or nothing, and which Mrs Tope would have found highly mystifying, but that her attention was divided by the service of the table.

'You will take something with me?' said Jasper, as the cloth was laid.

'I couldn't get a morsel down my throat, I thank you,' answered Mr Grewgious.

Jasper both ate and drank almost voraciously. Combined with the hurry in his mode of doing it, was an evident indifference to the taste of what he took, suggesting that he ate and drank to fortify himself against any other failure of the spirits, far more than to gratify his palate. Mr Grewgious in the meantime sat upright, with no expression in his face, and a hard kind of imperturbably polite protest all over him: as though he would have said, in reply to some invitation to discourse: 'I couldn't originate the faintest approach to an observation on any subject whatever, I thank you.'

'Do you know,'[2] said Jasper, when he had pushed away his plate and glass, and had sat meditating for a few minutes: 'do you know that I find some crumbs of comfort in the communication with which you have so much amazed me?'

'*Do* you?' returned Mr Grewgious; pretty plainly adding the unspoken clause, 'I don't, I thank you!'

'After recovering from the shock of a piece of news of my dear boy, so entirely unexpected, and so destructive of all the castles I had built for him; and after having had time to think of it; yes.'

'I shall be glad to pick up your crumbs,' said Mr Grewgious, dryly.

'Is there not, or is there – if I deceive myself, tell me so, and shorten my pain – is there not, or is there, hope that, finding himself in this new position, and becoming sensitively alive to the awkward burden of explanation, in this quarter, and that, and the other, with which it would load him, he avoided the awkwardness, and took to flight?'

'Such a thing might be,' said Mr Grewgious, pondering.

'Such a thing has been. I have read of cases in which people, rather than face a seven days' wonder,³ and have to account for themselves to the idle and impertinent, have taken themselves away, and been long unheard of.'

'I believe such things have happened,' said Mr Grewgious, pondering still.

'When I had, and could have, no suspicion,' pursued Jasper, eagerly following the new track, 'that the dear lost boy had withheld anything from me – most of all, such a leading matter as this – what gleam of light was there for me in the whole black sky? When I supposed that his intended wife was here, and his marriage close at hand, how could I entertain the possibility of his voluntarily leaving this place, in a manner that would be so unaccountable, capricious, and cruel? But now that I know what you have told me, is there no little chink through which day pierces? Supposing him to have disappeared of his own act, is not his disappearance more accountable and less cruel? The fact of his having just parted from your ward, is in itself a sort of reason for his going away. It does not make his mysterious departure the less cruel to me, it is true; but it relieves it of cruelty to her.'

Mr Grewgious could not but assent to this.

'And even as to me,' continued Jasper, still pursuing the new track, with ardor, and, as he did so, brightening with hope: 'he knew that you were coming to me; he knew that you were entrusted to tell me what you have told me; if your doing so has wakened a new train of thought in my perplexed mind, it reasonably follows that, from the same premises, he might have foreseen the inferences that I should draw. Grant that he did foresee them; and even the cruelty to me – and who am I! – John Jasper, Music Master! – vanishes.'

Once more, Mr Grewgious could not but assent to this.

'I have had my distrusts, and terrible distrusts they have been,' said Jasper; 'but your disclosure, overpowering as it was at first – showing me that my own dear boy had had a great disappointing reservation from me, who so fondly loved him – kindles hope within me. You do not extinguish it when I state it, but admit it to be a reasonable hope. I begin to believe it possible;' here he clasped his hands: 'that he may have disappeared from among us of his own accord, and that he may yet be alive and well!'

Mr Crisparkle came in at the moment. To whom Mr Jasper repeated:

'I begin to believe it possible that he may have disappeared of his own accord, and may yet be alive and well!'

Mr Crisparkle taking a seat, and enquiring: 'Why so?' Mr Jasper repeated the arguments he had just set forth. If they had been less plausible than they were, the good Minor Canon's mind would have been in a state of preparation to receive them, as exculpatory of his unfortunate pupil. But he, too, did really attach great importance to the lost young man's having been, so immediately before his disappearance, placed in a new and embarrassing relation towards every one acquainted with his projects and affairs; and the fact seemed to him to present the question in a new light.

'I stated to Mr Sapsea, when we waited on him,' said Jasper: as he really had done: 'that there was no quarrel or difference between the two young men at their last meeting. We all know that their first meeting was, unfortunately, very far from amicable; but all went smoothly and quietly when they were last together at my house. My dear boy was not in his usual spirits; he was depressed – I noticed that – and I am bound henceforth to dwell upon the circumstance the more now that I know there was a special reason for his being depressed: a reason, moreover, which may possibly have induced him to absent himself.'

'I pray to Heaven it may turn out so!' exclaimed Mr Crisparkle.

'*I* pray to Heaven it may turn out so!' repeated Jasper. 'You know

– and Mr Grewgious should now know likewise – that I took a great prepossession against Mr Neville Landless, arising out of his furious conduct on that first occasion. You know that I came to you, extremely apprehensive, on my dear boy's behalf, of his mad violence. You know that I even entered in my Diary, and showed the entry to you, that I had dark forebodings against him. Mr Grewgious ought to be possessed of the whole case. He shall not, through any suppression of mine, be informed of a part of it, and kept in ignorance of another part of it. I wish him to be good enough to understand that the communication he has made to me has hopefully influenced my mind, in spite of its having been, before this mysterious occurrence took place, profoundly impressed against young Landless.'

This fairness troubled the Minor Canon much. He felt that he was not as open in his own dealing. He charged against himself reproachfully that he had suppressed, so far, the two points of a second strong outbreak of temper against Edwin Drood on the part of Neville, and of the passion of jealousy having, to his own certain knowledge, flamed up in Neville's breast against him. He was convinced of Neville's innocence of any part in the ugly disappearance, and yet so many little circumstances combined so wofully against him, that he dreaded to add two more to their cumulative weight. He was among the truest of men; but he had been balancing in his mind, much to its distress, whether his volunteering to tell these two fragments of truth, at this time, would not be tantamount to a piecing together of falsehood in the place of truth.

However, here was a model before him. He hesitated no longer. Addressing Mr Grewgious, as one placed in authority by the revelation he had brought to bear on the mystery (and surpassingly Angular Mr Grewgious became when he found himself in that unexpected position), Mr Crisparkle bore his testimony to Mr Jasper's strict sense of justice, and, expressing his absolute confidence in the complete clearance of his pupil from the least taint of suspicion, sooner or later, avowed that his confidence in that young gentleman had been formed, in spite of his confidential knowledge that his temper was of the hottest and fiercest, and that it was directly incensed against Mr Jasper's nephew, by the circumstance of his romantically supposing himself to be

enamored of the same young lady. The sanguine reaction manifest in
Mr Jasper was proof even against this unlooked-for declaration. It
turned him paler; but he repeated that he would cling to the hope he
had derived from Mr Grewgious; and that if no trace of his dear boy
were found, leading to the dreadful inference that he had been made
away with, he would cherish unto the last stretch of possibility the
idea, that he might have absconded of his own wild will.

Now, it fell out that Mr Crisparkle, going away from this conference
still very uneasy in his mind, and very much troubled on behalf of the
young man whom he held as a kind of prisoner in his own house, took
a memorable night walk.

He walked to Cloisterham Weir.

He often did so, and consequently there was nothing remarkable in
his footsteps tending that way. But the preoccupation of his mind so
hindered him from planning any walk, or taking heed of the objects
he passed, that his first consciousness of being near the Weir was
derived from the sound of the falling water close at hand.

'How did I come here!'[4] was his first thought, as he stopped.

'Why did I come here!' was his second.

Then he stood intently listening to the water. A familiar passage in
his reading, about airy tongues that syllable men's names,[5] rose so
unbidden to his ear, that he put it from him with his hand, as if it were
tangible.

It was starlight. The Weir was full two miles above the spot to
which the young men had repaired to watch the storm. No search had
been made up here, for the tide had been running strongly down, at
that time of the night of Christmas Eve, and the likeliest places for the
discovery of a body, if a fatal accident had happened under such
circumstances, all lay – both when the tide ebbed, and when it flowed
again – between that spot and the sea. The water came over the Weir,
with its usual sound on a cold starlight night, and little could be seen
of it; yet Mr Crisparkle had a strange idea that something unusual
hung about the place.

He reasoned with himself: What was it? Where was it? Put it to the
proof. Which sense did it address?

No sense reported anything unusual there. He listened again, and his sense of hearing again checked the water coming over the Weir, with its usual sound on a cold starlight night.

Knowing very well that the mystery with which his mind was occupied, might of itself give the place this haunted air, he strained those hawk's eyes of his for the correction of his sight. He got closer to the Weir, and peered at its well-known posts and timbers. Nothing in the least unusual was remotely shadowed forth. But he resolved that he would come back early in the morning.

The Weir ran through his broken sleep, all night, and he was back again at sunrise. It was a bright frosty morning. The whole composition before him, when he stood where he had stood last night, was clearly discernible in its minutest details. He had surveyed it closely for some minutes, and was about to withdraw his eyes, when they were attracted keenly to one spot.

He turned his back upon the Weir, and looked far away at the sky, and at the earth, and then looked again at that one spot. It caught his sight again immediately, and he concentrated his vision upon it. He could not lose it now, though it was but such a speck in the landscape. It fascinated his sight. His hands began plucking off his coat. For it struck him that at that spot – a corner of the Weir – something glistened, which did not move and come over with the glistening water-drops, but remained stationary.

He assured himself of this, he threw off his clothes, he plunged into the icy water, and swam for the spot. Climbing the timbers, he took from them, caught among their interstices by its chain, a gold watch,[6] bearing engraved upon its back, E. D.

He brought the watch to the bank, swam to the Weir again, climbed it, and dived off. He knew every hole and corner of all the depths, and dived and dived and dived, until he could bear the cold no more. His notion was, that he would find the body; he only found a shirt-pin sticking in some mud and ooze.

With these discoveries he returned to Cloisterham, and, taking Neville Landless with him, went straight to the Mayor. Mr Jasper was sent for, the watch and shirt-pin were identified, Neville was detained, and the wildest frenzy and fatuity of evil report arose against him. He was of that vindictive and violent nature, that but for his poor sister, who alone had influence over him, and out of whose sight he was never to be trusted, he would be in the daily commission of murder. Before coming to England he had caused to be whipped to death sundry 'Natives' – nomadic persons, encamping now in Asia, now in Africa, now in the West Indies, and now at the North Pole – vaguely supposed in Cloisterham to be always black, always of great virtue, always calling themselves Me, and everybody else Massa or Missie (according to sex), and always reading tracts[7] of the obscurest meaning, in broken English, but always accurately understanding them in the purest mother tongue. He had nearly brought Mrs Crisparkle's grey hairs with sorrow to the grave.[8] (Those original expressions were Mr Sapsea's.) He had repeatedly said he would have Mr Crisparkle's life. He had repeatedly said he would have everybody's life, and become in effect the last man. He had been brought down to Cloisterham, from London, by an eminent Philanthropist, and why? Because that Philanthropist had expressly declared: 'I owe it to my fellow-creatures that he should be, in the words of BENTHAM, where he is the cause of the greatest danger to the smallest number.'[9]

These dropping shots from the blunderbusses of blunderheadedness might not have hit him in a vital place. But he had to stand against a trained and well-directed fire of arms of precision[10] too. He had notoriously threatened the lost young man, and had, according to the showing of his own faithful friend and tutor who strove so hard for him, a cause of bitter animosity (created by himself, and stated by himself), against that ill-starred fellow. He had armed himself with an offensive weapon for the fatal night, and he had gone off early in the morning, after making preparations for departure. He had been found with traces of blood on him; truly, they might have been wholly caused as he represented, but they might not, also. On a search-warrant being issued for the examination of his room, clothes, and so forth, it was discovered that he had destroyed all his papers, and rearranged all his possessions, on the very afternoon of the disappearance. The watch found at the Weir was challenged by the jeweller as one he had wound and set for Edwin Drood, at twenty minutes past two on that same afternoon; and it had run down, before being cast into the water; and it was the jeweller's positive opinion that it had never been re-wound.

This would justify the hypothesis that the watch was taken from him not long after he left Mr Jasper's house at midnight, in company with the last person seen with him, and that it had been thrown away after being retained some hours. Why thrown away? If he had been murdered, and so artfully disfigured, or concealed, or both, as that the murderer hoped identification to be impossible, except from something that he wore, assuredly the murderer would seek to remove from the body the most lasting, the best known, and the most easily recognizable, things upon it. Those things would be the watch and shirt-pin. As to his opportunities of casting them into the river; if he were the object of these suspicions, they were easy. For, he had been seen by many persons, wandering about on that side of the city – indeed on all sides of it – in a miserable and seemingly half-distracted manner. As to the choice of the spot, obviously such criminating evidence had better take its chance of being found anywhere, rather than upon himself, or in his possession. Concerning the reconciliatory nature of the appointed meeting between the two young men, very little could be made of that in young Landless's favor; for it distinctly appeared that the meeting originated, not with him, but with Mr Crisparkle, and that it had been urged on by Mr Crisparkle; and who could say how unwillingly, or in what ill-conditioned mood, his enforced pupil had gone to it? The more his case was looked into, the weaker it became in every point.[11] Even the broad suggestion that the lost young man had absconded, was rendered additionally improbable on the showing of the young lady from whom he had so lately parted; for, what did she say, with great earnestness and sorrow, when interrogated? That he had, expressly and enthusiastically, planned with her, that he would await the arrival of her guardian, Mr Grewgious. And yet, be it observed, he disappeared before that gentleman appeared.

On the suspicions thus urged and supported, Neville was detained and re-detained, and the search was pressed on every hand, and Jasper labored night and day.[12] But nothing more was found. No discovery being made, which proved the lost man to be dead, it at length became necessary to release the person suspected of having made away with him. Neville was set at large. Then, a consequence ensued which Mr Crisparkle had too well foreseen. Neville must leave the place, for the place shunned him and cast him out. Even had it not been so, the dear old china shepherdess would have worried herself to death with fears for her son, and with general trepidation occasioned by their having such an inmate. Even had that not been so, the authority to which the Minor Canon deferred officially, would have settled the point.

'Mr Crisparkle,' quoth the Dean, 'human justice may err, but it must act according to its lights. The days of taking sanctuary are past.[13] This young man must not take sanctuary with us.'

'You mean that he must leave my house, sir?'

'Mr Crisparkle,' returned the prudent Dean, 'I claim no authority in your house. I merely confer with you, on the painful necessity you find yourself under, of depriving this young man of the great advantages of your counsel and instruction.'

'It is very lamentable, sir,'[14] Mr Crisparkle represented.

'Very much so,' the Dean assented.

'And if it be a necessity —' Mr Crisparkle faltered.

'As you unfortunately find it to be,' returned the Dean.

Mr Crisparkle bowed submissively: 'It is hard to prejudge his case, sir, but I am sensible that —'

'Just so. Perfectly. As you say, Mr Crisparkle,' interposed the Dean, nodding his head smoothly, 'there is nothing else to be done. No doubt, no doubt. There is no alternative, as your good sense has discovered.'

'I am entirely satisfied of his perfect innocence, sir, nevertheless.'

'We-e-ell!' said the Dean, in a more confidential tone, and slightly glancing around him, 'I would not say so, generally. Not generally. Enough of suspicion attaches to him to — no, I think I would not say so, generally.'

Mr Crisparkle bowed again.

'It does not become us, perhaps,' pursued the Dean, 'to be partizans. Not partizans. We clergy keep our hearts warm and our heads cool, and we hold a judicious middle course.'

'I hope you do not object, sir, to my having stated in public, emphatically, that he will reappear here, whenever any new suspicion may be awakened, or any new circumstance may come to light in this extraordinary matter?'

'Not at all,' returned the Dean. 'And yet, do you know, I don't think,' with a very nice and neat emphasis on those two words: 'I *don't think* I would state it emphatically. State it? Ye-e-es! But emphatically? No-o-o. I *think* not. In point of fact, Mr Crisparkle, keeping our hearts warm and our heads cool, we clergy need do nothing emphatically.'[15]

So Minor Canon Row knew Neville Landless no more; and he went whithersoever he would, or could, with a blight upon his name and fame.[16]

It was not until then that John Jasper silently resumed his place in the choir. Haggard and red-eyed, his hopes plainly had deserted him, his sanguine mood was gone, and all his worst misgivings had come back. A day or two afterwards, while unrobing, he took his Diary from a pocket of his coat, turned the leaves, and with an impressive look, and without one spoken word, handed this entry to Mr Crisparkle to read:

My dear boy is murdered. The discovery of the watch and shirt-pin convinces me that he was murdered that night, and that his jewellery was taken from him to prevent identification by its means. All the delusive hopes I had founded on his separation from his betrothed wife, I give to the winds. They perish before this fatal discovery. I now swear, and record the oath on this page, That I nevermore will discuss this mystery with any human creature, until I hold the clue to it in my hand. That I never will relax in my secrecy or in my search. That I will fasten the crime of the murder of my dear dead boy upon the murderer.[17] And That I devote myself to his destruction.

*

CHAPTER 17

Philanthropy, Professional and Unprofessional[1]

Full half a year had come and gone, and Mr Crisparkle sat in a waiting-room in the London chief offices of the Haven of Philanthropy, until he could have audience of Mr Honeythunder.

In his college-days of athletic exercises,[2] Mr Crisparkle had known professors of the Noble Art of fisticuffs,[3] and had attended two or three of their gloved gatherings. He had now an opportunity of observing that as to the phrenological formation[4] of the backs of their heads, the Professing Philanthropists were uncommonly like the Pugilists. In the development of all those organs which constitute, or attend, a propensity to 'pitch into' your fellow-creatures, the Philanthropists were remarkably favored. There were several Professors passing in and out, with exactly the aggressive air upon them of being ready for a turn-up with any Novice who might happen to be on hand, that Mr Crisparkle well remembered in the circles of the Fancy. Preparations were in progress for a moral little Mill somewhere on the rural circuit, and other Professors were backing this or that Heavy-Weight as good for such or such speech-making hits, so very much after the manner of the sporting publicans, that the intended Resolutions might have been Rounds.[5] In an official manager of these displays much celebrated for his platform tactics, Mr Crisparkle recognized (in a suit of black) the counterpart of a deceased benefactor of his species, an eminent public character, once known to fame as Frosty-faced Fogo, who in days of yore superintended the formation of the magic circle with the ropes and stakes. There were only three conditions of resemblance wanting between these Professors and those. Firstly, the Philanthropists were in very bad training: much too fleshy, and presenting, both in face and figure, a superabundance of what is known to Pugilistic Experts as Suet Pudding. Secondly, the Philanthropists had not the good temper of the Pugilists, and used worse language. Thirdly, their fighting code stood in great need of revision, as empowering them not only to bore their man to the ropes, but to bore him to the confines of distraction; also to hit him when he was down, hit him anywhere and anyhow, kick him, stamp upon him, gouge him, and maul him behind his back without mercy. In these last particulars the Professors of the Noble Art were much nobler than the Professors of Philanthropy.

Mr Crisparkle was so completely lost in musing on these similarities and dissimilarities, at the same time watching the crowd which came and went, always, as it seemed, on errands of antagonistically snatching something from somebody, and never giving anything to anybody: that his name was twice called before he heard it. On his at length responding, he was shown by a miserably shabby and underpaid stipendiary Philanthropist (who could hardly have done worse if he had taken service with a declared enemy of the human race) to Mr Honeythunder's room.

'Sir,' said Mr Honeythunder, in his tremendous voice, like a schoolmaster issuing orders to a boy of whom he had a bad opinion, 'sit down.'

Mr Crisparkle seated himself.

Mr Honeythunder, having signed the remaining few score of a few thousand circulars, calling upon a corresponding number of families without means to come forward, stump up instantly, and be Philanthropists, or go to the Devil, another shabby stipendiary Philanthropist (highly disinterested, if in earnest) gathered these into a basket and walked off with them.

'Now, Mr Crisparkle,' said Mr Honeythunder,[6] turning his chair half round towards him when they were alone, and squaring his arms with his hands on his knees, and his brows knitted, as if he added, I am going to make short work of *you:* 'Now, Mr Crisparkle, we entertain different views, you and I, sir, of the sanctity of human life.'

'Do we?' returned the Minor Canon.

'We do, sir.'

'Might I ask you,' said the Minor Canon: 'what are your views on that subject?'

'That human life is a thing to be held sacred, sir.'

'Might I ask you,' pursued the Minor Canon as before: 'what you suppose to be my views on that subject?'

'By George, sir!' returned the Philanthropist, squaring his arms still more, as he frowned on Mr Crisparkle: 'they are best known to yourself.'

'Readily admitted. But you began by saying that we took different views, you know. Therefore (or you could not say so) you must have set up some views as mine. Pray, what views *have* you set up as mine?'

'Here is a man – and a young man,' said Mr Honeythunder, as if that made the matter infinitely worse, and he could have easily borne the loss of an old one: 'swept off the face of the earth[7] by a deed of violence. What do you call that?'

'Murder,' said the Minor Canon.

'What do you call the doer of that deed, sir?'

'A murderer,' said the Minor Canon.

'I am glad to hear you admit so much, sir,' retorted Mr Honeythunder, in his most offensive manner; 'and I candidly tell you that I didn't expect it.' Here he lowered heavily at Mr Crisparkle again.

'Be so good as to explain what you mean by those very unjustifiable expressions.'

'I don't sit here, sir,' returned the Philanthropist, raising his voice to a roar, 'to be browbeaten.'

'As the only other person present, no one can possibly know that better than I do,' returned the Minor Canon very quietly. 'But I interrupt your explanation.'

'Murder!' proceeded Mr Honeythunder, in a kind of boisterous reverie, with his platform folding of his arms, and his platform nod of abhorrent reflection after each short sentiment of a word. 'Bloodshed! Abel! Cain![8] I hold no terms with Cain. I repudiate with a shudder the red hand when it is offered me.'

Instead of instantly leaping into his chair and cheering himself hoarse, as the Brotherhood in public meeting assembled would infallibly have done on this cue, Mr Crisparkle merely reversed the quiet crossing of his legs, and said mildly: 'Don't let me interrupt your explanation – when you begin it.'

'The Commandments say no murder.[9] NO murder, sir!' proceeded Mr Honeythunder, platformally pausing as if he took Mr Crisparkle to task for having distinctly asserted that they said, You may do a little murder and then leave off.

'And they also say, you shall bear no false witness,'[10] observed Mr Crisparkle.

'Enough!' bellowed Mr Honeythunder, with a solemnity and severity that would have brought the house down at a meeting. 'E-e-nough! My late wards being now of age, and I being released from a trust which I cannot contemplate without a thrill of horror, there are the accounts which you have undertaken to accept on their behalf, and there is a statement of the balance which you have undertaken to receive, and which you cannot receive too soon. And let me tell you, sir, I wish, that as a man and a Minor Canon, you were better employed,' with a nod. 'Better employed,' with another nod. 'Bet-ter em-ployed!' with another and the three nods added up.

Mr Crisparkle rose;[11] a little heated in the face, but with perfect command of himself.

'Mr Honeythunder,' he said, taking up the papers referred to: 'my being better or worse employed than I am at present is a matter of taste and opinion. You might think me better employed in enrolling myself a member of your Society.'

'Ay, indeed, sir!' retorted Mr Honeythunder, shaking his head in a threatening manner. 'It would have been better for you if you had done that long ago!'

'I think otherwise.'

'Or,' said Mr Honeythunder, shaking his head again, 'I might think one of your profession better employed in devoting himself to the discovery and punishment of guilt than in leaving that duty to be undertaken by a layman.'

'I may regard my profession from a point of view which teaches me that its first duty is towards those who are in necessity and tribulation,[12] who are desolate and oppressed,' said Mr Crisparkle. 'However, as I have quite clearly satisfied myself that it is no part of my profession to make professions, I say no more of that. But I owe it to Mr Neville, and to Mr Neville's sister (and in a much lower degree to myself), to say to you that I *know* I was in the full possession and understanding of Mr Neville's mind and heart at the time of this occurrence; and that, without in the least coloring or concealing what was to be deplored in him and required to be corrected, I feel certain that his tale is true.

Feeling that certainty, I befriend him. As long as that certainty shall last, I will befriend him. And if any consideration could shake me in this resolve, I should be so ashamed of myself for my meanness that no man's good opinion – no, nor no woman's – so gained, could compensate me for the loss of my own.'

Good fellow! Manly fellow! And he was so modest, too. There was no more self-assertion in the Minor Canon than in the schoolboy who had stood in the breezy playing-fields keeping a wicket.[13] He was simply and staunchly true to his duty alike in the large case and in the small. So all true souls ever are. So every true soul ever was, ever is, and ever will be. There is nothing little to the really great in spirit.

'Then who do you make out did the deed?' asked Mr Honeythunder, turning on him abruptly.

'Heaven forbid,' said Mr Crisparkle, 'that in my desire to clear one man I should lightly criminate another! I accuse no one.'

'Tcha!' ejaculated Mr Honeythunder with great disgust; for this was by no means the principle on which the Philanthropic Brotherhood usually proceeded. 'And, sir, you are not a disinterested witness, we must bear in mind.'

'How am I an interested one?' enquired Mr Crisparkle, smiling innocently, at a loss to imagine.

'There was a certain stipend, sir, paid to you for your pupil, which may have warped your judgment a bit,' said Mr Honeythunder, coarsely.

'Perhaps I expect to retain it still?' Mr Crisparkle returned, enlightened; 'do you mean that too?'

'Well, sir,' returned the professional Philanthropist, getting up, and thrusting his hands down into his trousers pockets; 'I don't go about measuring people for caps.[14] If people find I have any about me that fit 'em, they can put 'em on and wear 'em, if they like. That's their look out: not mine.'

Mr Crisparkle eyed him with a just indignation, and took him to task thus:

'Mr Honeythunder, I hoped when I came in here that I might be under no necessity of commenting on the introduction of platform manners or platform manœuvres among the decent forbearances of private life. But you have given me such a specimen of both, that I should be a fit subject for both if I remained silent respecting them. They are detestable.'

'They don't suit *you*, I dare say, sir.'

'They are,' repeated Mr Crisparkle, without noticing the interruption, 'detestable. They violate equally the justice that should belong to Christians, and the restraints that should belong to gentlemen. You assume a great crime to have been committed by one whom I, acquainted with the attendant circumstances, and having numerous reasons on my side, devoutly believe to be innocent of it. Because I differ from you on that vital point, what is your platform resource? Instantly to turn upon me, charging that I have no sense of the enormity of the crime itself, but am its aider and abettor! So, another time – taking me as representing your opponent in other cases – you set up a platform credulity: a moved and seconded and carried unanimously profession of faith in some ridiculous delusion or mischievous imposition. I decline to believe it, and you fall back upon your platform resource of proclaiming that I believe nothing; that because I will not bow down to a false God of your making,[15] I deny the true God! Another time, you make the platform discovery that War is a calamity,[16] and you propose to abolish it by a string of twisted resolutions tossed into the air like the tail of a kite. I do not admit the discovery to be yours in the least, and I have not a grain of faith in your remedy. Again, your platform resource of representing me as revelling in the horrors of a battle field like a fiend incarnate! Another time, in another of your undiscriminating platform rushes, you would punish the sober for the drunken.[17] I claim consideration for the comfort, convenience, and refreshment of the sober; and you presently make platform proclamation that I have a depraved desire to turn Heaven's creatures into swine and wild beasts![18] In all such cases your movers, and your seconders, and your supporters – your regular Professors of all degrees – run amuck like so many mad Malays;[19] habitually attributing the lowest and basest motives with the utmost recklessness (let me call your attention to a recent instance in yourself for which you should blush), and quoting figures which you know to be as wilfully onesided as a statement of any complicated account that should be all Creditor side and no Debtor, or all Debtor side and no Creditor. Therefore it is, Mr Honeythunder, that I consider the platform a sufficiently bad example and a sufficiently bad school, even in public life; but hold that, carried into private life, it becomes an unendurable nuisance.'

'These are strong words, sir!' exclaimed the Philanthropist.

'I hope so,' said Mr Crisparkle. 'Good morning.'

He walked out of the Haven at a great rate, but soon fell into his regular brisk pace, and soon had a smile upon his face as he went along, wondering what the china shepherdess would have said if she had seen him pounding Mr Honeythunder in the late little lively affair. For Mr Crisparkle had just enough of harmless vanity to hope that he had hit hard, and to glow with the belief that he had trimmed the Philanthropic jacket pretty handsomely.

He took himself to Staple Inn, but not to P. J. T. and Mr Grewgious. Full many a creaking stair he climbed before he reached some attic rooms in a corner, turned the latch of their unbolted door, and stood beside the table of Neville Landless.

An air of retreat and solitude hung about the rooms, and about their inhabitant. He was much worn, and so were they. Their sloping ceilings, cumbrous rusty locks and grates, and heavy wooden bins and beams, slowly mouldering withal, had a prisonous look, and he had the haggard face of a prisoner. Yet the sunlight shone in at the ugly garret window, which had a penthouse to itself thrust out among the tiles; and on the cracked and smoke-blackened parapet beyond, some of the deluded sparrows of the place rheumatically hopped, like little feathered cripples who had left their crutches in their nests; and there was a play of living leaves at hand that changed the air, and made an imperfect sort of music in it that would have been melody in the country.

The rooms were sparely furnished, but with good store of books. Everything expressed the abode of a poor student. That Mr Crisparkle had been either chooser, lender, or donor of the books, or that he combined the three characters, might have been easily seen in the friendly beam of his eyes upon them as he entered.

'How goes it, Neville?'

'I am in good heart, Mr Crisparkle, and working away.'

'I wish your eyes were not quite so large and not quite so bright,'[20] said the Minor Canon, slowly releasing the hand he had taken in his.

'They brighten at the sight of you,' returned Neville. 'If you were to fall away from me, they would soon be dull enough.'

'Rally, rally!' urged the other, in a stimulating tone. 'Fight for it, Neville!'

'If I were dying, I feel as if a word from you would rally me; if my pulse had stopped, I feel as if your touch would make it beat again,' said Neville. 'But I *have* rallied, and am doing famously.'

Mr Crisparkle turned him with his face a little more towards the light.

'I want to see a ruddier touch here, Neville,' he said, indicating his own healthy cheek by way of pattern; 'I want more sun to shine upon you.'

Neville drooped suddenly, as he replied in a lowered voice: 'I am not hardy enough for that, yet. I may become so, but I cannot bear it yet. If you had gone through those Cloisterham streets as I did; if you had seen, as I did, those averted eyes, and the better sort of people silently giving me too much room to pass, that I might not touch them or come near them, you wouldn't think it quite unreasonable that I cannot go about in the daylight.'

'My poor fellow!' said the Minor Canon, in a tone so purely sympathetic that the young man caught his hand: 'I never said it was unreasonable: never thought so. But I should like you to do it.'

'And that would give me the strongest motive to do it. But I cannot yet. I cannot persuade myself that the eyes of even the stream of strangers I pass in this vast city look at me without suspicion. I feel marked and tainted,[21] even when I go out – as I do only – at night. But the darkness covers me then, and I take courage from it.'

Mr Crisparkle laid a hand upon his shoulder, and stood looking down at him.

'If I could have changed my name,' said Neville, 'I would have done so. But as you wisely pointed out to me, I can't do that, for it would look like guilt. If I could have gone to some distant place, I might have found relief in that, but the thing is not to be thought of, for the same reason. Hiding and escaping would be the construction in either case. It seems a little hard to be so tied to a stake, and innocent; but I don't complain.'

'And you must expect no miracle to help you, Neville,' said Mr Crisparkle, compassionately.

'No, sir, I know that. The ordinary fulness of time and circumstance is all I have to trust to.'

'It will right you at last, Neville.'

'So I believe, and I hope I may live to know it.'

But perceiving that the despondent mood into which he was falling cast a shadow on the Minor Canon, and (it may be) feeling that the broad hand upon his shoulder was not then quite as steady as its own natural strength had rendered it when it first touched him just now, he brightened and said:

'Excellent circumstances for study, anyhow! and you know, Mr Crisparkle, what need I have of study in all ways. Not to mention that you have advised me to study for the difficult profession of the law, specially, and that of course I am guiding myself by the advice of such a friend and helper. Such a good friend and helper!'

He took the fortifying hand from his shoulder, and kissed it. Mr Crisparkle beamed at the books, but not so brightly as when he had entered.

'I gather from your silence on the subject that my late guardian is adverse, Mr Crisparkle?'

The Minor Canon answered: 'Your late guardian is a – a most unreasonable person, and it signifies nothing to any reasonable person whether he is *ad*verse or *per*verse, or the *re*verse.'

'Well for me that I have enough with economy to live upon,' sighed Neville, half wearily and half cheerily, 'while I wait to be learned, and wait to be righted! Else I might have proved the proverb, that while the grass grows, the steed starves!'[22]

He opened some books as he said it, and was soon immersed in their interleaved and annotated passages, while Mr Crisparkle sat beside him, expounding, correcting, and advising. The Minor Canon's Cathedral duties made these visits of his difficult to accomplish, and only to be compassed at intervals of many weeks. But they were as serviceable as they were precious to Neville Landless.

When they had got through such studies as they had in hand, they stood leaning on the window-sill, and looking down upon the patch of garden. 'Next week,' said Mr Crisparkle, 'you will cease to be alone, and will have a devoted companion.'

'And yet,' returned Neville, 'this seems an uncongenial place to bring my sister to!'

'I don't think so,' said the Minor Canon. 'There is duty to be done here; and there are womanly feeling, sense, and courage wanted here.'

'I meant,' explained Neville, 'that the surroundings are so dull and unwomanly, and that Helena can have no suitable friend or society here.'

'You have only to remember,' said Mr Crisparkle, 'that you are here yourself, and that she has to draw you into the sunlight.'

They were silent for a little while, and then Mr Crisparkle began anew.

'When we first spoke together, Neville, you told me that your sister had risen out of the disadvantages of your past lives as superior to you as the tower of Cloisterham Cathedral is higher than the chimneys of Minor Canon Corner. Do you remember that?'

'Right well!'

'I was inclined to think it at the time an enthusiastic flight. No matter what I think it now. What I would emphasize is, that under the head of Pride your sister is a great and opportune example to you.'

'Under *all* heads that are included in the composition of a fine character, she is.'

'Say so; but take this one. Your sister has learnt how to govern what is proud in her nature. She can dominate it even when it is wounded through her sympathy with you. No doubt she has suffered deeply in those same streets where you suffered deeply. No doubt her life is darkened by the cloud that darkens yours. But bending her pride into a grand composure that is not haughty or aggressive, but is a sustained confidence in you and in the truth, she has won her way through those streets until she passes along them as high in the general respect as any one who treads them. Every day and hour of her life since Edwin Drood's disappearance, she has faced malignity and folly – for you – as only a brave nature well directed can. So it will be with her to the end. Another and weaker kind of pride might sink broken-hearted, but never such a pride as hers: which knows no shrinking, and can get no mastery of her.'

The pale cheek beside him flushed under the comparison and the hint implied in it. 'I will do all I can to imitate her,' said Neville.

'Do so, and be a truly brave man as she is a truly brave woman,' answered Mr Crisparkle, stoutly. 'It is growing dark. Will you go my way with me, when it is quite dark? Mind! It is not I who wait for darkness.'

Neville replied that he would accompany him directly. But Mr Crisparkle said he had a moment's call to make on Mr Grewgious as an act of courtesy, and would run across to that gentleman's chambers, and rejoin Neville on his own doorstep, if he would come down there to meet him.

Mr Grewgious, bolt upright as usual, sat taking his wine in the dusk at his open window; his wineglass and decanter on the round table at his elbow; himself and his legs on the windowseat; only one hinge in his whole body, like a bootjack.

'How do you do, reverend sir?' said Mr Grewgious, with abundant offers of hospitality, which were as cordially declined as made. 'And how is your charge getting on over the way in the set that I had the pleasure of recommending to you as vacant and eligible?'

Mr Crisparkle replied suitably.

'I am glad you approve of them,' said Mr Grewgious, 'because I entertain a sort of fancy for having him under my eye.'

As Mr Grewgious had to turn his eye up considerably, before he could see the chambers, the phrase was to be taken figuratively and not literally.

'And how did you leave Mr Jasper, reverend sir?' said Mr Grewgious.

Mr Crisparkle had left him pretty well.

'And where did you leave Mr Jasper, reverend sir?'

Mr Crisparkle had left him at Cloisterham.

'And when did you leave Mr Jasper, reverend sir?'

That morning.

'Umps!' said Mr Grewgious. 'He didn't say he was coming, perhaps?'

'Coming where?'

'Anywhere, for instance?' said Mr Grewgious.

'No.'

'Because here he is,' said Mr Grewgious, who had asked all these questions, with his preoccupied glance directed out at window. 'And he don't look agreeable, does he?'

Mr Crisparkle was craning towards the window, when Mr Grewgious added:

'If you will kindly step round here behind me, in the gloom of the room, and will cast your eye at the second-floor landing window, in yonder house, I think you will hardly fail to see a slinking individual in whom I recognize our local friend.'

'You are right!' cried Mr Crisparkle.

'Umps!' said Mr Grewgious. Then he added, turning his face so abruptly that his head nearly came into collision with Mr Crisparkle's: 'what should you say that our local friend was up to?'

The last passage he had been shown in the Diary returned on Mr Crisparkle's mind with the force of a strong recoil, and he asked Mr Grewgious if he thought it possible that Neville was to be harassed by the keeping of a watch upon him?

'A watch,' repeated Mr Grewgious, musingly. 'Aye!'

'Which would not only of itself haunt and torture his life,' said Mr Crisparkle, warmly, 'but would expose him to the torment of a perpetually reviving suspicion, whatever he might do, or wherever he might go?'

'Aye!' said Mr Grewgious, musingly still. 'Do I see him waiting for you?'

'No doubt you do.'

'Then *would* you have the goodness to excuse my getting up to see you out, and to go out to join him, and to go the way that you were going, and to take no notice of our local friend?' said Mr Grewgious. 'I entertain a sort of fancy for having *him* under my eye to-night, do you know?'

Mr Crisparkle, with a significant nod, complied, and rejoining Neville, went away with him. They dined together and parted at the yet unfinished and undeveloped railway station:[23] Mr Crisparkle to get home; Neville to walk the streets, cross the bridges, make a wide round of the city in the friendly darkness, and tire himself out.

It was midnight when he returned from his solitary expedition, and climbed his staircase. The night was hot, and the windows of the staircase were all wide open. Coming to the top, it gave him a passing chill of surprise (there being no rooms but his up there) to find a stranger sitting on the window-sill, more after the manner of a venturesome glazier than an amateur ordinarily careful of his neck; in fact, so much more outside the window than inside, as to suggest the thought that he must have come up by the waterspout instead of the stairs.

The stranger said nothing until Neville put his key in his door; then, seeming to make sure of his identity from the action, he spoke:

'I beg your pardon,' he said, coming from the window with a frank and smiling air, and a prepossessing address; 'the beans.'

Neville was quite at a loss.

'Runners,' said the visitor. 'Scarlet. Next door at the back.'

'Oh!' returned Neville. 'And the mignonette and wallflower?'

'The same,' said the visitor.

'Pray walk in.'

'Thank you.'

Neville lighted his candles, and the visitor sat down. A handsome gentleman, with a young face, but with an older figure in its robustness and its breadth of shoulder; say a man of eight-and-twenty, or at the utmost thirty: so extremely sunburnt that the contrast between his brown visage and the white forehead shaded out of doors by his hat, and the glimpse of white throat below the neckerchief, would have been almost ludicrous but for his broad temples, bright blue eyes, clustering brown hair, and laughing teeth.

'I have noticed,' said he; ' – my name is Tartar.'[24]

Neville inclined his head.

'I have noticed (excuse me) that you shut yourself up a good deal, and that you seem to like my garden aloft here.[25] If you would like a little more of it, I could throw out a few lines and stays between my windows and yours, which the runners would take to directly. And I have some boxes, both of mignonette and wallflower, that I could shove on along the gutter (with a boat-hook I have by me) to your windows, and draw back again when they wanted watering or gardening, and shove on again when they were shipshape, so that they would cause you no trouble. I couldn't take this liberty without asking your permission, so I venture to ask it. Tartar, corresponding set, next door.'

'You are very kind.'

'Not at all. I beg you will not think so. I ought to apologize for looking in so late. But having noticed (excuse me) that you generally walk out at night, I thought I should inconvenience you least by awaiting your return. I am always afraid of inconveniencing busy men, being an idle man.'

'I should not have thought so, from your appearance.'

'No? I take it as a compliment. In fact, I was bred in the Royal Navy[26] and was First Lieutenant when I quitted it. But an uncle disappointed in the service leaving me his property on condition that I left the Navy, I accepted the fortune and resigned my commission.'

'Lately, I presume?'

'Well, I had had twelve or fifteen years of knocking about first. I came here some nine months before you; I had had one crop before you came. I chose this place, because, having served last in a little Corvette, I knew I should feel more at home where I had a constant opportunity of knocking my head against the ceiling. Besides: it would never do for a man who had been aboard ship from his boyhood to turn luxurious all at once. Besides, again: having been accustomed to a very short allowance of land all my life, I thought I'd feel my way to the command of a landed estate, by beginning in boxes.'

Whimsically as this was said, there was a touch of merry earnestness in it that made it doubly whimsical.

'However,' said the Lieutenant, 'I have talked quite enough about myself. It is not my way, I hope; it has merely been to present myself to you naturally. If you will allow me to take the liberty I have described, it will be a charity, for it will give me something more to do. And you are not to suppose that it will entail any interruption or intrusion on you, for that is far from my intention.'

Neville replied that he was greatly obliged, and that he thankfully accepted the kind proposal.

'I am very glad to take your windows in tow,' said the Lieutenant. 'From what I have seen of you when I have been gardening at mine, and you have been looking on, I have thought you (excuse me) rather too studious and delicate! May I ask, is your health at all affected?'

'I have undergone some mental distress,' said Neville, confused, 'which has stood me in the stead of illness.'

'Pardon me,' said Mr Tartar.

With the greatest delicacy he shifted his ground to the windows again, and asked if he could look at one of them. On Neville's opening it, he immediately sprang out, as if he were going aloft with a whole watch in an emergency, and were setting a bright example.

'For Heaven's sake!' cried Neville, 'don't do that! Where are you going, Mr Tartar? You'll be dashed to pieces!'

'All well!' said the Lieutenant, coolly looking about him on the housetop. 'All taut and trim here. Those lines and stays shall be rigged before you turn out in the morning. May I take this short cut home and say, Good-night?'

'Mr Tartar!' urged Neville. 'Pray! It makes me giddy to see you!'

But Mr Tartar, with a wave of his hand and the deftness of a cat, had already dipped through his scuttle of scarlet runners without breaking a leaf, and 'gone below.'

Mr Grewgious, his bedroom window-blind held aside with his hand, happened at that moment to have Neville's chambers under his eye for the last time that night. Fortunately his eye was on the front of the house and not the back, or this remarkable appearance and disappearance might have broken his rest as a phenomenon. But, Mr Grewgious seeing nothing there, not even a light in the windows, his gaze wandered from the windows to the stars, as if he would have read in them something that was hidden from him.[27] Many of us would, if we could; but none of us so much as know our letters in the stars yet – or seem likely to, in this state of existence – and few languages can be read until their alphabets are mastered.

CHAPTER 18

A Settler in Cloisterham[1]

At about this time a stranger appeared in Cloisterham; a white-haired personage with black eyebrows. Being buttoned up in a tightish blue surtout,[2] with a buff waistcoat and grey trousers, he had something of a military air; but he announced himself at the Crozier[3] (the orthodox hotel, where he put up with a portmanteau) as an idle dog who lived upon his means; and he further announced that he had a mind to take a lodging in the picturesque old city for a month or two, with a view of settling down there altogether. Both announcements were made in the coffee-room of the Crozier, to all whom it might, or might not, concern, by the stranger as he stood with his back to the empty fireplace, waiting for his fried sole, veal cutlet, and pint of sherry.[4] And the waiter (business being chronically slack at the Crozier) represented all whom it might or might not concern, and absorbed the whole of the information.

This gentleman's white head was unusually large, and his shock of white hair was unusually thick and ample. 'I suppose, waiter,' he said, shaking his shock of hair, as a Newfoundland dog might shake[5] his before sitting down to dinner, 'that a fair lodging for a single buffer[6] might be found in these parts, eh?'

The waiter had no doubt of it.

'Something old,' said the gentleman. 'Take my hat down for a moment from that peg, will you? No, I don't want it; look into it. What do you see written there?'

The waiter read: 'Datchery.'

'Now you know my name,' said the gentleman; 'Dick Datchery. Hang it up again. I was saying something old is what I should prefer, something odd and out of the way; something venerable, architectural, and inconvenient.'

'We have a good choice of inconvenient lodgings in the town, sir, I think,' replied the waiter, with modest confidence in its resources that way; 'indeed, I have no doubt that we could suit you that far, however particular you might be. But a architectural lodging!' That seemed to trouble the waiter's head, and he shook it.

'Anything Cathedraly, now,' Mr Datchery suggested.

'Mr Tope,' said the waiter, brightening, as he rubbed his chin with his hand, 'would be the likeliest party to inform in that line.'

'Who is Mr Tope?' enquired Dick Datchery.

The waiter explained that he was the Verger, and that Mrs Tope had indeed once upon a time let lodgings herself – or offered to let them; but that as nobody had ever taken them, Mrs Tope's window-bill, long a Cloisterham Institution, had disappeared; probably had tumbled down one day, and never been put up again.

'I'll call on Mrs Tope,' said Mr Datchery, 'after dinner.'

So when he had done his dinner, he was duly directed to the spot, and sallied out for it. But the Crozier being an hotel of a most retiring disposition, and the waiter's directions being fatally precise, he soon became bewildered, and went boggling about and about the Cathedral Tower, whenever he could catch a glimpse of it, with a general impression on his mind[7] that Mrs Tope's was somewhere very near it, and that, like the children in the game of hot boiled beans and very good butter,[8] he was warm in his search when he saw the Tower, and cold when he didn't see it.

He was getting very cold indeed when he came upon a fragment of burial-ground in which an unhappy sheep was grazing. Unhappy, because a hideous small boy was stoning it through the railings, and had already lamed it in one leg, and was much excited by the benevolent sportsmanlike purpose of breaking its other three legs, and bringing it down.

''It 'im agin!' cried the boy, as the poor creature leaped; 'and made a dint in 'is wool.'

'Let him be!' said Mr Datchery. 'Don't you see you have lamed him?'

'Yer lie,' returned the sportsman. ''E went and lamed 'isself. I see 'im do it, and I giv' 'im a shy as a Widdy-warning to 'im not to go a bruisin 'is master's mutton any more.'

'Come here.'

'I won't; I'll come when yer can ketch me.'

'Stay there then, and show me which is Mr Tope's.'

''Ow can I stay here and show you which is Topeseses, when Topeseses is t'other side the Kinfreederal, and over the crossings, and round ever so many corners? Stoo-pid! Ya-a-ah!'

'Show me where it is, and I'll give you something.'

'Come on, then!'

This brisk dialogue concluded, the boy led the way, and by-and-bye stopped at some distance from an arched passage, pointing.

'Look'ee yonder. You see that there winder and door?'

'That's Tope's?'

'Yer lie; it ain't. That's Jarsper's.'

'Indeed?' said Mr Datchery, with a second look of some interest.'

'Yes, and I ain't a goin no nearer 'IM, I tell yer.'

'Why not?'

''Cos I ain't a goin to be lifted off my legs and 'ave my braces bust and be choked; not if I knows it, and not by 'Im. Wait till I set a jolly good flint a flyin at the back o' 'is jolly old 'ed some day! Now look t'other side the harch; not the side where Jarsper's door is; t'other side.'

'I see.'

'A little way in, o' that side, there's a low door, down two steps. That's Topeseses with 'is name on a hoval plate.'

'Good. See here,' said Mr Datchery, producing a shilling. 'You owe me half of this.'

'Yer lie; I don't owe yer nothing; I never seen yer.'

'I tell you you owe me half of this, because I have no sixpence in my pocket. So the next time you meet me you shall do something else for me, to pay me.'

'All right, give us 'old.'

'What is your name, and where do you live?'

'Deputy. Travellers' Twopenny, 'cross the green.'

The boy instantly darted off with the shilling, lest Mr Datchery should repent, but stopped at a safe distance, on the happy chance of his being uneasy in his mind about it, to goad him with a demon dance expressive of its irrevocability.

Mr Datchery, taking off his hat to give that shock of white hair of his another shake, seemed quite resigned, and betook himself whither he had been directed.[10]

Mr Tope's official dwelling, communicating by an upper stair with Mr Jasper's (hence Mrs Tope's attendance on that gentleman), was of very modest proportions, and partook of the character of a cool dungeon. Its ancient walls were massive and its rooms rather seemed to have been dug out of them, than to have been designed beforehand with any reference to them. The main door opened at once on a chamber of no describable shape, with a groined roof, which in its turn opened on another chamber of no describable shape, with another groined roof: their windows small, and in the thickness of the walls. These two chambers, close as to their atmosphere and swarthy as to their illumination by natural light, were the apartments which Mrs Tope had so long offered to an unappreciative city. Mr Datchery, however, was more appreciative. He found that if he sat with the main door open he would enjoy the passing society of all comers to and fro by the gateway, and would have light enough. He found that if Mr and Mrs Tope, living overhead, used for their own egress and ingress a little side stair that came plump into the Precincts by a door opening outward, to the surprise and inconvenience of a limited public of pedestrians in a narrow way, he would be alone, as in a separate residence. He found the rent moderate, and everything as quaintly inconvenient as he could desire. He agreed therefore to take the lodging then and there, and money down, possession to be had next evening, on condition that reference was permitted him to Mr Jasper as occupying the Gate House, of which, on the other side of the gateway, the Verger's hole-in-the-wall was an appanage or subsidiary part.

The poor dear gentleman was very solitary and very sad, Mrs Tope said, but she had no doubt he would 'speak for her.' Perhaps Mr Datchery had heard something of what had occurred there last winter?[11]

Mr Datchery had as confused a knowledge of the event in question, on trying to recall it, as he well could have. He begged Mrs Tope's pardon when she found it incumbent on her to correct him in every detail of his summary of the facts, but pleaded that he was merely a single buffer getting through life upon his means as idly as he could, and that so many people were so constantly making away with so many other people, as to render it difficult for a buffer of an easy temper to preserve the circumstances of the several cases unmixed in his mind.[12]

Mr Jasper proving willing to speak for Mrs Tope, Mr Datchery, who had sent up his card, was invited to ascend the postern staircase. The Mayor was there, Mrs Tope said; but he was not to be regarded in the light of company, as he and Mr Jasper were great friends.

'I beg pardon,' said Mr Datchery, making a leg with his hat under his arm, as he addressed himself equally to both gentlemen; 'a selfish precaution on my part, and not personally interesting to anybody but myself. But as a buffer living on his means, and having an idea of doing it in this lovely place in peace and quiet, for remaining span of life, beg to ask if the Tope family are quite respectable?'

Mr Jasper could answer for that without the slightest hesitation.

'That is enough, sir,' said Mr Datchery.

'My friend the Mayor,' added Mr Jasper, presenting Mr Datchery with a courtly motion of his hand towards that potentate; 'whose recommendation is actually much more important to a stranger than that of an obscure person like myself, will testify in their behalf, I am sure.'

'The Worshipful the Mayor,' said Mr Datchery, with a low bow, 'places me under an infinite obligation.'

'Very good people, sir, Mr and Mrs Tope,' said Mr Sapsea, with condescension. 'Very good opinions. Very well behaved. Very respectful. Much approved by the Dean and Chapter.'

'The Worshipful the Mayor gives them a character,' said Mr Datchery, 'of which they may indeed be proud. I would ask His Honor (if I might be permitted) whether there are not many objects of great interest in the city which is under his beneficent sway?'

'We are, sir,' returned Mr Sapsea, 'an ancient city, and an ecclesiastical city. We are a constitutional city, as it becomes such a city to be, and we uphold and maintain our glorious privileges.'

'His Honor,' said Mr Datchery, bowing, 'inspires me with a desire to know more of the city, and confirms me in my inclination to end my days in the city.'

'Retired from the Army, sir?' suggested Mr Sapsea.

'His Honor the Mayor does me too much credit,' returned Mr Datchery.

'Navy, sir?' suggested Mr Sapsea.

'Again,' repeated Mr Datchery, 'His Honor the Mayor does me too much credit.'

'Diplomacy is a fine profession,' said Mr Sapsea, as a general remark.

'There, I confess, His Honor the Mayor is too many for me,' said Mr Datchery, with an ingenuous smile and bow; 'even a diplomatic bird must fall to such a gun.'

Now, this was very soothing. Here was a gentleman of a great – not to say a grand – address, accustomed to rank and dignity, really setting a fine example how to behave to a Mayor. There was something in that third person style of being spoken to, that Mr Sapsea found particularly recognisant of his merits and position.

'But I crave pardon,' said Mr Datchery. 'His Honor the Mayor will bear with me, if for a moment I have been deluded into occupying his time, and have forgotten the humble claims upon my own, of my hotel, the Crozier.'

'Not at all, sir,' said Mr Sapsea. 'I am returning home, and if you would like to take the exterior of our Cathedral in your way, I shall be glad to point it out.'

'His Honor the Mayor,' said Mr Datchery, 'is more than kind and gracious.'

As Mr Datchery, when he had made his acknowledgments to Mr Jasper, could not be induced to go out of the room before the Worshipful, the Worshipful led the way down stairs; Mr Datchery following with his hat under his arm, and his shock of white hair streaming in the evening breeze.

'Might I ask His Honor,'[13] said Mr Datchery, 'whether that gentleman we have just left is the gentleman of whom I have heard in the neighbourhood as being much afflicted by the loss of a nephew, and concentrating his life on avenging the loss?'

'That is the gentleman. John Jasper, sir.'

'Would His Honor allow me to enquire whether there are strong suspicions of any one?'

'More than suspicions, sir,' returned Mr Sapsea, 'all but certainties.'

'Only think now!' cried Mr Datchery.

'But proof, sir, proof must be built up stone by stone,' said the Mayor. 'As I say, the end crowns the work.[14] It is not enough that Justice should be morally certain; she must be *im*morally certain – legally, that is.'

'His Honor,' said Mr Datchery, 'reminds me of the nature of the law. Immoral. How true!'

'As I say, sir,' pompously went on the Mayor, 'the arm of the law is a strong arm, and a long arm. That is the way *I* put it. A strong arm and a long arm.'

'How forcible! – And yet, again, how true!' murmured Mr Datchery.

'And without betraying what I call the secrets of the prison-house,'[15] said Mr Sapsea; 'the secrets of the prison-house is the term I used on the bench.'

'And what other term than His Honor's would express it?' said Mr Datchery.

'Without, I say, betraying them, I predict to you, knowing the iron will of the gentleman we have just left (I take the bold step of calling it iron, on account of its strength), that in this case the long arm will reach, and the strong arm will strike. – This is our Cathedral, sir. The best judges are pleased to admire it, and the best among our townsmen own to being a little vain of it.'

All this time Mr Datchery had walked with his hat under his arm, and his white hair streaming. He had an odd momentary appearance upon him of having forgotten his hat, when Mr Sapsea now touched it; and he clapped his hand up to his head as if with some vague expectation of finding another hat upon it.

'Pray be covered, sir,' entreated Mr Sapsea; magnificently implying: 'I shall not mind it, I assure you.'

'His Honor is very good, but I do it for coolness,' said Mr Datchery.

Then Mr Datchery admired the Cathedral, and Mr Sapsea pointed it out as if he himself had invented and built it; there were a few details indeed of which he did not approve, but those he glossed over, as if the workmen had made mistakes in his absence. The Cathedral disposed of, he led the way by the churchyard, and stopped to extol the beauty of the evening – by chance – in the immediate vicinity of Mrs Sapsea's epitaph.

'And by-the-bye,' said Mr Sapsea, appearing to descend from an elevation to remember it all of a sudden; like Apollo shooting down from Olympus to pick up his forgotten lyre;[16] '*that* is one of our small lions.[17] The partiality of our people has made it so, and strangers have been seen taking a copy of it now and then. I am not a judge of it myself, for it is a little work of my own. But it was troublesome to turn, sir; I may say, difficult to turn with elegance.'

Mr Datchery became so ecstatic over Mr Sapsea's composition that, in spite of his intention to end his days in Cloisterham, and therefore his probably having in reserve many opportunities of copying it, he would have transcribed it into his pocket-book on the spot, but for the slouching towards them of its material producer and perpetuator, Durdles, whom Mr Sapsea hailed, not sorry to show him a bright example of behavior to superiors.

'Ah, Durdles! This is the mason, sir; one of our Cloisterham worthies; everybody here knows Durdles. Mr Datchery, Durdles; a gentleman who is going to settle here.'

'I wouldn't do it if I was him,' growled Durdles. 'We're a heavy lot.'

'You surely don't speak for yourself, Mr Durdles,' returned Mr Datchery, 'any more than for His Honor.'

'Who's His Honor?' demanded Durdles.

'His Honor the Mayor.'

'I never was brought afore him,' said Durdles, with anything but the look of a loyal subject of the mayoralty, 'and it'll be time enough for me to Honor him when I am. Until which, and when, and where:

> 'Mister Sapsea is his name[18]
> England is his nation,
> Cloisterham's his dwelling-place,
> Aukshneer's his occupation.'

Here, Deputy (preceded by a flying oyster-shell) appeared upon the scene, and requested to have the sum of threepence instantly 'chucked' to him by Mr Durdles, whom he had been vainly seeking up and down, as lawful wages overdue. While that gentleman, with his bundle under his arm, slowly found and counted out the money, Mr Sapsea informed the new settler of Durdles's habits, pursuits, abode, and reputation. 'I suppose a curious stranger might come to see you, and your works, Mr Durdles, at any odd time?' said Mr Datchery upon that.

'Any gentleman is welcome to come and see me any evening if he brings liquor for two with him,' returned Durdles, with a penny between his teeth and certain halfpence in his hands. 'Or if he likes to make it twice two, he'll be double welcome.'

'I shall come. Master Deputy, what do you owe me?'

'A job.'

'Mind you pay me honestly with the job of showing me Mr Durdles's house when I want to go there.'

Deputy, with a piercing broadside of whistle through the whole gap in his mouth, vanished.

The Worshipful and the Worshipper then passed on together until they parted, with many ceremonies, at the Worshipful's door; even then, the Worshipper carried his hat under his arm, and gave his streaming white hair to the breeze.

Said Mr Datchery to himself that night, as he looked at his white hair in the gas-lighted looking-glass over the coffee-room chimneypiece at the Crozier, and shook it out: 'For a single buffer, of an easy temper, living idly on his means, I have had a rather busy afternoon!'

CHAPTER 19

Shadow on the Sun-Dial[1]

Again Miss Twinkleton has delivered her valedictory address, with the accompaniments of white wine and pound cake, and again the young ladies have departed to their several homes. Helena Landless has left the Nuns' House to attend her brother's fortunes, and pretty Rosa is alone.

Cloisterham is so bright and sunny in these summer days, that the Cathedral and the monastery-ruin show as if their strong walls were transparent. A soft glow seems to shine from within them, rather than upon them from without, such is their mellowness as they look forth on the hot corn-fields and the smoking roads that distantly wind among them. The Cloisterham gardens blush with ripening fruit. Time was when travel-stained pilgrims rode in clattering parties through the city's welcome shades; time is when wayfarers, leading a gipsy life between haymaking time and harvest, and looking as if they were just made of the dust of the earth, so very dusty are they, lounge about on cool doorsteps, trying to mend their unmendable shoes, or giving them to the city kennels[2] as a hopeless job, and seeking others in the bundles that they carry, along with their yet unused sickles swathed in bands of straw. At all the more public pumps there is much cooling of bare feet, together with much bubbling and gurgling of drinking with hand to spout on the part of these Bedouins; the Cloisterham police meanwhile looking askant from their beats with suspicion, and manifest impatience that the intruders should depart from within the civic bounds, and once more fry themselves on the simmering highroads.

On the afternoon of such a day, when the last Cathedral service is done, and when that side of the High Street on which the Nuns' House stands is in grateful shade, save where its quaint old garden opens to the west between the boughs of trees, a servant informs Rosa, to her terror, that Mr Jasper desires to see her.

If he had chosen his time for finding her at a disadvantage, he could have done no better. Perhaps he has chosen it. Helena Landless is gone, Mrs Tisher is absent on leave, Miss Twinkleton (in her amateur state of existence) has contributed herself and a veal pie to a picnic.

'Oh why, why, why, did you say I was at home!' cries Rosa, helplessly.

The maid replies, that Mr Jasper never asked the question. That he said he knew she was at home, and begged she might be told that he asked to see her.

'What shall I do, what shall I do?' thinks Rosa, clasping her hands.

Possessed by a kind of desperation, she adds in the next breath that she will come to Mr Jasper in the garden. She shudders at the thought of being shut up with him in the house; but many of its windows command the garden, and she can be seen as well as heard there, and can shriek in the free air and run away. Such is the wild idea that flutters through her mind.

She has never seen him since the fatal night, except when she was questioned before the Mayor, and then he was present in gloomy watchfulness, as representing his lost nephew and burning to avenge him. She hangs her garden-hat on her arm, and goes out. The moment she sees him from the porch, leaning on the sun-dial, the old horrible feeling of being compelled by him, asserts its hold upon her. She feels that she would even then go back, but that he draws her feet towards him. She cannot resist, and sits down, with her head bent, on the garden-seat beside the sun-dial. She cannot look up at him for abhorrence, but she has perceived that he is dressed in deep mourning.[3] So is she. It was not so at first; but the lost has long been given up, and mourned for, as dead.

He would begin by touching her hand. She feels the intention, and draws her hand back. His eyes are then fixed upon her, she knows, though her own see nothing but the grass.

'I have been waiting,' he begins, 'for some time, to be summoned back to my duty near you.'

After several times forming her lips, which she knows he is closely watching, into the shape of some other hesitating reply, and then into none, she answers: 'Duty, sir?'

'The duty of teaching you, serving you as your faithful music-master.'

'I have left off that study.'

'Not left off, I think. Discontinued. I was told by your guardian that you discontinued it under the shock that we have all felt so acutely. When will you resume?'

'Never, sir.'

'Never? You could have done no more if you had loved my dear boy.'

'I did love him!' cries Rosa, with a flash of anger.

'Yes; but not quite – not quite in the right way, shall I say? Not in the intended and expected way. Much as my dear boy was, unhappily, too self-conscious and self-satisfied (but I draw no parallel between him and you in that respect) to love as he should have loved, or as any one in his place would have loved – must have loved!'

She sits in the same still attitude, but shrinking a little more.

'Then, to be told that you discontinued your study with me, was to be politely told that you abandoned it altogether?' he suggests.

'Yes,' says Rosa, with sudden spirit. 'The politeness was my guardian's, not mine. I told him that I was resolved to leave off, and that I was determined to stand by my resolution.'

'And you still are?'

'I still am, sir. And I beg not to be questioned any more about it. At all events, I will not answer any more; I have that in my power.'

She is so conscious of his looking at her with a gloating admiration of the touch of anger on her, and the fire and animation it brings with it, that even as her spirit rises, it falls again, and she struggles with a sense of shame, affront, and fear, much as she did that night at the piano.

'I will not question you any more, since you object to it so much; I will confess.'

'I do not wish to hear you, sir,' cries Rosa, rising.

This time he does touch her with his outstretched hand. In shrinking from it, she shrinks into her seat again.

'We must sometimes act in opposition to our wishes,' he tells her in a low voice. 'You must do so now, or do more harm to others than you can ever set right.'

'What harm?'

'Presently, presently. You question *me*, you see, and surely that's

213

not fair when you forbid me to question you. Nevertheless, I will answer the question presently. Dearest Rosa! Charming Rosa!'

She starts up again.

This time he does not touch her. But his face looks so wicked and menacing, as he stands leaning against the sun-dial – setting, as it were, his black mark upon the very face of day – that her flight is arrested by horror as she looks at him.

'I do not forget how many windows command a view of us,' he says, glancing towards them. 'I will not touch you again, I will come no nearer to you than I am. Sit down, and there will be no mighty wonder in your music-master's leaning idly against a pedestal and speaking with you, remembering all that has happened and our shares in it. Sit down, my beloved.'

She would have gone once more – was all but gone – and once more his face, darkly threatening what would follow if she went, has stopped her. Looking at him with the expression of the instant frozen on her face, she sits down on the seat again.

'Rosa, even when my dear boy was affianced to you, I loved you madly; even when I thought his happiness in having you for his wife was certain, I loved you madly; even when I strove to make him more ardently devoted to you, I loved you madly; even when he gave me the picture of your lovely face so carelessly traduced by him, which I feigned to hang always in my sight for his sake, but worshipped in torment for yours, I loved you madly. In the distasteful work of the day, in the wakeful misery of the night, girded by sordid realities, or wandering through Paradises and Hells of visions in which I rushed, carrying your image in my arms, I loved you madly.'

If anything could make his words more hideous[4] to her than they are in themselves, it would be the contrast between the violence of his look and delivery, and the composure of his assumed attitude.

'I endured it all in silence. So long as you were his, or so long as I supposed you to be his, I hid my secret loyally. Did I not?'

This lie, so gross, while the mere words in which it is told are so true, is more than Rosa can endure. She answers with kindling indignation: 'You were as false throughout, sir, as you are now. You were false to him, daily and hourly. You know that you made my life unhappy by your pursuit of me. You know that you made me afraid to open his generous eyes, and that you forced me, for his own trusting, good, good sake, to keep the truth from him, that you were a bad, bad man!'

His preservation of his easy attitude rendering his working features and his convulsive hands absolutely diabolical, he returns, with a fierce extreme of admiration:

'How beautiful you are! You are more beautiful in anger than in repose. I don't ask you for your love; give me yourself and your hatred; give me yourself and that pretty rage; give me yourself and that enchanting scorn; it will be enough for me.'

Impatient tears rise to the eyes of the trembling little beauty, and her face flames; but as she again rises to leave him in indignation, and seek protection within the house, he stretches out his hand towards the porch, as though he invited her to enter it.

'I told you, you rare charmer, you sweet witch, that you must stay and hear me, or do more harm than can ever be undone. You asked me what harm. Stay, and I will tell you. Go, and I will do it!'

Again Rosa quails before his threatening face, though innocent of its meaning, and she remains. Her panting breathing comes and goes as if it would choke her; but with a repressive hand upon her bosom, she remains.

'I have made my confession that my love is mad. It is so mad that, had the ties between me and my dear lost boy been one silken thread less strong, I might have swept even him from your side when you favored him.'

A film comes over the eyes she raises for an instant, as though he had turned her faint.

'Even him,' he repeats. 'Yes, even him! Rosa, you see me and you hear me. Judge for yourself whether any other admirer shall love you and live, whose life is in my hand.'

'What do you mean, sir?'

'I mean to show you how mad my love is. It was hawked through the late enquiries by Mr Crisparkle, that young Landless had confessed to him that he was a rival of my lost boy.[5] That is an inexpiable offence in my eyes. The same Mr Crisparkle knows under my hand that I have devoted myself to the murderer's discovery and destruction, be he who he might, and that I determined to discuss the mystery with no one until I should hold the clue in which to entangle the murderer as in a net. I have since worked patiently to wind and wind it round him; and it is slowly winding as I speak.'

'Your belief, if you believe in the criminality of Mr Landless, is not Mr Crisparkle's belief, and he is a good man,' Rosa retorts.

'My belief is my own; and I reserve it, worshipped of my soul! Circumstances may accumulate so strongly *even against an innocent man*, that, directed, sharpened, and pointed, they may slay him. One wanting link discovered by perseverance against a guilty man, proves his guilt, however slight its evidence before, and he dies. Young Landless stands in deadly peril either way.'

'If you really suppose,' Rosa pleads with him, turning paler, 'that I favor Mr Landless, or that Mr Landless has ever in any way addressed himself to me, you are wrong.'

He puts that from him with a slighting action of his hand and a curled lip.

'I was going to show you how madly I love you. More madly now than ever, for I am willing to renounce the second object that has arisen in my life to divide it with you; and henceforth to have no object in existence but you only. Miss Landless has become your bosom friend. You care for her peace of mind?'

'I love her dearly.'

'You care for her good name?'

'I have said, sir, I love her dearly.'

'I am unconsciously,' he observes with a smile, as he folds his hands upon the sun-dial and leans his chin upon them, so that his talk would seem from the windows (faces occasionally come and go there) to be of the airiest and playfullest: 'I am unconsciously giving offence by questioning again. I will simply make statements, therefore, and not put questions. You do care for your bosom friend's good name, and you do care for her peace of mind. Then remove the shadow of the gallows from her, dear one!'

'You dare propose to me to —'

'Darling, I dare propose to you. Stop there. If it be bad to idolize you, I am the worst of men; if it be good, I am the best. My love for you is above all other love, and my truth to you is above all other truth. Let me have hope and favor, and I am a forsworn man for your sake.'

Rosa puts her hands to her temples, and, pushing back her hair, looks wildly and abhorrently at him, as though she were trying to piece together what it is his deep purpose to present to her only in fragments.

'Reckon up nothing at this moment, angel, but the sacrifices that I lay at those dear feet, which I could fall down among the vilest ashes and kiss, and put upon my head as a poor savage might. There is my fidelity to my dear boy after death. Tread upon it!'

With an action of his hands, as though he cast down something precious.

'There is the inexpiable offence against my adoration of you. Spurn it!'

With a similar action.

'There are my labors in the cause of a just vengeance for six toiling months. Crush them!'

With another repetition of the action.

'There is my past and my present wasted life. There is the desolation of my heart and my soul. There is my peace; there is my despair. Stamp them into the dust, so that you take me, were it even mortally hating me!'

The frightful vehemence of the man, now reaching its full height, so additionally terrifies her as to break the spell that has held her to the spot. She swiftly moves towards the porch; but in an instant he is at her side, and speaking in her ear.

'Rosa, I am self-repressed again. I am walking calmly beside you to the house. I shall wait for some encouragement and hope. I shall not strike too soon. Give me a sign that you attend to me.'

She slightly and constrainedly moves her hand.

'Not a word of this to any one or it will bring down the blow, as certainly as night follows day.[6] Another sign that you attend to me.'

She moves her hand once more.

Jasper's sacrifices

'I love you, love you, love you. If you were to cast me off now – but you will not – you would never be rid of me. No one should come between us. I would pursue you to the death.'

The handmaid coming out to open the gate for him, he quietly pulls off his hat as a parting salute, and goes away with no greater show of agitation than is visible in the effigy of Mr Sapsea's father opposite. Rosa faints in going up-stairs, and is carefully carried to her room and laid down on her bed. A thunderstorm is coming on, the maids say, and the hot and stifling air has overset the pretty dear; no wonder; they have felt their own knees all of a tremble all day long.

CHAPTER 20

A Flight[1]

Rosa no sooner came to herself than the whole of the late interview was before her. It even seemed as if it had pursued her into her insensibility, and she had not had a moment's unconsciousness of it. What to do, she was at a frightened loss to know: the only one clear thought in her mind was, that she must fly from this terrible man.

But where could she take refuge, and how could she go? She had never breathed her dread of him to any one but Helena. If she went to Helena, and told her what had passed, that very act might bring down the irreparable mischief that he threatened he had the power, and that she knew he had the will, to do. The more fearful he appeared to her excited memory and imagination, the more alarming her responsibility appeared: seeing that a slight mistake on her part, either in action or delay, might let his malevolence loose on Helena's brother.

Rosa's mind throughout the last six months had been stormily confused. A half-formed, wholly unexpressed suspicion tossed in it, now heaving itself up, and now sinking into the deep; now gaining palpability, and now losing it. Jasper's self-absorption in his nephew when he was alive, and his unceasing pursuit of the enquiry how he came by his death, if he were dead, were themes so rife in the place, that no one appeared able to suspect the possibility of foul play at his hands. She had asked herself the question, 'Am I so wicked in my thoughts as to conceive a wickedness that others cannot imagine?' Then she had considered, Did the suspicion come of her previous recoiling from him before the fact? And if so, was not that a proof of its baselessness? Then she had reflected. 'What motive could he have, according to my accusation?' She was ashamed to answer in her mind, 'The motive of gaining *me!*' And covered her face, as if the lightest shadow of the idea of founding murder on such an idle vanity were a crime almost as great.

She ran over in her mind again, all that he had said by the sun-dial in the garden. He had persisted in treating the disappearance as murder, consistently with his whole public course since the finding of the watch and shirt-pin. If he were afraid of the crime being traced out, would he not rather encourage the idea of a voluntary disappearance? He had even declared that if the ties between him and his nephew had been less strong, he might have swept 'even him' away from her side. Was that like his having really done so? He had spoken of laying his six months' labors in the cause of a just vengeance at her feet. Would he have done that, with that violence of passion, if they were a pretence? Would he have ranged them with his desolate heart and soul, his wasted life, his peace, and his despair? The very first sacrifice that he represented himself as making for her, was his fidelity to his dear boy after death. Surely these facts were strong against a fancy that scarcely dared to hint itself. And yet he was so terrible a man! In short, the poor girl (for what could she know of the criminal intellect, which its own professed students perpetually misread, because they persist in trying to reconcile it with the average intellect of average men, instead of identifying it as a horrible wonder apart[2]) could get by no road to any other conclusion than that he *was* a terrible man, and must be fled from.

She had been Helena's stay and comfort during the whole time. She had constantly assured her of her full belief in her brother's innocence, and of her sympathy with him in his misery. But she had never seen him since the disappearance, nor had Helena ever spoken one word of his avowal to Mr Crisparkle in regard of Rosa, though as a part of the interest of the case it was well known far and wide. He was Helena's unfortunate brother, to her, and nothing more. The assurance she had given her odious suitor was strictly true, though it would have been better (she considered now) if she could have restrained herself from giving it. Afraid of him as the bright and delicate little creature was, her spirit swelled at the thought of his knowing it from her own lips.

But where was she to go? Anywhere beyond his reach, was no reply to the question. Somewhere must be thought of. She determined to go to her guardian, and to go immediately. The feeling she had imparted to Helena on the night of their first confidence, was so strong upon her – the feeling of not being safe from him, and of the solid walls of the old convent being powerless to keep out his ghostly following of her – that no reasoning of her own could calm her terrors. The fascination of repulsion[3] had been upon her so long, and now culminated so darkly, that she felt as if he had power to bind her by a spell. Glancing out at window, even now, as she rose to dress, the sight of the sun-dial on which he had leaned when he declared himself, turned her cold, and made her shrink from it, as though he had invested it with some awful quality from his own nature.

She wrote a hurried note to Miss Twinkleton, saying that she had sudden reason for wishing to see her guardian promptly, and had gone to him; also, entreating the good lady not to be uneasy, for all was well with her. She hurried a few quite useless articles into a very little bag, left the note in a conspicuous place, and went out, softly closing the gate after her.

It was the first time she had ever been even in Cloisterham High Street alone. But knowing all its ways and windings very well, she hurried straight to the corner from which the omnibus departed. It was, at that very moment, going off.

'Stop and take me, if you please, Joe. I am obliged to go to London.'

In less than another minute she was on her road to the railway, under Joe's protection. Joe waited on her when she got there, put her safely into the railway carriage, and handed in the very little bag after her, as though it were some enormous trunk, hundredweights heavy, which she must on no account endeavour to lift.

'Can you go round when you get back, and tell Miss Twinkleton that you saw me safely off, Joe?'

'It shall be done, Miss.'

'With my love, please, Joe.'

'Yes, Miss – and I wouldn't mind having it myself!' But Joe did not articulate the last clause; only thought it.

Now that she was whirling away for London in real earnest, Rosa was at leisure to resume the thoughts which her personal hurry had checked. The indignant thought that his declaration of love soiled her; that she could only be cleansed from the stain of its impurity by appealing to the honest and true; supported her for a time against her fears, and confirmed her in her hasty resolution. But as the evening grew darker and darker, and the great city impended nearer and nearer, the doubts usual in such cases began to arise. Whether this was not a wild proceeding, after all; how Mr Grewgious might regard it; whether she should find him at the journey's end; how she would act if he were absent; what might become of her, alone, in a place so strange and crowded; how if she had but waited and taken counsel first; whether, if she could now go back, she would not do it thankfully: a multitude of such uneasy speculations disturbed her, more and more as they accumulated. At length the train came into London over the housetops;[4] and down below lay the gritty streets with their yet un-needed lamps aglow, on a hot light summer night.

'Hiram[5] Grewgious, Esquire, Staple Inn, London.' This was all Rosa knew of her destination; but it was enough to send her rattling away again in a cab,[6] through deserts of gritty streets, where many people crowded at the corners of courts and byways to get some air, and where many other people walked with a miserably monotonous noise of shuffling feet on hot paving-stones, and where all the people and all their surroundings were so gritty and so shabby.

There was music playing here and there,[7] but it did not enliven the case. No barrel-organ mended the matter, and no big drum beat dull care away. Like the chapel bells that were also going here and there, they only seemed to evoke echoes from brick surfaces, and dust from everything. As to the flat wind-instruments, they seemed to have cracked their hearts and souls in pining for the country.

Her jingling conveyance stopped at last at a fast-closed gateway, which appeared to belong to somebody who had gone to bed very early, and was much afraid of housebreakers; Rosa, discharging her conveyance, timidly knocked at this gateway, and was let in, very little bag and all, by a watchman.

'Does Mr Grewgious live here?'

'Mr Grewgious lives there, Miss,' said the watchman, pointing further in.

So Rosa went further in, and, when the clocks were striking ten, stood on P. J. T.'s doorsteps, wondering what P. J. T. had done with his street door.

Guided by the painted name of Mr Grewgious, she went up-stairs and softly tapped and tapped several times. But no one answering, and Mr Grewgious's door-handle yielding to her touch, she went in, and saw her guardian sitting on a windowseat at an open window, with a shaded lamp placed far from him on a table in a corner.

Rosa drew nearer to him in the twilight of the room. He saw her, and he said in an under-tone: 'Good Heaven!'

Rosa fell upon his neck, with tears, and then he said, returning her embrace:

'My child, my child! I thought you were your mother!'

'But what, what, what,' he added, soothingly, 'has happened? My dear, what has brought you here? Who has brought you here?'

'No one. I came alone.'

'Lord bless me!' ejaculated Mr Grewgious. 'Came alone! Why didn't you write to me to come and fetch you?'

'I had no time. I took a sudden resolution. Poor, poor Eddy!'

'Ah, poor fellow, poor fellow!'

'His uncle has made love to me. I cannot bear it,' said Rosa, at once with a burst of tears, and a stamp of her little foot; 'I shudder with horror of him, and I have come to you to protect me and all of us from him, if you will?'

'I will!' cried Mr Grewgious, with a sudden rush of amazing energy. 'Damn him!

'Confound his politics![8]
Frustrate his knavish tricks!
On Thee his hopes to fix?
Damn him again!'

After this most extraordinary outburst, Mr Grewgious, quite beside himself, plunged about the room, to all appearance undecided whether he was in a fit of loyal enthusiasm, or combative denunciation.

He stopped and said, wiping his face: 'I beg your pardon, my dear, but you will be glad to know I feel better. Tell me no more just now, or I might do it again. You must be refreshed and cheered. What did you take last? Was it breakfast, lunch, dinner, tea, or supper? And what will you take next? Shall it be breakfast, lunch, dinner, tea, or supper?'

The respectful tenderness with which, on one knee before her, he helped her to remove her hat, and disentangle her pretty hair from it, was quite a chivalrous sight. Yet who, knowing him only on the surface, would have expected chivalry — and of the true sort, too: not the spurious — from Mr Grewgious?

'Your rest too must be provided for,' he went on; 'and you shall have the prettiest chamber in Furnival's. Your toilet must be provided for, and you shall have everything that an unlimited head chambermaid — by which expression I mean a head chambermaid not limited as to outlay — can procure. Is that a bag?' he looked hard at it; sooth to say, it required hard looking at to be seen at all in a dimly-lighted room: 'and is it your property, my dear?'

'Yes, sir. I brought it with me.'

'It is not an extensive bag,' said Mr Grewgious, candidly, 'though admirably calculated to contain a day's provision for a canary bird. Perhaps you brought a canary bird?'

Rosa smiled, and shook her head.

'If you had, he should have been made welcome,' said Mr Grewgious, 'and I think he would have been pleased to be hung upon a nail outside and pit himself against our Staple sparrows; whose execution must be admitted to be not quite equal to their intention. Which is the case with so many of us! You didn't say what meal, my dear. Have a nice jumble of all meals.'

Rosa thanked him, but said she could only take a cup of tea. Mr Grewgious, after several times running out, and in again, to mention such supplementary items as marmalade, eggs, watercresses, salted fish, and frizzled ham, ran across to Furnival's without his hat, to give his various directions. And soon afterwards they were realized in practice, and the board was spread.

'Lord bless my soul!' cried Mr Grewgious, putting the lamp upon it, and taking his seat opposite Rosa; 'what a new sensation for a poor old Angular bachelor, to be sure!'

Rosa's expressive little eyebrows asked him what he meant!

'The sensation of having a sweet young presence in the place that whitewashes it, paints it, papers it, decorates it with gilding, and makes it Glorious!' said Mr Grewgious. 'Ah me! Ah me!'

As there was something mournful in his sigh, Rosa, in touching him with his tea-cup, ventured to touch him with her small hand too.

'Thank you, my dear,' said Mr Grewgious. 'Ahem! Let's talk!'

'Do you always live here, sir?' asked Rosa.

'Yes, my dear.'

'And always alone?'

'Always alone; except that I have daily companion in a gentleman by the name of Bazzard; my clerk.'

'*He* doesn't live here?'

'No, he goes his ways after office hours. In fact, he is off duty here, altogether, just at present; and a Firm down stairs, with which I have business relations, lend me a substitute. But it would be extremely difficult to replace Mr Bazzard.'

'He must be very fond of you,' said Rosa.

'He bears up against it with commendable fortitude if he is,' returned Mr Grewgious, after considering the matter. 'But I doubt if he is. Not particularly so. You see, he is discontented, poor fellow.'

'Why isn't he contented?' was the natural enquiry.

'Misplaced,' said Mr Grewgious, with great mystery.

Rosa's eyebrows resumed their inquisitive and perplexed expression.

'So misplaced,' Mr Grewgious went on, 'that I feel constantly apologetic towards him. And he feels (though he doesn't mention it) that I have reason to be.'

Mr Grewgious experiences a new sensation

Mr Grewgious had by this time grown so very mysterious, that Rosa did not know how to go on. While she was thinking about it Mr Grewgious suddenly jerked out of himself for the second time:

'Let's talk. We were speaking of Mr Bazzard. It's a secret, and moreover it is Mr Bazzard's secret; but the sweet presence at my table makes me so unusually expansive, that I feel I must impart it in inviolable confidence. What do you think Mr Bazzard has done?'

'Oh dear!' cried Rosa, drawing her chair a little nearer, and her mind reverting to Jasper, 'nothing dreadful, I hope?'

'He has written a play,' said Mr Grewgious, in a solemn whisper. 'A tragedy.'

Rosa seemed much relieved.

'And nobody,' pursued Mr Grewgious in the same tone, 'will hear, on any account whatever, of bringing it out.'

Rosa looked reflective, and nodded her head slowly; as who should say: 'Such things are, and why are they!'

'Now, you know,' said Mr Grewgious, '*I* couldn't write a play.'

'Not a bad one, sir?' asked Rosa, innocently, with her eyebrows again in action.

'No. If I was under sentence of decapitation, and was about to be instantly decapitated, and an express arrived with a pardon for the condemned convict Grewgious if he wrote a play, I should be under the necessity of resuming the block and begging the executioner to proceed to extremities, – meaning,' said Mr Grewgious, passing his hand under his chin, 'the singular number, and this extremity.'

Rosa appeared to consider what she would do if the awkward supposititious case were hers.

'Consequently,' said Mr Grewgious, 'Mr Bazzard would have a sense of my inferiority to himself under any circumstances; but when I am his master, you know, the case is greatly aggravated.'

Mr Grewgious shook his head seriously, as if he felt the offence to be a little too much, though of his own committing.

'How came you to be his master, sir?' asked Rosa.

'A question that naturally follows,' said Mr Grewgious. 'Let's talk. Mr Bazzard's father, being a Norfolk farmer, would have furiously laid about him with a flail, a pitchfork, and every agricultural implement available for assaulting purposes, on the slightest hint of his son's having written a play. So the son, bringing to me the father's rent (which I receive), imparted his secret, and pointed out that he was determined to pursue his genius, and that it would put him in peril of starvation, and that he was not formed for it.'

'For pursuing his genius, sir?'

'No, my dear,' said Mr Grewgious, 'for starvation. It was impossible to deny the position that Mr Bazzard was not formed to be starved, and Mr Bazzard then pointed out that it was desirable that I should stand between him and a fate so perfectly unsuited to his formation. In that way Mr Bazzard became my clerk, and he feels it very much.'

'I am glad he is grateful,' said Rosa.

'I didn't quite mean that, my dear. I mean that he feels the degradation. There are some other geniuses that Mr Bazzard has become acquainted with, who have also written tragedies,' which likewise nobody will on any account whatever hear of bringing out, and these choice spirits dedicate their plays to one another in a highly panegyrical manner. Mr Bazzard has been the subject of one of these dedications. Now, you know, *I* never had a play dedicated to *me!*'

Rosa looked at him as if she would have liked him to be the recipient of a thousand dedications.

'Which again, naturally, rubs against the grain of Mr Bazzard,' said Mr Grewgious. 'He is very short with me sometimes, and then I feel that he is meditating "This blockhead is my master! A fellow who couldn't write a tragedy on pain of death, and who will never have one dedicated to him with the most complimentary congratulations on the high position he has taken in the eyes of posterity!" Very trying, very trying. However, in giving him directions, I reflect beforehand: "Perhaps he may not like this," or "He might take it ill if I asked that," and so we get on very well. Indeed, better than I could have expected.'

'Is the tragedy named, sir?' asked Rosa.

'Strictly between ourselves,' answered Mr Grewgious, 'it has a dreadfully appropriate name. It is called The Thorn of Anxiety. But Mr Bazzard hopes – and I hope – that it will come out at last.'

It was not hard to divine that Mr Grewgious had related the Bazzard history thus fully, at least quite as much for the recreation of his ward's mind from the subject that had driven her there, as for the gratification of his own tendency to be social and communicative. 'And now, my dear,' he said at this point, 'if you are not too tired to tell me more of what passed to-day – but only if you feel quite able – I should be glad to hear it. I may digest it the better, if I sleep on it to-night.'

Rosa, composed now, gave him a faithful account of the interview. Mr Grewgious often smoothed his head while it was in progress, and begged to be told a second time those parts which bore on Helena and Neville. When Rosa had finished, he sat grave, silent, and meditative, for a while.

'Clearly narrated,' was his only remark at last, 'and, I hope, clearly put away here,' smoothing his head again. 'See, my dear,' taking her to the open window, 'where they live! The dark windows over yonder.'

'I may go to Helena to-morrow?' asked Rosa.

'I should like to sleep on that question to-night,' he answered, doubtfully. 'But let me take you to your own rest, for you must need it.'

With that, Mr Grewgious helped her to get her hat on again, and hung upon his arm the very little bag that was of no earthly use, and led her by the hand (with a certain stately awkwardness, as if he were going to walk a minuet) across Holborn, and into Furnival's Inn. At the hotel[10] door, he confided her to the Unlimited head chambermaid, and said that while she went up to see her room, he would remain below, in case she should wish it exchanged for another, or should find that there was anything she wanted.

Rosa's room was airy, clean, comfortable, almost gay. The Unlimited had laid in everything omitted from the very little bag (that is to say, everything she could possibly need), and Rosa tripped down the great many stairs again, to thank her guardian for his thoughtful and affectionate care of her.

'Not at all, my dear,' said Mr Grewgious, infinitely gratified; 'it is I who thank you for your charming confidence and for your charming company. Your breakfast will be provided for you in a neat, compact, and graceful little sitting-room (appropriate to your figure), and I will come to you at ten o'clock in the morning. I hope you don't feel very strange indeed, in this strange place.'

'Oh no, I feel so safe!'

'Yes, you may be sure that the stairs are fire-proof,'[11] said Mr Grewgious, 'and that any outbreak of the devouring element would be perceived and suppressed by the watchmen.'

'I did not mean that,' Rosa replied. 'I mean, I feel so safe from him.'

'There is a stout gate of iron bars to keep him out,' said Mr Grewgious, 'and Furnival's is specially watched and lighted, and *I* live over the way!' In the stoutness of his knight-errantry, he seemed to think the last-named protection all-sufficient. In the same spirit, he said to the gate-porter as he went out, 'If some one staying in the hotel should wish to send across the road to me in the night, a crown will be ready for the messenger.' In the same spirit, he walked up and down outside the iron gate for the best part of an hour, with some solicitude: occasionally looking in between the bars, as if he had laid a dove in a high roost in a cage of lions, and had it on his mind that she might tumble out.

*

CHAPTER 21

A Recognition[1]

Nothing occurred in the night to flutter the tired dove, and the dove arose refreshed. With Mr Grewgious, when the clock struck ten in the morning, came Mr Crisparkle, who had come at one plunge out of the river at Cloisterham.

'Miss Twinkleton was so uneasy, Miss Rosa,' he explained to her, 'and came round to Ma and me with your note, in such a state of wonder, that, to quiet her, I volunteered on this service by the very first train to be caught in the morning. I wished at the time[2] that you had come to me; but now I think it best that you did *as* you did, and came to your guardian.'

'I did think of you,' Rosa told him; 'but Minor Canon Corner was so near him –'

'I understand. It was quite natural.'

'I have told Mr Crisparkle,' said Mr Grewgious, 'all that you told me last night, my dear. Of course I should have written it to him immediately; but his coming was most opportune. And it was particularly kind of him to come, for he had but just gone.'

'Have you settled,'³ asked Rosa, appealing to them both, 'what is to be done for Helena and her brother?'

'Why, really,' said Mr Crisparkle, 'I am in great perplexity. If even Mr Grewgious, whose head is much longer than mine and who is a whole night's cogitation in advance of me, is undecided, what must I be!'

The Unlimited here put her head in at the door – after having rapped, and been authorized to present herself – announcing that a gentleman wished for a word with another gentleman named Crisparkle, if any such gentleman were there. If no such gentleman were there, he begged pardon for being mistaken.

'Such a gentleman is here,' said Mr Crisparkle, 'but is engaged just now.'

'Is it a dark gentleman?' interposed Rosa, retreating on her guardian.

'No, Miss, more of a brown gentleman.'

'You are sure not with black hair?' asked Rosa, taking courage.

'Quite sure of that, Miss. Brown hair and blue eyes.'

'Perhaps,' hinted Mr Grewgious, with habitual caution, 'it might be well to see him, reverend sir, if you don't object. When one is in a difficulty, or at a loss, one never knows in what direction a way out may chance to open. It is a business principle of mine, in such a case, not to close up any direction, but to keep an eye on every direction that may present itself. I could relate an anecdote in point, but that it would be premature.'

'If Miss Rosa will allow me, then? Let the gentleman come in,' said Mr Crisparkle.

The gentleman came in; apologized, with a frank but modest grace, for not finding Mr Crisparkle alone; turned to Mr Crisparkle, and smilingly asked the unexpected question: 'Who am I?'

'You are the gentleman I saw smoking under the trees in Staple Inn a few minutes ago.'

'True. There I saw you. Who else am I?'

Mr Crisparkle concentrated his attention on a handsome face, much sunburnt; and the ghost of some departed boy seemed to rise, gradually and dimly, in the room.

The gentleman saw a struggling recollection lighten up the Minor Canon's features, and smiling again, said: 'What will you have for breakfast this morning? You are out of jam.'

'Wait a moment!' cried Mr Crisparkle, raising his right hand. 'Give me another instant! Tartar!'

The two shook hands with the greatest heartiness, and then went the wonderful length – for Englishmen – of laying their hands each on the other's shoulders, and looking joyfully each into the other's face.

'My old fag!'[4] said Mr Crisparkle.

'My old master!' said Mr Tartar.

'You saved me from drowning!' said Mr Crisparkle.

'After which you took to swimming, you know!' said Mr Tartar.

'God bless my soul!' said Mr Crisparkle.

'Amen!' said Mr Tartar.

And then they fell to shaking hands most heartily again.

'Imagine,' exclaimed Mr Crisparkle, with glistening eyes: 'Miss Rosa Bud and Mr Grewgious, imagine Mr Tartar, when he was the smallest of juniors, diving for me, catching me, a big heavy senior, by the hair of the head, and striking out for the shore with me like a water-giant!'

'Imagine my not letting him sink, as I was his fag!' said Mr Tartar. 'But the truth being that he was my best protector and friend, and did me more good than all the masters put together, an irrational impulse seized me to pick him up, or go down with him.'

'Hem! Permit me, sir, to have the honor,' said Mr Grewgious, advancing with extended hand, 'for an honor I truly esteem it. I am proud to make your acquaintance. I hope you didn't take cold. I hope you were not inconvenienced by swallowing too much water. How have you been since?'

It was by no means apparent that Mr Grewgious knew what he said, though it was very apparent that he meant to say something highly friendly and appreciative.

If Heaven, Rosa thought, had but sent such courage and skill to her poor mother's aid! And he to have been so slight and young then!

'I don't wish to be complimented upon it, I thank you, but I think I have an idea,' Mr Grewgious announced, after taking a jog-trot or two across the room, so unexpected and unaccountable that they had all stared at him, doubtful whether he was choking or had the cramp. 'I *think* I have an idea. I believe I have had the pleasure of seeing Mr Tartar's name as tenant of the top set in the house next the top set in the corner?'

'Yes, sir,' returned Mr Tartar. 'You are right so far.'

'I am right so far,' said Mr Grewgious. 'Tick that off,' which he did, with his right thumb on his left. 'Might you happen to know the name of your neighbour in the top set on the other side of the party-wall?' coming very close to Mr Tartar, to lose nothing of his face, in his shortness of sight.

'Landless.'

'Tick that off,' said Mr Grewgious, taking another trot, and then coming back. 'No personal knowledge, I suppose, sir?'

'Slight, but some.'

'Tick that off,' said Mr Grewgious, taking another trot, and again coming back. 'Nature of knowledge, Mr Tartar?'

'I thought he seemed to be a young fellow in a poor way, and I asked his leave – only within a day or so – to share my flowers up there with him; that is to say, to extend my flower-garden to his windows.'

'Would you have the kindness to take seats?' said Mr Grewgious. '*I have* an idea!'

They complied; Mr Tartar none the less readily, for being all abroad; and Mr Grewgious, seated in the centre, with his hands upon his knees, thus stated his idea, with his usual manner of having got the statement by heart.

'I cannot as yet make up my mind whether it is prudent to hold open communication under present circumstances, and on the part of the fair member of the present company, with Mr Neville or Miss Helena. I have reason to know that a local friend of ours (on whom I beg to bestow a passing but a hearty malediction, with the kind permission of my reverend friend) sneaks to and fro, and dodges up and down. When not doing so himself, he may have some informant skulking about, in the person of a watchman, porter, or such-like hanger-on of Staple. On the other hand, Miss Rosa very naturally wishes to see her friend Miss Helena, and it would seem important that at least Miss Helena (if not her brother too, through her) should privately know from Miss Rosa's lips what has occurred, and what has been threatened. Am I agreed with generally[5] in the views I take?'

'I entirely coincide with them,' said Mr Crisparkle, who had been very attentive.

'As I have no doubt I should,' added Mr Tartar, smiling, 'if I understood them.'

'Fair and softly, sir,' said Mr Grewgious; 'we shall fully confide in you directly, if you will favor us with your permission. Now, if our local friend should have any informant on the spot, it is tolerably clear that such informant can only be set to watch the chambers in the occupation of Mr Neville. He reporting, to our local friend, who comes and goes there, our local friend would supply for himself, from his own previous knowledge, the identity of the parties. Nobody can be set to watch all Staple, or to concern himself with comers and goers to other sets of chambers: unless, indeed, mine.'

'I begin to understand[6] to what you tend,' said Mr Crisparkle, 'and highly approve of your caution.'

'I needn't repeat that I know nothing yet of the why and wherefore,' said Mr Tartar; 'but I also understand to what you tend, so let me say at once that my chambers are freely at your disposal.'

'There!' cried Mr Grewgious, smoothing his head triumphantly. 'Now we have all got the idea. You have it, my dear?'

'I think I have,' said Rosa, blushing a little as Mr Tartar looked quickly towards her.

'You see, you go over to Staple with Mr Crisparkle and Mr Tartar,' said Mr Grewgious; 'I going in and out and out and in, alone, in my usual way; you go up with those gentlemen to Mr Tartar's rooms; you look into Mr Tartar's flower-garden; you wait for Miss Helena's appearance there, or you signify to Miss Helena that you are close by; and you communicate with her freely, and no spy can be the wiser.'

'I am very much afraid I shall be –'

'Be what, my dear?' asked Mr Grewgious, as she hesitated. 'Not frightened?'

'No, not that,' said Rosa, shyly; – 'in Mr Tartar's way. We seem to be appropriating Mr Tartar's residence so very coolly.'

'I protest to you,' returned that gentleman, 'that I shall think the better of it for evermore, if your voice sounds in it only once.'

Rosa, not quite knowing what to say about that, cast down her eyes, and turning to Mr Grewgious, dutifully asked if she should put her hat on? Mr Grewgious being of opinion that she could not do better, she withdrew for the purpose. Mr Crisparkle took the opportunity of giving Mr Tartar a summary of the distresses of Neville and his sister; the opportunity was quite long enough, as the hat happened to require a little extra fitting on.

Mr Tartar gave his arm to Rosa, and Mr Crisparkle walked, detached, in front.

'Poor, poor Eddy!' thought Rosa, as they went along.

Mr Tartar waved his right hand as he bent his head down over Rosa, talking in an animated way.

'It was not so powerful or so sun-browned when it saved Mr Crisparkle,' thought Rosa, glancing at it; 'but it must have been very steady and determined even then.'

Mr Tartar told her he had been a sailor, roving everywhere for years and years.

'When are you going to sea again?' asked Rosa.

'Never!'

Rosa wondered what the girls would say if they could see her crossing the wide street on the sailor's arm. And she fancied that the passers-by must think her very little and very helpless, contrasted with the strong figure that could have caught her up and carried her out of any danger, miles and miles without resting.

She was thinking further, that his far-seeing blue eyes looked as if they had been used to watch danger afar off, and to watch it without flinching, drawing nearer and nearer: when, happening to raise her own eyes, she found that he seemed to be thinking something about *them*.

This a little confused Rosebud, and may account for her never afterwards quite knowing how she ascended (with his help) to his garden in the air,[7] and seemed to get into a marvellous country that came into sudden bloom like the country on the summit of the magic bean-stalk. May it flourish for ever!

CHAPTER 22

A Gritty State of Things comes on[1]

Mr Tartar's chambers were the neatest, the cleanest, and the best-ordered chambers[2] ever seen under the sun, moon, and stars.[3] The floors were scrubbed to that extent, that you might have supposed the London blacks[4] emancipated for ever, and gone out of the land for good. Every inch of brass-work in Mr Tartar's possession was polished and burnished, till it shone like a brazen mirror. No speck, nor spot, nor spatter soiled the purity of any of Mr Tartar's household gods,[5] large, small, or middle sized. His sitting-room was like the admiral's cabin, his bath room was like a dairy, his sleeping chamber, fitted all about with lockers and drawers, was like a seedsman's shop,[6] and his nicely-balanced cot[7] just stirred in the midst, as if it breathed. Everything belonging to Mr Tartar had quarters of its own assigned to it: his maps and charts had their quarters; his books had theirs; his brushes had theirs; his boots had theirs; his clothes had theirs; his case-bottles had theirs; his telescopes and other instruments had theirs. Everything was readily accessible. Shelf, bracket, locker, hook, and drawer were equally within reach, and were equally contrived with a view to avoiding waste of room, and providing some snug inches of stowage for something that would have exactly fitted nowhere else. His gleaming little service of plate was so arranged upon his sideboard as that a slack salt-spoon would have instantly betrayed itself; his toilet implements were so arranged upon his dressing-table as that a toothpick of slovenly deportment could have been reported at a glance. So with the curiosities he had brought home from various voyages. Stuffed, dried, repolished, or otherwise preserved, according to their kind; birds, fishes, reptiles, arms, articles of dress, shells, seaweeds, grasses, or memorials of coral reef; each was displayed in its especial place, and each could have been displayed in no better place. Paint and varnish seemed to be kept somewhere out of sight, in constant readiness to obliterate stray finger-marks wherever any might become perceptible in Mr Tartar's chambers. No man-of-war was ever kept more spick and span from careless touch. On this bright summer day, a neat awning was rigged over Mr Tartar's flower-garden as only a sailor could rig it; and there was a sea-going air upon the whole effect, so delightfully complete, that the flower-garden might have appertained to stern-windows afloat, and the whole concern might have bowled away gallantly with all on board, if Mr Tartar had only clapped to his lips the speaking trumpet that was slung in a corner, and given hoarse orders to have the anchor up, look alive there, men, and get all sail upon her!

Mr Tartar doing the honors[8] of this gallant craft was of a piece with the rest. When a man rides an amiable hobby[9] that shies at nothing and kicks nobody, it is always agreeable to find him riding it with a humorous sense of the droll side of the creature. When the man is a cordial and an earnest man by nature, and withal is perfectly fresh and genuine, it may be doubted whether he is ever seen to greater advantage than at such a time. So Rosa would have naturally thought (even if she *hadn't* been conducted over the ship with all the homage due to the First Lady of the Admiralty,[10] or First Fairy of the Sea), that it was charming to see and hear Mr Tartar half laughing at, and half rejoicing in, his various contrivances. So Rosa would have naturally thought, anyhow, that the sunburnt sailor showed to great advantage when, the inspection finished, he delicately withdrew out of his admiral's cabin, beseeching her to consider herself its Queen, and waving her free of his flower-garden with the hand that had had Mr Crisparkle's life in it.

'Helena! Helena Landless! Are you there?'

'Who speaks to me? Not Rosa?' Then a second handsome face appearing.

'Yes, my darling!'

'Why, how did you come here, dearest?'

'I – I don't quite know,' said Rosa with a blush; 'unless I am dreaming!'

Why with a blush? For their two faces were alone with the other flowers. Are blushes among the fruits of the country of the magic bean-stalk?

'*I* am not dreaming,' said Helena, smiling. 'I should take more for granted if I were. How do we come together – or so near together – so very unexpectedly?'

Unexpectedly indeed, among the dingy gables and chimneypots of P. J. T.'s connexion, and the flowers that had sprung from the salt sea. But Rosa, waking, told in a hurry how they came to be together, and all the why and wherefore of that matter.

'And Mr Crisparkle is here,' said Rosa, in rapid conclusion; 'and, could you believe it? Long ago, he saved his life!'

'I could believe any such thing of Mr Crisparkle,' returned Helena, with a mantling face.

(More blushes in the bean-stalk country!)

'Yes, but it wasn't Mr Crisparkle,' said Rosa, quickly putting in the correction.

'I don't understand, love.'

'It was very nice of Mr Crisparkle to be saved,' said Rosa, 'and he couldn't have shown his high opinion of Mr Tartar more expressively. But it was Mr Tartar who saved him.'

Helena's dark eyes looked very earnestly at the bright face among the leaves, and she asked, in a slower and more thoughtful tone:

'Is Mr Tartar with you now, dear?'

'No; because he has given up his rooms to me – us, I mean. It *is* such a beautiful place!'

'Is it?'

'It is like the inside of the most exquisite ship that ever sailed. It is like – it is like –!'

'Like a dream?' suggested Helena.

Rosa answered with a little nod, and smelled the flowers.

Helena resumed, after a short pause of silence, during which she seemed (or it was Rosa's fancy) to compassionate somebody: 'My poor Neville is reading in his own room, the sun being so very bright on this side just now. I think he had better not know that you are so near.'

'Oh, I think so too!' cried Rosa very readily.

'I suppose,' pursued Helena, doubtfully, 'that he must know by-and-bye all you have told me; but I am not sure. Ask Mr Crisparkle's advice, my darling. Ask him whether I may tell Neville as much or as little of what you have told me as I think best.'

Rosa subsided into her State Cabin, and propounded the question. The Minor Canon was for the free exercise of Helena's judgment.

'I thank him very much,' said Helena, when Rosa emerged again with her report. 'Ask him whether it would be best to wait until any new maligning and pursuing of Neville on the part of this wretch shall disclose itself, or to try to anticipate it: I mean, so far as to find out whether any such goes on darkly about us?'

The Minor Canon found this point so difficult to give a confident opinion on, that, after two or three attempts and failures, he suggested a reference to Mr Grewgious. Helena acquiescing, he betook himself (with a most unsuccessful assumption of lounging indifference) across the quadrangle to P. J. T.'s, and stated it. Mr Grewgious held decidedly to the general principle, that if you could steal a march upon a brigand or a wild beast, you had better do it; he also held decidedly to the special case, that John Jasper was a brigand *and* a wild beast in combination.

Thus advised, Mr Crisparkle came back again and reported to Rosa, who in her turn reported to Helena. She, now steadily pursuing her train of thought at her window, considered thereupon.

'We may count on Mr Tartar's readiness to help us, Rosa?' she enquired.

O yes! Rosa shyly thought so. O yes, Rosa shyly believed she could almost answer for it. But should she ask Mr Crisparkle? 'I think your authority on the point as good as his, my dear,' said Helena, sedately, 'and you needn't disappear again for that.' Odd of Helena!

'You see: Neville,' Helena pursued after more reflection, 'knows no one else here: he has not so much as exchanged a word with any one else here. If Mr Tartar would call to see him openly and often; if he would spare a minute for the purpose, frequently; if he would even do so, almost daily; something might come of it.'

'Something might come of it, dear?' repeated Rosa, surveying her friend's beauty with a highly perplexed face. 'Something might?'

'If Neville's movements are really watched, and if the purpose really is to isolate him from all friends and acquaintance and wear his daily life out grain by grain (which would seem to be in the threat to you), does it not appear likely,' said Helena, 'that his enemy would in some way communicate with Mr Tartar to warn him off from Neville? In which case, we might not only know the fact, but might know from Mr Tartar what the terms of the communication were.'

'I see!' cried Rosa. And immediately darted into her State Cabin again.

Presently her pretty face reappeared, with a heightened color, and she said that she had told Mr Crisparkle, and that Mr Crisparkle had fetched in Mr Tartar, and that Mr Tartar – 'who is waiting now, in case you want him,' added Rosa, with a half look back, and in not a little confusion between the inside of the State Cabin and the out – had declared his readiness to act as she had suggested, and to enter on his task that very day.

'I thank him from my heart,' said Helena. 'Pray tell him so.'

Again not a little confused between the Flower Garden and the Cabin, Rosa dipped in with her message, and dipped out again with more assurances from Mr Tartar, and stood wavering in a divided state between Helena and him, which proved that confusion is not always necessarily awkward, but may sometimes present a very pleasant appearance.

'And now, darling,' said Helena, 'we will be mindful of the caution that has restricted us to this interview for the present, and will part. I hear Neville moving too. Are you going back?'

'To Miss Twinkleton's?' asked Rosa.

'Yes.'

'Oh, I could never go there any more. I couldn't indeed, after that dreadful interview!' said Rosa.

'Then where *are* you going, pretty one?'

'Now I come to think of it, I don't know,' said Rosa. 'I have settled nothing at all yet, but my guardian will take care of me. Don't be uneasy, dear. I shall be sure to be somewhere.'

(It did seem likely.)

'And I shall hear of my Rosebud from Mr Tartar?' enquired Helena.

'Yes, I suppose so; from –' Rosa looked back again in a flutter, instead of supplying the name. 'But tell me one thing before we part, dearest Helena. Tell me that you are sure, sure, sure, I couldn't help it.'

'Help it, love?'

'Help making him malicious and revengeful. I couldn't hold any terms with him, could I?'

'You know how I love you, darling,' answered Helena, with indignation; 'but I would sooner see you dead at his wicked feet.'[11]

'That's a great comfort to me! And you will tell your poor brother so, won't you? And you will give him my remembrance and my sympathy? And you will ask him not to hate me?'

With a mournful shake of the head, as if that would be quite a superfluous entreaty, Helena lovingly kissed her two hands to her friend, and her friend's two hands were kissed to her; and then she saw a third hand (a brown one) appear among the flowers and leaves, and help her friend out of sight.

The refection that Mr Tartar produced in the Admiral's Cabin by merely touching the spring knob of a locker and the handle of a drawer, was a dazzling enchanted repast. Wonderful macaroons, glittering liqueurs, magically preserved tropical spices, and jellies of celestial tropical fruits, displayed themselves profusely at an instant's notice. But Mr Tartar could not make time stand still; and time, with his hard-hearted fleetness, strode on so fast, that Rosa was obliged to come down from the bean-stalk country to earth and her guardian's chambers.

'And now, my dear,' said Mr Grewgious, 'what is to be done next? To put the same thought in another form; what is to be done with you?'

Rosa could only look apologetically sensible of being very much in her own way, and in everybody else's. Some passing idea of living, fireproof, up a good many stairs in Furnival's Inn for the rest of her life, was the only thing in the nature of a plan that occurred to her.

'It has come into my thoughts,' said Mr Grewgious, 'that the respected lady, Miss Twinkleton, occasionally repairs to London in the recess, with the view of extending her connexion, and being available for interviews with metropolitan parents, if any; whether, until we have time in which to turn ourselves round, we might invite Miss Twinkleton to come and stay with you for a month?'

'Stay where, sir?'

'Whether,' explained Mr Grewgious, 'we might take a furnished lodging in town for a month, and invite Miss Twinkleton to assume the charge of you in it for that period?'

'And afterwards?' hinted Rosa.

'And afterwards,' said Mr Grewgious, 'we should be no worse off than we are now.'

'I think that might smooth the way,' assented Rosa.

'Then let us,' said Mr Grewgious, rising, 'go and look for a furnished lodging. Nothing could be more acceptable to me than the sweet presence of last evening, for all the remaining evenings of my existence; but these are not fit surroundings for a young lady. Let us set out in quest of adventures, and look for a furnished lodging. In the meantime, Mr Crisparkle here, about to return home immediately, will no doubt kindly see Miss Twinkleton, and invite that lady to co-operate in our plan.'

Mr Crisparkle, willingly accepting the commission, took his departure; Mr Grewgious and his ward set forth on their expedition.

As Mr Grewgious's idea of looking at a furnished lodging was to get on the opposite side of the street to a house with a suitable bill in the window, and stare at it; and then work his way tortuously to the back of the house and stare at that; and then not go in, but make similar trials of another house, with the same result; their progress was but slow. At length he bethought himself of a widowed cousin, divers times removed, of Mr Bazzard's, who had once solicited his influence in the lodger world and who lived in Southampton Street, Bloomsbury Square.[12] This lady's name, stated in uncompromising capitals of considerable size on a brass door-plate, and yet not lucidly stated as to sex or condition, was BILLICKIN.

Personal faintness, and an overpowering personal candour, were the distinguishing features of Mrs Billickin's organization. She came languishing out from her own exclusive back parlor, with the air of having been expressly brought-to for the purpose, from an accumulation of several swoons.

'I hope I see you well, sir,' said Mrs Billickin, recognizing her visitor with a bend.

'Thank you, quite well. And you, ma'am?' returned Mr Grewgious.

'I am as well,' said Mrs Billickin, becoming aspirational with excess of faintness, 'as I hever ham.'[13]

'My ward and an elder lady,' said Mr Grewgious, 'wish to find a genteel lodging for a month or so. Have you any apartments available, ma'am?'

'Mr Grewgious,' returned Mrs Billickin, 'I will not deceive you; far from it. I *have* apartments available.'

This with the air of adding: 'Convey me to the stake, if you will; but while I live, I will be candid.'

'And now, what apartments, ma'am?' asked Mr Grewgious, cosily. To tame a certain severity apparent on the part of Mrs Billickin.

'There is this sitting-room – which, call it what you will, it is the front parlior, Miss,' said Mrs Billickin, impressing Rosa into the conversation: 'the back parlior being what I cling to and never part with; and there is two bedrooms at the top of the 'ouse with gas laid on.[14] I do not tell you that your bedroom floors is firm, for firm they are not. The gas-fitter himself allowed that to make a firm job, he must go right under your jistes,[15] and it were not worth the outlay as a yearly tenant so to do. The piping is carried above your jistes, and it is best that it should be made known to you.'

Mr Grewgious, and Rosa exchanged looks of some dismay, though they had not the least idea what latent horrors this carriage of the piping might involve. Mrs Billickin put her hand to her heart, as having eased it of a load.

'Well! The roof is all right, no doubt,' said Mr Grewgious, plucking up a little.

'Mr Grewgious,' returned Mrs Billickin, 'if I was to tell you, sir, that to have nothink above you is to have a floor above you, I should put a deceptin upon you which I will not do. No, sir. Your slates WILL rattle loose at that elewation in windy weather, do your utmost, best or worst! I defy you, sir, be you who you may, to keep your slates tight, try how you can.' Here Mrs Billickin, having been warm with Mr Grewgious, cooled a little, not to abuse the moral power she held over him. 'Consequent,' proceeded Mrs Billickin, more mildly, but still firmly in her incorruptible candour; 'consequent it would be worse than of no use for me to trapse and travel up to the top of the 'ouse with you, and for you to say, "Mrs Billickin, what stain do I notice in the ceiling, for a stain I do consider it?" and for me to answer, "I do not understand you, sir." No, sir; I will not be so underhand. I *do* understand you before you pint it out. It is the wet, sir. It do come in, and it do not come in. You may lay dry there half your lifetime; but the time will come, and it is best that you should know it, when a dripping sop would be no name for you.'

Mr Grewgious looked much disgraced by being prefigured in this pickle.

'Have you any other apartments, ma'am?' he asked.

'Mr Grewgious,' returned Mrs Billickin, with much solemnity, 'I have. You ask me have I, and my open and my honest answer air, I have. The first and second floors is wacant, and sweet rooms.'

'Come, come! There's nothing against *them*,' said Mr Grewgious, comforting himself.

'Mr Grewgious,' replied Mrs Billickin, 'pardon me, there is the stairs. Unless your mind is prepared for the stairs, it will lead to inevitable disapintmink. You cannot, Miss,' said Mrs Billickin, addressing Rosa reproachfully, 'place a first floor, and far less a second, on the level footing of a parlor. No, you cannot do it, Miss, it is beyond your power, and wherefore try?'

Mrs Billickin put it very feelingly, as if Rosa had shown a headstrong determination to hold the untenable position.

'Can we see these rooms, ma'am?' enquired her guardian.

'Mr Grewgious,' returned Mrs Billickin, 'you can. I will not disguise it from you, sir, you can.'

Mrs Billickin then sent into her back parlor for her shawl (it being a state fiction, dating from immemorial antiquity, that she could never go anywhere without being wrapped up), and having been enrobed by her attendant, led the way. She made various genteel pauses on the stairs for breath, and clutched at her heart in the drawing-room as if it had very nearly got loose, and she had caught it in the act of taking wing.

'And the second floor?' said Mr Grewgious, on finding the first satisfactory.

'Mr Grewgious,' replied Mrs Billickin, turning upon him with ceremony, as if the time had now come when a distinct understanding on a difficult point must be arrived at, and a solemn confidence established: 'the second floor is over this.'

'Can we see that too, ma'am?'

'Yes, sir,' returned Mrs Billickin, 'it is open as the day.'[16]

That also proving satisfactory, Mr Grewgious retired into a window with Rosa for a few words of consultation, and then asking for pen and ink, sketched out a line or two of agreement. In the meantime Mrs Billickin took a seat, and delivered a kind of Index to, or Abstract of, the general question.

'Five-and-forty shillings per week by the month certain at the time of year,' said Mrs Billickin, 'is only reasonable to both parties. It is not Bond Street nor yet St James's Palace;[17] but it is not pretended that it is. Neither is it attempted to be denied – for why should it? – that the Archway leads to a Mews. Mewses must exist.[18] Respectin' attendance; two is kep',[19] at liberal wages. Words *has* arisen as to tradesmen, but dirty shoes on fresh hearthstoning was attributable, and no wish for a commission on your orders. Coals is either *by* the fire, or *per* the scuttle.'[20] She emphasized the prepositions as marking a subtle but immense difference. 'Dogs is not viewed with faviour. Besides litter, they gets stole[21] and sharing suspicions is apt to creep in, and unpleasantness takes place.'

By this time Mr Grewgious had his agreement-lines and his earnest-money ready. 'I have signed it for the ladies, ma'am,' he said, 'and you'll have the goodness to sign it for yourself, Christian and Surname, here, if you please.'

'Mr Grewgious,' said Mrs Billickin in a new burst of candour, 'no, sir! You must excuse the Chris'en name.'

Mr Grewgious stared at her.

'The door plate is used as a protection,' said Mrs Billickin, 'and acts as such, and go from it I will not!'

Mr Grewgious stared at Rosa.

'No, Mr Grewgious, you must excuse me. So long as this 'ouse is known indefinite as Billickin's, and so long as it is a doubt with the riff-raff where Billickin may be hidin', near the street door or down the airy,[22] and what his weight and size, so long I feel safe. But commit myself to a solitary female statement, no, Miss![23] Nor would you for a moment wish,' said Mrs Billickin, with a strong sense of injury, 'to take that advantage of your sex, if you was not brought to it by inconsiderate example.'

Rosa reddening as if she had made some most disgraceful attempt to over-reach the good lady, besought Mr Grewgious to rest content with any signature. And accordingly, in a baronial way,[24] the sign-manual BILLICKIN got appended to the document.

Details were then settled for taking possession on the next day but one, when Miss Twinkleton might be reasonably expected, and Rosa went back to Furnival's Inn on her guardian's arm.

Behold Mr Tartar walking up and down Furnival's Inn, checking himself when he saw them coming, and advancing towards them!

'It occurred to me,' hinted Mr Tartar, 'that we might go up the river, the weather being so delicious and the tide serving. I have a boat of my own at the Temple Stairs.'[25]

'I have not been up the river for this many a day,' said Mr Grewgious, tempted.

'I was never up the river,' added Rosa.

Within half an hour they were setting this matter right by going up the river. The tide was running with them, the afternoon was charming. Mr Tartar's boat was perfect. Mr Tartar and Lobley (Mr Tartar's man) pulled a pair of oars. Mr Tartar had a yacht, it seemed, lying somewhere down by Greenhithe;[26] and Mr Tartar's man had charge of this yacht, and was detached upon his present service. He was a jolly-favored man, with tawny hair and whiskers, and a big red face. He was the dead image of the sun in old wood-cuts,[27] his hair and whiskers answering for rays all round him. Resplendent in the bow of the boat, he was a shining sight, with a man-of-war's man's shirt on – or off, according to opinion – and his arms and breast tattoo'd all sorts of patterns. Lobley seemed to take it easily, and so did Mr Tartar; yet their oars bent as they pulled, and the boat bounded under them. Mr Tartar talked as if he were doing nothing, to Rosa who was really doing nothing, and to Mr Grewgious who was doing this much that he steered all wrong – but what did that matter, when a turn of Mr Tartar's skilful wrist, or a mere grin of Mr Lobley's over the bow, put all to rights! The tide bore them on in the gayest and most sparkling manner, until they stopped to dine in some everlastingly green garden, needing no matter of fact identification here; and then the tide obligingly turned – being devoted to that party alone for that day – and as they floated idly among some osier beds, Rosa tried what she could do in the rowing way, and came off splendidly, being much assisted; and Mr Grewgious tried what he could do, and came off on his back, doubled up with an oar under his chin, being not assisted at all. Then there was an interval of rest under boughs (such rest!) what time Mr Lobley mopped, and, arranging cushions, stretchers, and the like, danced the tight-rope the whole length of the boat like a man to whom shoes were a superstition and stockings slavery;[28] and then came the sweet return among delicious odours of limes in bloom, and musical ripplings; and, all too soon, the great black city cast its shadow on the waters, and its dark bridges[29] spanned them as death spans life, and the everlastingly green garden seemed to be left for everlasting, unregainable and far away.

'Cannot people get through life without gritty stages, I wonder!' Rosa thought next day, when the town was very gritty again, and everything had a strange and an uncomfortable appearance on it of seeming to wait for something that wouldn't come. No. She began to think, that, now the Cloisterham school days had glided past and gone, the gritty stages would begin to set in at intervals and make themselves wearily known.

Yet what did Rosa expect? Did she expect Miss Twinkleton? Miss Twinkleton duly came. Forth from her back parlor issued the Billickin

Up the river

to receive Miss Twinkleton, and War was in the Billickin's eye from that fell moment.

Miss Twinkleton brought a quantity of luggage with her, having all Rosa's as well as her own. The Billickin took it ill that Miss Twinkleton's mind, being sorely disturbed by this luggage, failed to take in her personal identity with that clearness of perception which was due to its demands. Stateliness mounted her gloomy throne upon the Billickin's brow in consequence. And when Miss Twinkleton, in agitation taking stock of her trunks and packages, of which she had seventeen, particularly counted in the Billickin herself as number eleven, the B found it necessary to repudiate.

'Things cannot too soon be put upon the footing,' said she, with a candour so demonstrative as to be almost obtrusive, 'that the person of the Ouse is not a box nor yet a bundle, nor a carpet bag – no, I am ily obleeged to you, Miss Twinkleton, nor yet a beggar.' This last disclaimer had reference to Miss Twinkleton's distractedly pressing two and sixpence on her, instead of the cabman.

Thus cast off, Miss Twinkleton wildly enquired 'which gentleman' was to be paid? There being two gentlemen in that position (Miss Twinkleton having arrived with two cabs), each gentleman on being paid held forth his two and sixpence on the flat of his open hand, and, with a speechless stare and a dropped jaw, displayed his wrong to Heaven and Earth. Terrified by this alarming spectacle, Miss Twinkleton placed another shilling in each hand, at the same time appealing to the law in flurried accents, and recounting her luggage; this time with the two gentlemen in, who caused the total to come out complicated. Meanwhile the two gentlemen, each looking very hard at the last shilling, as if it might become eighteenpence if he kept his eyes on it, grumblingly descended the doorsteps, ascended their carriages, and drove away, leaving Miss Twinkleton bewildered on a bonnet-box in tears.

The Billickin beheld this manifestation of weakness without sympathy, and gave directions for 'a young man to be got in,' to wrestle with the luggage. When that gladiator had disappeared from the arena, peace ensued, and the new lodgers dined.

But the Billickin had somehow come to the knowledge that Miss

Twinkleton kept a school. The leap from that knowledge to the inference that Miss Twinkleton would set herself to teach *her* something, was easy. 'But you don't do it,' soliloquized the Billickin; '*I* am not your pupil, whatever she,' meaning Rosa, 'may be, poor thing!'

Miss Twinkleton, on the other hand, having changed her dress and recovered her spirits, was animated by a bland desire to improve the occasion in all ways, and to be as serene a model as possible. In a happy compromise between her two states of existence, she had already become, with her work-basket before her, the equally vivacious companion with a slight judicious flavoring of information, when the Billickin announced herself.

'I will not hide from you, ladies,' said the B, enveloped in the shawl of state, 'for it is not my character to hide neither my motives nor my actions, that I take the liberty to look in upon you to express a 'ope that your dinner was to your liking. Though not Professed but Plain,[30] still her wages should be a sufficient object to her to stimilate to soar above mere roast and biled.'

'We dined very well indeed,' said Rosa, 'thank you.'

'Accustomed,' said Miss Twinkleton, with a gracious air which to the jealous ears of the Billickin seemed to add 'my good woman': – 'Accustomed to a liberal and nutritious, yet plain and salutary diet, we have found no reason to bemoan our absence from the ancient city, and the methodical household, in which the quiet routine of our lot has been hitherto cast.'

'I did think it well to mention to my cook,' observed the Billickin with a gush of candour, 'which I 'ope you will agree with me, Miss Twinkleton, was a right precaution, that the young lady being used to what we should consider here but poor diet, had better be brought forard by degrees. For a rush from scanty feeding to generous feeding, and from what you may call messing to what you may call method, do require a power of constitution which is not often found in youth, particular when undermined by boarding-school.'

It will be seen that the Billickin now openly pitted herself against Miss Twinkleton, as one whom she had fully ascertained to be her natural enemy.

'Your remarks,' returned Miss Twinkleton, from a remote moral eminence, 'are well meant, I have no doubt; but you will permit me to observe that they develop a mistaken view of the subject, which can only be imputed to your extreme want of accurate information.'

'My informiation,' retorted the Billickin, throwing in an extra syllable for the sake of an emphasis at once polite and powerful; 'my informiation, Miss Twinkleton, were my own experience, which I believe is usually considered to be good guidance. But whether so or not, I was put in youth to a very genteel boarding-school, the mistress being no less a lady than yourself, of about your own age or it may be some years younger, and a poorness of blood flowed from the table which has run through my life.'

'Very likely,' said Miss Twinkleton, still from her distant eminence; 'and very much to be deplored. Rosa, my dear, how are you getting on with your work?'

'Miss Twinkleton,' resumed the Billickin, in a courtly manner, 'before retiring on the 'Int, as a lady should, I wish to ask of yourself, as a lady, whether I am to consider that my words is doubted?'

'I am not aware on what ground you cherish such a supposition,' began Miss Twinkleton, when the Billickin neatly stopped her.

'Do not, if you please, put suppositions betwixt my lips where none such have been imported by myself. Your flow of words is great, Miss Twinkleton, and no doubt is expected from you by your pupils, and no doubt is considered worth the money. *No* doubt, I am sure. But not paying for flows of words, and not asking to be faviored with them here, I wish to repeat my question.'

'If you refer to the poverty of your circulation –' began Miss Twinkleton again, when again the Billickin neatly stopped her.

'I have used no such expressions.'

'If you refer, then, to the poorness of your blood –'

'Brought upon me,' stipulated the Billickin, expressly, 'at a boarding-school.'

'Then,' resumed Miss Twinkleton, 'all I can say is, that I am bound to believe, on your asseveration, that it is very poor indeed. I cannot forbear adding, that if that unfortunate circumstance influences your conversation, it is much to be lamented, and it is eminently desirable that your blood were richer. Rosa, my dear, how are you getting on with your work?'

'Hem! Before retiring, Miss,' proclaimed the Billickin to Rosa, loftily cancelling Miss Twinkleton, 'I should wish it to be understood between yourself and me that my transactions in future is with you alone. I know no elderly lady here, Miss; none older than yourself.'

'A highly desirable arrangement, Rosa my dear,' observed Miss Twinkleton.

'It is not, Miss,' said the Billickin, with a sarcastic smile, 'that I possess the Mill I have heard of, in which old single ladies could be ground up young[31] (what a gift it would be to some of us!), but that I limit myself to you totally.'

'When I have any desire to communicate a request to the person of the house, Rosa my dear,' observed Miss Twinkleton with majestic cheerfulness, 'I will make it known to you, and you will kindly undertake, I am sure, that it is conveyed to the proper quarter.'

'Good-evening, Miss,' said the Billickin, at once affectionately and distantly. 'Being alone in my eyes, I wish you good-evening with best wishes, and do not find myself drove, I am truly 'appy to say, into expressing my contempt for any indiwidual, unfortunately for yourself, belonging to you.'

The Billickin gracefully withdrew with this parting speech, and from that time Rosa occupied the restless position of shuttlecock between these two battledores. Nothing could be done without a smart match being played out. Thus, on the daily-arising question of dinner, Miss Twinkleton would say; the three being present together:

'Perhaps, my love, you will consult with the person of the house, whether she could procure us a lamb's fry;[32] or, failing that, a roast fowl.'

On which the Billickin would retort (Rosa not having spoken a word), 'If you was better accustomed to butcher's-meat, Miss, you would not entertain the idea of a lamb's fry. Firstly, because lambs has long been sheep, and secondly, because there is such things as killing-days,[33] and there is not. As to roast fowls, Miss, why you must be quite surfeited with roast fowls, letting alone your buying, when you market for yourself, the agedest of poultry with the scaliest of legs, quite as if you was accustomed to picking 'em out for cheapness. Try a little inwention, Miss. Use yourself to 'ousekeeping a bit. Come now, think of somethink else.'

To this encouragement, offered with the indulgent toleration of a wise and liberal expert, Miss Twinkleton would rejoin, reddening:

'Or, my dear, you might propose to the person of the house, a duck.'

'Well, Miss!' the Billickin would exclaim (still no word being spoken by Rosa), 'you do surprise me when you speak of ducks! Not to mention that they're getting out of season and very dear, it really strikes to my heart to see you have a duck; for the breast, which is the only delicate cuts in a duck, always goes in a direction which I cannot imagine where, and your own plate comes down so miserable skin-and-bony! Try again, Miss. Think more of yourself and less of others. A dish of sweetbreads, now, or a bit of mutton. Somethink at which you can get your equal chance.'

Occasionally the game would wax very brisk indeed, and would be kept up with a smartness rendering such an encounter as this quite tame. But the Billickin almost invariably made by far the higher score; and would come in with side hits of the most unexpected and extraordinary description, when she seemed without a chance.

All this did not improve the gritty state of things in London, or the air that London had acquired in Rosa's eyes of waiting for something that never came. Tired of working and conversing with Miss Twinkleton, she suggested working and reading: to which Miss Twinkleton readily assented, as an admired reader, of tried powers. But Rosa soon made the discovery that Miss Twinkleton didn't read fairly. She cut the love scenes, interpolated passages in praise of female celibacy, and was guilty of other glaring pious frauds. As an instance in point, take the glowing passage: 'Ever dearest and best adored, said Edward, clasping the dear head to his breast, and drawing the silken hair through his caressing fingers, from which he suffered it to fall like golden rain; ever dearest and best adored, let us fly from the unsympathetic world and the sterile coldness of the stony-hearted, to the rich warm Paradise of Trust and Love.' Miss Twinkleton's fraudulent version tamely ran thus: 'Ever engaged to me with the consent of our parents on both sides, and the approbation of the silver-haired rector of the district, said Edward, respectfully raising to his lips the taper fingers so skilful in embroidery, tambour, crochet, and other truly feminine arts; let me call on thy papa ere to-morrow's dawn has sunk into the west, and propose a suburban establishment, lowly it may be, but within our means, where he will be always welcome as an evening guest, and where every arrangement shall invest economy and the constant interchange of scholastic acquirements with the attributes of the ministering angel to domestic bliss.'

As the days crept on and nothing happened, the neighbours began to say that the pretty girl at Billickin's, who looked so wistfully and so much out of the gritty windows of the drawing-room, seemed to be losing her spirits. The pretty girl might have lost them but for the accident of lighting on some books of voyages and sea-adventure. As a compensation against their romance, Miss Twinkleton, reading aloud, made the most of all the latitudes and longitudes, bearings, winds, currents, offsets, and other statistics (which she felt to be none the less improving because they expressed nothing whatever to her); while Rosa, listening intently, made the most of what was nearest to her heart. So they both did better than before.

CHAPTER 23

The Dawn Again

Although Mr Crisparkle and John Jasper met daily under the Cathedral roof, nothing at any time passed between them bearing reference to Edwin Drood after the time, more than half a year gone by, when Jasper mutely showed the Minor Canon the conclusion and the resolution entered in his Diary. It is not likely that they ever met, though so often, without the thoughts of each reverting to the subject. It is not likely that they ever met, though so often, without a sensation on the part of each that the other was a perplexing secret to him. Jasper as the denouncer and pursuer of Neville Landless, and Mr Crisparkle as his consistent advocate and protector, must at least have stood sufficiently in opposition to have speculated with keen interest each on the steadiness and next direction of the other's designs. But neither ever broached the theme.

False pretence not being in the Minor Canon's nature, he doubtless displayed openly that he would at any time have revived the subject, and even desired to discuss it. The determined reticence of Jasper, however, was not to be so approached. Impassive, moody, solitary, resolute, concentrated on one idea, and on its attendant fixed purpose that he would share it with no fellow creature, he lived apart from human life. Constantly exercising an Art which brought him into mechanical harmony with others, and which could not have been pursued unless he and they had been in the nicest mechanical relations and unison, it is curious to consider that the spirit of the man was in moral accordance or interchange with nothing around him. This indeed he had confided to his lost nephew, before the occasion for his present inflexibility arose.

That he must know of Rosa's abrupt departure, and that he must divine its cause, was not to be doubted. Did he suppose that he had terrified her into silence, or did he suppose that she had imparted to any one – to Mr Crisparkle himself, for instance – the particulars of his last interview with her? Mr Crisparkle could not determine this in his mind. He could not but admit, however, as a just man, that it was not, of itself, a crime to fall in love with Rosa, any more than it was a crime to offer to set love above revenge.

The dreadful suspicion of Jasper, which Rosa was so shocked to have received into her imagination, appeared to have no harbour in Mr Crisparkle's. If it ever haunted Helena's thoughts or Neville's, neither gave it one spoken word of utterance. Mr Grewgious took no pains to conceal his implacable dislike of Jasper, yet he never referred it, however distantly, to such a source. But he was a reticent as well as an eccentric man; and he made no mention of a certain evening when he warmed his hands at the Gate House fire, and looked steadily down upon a certain heap of torn and miry clothes upon the floor.

Drowsy Cloisterham, whenever it awoke to a passing reconsideration of a story above six months old and dismissed by the bench of magistrates, was pretty equally divided in opinion whether John Jasper's beloved nephew had been killed by his passionate rival treacherously, or in an open struggle; or had, for his own purposes, spirited himself away. It then lifted up its head, to notice that the bereaved Jasper was still ever devoted to discovery and revenge; and then dozed off again. This was the condition of matters, all round, at the period to which the present history has now attained.

The Cathedral doors have closed for the night; and the Choir-Master, on a short leave of absence for two or three services, sets his face towards London. He travels thither by the means by which Rosa travelled, and arrives, as Rosa arrived, on a hot, dusty evening.

His travelling baggage is easily carried in his hand, and he repairs with it, on foot, to a hybrid hotel in a little square behind Aldersgate Street, near the General Post Office.[1] It is hotel, boarding-house, or lodging-house, at its visitor's option. It announces itself as a novel enterprise in the new Railway Advertisers[2] timidly beginning to spring up. It bashfully, almost apologetically, gives the traveller to understand that it does not expect him, on the good old constitutional hotel plan, to order a pint of sweet blacking[3] for his drinking, and throw it away; but insinuates that he may have his boots blacked instead of his stomach, and maybe also have bed, breakfast, attendance, and a porter up all night, for a certain fixed charge. From these and similar premises, many true Britons in the lowest spirits deduce that the times are levelling times, except in the article of high roads, of which there will shortly be not one in England.[4]

He eats without appetite, and soon goes forth again. Eastward and still eastward through the stale streets he takes his way, until he reaches his destination: a miserable court, specially miserable among many such.

He ascends a broken staircase, opens a door, looks into a dark stifling room, and says: 'Are you alone here?'

'Alone, deary; worse luck for me, and better for you,' replies a croaking voice. 'Come in, come in, whoever you be: I can't see you till I light a match, yet I seem to know the sound of your speaking. I am acquainted with you; ain't I?'

'Light your match, and try.'

'So I will, deary, so I will; but my hand that shakes, as I can't lay it on a match all in a moment. And I cough so, that, put my matches where I may, I never find 'em there. They jump and start as I cough and cough, like live things. Are you off a voyage, deary?'

'No.'

'Not seafaring?'

'No.'

'Well, there's land customers, and there's water customers. I'm a mother to both. Different from Jack Chinaman t'other side the court. He ain't a father to neither. It ain't in him. And he ain't got the true secret of mixing, though he charges as much as me that has, and more if he can get it. Here's a match, and now where's the candle? If my cough takes me, I shall cough out twenty matches afore I gets a light.'

But she finds the candle, and lights it, before the cough comes on. It seizes her in the moment of success, and she sits down rocking herself to and fro, and gasping at intervals, 'Oh, my lungs is awful bad, my lungs is wore away to cabbage-nets!'[5] until the fit is over. During its continuance she has had no power of sight, or any other power not absorbed in the struggle; but as it leaves her, she begins to strain her eyes, and as soon as she is able to articulate, she cries, staring:

'Why, it's you!'

'Are you so surprised to see me?'

'I thought I never should have seen you again, deary. I thought you was dead, and gone to Heaven.'

'Why?'

'I didn't suppose you could have kept away, alive, so long, from the poor old soul with the real receipt for mixing it! And you are in mourning too! Why didn't you come and have a pipe or two of comfort? Did they leave you money, perhaps, and so you didn't want comfort?'

'No!'

'Who was they as died, deary?'

'A relation.'

'Died of what, lovey?'[6]

'Probably, Death.'

'We are short to-night!' cries the woman, with a propitiatory laugh. 'Short and snappish, we are! But we're out of sorts for want of a smoke. We've got the all-overs,[7] haven't us, deary? But this is the place to cure 'em in; this is the place where the all-overs is smoked off.'

'You may make ready, then,' replies the visitor, 'as soon as you like.'

He divests himself of his shoes, loosens his cravat, and lies across the foot of the squalid bed, with his head resting on his left hand.

'Now, you begin to look like yourself,' says the woman, approvingly. 'Now I begin to know my old customer indeed! Been trying to mix for yourself this long time, poppet?'

'I have been taking it now and then in my own way.'

'Never take it your own way. It ain't good for trade and it ain't good for you. Where's my ink bottle, and where's my thimble, and where's my little spoon? He's going to take it in a artful form now, my deary dear!'

Entering on her process, and beginning to bubble and blow at the faint spark enclosed in the hollow of her hands, she speaks from time to time, in a tone of snuffling satisfaction, without breaking off; when he speaks, he does so without looking at her, and as if his thoughts were already roaming away by anticipation.

'I've got a pretty many smokes ready for you, first and last; haven't I, chuckey?'

'A good many.'

'When you first come, you was quite new to it; warn't ye?'

'Yes, I was easily disposed of, then.'

'But you got on in the world, and was able by-and-bye to take your pipes with the best of 'em, warn't ye?'

'Aye. And the worst.'

'It's just ready for you. What a sweet singer you was when you first come! Used to drop your head, and sing yourself off, like a bird! It's ready for you now, deary.'

He takes it from her with great care, and puts the mouthpiece to his lips. She seats herself beside him, ready to refill the pipe. After inhaling a few whiffs in silence, he doubtingly accosts her with:

'Is it as potent as it used to be?'

'What do you speak of, deary?'

'What should I speak of, but what I have in my mouth!'

'It's just the same. Always the identical same.'

'It doesn't taste so. And it's slower.'

'You've got more used to it, you see.'

'That may be the cause, certainly. Look here.' He stops, becomes dreamy, and seems to forget that he has invited her attention. She bends over him, and speaks in his ear.

'I'm attending to you. Says you just now, look here. Says I now, I am attending to ye. We was talking just before of your being used to it.'

'I know all that. I was only thinking. Look here. Suppose you had something in your mind; something you were going to do.'

'Yes, deary; something I was going to do?'

'But had not quite determined to do.'

'Yes, deary.'

'Might or might not do, you understand.'

'Yes.' With the point of a needle she stirs the contents of the bowl.

'Should you do it in your fancy, when you were lying here doing this?'

She nods her head. 'Over and over again.'

'Just like me! I did it over and over again.[8] I have done it hundreds of thousands of times in this room.'

'It's to be hoped it was pleasant to do, deary.'

'It *was* pleasant to do!'

He says this with a savage air, and a spring or start at her. Quite unmoved, she retouches or replenishes the contents of the bowl with her little spatula. Seeing her intent upon the occupation, he sinks into his former attitude.

'It was a journey, a difficult and dangerous journey. That was the subject in my mind. A hazardous and perilous journey, over abysses where a slip would be destruction. Look down, look down! You see what lies at the bottom there?'

He has darted forward to say it, and to point at the ground, as though at some imaginary object far beneath. The woman looks at him, as his spasmodic face approaches close to hers, and not at his pointing. She seems to know what the influence of her perfect quietude will be; if so, she has not miscalculated it, for he subsides again.

'Well; I have told you. I did it, here, hundreds of thousands of times. What do I say? I did it millions and billions of times. I did it so often, and through such vast expanses of time, that when it was really done, it seemed not worth the doing,[9] it was done so soon.'

'That's the journey you have been away upon?' she quietly remarks.

He glares at her as he smokes; and then, his eyes becoming filmy, answers: 'That's the journey.'

Silence ensues. His eyes are sometimes closed and sometimes open. The woman sits beside him, very attentive to the pipe, which is all the while at his lips.

'I'll warrant,' she observes, when he has been looking fixedly at her for some consecutive moments, with a singular appearance in his eyes of seeming to see her a long way off, instead of so near him: 'I'll warrant you made the journey in a many ways, when you made it so often?'

'No, always in one way.'

'Always in the same way?'

'Aye.'

'In the way in which it was really made at last?'

'Aye.'

'And always took the same pleasure in harping on it?'

'Aye.'

For the time he appears unequal to any other reply than this lazy monosyllabic assent. Probably to assure herself that it is not the assent of a mere automaton, she reverses the form of her next sentence.

'Did you never get tired of it, deary, and try to call up something else for a change?'

He struggles into a sitting posture, and retorts upon her: 'What do you mean? What did I want? What did I come for?'

She gently lays him back again, and, before returning him the instrument he has dropped, revives the fire in it with her own breath; then says to him, coaxingly:

'Sure, sure, sure! Yes, yes, yes! Now I go along with you. You was too quick for me. I see now. You come o' purpose to take the journey. Why, I might have known it, through its standing by you so.'

He answers, first with a laugh, and then with a passionate setting of his teeth: 'Yes, I came on purpose. When I could not bear my life, I came to get the relief, and I got it. It WAS one! It WAS one!' This repetition with extraordinary vehemence, and the snarl of a wolf.

She observes him very cautiously, as though mentally feeling her way to her next remark. It is: 'There was a fellow-traveller, deary.'

'Ha ha ha!' He breaks into a ringing laugh, or rather yell.

'To think,' he cries, 'how often fellow-traveller, and yet not know it! To think how many times he went the journey, and never saw the road!'

The woman kneels upon the floor, with her arms crossed on the coverlet of the bed, close by him, and her chin upon them. In this crouching attitude she watches him. The pipe is falling from his mouth. She puts it back, and, laying her hand upon his chest, moves him slightly from side to side. Upon that he speaks, as if she had spoken.

'Yes! I always made the journey first, before the changes of colors and the great landscapes and glittering processions began. They couldn't begin till it was off my mind. I had no room till then for anything else.'

Once more he lapses into silence. Once more she lays her hand upon his chest, and moves him slightly to and fro, as a cat might stimulate a half-slain mouse. Once more he speaks, as if she had spoken.

'What? I told you so. When it comes to be real at last, it is so short that it seems unreal for the first time. Hark!'

'Yes, deary. I'm listening.'

'Time and place are both at hand.'[10]

He is on his feet, speaking in a whisper, and as if in the dark.

'Time, place, and fellow-traveller,' she suggests, adopting his tone, and holding him softly by the arm.

'How could the time be at hand unless the fellow-traveller was? Hush! The journey's made. It's over.'

'So soon?'

'That's what I said to you. So soon. Wait a little. This is a vision. I

Sleeping it off

shall sleep it off. It has been too short and easy. I must have a better vision than this; this is the poorest of all. No struggle, no consciousness of peril, no entreaty – and yet I never saw *that* before.' With a start.

'Saw what, deary?'

'Look at it! Look what a poor, mean, miserable thing it is! *That* must be real. It's over!'

He has accompanied this incoherence with some wild unmeaning gestures; but they trail off into the progressive inaction of stupor, and he lies a log upon the bed.

The woman, however, is still inquisitive. With a repetition of her catlike action she slightly stirs his body again, and listens; stirs it again, and listens; whispers to it, and listens. Finding it past all rousing for the time, she slowly gets upon her feet, with an air of disappointment, and flicks the face with the back of her hand in turning from it.

But she goes no further away[11] from it than the chair upon the hearth. She sits in it, with an elbow on one of its arms, and her chin upon that hand, intent upon him. 'I heard ye say once,' she croaks under her breath, 'I heard ye say once, when I was lying where you're lying, and you were making your speculations upon me, "Unintelligible!" I heard you say so, of two more than me. But don't ye be too sure always; don't ye be too sure, beauty!'

Unwinking, catlike, and intent, she presently adds: 'Not so potent as it once was? Ah! Perhaps not at first. Ye may be more right there. Practice makes perfect. I may have learned the secret how to make ye talk, my deary.'

He talks no more, whether or no. Twitching in an ugly way from time to time, both as to his face and limbs, he lies heavy and silent. The wretched candle burns down; the woman takes its expiring end between her fingers, lights another at it, crams the guttering frying morsel deep into the candlestick, and rams it home with the new candle, as if she were loading some ill-savoured and unseemly weapon of witchcraft; the new candle in its turn burns down; and still he lies insensible. At length what remains of the last candle is blown out, and daylight looks into the room.

It has not looked very long, when he sits up, chilled and shaking, slowly recovers consciousness of where he is, and makes himself ready to depart. The woman receives what he pays her with a grateful 'Bless ye, bless ye, deary!' and seems, tired out, to begin making herself ready for sleep as he leaves the room.

But seeming may be false or true. It is false in this case, for the moment the stairs had ceased to creak under his tread, she glides after him, muttering emphatically: 'I'll not miss ye twice!'

There is no egress from the court but by its entrance. With a weird peep from the doorway, she watches for his looking back. He does not look back before disappearing, with a wavering step. She follows him, peeps from the court, sees him still faltering on without looking back, and holds him in view.

He repairs to the back of Aldersgate Street, where a door immediately opens to his knocking. She crouches in another doorway, watching that one, and easily comprehending that he puts up temporarily at that house. Her patience is unexhausted by hours. For sustenance she can, and does, buy bread within a hundred yards, and milk as it is carried past her.[12]

He comes forth again at noon, having changed his dress, but carrying nothing in his hand, and having nothing carried for him. He is not going back into the country, therefore, just yet. She follows him a little way, hesitates instantaneously, turns confidently and goes straight into the house he has quitted.

Is the gentleman from Cloisterham indoors?

Just gone out.

Unlucky. When does the gentleman return to Cloisterham?

At six this evening.

Bless ye and thank ye. May the Lord prosper a business where a civil question, even from a poor soul, is so civilly answered!

'I'll not miss ye twice!' repeats the poor soul in the street, and not so civilly. 'I lost ye last, where that omnibus you got into nigh your journey's end plied betwixt the station and the place. I wasn't so much as certain that you even went right on to the place. Now I know ye did. My gentleman from Cloisterham, I'll be there before ye and bide your coming. I've swore my oath that I'll not miss ye twice!'

Accordingly, that same evening the poor soul stands in Cloisterham High Street, looking at the many quaint gables of the Nuns' House, and getting through the time as she best can until nine o'clock; at which hour she has reason to suppose that the arriving omnibus passengers may have some interest for her. The friendly darkness, at that hour, renders it easy for her to ascertain whether this be so or not; and it is so, for the passenger not to be missed twice arrives among the rest.

'Now, let me see what becomes of you. Go on!'

An observation addressed to the air. And yet it might be addressed to the passenger, so compliantly does he go on along the High Street until he comes to an arched gateway, at which he unexpectedly vanishes. The poor soul quickens her pace; is swift, and close upon him in turning under the gateway; but only sees a postern staircase on one side of it, and on the other side an ancient vaulted room, in which a large-headed, grey-haired gentleman[13] is writing, under the odd circumstances of sitting open to the thoroughfare and eyeing all who pass, as if he were toll-taker at the gateway: though the way is free.

'Halloa!' he cries in a low voice, seeing her brought to a standstill: 'Who are you looking for?'

'There was a gentleman passed in here this minute, sir. Gentleman in mourning.'

'Of course there was. What do you want with him?'

'Where do he live, deary?'

'Live? Up that staircase.'

'Bless ye! Whisper. What's his name, deary?'

'Surname Jasper, Christian name John. Mr John Jasper.'

'Has he a calling, good gentleman?'

'Calling? Yes. Sings in the choir.'

'In the spire?'

'Choir.'

'What's that?'

Mr Datchery rises from his papers, and comes to his doorstep. 'Do you know what a cathedral is?' he asks, jocosely.

The woman nods.

'What is it?'

She looks puzzled, casting about in her mind to find a definition, when it occurs to her that it is easier to point out the substantial object itself, massive against the dark-blue sky and the early stars.

'That's the answer. Go in there at seven to-morrow morning, and you may see Mr John Jasper, and hear him too.'

'Thank ye! Thank ye!'

The burst of triumph in which she thanks him does not escape the notice of the single buffer of an easy temper living idly on his means. He glances at her; clasps his hands behind him, as the wont of such buffers is, and lounges along the echoing Precincts at her side.

'Or,' he suggests, with a backward hitch of his head, 'you can go up at once to Mr Jasper's rooms there.'

The woman eyes him with a cunning smile, and shakes her head.

'Oh! You don't want to speak to him?'

She repeats her dumb reply, and forms with her lips a soundless 'No.'

'You can admire him at a distance three times a day, whenever you like. It's a long way to come for that, though.'

The woman looks up quickly. If Mr Datchery thinks she is to be so induced to declare where she comes from, he is of a much easier temper than she is. But she acquits him of such an artful thought, as he lounges along, like the chartered bore of the city, with his uncovered grey hair blowing about, and his purposeless hands rattling the loose money in the pockets of his trousers.

The chink of the money has an attraction for her greedy ears. 'Wouldn't you help me to pay for my traveller's lodging, dear gentleman, and to pay my way along? I am a poor soul, I am indeed, and troubled with a grievous cough.'

'You know the travellers' lodging, I perceive, and are making direct for it,' is Mr Datchery's bland comment, still rattling his loose money. 'Been here often, my good woman?'

'Once in all my life.'

'Aye, aye?'

They have arrived at the entrance to the Monks' Vineyard. An appropriate remembrance, presenting an exemplary model for imitation, is revived in the woman's mind by the sight of the place. She stops at the gate, and says energetically:

'By this token, though you mayn't believe it, that a young gentleman gave me three and sixpence as I was coughing my breath away
on this very grass. I asked him for three and sixpence, and he gave it
me.'

'Wasn't it a little cool to name your sum?' hints Mr Datchery, still
rattling. 'Isn't it customary to leave the amount open? Mightn't it have
had the appearance, to the young gentleman – only the appearance –
that he was rather dictated to?'

'Look'ee here, deary,' she replies, in a confidential and persuasive
tone, 'I wanted the money to lay it out on a medicine as does me good,
and as I deal in. I told the young gentleman so, and he gave it me, and
I laid it out honest to the last brass farden. I want to lay out the same
sum in the same way now; and if you'll give it me, I'll lay it out honest
to the last brass farden again, upon my soul!'

'What's the medicine?'

'I'll be honest with you beforehand, as well as after. It's opium.'

Mr Datchery, with a sudden change of countenance, gives her a
sudden look.[14]

'It's opium, deary. Neither more nor less. And it's like a human
creetur so far, that you always hear what can be said against it, but
seldom what can be said in its praise!'

Mr Datchery begins very slowly to count out the sum demanded of
him. Greedily watching his hands, she continues to hold forth on the
great example set him.

'It was last Christmas Eve, just arter dark, the once that I was here
afore, when the young gentleman gave me the three and six.'

Mr Datchery stops in his counting, finds he has counted wrong,
shakes his money together, and begins again.

'And the young gentleman's name,' she adds, 'was Edwin.'

Mr Datchery drops some money, stoops to pick it up, and reddens
with the exertion as he asks:

'How do you know the young gentleman's name?'

'I asked him for it, and he told it me. I only asked him the two
questions, what was his Chris'en name, and whether he'd a sweetheart?
And he answered, Edwin, and he hadn't.'

Mr Datchery pauses with the selected coins in his hand, rather as if he were falling into a brown study of their value, and couldn't bear to part with them. The woman looks at him distrustfully, and with her anger brewing for the event of his thinking better of the gift; but he bestows it on her as if he were abstracting his mind from the sacrifice, and with many servile thanks she goes her way.

John Jasper's lamp is kindled, and his Lighthouse is shining when Mr Datchery returns alone towards it. As mariners on a dangerous voyage, approaching an iron-bound coast, may look along the beams of the warning light to the haven lying beyond it that may never be reached, so Mr Datchery's wistful gaze is directed to this beacon, and beyond.

His object in now revisiting his lodging is merely to put on the hat which seems so superfluous an article in his wardrobe. It is half-past ten by the Cathedral clock when he walks out into the Precincts again; he lingers and looks about him, as though, the enchanted hour when Mr Durdles may be stoned home having struck, he had some expectation of seeing the Imp who is appointed to the mission of stoning him.

In effect, that Power of Evil is abroad. Having nothing living to stone at the moment, he is discovered by Mr Datchery in the unholy office of stoning the dead, through the railings of the churchyard. The Imp finds this a relishing and piquing pursuit; firstly, because their resting-place is announced to be sacred; and secondly, because the tall headstones are sufficiently like themselves, on their beat in the dark, to justify the delicious fancy that they are hurt when hit.

Mr Datchery hails him with: 'Halloa, Winks!'

He acknowledges the hail with: 'Halloa, Dick!' Their acquaintance seemingly having been established on a familiar footing.

'But, I say,' he remonstrates, 'don't yer go a making my name public. I never means to plead to no name, mind yer. When they says to me in the Lock-up, a goin to put me down in the book, "What's your name?" I says to them "Find out." Likeways when they says "What's your religion?" I says "Find out."' Which, it may be observed in passing, it would be immensely difficult for the State, however Statistical, to do.[15]

'Asides which,' adds the boy, 'there ain't no family of Winkses.'

'I think there must be.'

'Yer lie, there ain't. The travellers give me the name on account of my getting no settled sleep and being knocked up all night; whereby I gits one eye roused open afore I've shut the other. That's what Winks means. Deputy's the nighest name to indict me by: but yer wouldn't catch me pleading to that, neither.'

'Deputy be it always, then. We two are good friends; eh, Deputy?'

'Jolly good.'

'I forgave you the debt you owed me when we first became acquainted, and many of my sixpences have come your way since; eh, Deputy?'

'Ah! And what's more, yer ain't no friend o' Jarsper's. What did he go a histing me off my legs for?'

'What indeed! But never mind him now. A shilling of mine is coming your way to-night, Deputy. You have just taken in a lodger I have been speaking to; an infirm woman with a cough.'

'Puffer,' assents Deputy, with a shrewd leer of recognition, and smoking an imaginary pipe with his head very much on one side and his eyes rolling very much out of their places: 'Hopeum Puffer.'

'What is her name?'

'Er Royal Highness the Princess Puffer.'

'She has some other name than that. Where does she live?'

'Up in London. Among the Jacks.'

'The sailors?'

'I said so; Jacks. And Chaynermen. And hother Knifers.'[16]

'I should like to know, through you, exactly where she lives.'

'All right. Give us 'old.'

A shilling passes; and, in that spirit of confidence which should pervade all business transactions between principals of honor, this piece of business is considered done.

'But here's a lark!' cries Deputy. 'Where do yer think Er Royal Highness is a goin to to-morrow morning? Blest if she ain't a goin to the KIN-FREE-DER-EL!' He greatly prolongs the word in his ecstasy, and smites his leg, and doubles himself up in a fit of shrill laughter.

'How do you know that, Deputy?'

'Cos she told me so just now. She said she must be hup and hout o' purpose. She ses, "Deputy, I must 'ave a early wash, and make myself as swell as I can, for I'm a goin to take a turn at the KIN-FREE-DER-EL!"'

He separates the syllables with his former zest, and, not finding his sense of the ludicrous sufficiently relieved by stamping about on the pavement, breaks into a slow and stately dance, perhaps supposed to be performed by the Dean.

Mr Datchery receives the communication with a well satisfied though a pondering face, and breaks up the conference. Returning to his quaint lodging, and sitting long over the supper of bread and cheese and salad and ale which Mrs Tope has left prepared for him, he still sits when his supper is finished. At length he rises, throws open the door of a corner cupboard, and refers to a few uncouth chalked strokes on its inner side.

'I like,' says Mr Datchery, 'the old tavern way of keeping scores.[17] Illegible except to the scorer. The scorer not committed, the scored debited with what is against him. Humph! A very small score this, a very poor score!'

He sighs over the contemplation of its poverty, takes a bit of chalk from one of the cupboard shelves, and pauses with it in his hand, uncertain what addition to make to the account. 'I think a moderate stroke,' he concludes, 'is all I am justified in scoring up;' so, suits the action to the word, closes the cupboard, and goes to bed.

A brilliant morning shines[18] on the old city. Its antiquities and ruins are surpassingly beautiful, with the lusty ivy gleaming in the sun, and the rich trees waving in the balmy air. Changes of glorious light from moving boughs, songs of birds, scents from gardens, woods, and fields – or rather, from the one great garden of the whole cultivated island[19] in its yielding time – penetrate into the Cathedral, subdue its earthy odour, and preach the Resurrection and the Life.[20] The cold stone tombs of centuries ago grow warm, and flecks of brightness dart into the sternest marble corners of the building, fluttering there like wings.

Comes Mr Tope with his large keys, and yawningly unlocks and sets open. Come Mrs Tope and attendant sweeping sprites. Come, in due time, organist and bellows-boy, peeping down from the red curtains in the loft, fearlessly flapping dust from books up at that remote elevation, and whisking it from stops and pedals. Come sundry rooks, from various quarters of the sky, back to the great tower; who may be presumed to enjoy vibration, and to know that bell and organ are going to give it them. Come a very small and straggling congregation indeed: chiefly from Minor Canon Corner and the Precincts. Come Mr Crisparkle, fresh and bright; and his ministering brethren, not quite so fresh and bright. Come the Choir in a hurry (always in a hurry, and struggling into their nightgowns at the last moment, like children shirking bed), and comes John Jasper leading their line.[21] Last of all comes Mr Datchery into a stall, one of a choice empty collection very much at his service, and glancing about him for Her Royal Highness the Princess Puffer.

The service is pretty well advanced before Mr Datchery can discern Her Royal Highness. But by that time he has made her out, in the shade. She is behind a pillar, carefully withdrawn from the Choir Master's view, but regards him with the closest attention. All unconscious of her presence, he chants and sings. She grins when he is most musically fervid, and – yes, Mr Datchery sees her do it! – shakes her fist at him behind the pillar's friendly shelter.

Mr Datchery looks again to convince himself. Yes, again! As ugly and withered as one of the fantastic carvings on the under brackets of the stall seats, as malignant as the Evil One, as hard as the big brass eagle holding the sacred books upon his wings (and, according to the sculptor's presentation of his ferocious attributes, not at all converted by them), she hugs herself in her lean arms, and then shakes both fists at the leader of the Choir.

And at that moment, outside the grated door of the Choir, having eluded the vigilance of Mr Tope by shifty resources in which he is an adept, Deputy peeps, sharp-eyed, through the bars, and stares astounded from the threatener to the threatened.

The service comes to an end, and the servitors disperse to breakfast. Mr Datchery accosts his last new acquaintance outside, when the Choir (as much in a hurry to get their bedgowns off, as they were but now to get them on) have scuffled away.

'Well, mistress. Good morning. You have seen him?'

'*I*'ve seen him, deary; *I*'ve seen him!'

'And you know him?'

'Know him! Better far, than all the Reverend Parsons put together know him.'

Mrs Tope's care has spread a very neat, clean breakfast ready for her lodger. Before sitting down to it, he opens his corner-cupboard door; takes his bit of chalk from its shelf; adds one thick line to the score, extending from the top of the cupboard-door to the bottom; and then falls to with an appetite.[22]

The 'Sapsea Fragment'

Editors of *The Mystery of Edwin Drood* properly include the enigmatic 'Sapsea Fragment' and the few facts associated with these extant manuscript pages. Five in all, the half-sheets begin with a new paragraph and break off in mid-sentence. Each slip of paper measures approximately 7¼ by 4½ inches. All are numbered consecutively in Dickens's hand from 6 to 10 at the top centre; no trace of the preceding five survives. What remains is a portion of an incident told by Mr Sapsea. In it he describes the occasion of his expulsion from a cribbage club to which he belongs, and introduces three characters new to the novel. One of them, Poker, bears some resemblance to Mr Datchery when he and Mr Sapsea meet and converse. Possibly the pages that went before account for the circumstances of how Mr Sapsea came to be relating this episode.

The discovery of the fragment belongs to John Forster. 'Within the leaves of one of Dickens's other manuscripts', he explains, 'were found some detached slips of his writing.' Though cramped, interlined and blotted, they proved, on inspection, Forster continued, to relate to *The Mystery of Edwin Drood*. Accompanying his description of the incident is Forster's hypothesis that the pages represent Dickens's attempt to 'open some fresh veins of character' in order to divert attention from the catastrophe into which he had inadvertently plunged 'too soon'.[1] As a delaying tactic, Forster's explanation has little to offer. Rather, the fragment comes too late in the plot to offset speculation about Edwin's fate, and, as Margaret Cardwell notes, 'Poker's introduction is a parallel too close to that of Datchery to be a likely additional interest.'[2]

The speculations of subsequent commentators seem to rest on firmer grounds. Rather than serving as a possible narrative departure, the fragment represents an early trial, a first attempt to bring in the vitally important 'detective' character. Hesitating and then rewriting, Dickens makes headway after a start he subsequently abandoned in favour of the introduction of Datchery as the 'single buffer' of Chapter 18, who settles in Cloisterham in search of 'an architectural lodging', something 'Cathedraly'. Some differences exist between Margaret Cardwell and Arthur Cox, but both support the view that the fragment belongs to the period when Dickens was at work on the novel. Most reasonably, according to Cardwell, the extant pages represent a rejected draft of Datchery, written perhaps at the time of the composition of the fifth and sixth numbers. Cox, however, proposes an earlier date: possibly after Dickens learned that his first two monthly numbers were short. The fact that Sapsea is never referred to as 'Mayor' in the fragment prompts Cox to suggest that it was created as a trial chapter before 25 February 1870, when Dickens read the third number (in which Sapsea becomes Mayor) aloud to friends. Charles Forsyte offers a third possibility. He suggests that the fragment was left over from 'George Silverman's Explanation', a short story written from the perspective of an elderly narrator, who writes in order to overcome a sense of personal unworthiness that originated in his childhood (1868), and relates only peripherally to the unfinished novel.[3]

The text below is taken from the Penguin edition of 1974, which retained Dickens's spelling and punctuation, so far as Cox could discern them. The title Forster devised – 'HOW MR SAPSEA CEASED TO BE A MEMBER OF THE EIGHT CLUB. *Told by* Himself' – has been omitted since there is no warrant for it in the MS.

The extant text of the 'Sapsea Fragment' follows

Wishing to take the air, I proceeded by a circuitous route to the Club, it being our weekly night of meeting. I found that we mustered our full strength. We were enrolled under the denomination of the Eight Club. We were eight in number; we met at eight o'clock during eight months of the year; our annual subscription was eight shillings each; we played eight games of four handed cribbage, at eightpence the game; our frugal supper was composed of eight rolls, eight mutton chops, eight pork sausages, eight baked potatoes, eight marrow bones with eight toasts, and eight bottles of ale. There may or may not be a certain harmony of color in the ruling idea of this (to adopt a phrase of our lively neighbours) reunion. It was a little idea of mine.

A somewhat popular member of the Eight Club was a member by the name of Kimber. By profession, dancing-master. A commonplace hopeful sort of man, wholly destitute of dignity or knowledge of the world.

As I entered the Club-room, Kimber was making the remark: 'And he still half believes him to be very high in the Church.'

In the act of hanging up my hat on the Eighth peg by the door, I caught Kimber's visual ray. He lowered it, and passed a remark on the next change of the moon. I did not take particular notice of this at the moment, because the world was often pleased to be a little shy of Ecclesiastical topics in my presence. For I felt that I was picked out (though perhaps only through a coincidence) to a certain extent to represent what I call our glorious constitution in church and state. The phrase may be objected to by captious minds; but I own to it as mine. I threw it off in argument some little time back. I said, Our Glorious Constitution in Church and State.

Another member of the Eight Club was Peartree, also member of the Royal College of Surgeons. Mr Peartree is not accountable to me for his opinions, and I say no more of them here than that he attends the poor gratis whenever they want him, and is not the parish doctor. Mr Peartree may justify it to the grasp of *his* mind thus to do his republican utmost to bring an appointed officer into contempt. Suffice it that Mr Peartree can never justify it to the grasp of *mine*.

Between Peartree and Kimber there was a sickly sort of feeble-minded alliance. It came under my particular notice when I sold off Kimber by auction. (Goods taken in execution.) He was a widower in a white under waistcoat and slight shoes with bows, and had two daughters not ill-looking. Indeed, the reverse. Both daughters taught dancing in Scholastic Establishments for Young Ladies – had done so at Mrs Sapsea's; nay, Twinkleton's – and both, in giving lessons, presented the unwomanly spectacle of having little fiddles tucked under their chins. In spite of which the younger one might, if I am correctly informed – I will raise the veil so far as to say I KNOW she might – have soared for life from this degrading taint, but for having the class of mind allotted to what I call the common herd, and being so incredibly devoid of veneration as to become painfully ludicrous.

When I sold off Kimber without reserve, Peartree (as poor as he can hold together) had several prime household lots knocked down to him. *I* am not to be blinded, and of course it was as plain to me what he was going to do with them, as it was that he was a brown hulking sort of revolutionary subject who had been in India with the soldiers and ought (for the sake of society) to have his neck broke. I saw the lots shortly afterwards in Kimber's lodging – through the windows – and I easily made out that there had been a sneaking pretence of lending them 'till better times. A man with a smaller knowledge of the world than myself might have been led to suspect that Kimber had held back money from his creditors and fraudulently bought the goods. But besides that I knew for certain he had no money, I knew that this would involve a species of forethought not to be made compatible with the frivolity of a caperer, inoculating other people with capering, for his bread.

As it was the first time I had seen either of those two since the Sale, I kept myself in what I call Abeyance. When selling him up, I had delivered a few remarks – shall I say a little homily? – concerning Kimber, which the world did regard as more than usually worth notice. I had come up into my pulpit, it was said, uncommonly like; and a murmur of recognition had repeated his (I will not name whose) title, before I spoke. I had then gone on to say that all present would find, in the first page of the Catalogue that was lying before them, in the last paragraph before the first lot, the following words: 'Sold in pursuance of a Writ of execution issued by a Creditor'. I had then proceeded to remind my Friends that however frivolous, not to say contemptible, the pursuits by which a man got his goods together, still his goods were as dear to him, and as cheap to society (if sold without reserve) as though his pursuits had been of character that would bear serious contemplation. I had then divided my text (if I may be allowed so to call it) into three heads: firstly, Sold; secondly, In pursuance of a writ of execution; thirdly, Issued by a creditor; with a few moral reflections on each, and winding up with 'Now to the first lot' in a manner that was complimented when I afterwards mingled with my hearers.

So not being certain on what terms I and Kimber stood, I was grave, I was chilling. Kimber, however, moving to me, I moved to Kimber. (I was the creditor who had issued the writ. Not that it matters.)

'I was alluding, Mr Sapsea,' said Kimber, 'when you came in, to a stranger who entered into conversation with me in the street as I came to the club. He had been speaking to you just before, it seemed, by the churchyard; and though you had told him who you were, I could hardly persuade him that you were not high in the Church.'

'Idiot!' said Peartree.

'Ass!' said Kimber.

'Idiot and Ass!' said the other five members.

'Idiot and Ass, gentlemen,' I remonstrated, looking around me, 'are strong expressions to apply to a young man of good appearance and address.' My generosity was roused. I own it.

'You'll admit that he must be a Fool,' said Peartree.

'You can't deny that he must be a Blockhead,' said Kimber.

Their tone of disgust amounted to being offensive. Why should the young man be so calumniated? What had he done? He had only made an innocent and natural mistake. I controlled my generous indignation, and said so.

'Natural,' repeated Kimber. '*He*'s a Natural!'

The remaining six members of the Eight Club laughed unanimously. It stung me. It was a scornful laugh. My anger was roused in behalf of an absent friendless stranger. I rose (for I had been sitting down).

'Gentlemen,' I said with dignity, 'I will not remain one of this club allowing opprobrium to be cast on an unoffending person in his absence. I will not so violate what I call the sacred rites of hospitality. Gentlemen, until you know how to behave yourselves better, I leave you. Gentlemen, until then I withdraw from this place of meeting whatever personal qualifications I may have brought into it. Gentlemen, until then you cease to be the Eight Club, and must make the best you can of becoming the Seven.'

I put on my hat and retired. As I went down stairs I distinctly heard them give a suppressed cheer. Such is the power of demeanour and knowledge of mankind. – I had forced it out of them.

II

Whom should I meet in the street, within a few yards of the door of the inn where the Club was held, but the selfsame young man whose cause I had felt it my duty so warmly – and I will add so disinterestedly – to take up!

'Is it Mr Sapsea,' he said doubtfully, 'or is it –'

'It is Mr Sapsea,' I replied.

'Pardon me, Mr Sapsea; you appear warm, Sir.'

'I have been warm,' I said, 'and on your account.' Having stated the circumstances at some length (my generosity almost overpowered him), I asked him his name.

'Mr Sapsea,' he answered, looking down, 'your penetration is so acute, your glance into the souls of your fellow men is so penetrating, that if I was hardy enough to deny that my name is Poker, what would it avail me?'

I don't know that I had quite exactly made out to a fraction that his name *was* Poker, but I dare say I had been pretty near doing it.

'Well, well,' said I, trying to put him at his ease by nodding my head in a soothing way. 'Your name is Poker, and there is no harm in being named Poker.'

'Oh Mr Sapsea!' cried the young man in a very well behaved manner. 'Bless you for those words!' He then, as if ashamed of having given way to his feelings, looked down again.

'Come, Poker,' said I, 'let me hear more about you. Tell me. Where are you going to, Poker, and where do you come from?'

'Ah Mr Sapsea!' exclaimed the young man. 'Disguise from you is impossible. You know already that I come from somewhere, and am going somewhere else. If I was to deny it, what would it avail me?'

'Then don't deny it,' was my remark.

'Or,' pursued Poker, in a kind of despondent rapture, 'or if I was to deny that I came to this town to see and hear you, Sir, what would it avail me? Or if I was to deny

The Number Plans

The Number Plans for *The Mystery of Edwin Drood* resemble the notes Dickens made for *Dombey and Son* and for every novel from 1846, with the exception of his two last weekly serials, *A Tale of Two Cities* and *Great Expectations*. The plans are uniform in appearance and purpose. Reserving one sheet of paper for each monthly number, Dickens adopted the practice of folding the sheet and using the crease to set apart two sets of notes. The left-hand half-sheets contain general memoranda, jottings that set down ideas, names for characters and phrases of speech. Double underscoring, question marks and replies convey a mind in action, a sense of debate, hesitation and affirmation in recording thoughts as they appear to have occurred prior to composition.

The notes on the right-hand half-sheet are more systematic. Each indicates the novel's title, the monthly instalment and the chapter divisions within that number. In this respect the notes on the right seem to serve a double purpose: to rough out the direction the chapters will take and emphasize their main points. Their other role, in the words of John Butt and Kathleen Tillotson, was 'to summarize the contents and to put Dickens into the mood of the last monthly number when beginning upon another'.[1]

The notes and Number Plans for *The Mystery of Edwin Drood* are reproduced in type in the pages that follow. The transcription attempts to reproduce the notes as they appear by observing Dickens's arrangement within practical limits. His underscorings and the enclosing lines he used for emphasis are included; excluded are the slight diagonal lines present in the original notes which serve to separate consecutive items. The full point after 'Mr' has been omitted; two full points indicate the abbreviated form of Number. For photographic facsimiles of the notes and a typographic transcription of the text on facing pages, readers should consult Harry Stone's edition of *Dickens' Working Notes for His Novels* (1987).

The first page transcribes a list of projected names and titles. Thereafter follow the notes and plans for the first six numbers of the novel. Readers will notice discrepancies between the plans as they are transcribed and the published text of the chapters. 'Mr Durdles and Friend', which we know of as Chapter 5, appears here as Chapter 9, 'Birds in the Bush'. The explanation is that, after Dickens had written the first two numbers and delivered them together to his printer, the compositors discovered, on setting the pages in type, that each number was six printed pages too short. To correct this deficiency Dickens transposed the five-page 'Mr Durdles and Friend' from Number II to Number I, and wrote an extra page of text which he inserted into the middle of Chapter 3, 'The Nuns' House'. This solved the shortfall for the first number but created an eleven-page deficit in Number II. Accordingly, he wrote 'Birds in the Bush', using material which he had intended to use in Number III, as is shown by the query 'Rosa's guardian?' on the left-hand side of the plan for that month, which is followed by the notation 'Done in No. II'. The use of this material meant advancing and contracting the story somewhat beyond his original intentions. An examination of the notes in the plans for the third, fourth and fifth numbers bears out this point.

The other disparity occurs in the last two numbers, whose notes indicate his original scheme for Numbers V and VI. After his death in the midst of writing Number VI, John Forster made the decision to restore the deletions in Number V (made by Dickens when he discovered the overmatter after reading preliminary proofs for the number) and to break Number V in two. Forster left the initial portion in Number V, with a modified title ('A Flight') and transferred the remainder to Number VI. It appears there with a new title ('A Recognition') and serves to make the two final numbers close to each other in length and approximately the length of an ordinary number.

Sparse entries in the plans for Numbers V and VI indicate that these parts were in progress when Dickens died. The left-half or memo portion of Number VI is missing; the number-plan sheets for the remaining numbers exist but provide only the book title and plan number inscribed in Dickens's hand at the top of each right-half portion. They have not been reproduced here.

Friday Twentieth August, 1869.

Gilbert   Alfred
                                Edwin
                   Jasper   Edwyn
                        Michael   Oswald
                        Arthur
The loss of James Wakefield   Selwyn
        Edwyn   Edgar
                          Mr Honeythunder
                          Mr Honeyblast

        James's Disappearance

                        The Dean
                        Mrs Dean
                        Miss Dean

        Flight And Pursuit

          Sworn to avenge it

          One object in Life

A Kinsman's Devotion

                        The Two Kinsmen

The loss of Edwyn Brood

        The loss of Edwin Brude
           The Mystery in the Drood Family
        The loss of Edwyn Drood
           The flight of Edwyn Drood

                              Edwin Drood in hiding

        The loss of Edwin Drude
The Disappearance of Edwin Drood
   The Mystery of Edwin Drood

           Dead?   Or alive?

Opium-Smoking
>> Touch the key note
>>>> 'When the Wicked Man' ——

The Uncle and Nephew:
>>>> 'Pussy's' Portrait
> <u>You won't take warning then?</u>

Dean   <u>Mr</u> Jasper
> Minor Canon, Mr Crisparkle   Verger Peptune
> Uncle and Nephew   <u>change to Tope</u>
Gloves for the Nuns' House
>>> churchyard
>>> <u>Cathedral town running throughout</u>

> Inside the Nuns' House
>> Miss Twinkleton and her double existence
>>>> Mrs Tisher
>>>> Rosebud
The affianced young people.   <u>Every love scene of theirs, a</u>

>>>> <u>quarrel more or less</u>

> Mr Sapsea.   <u>old Tory Jackass</u>
>>>> His wife's epitaph

> Jasper and the keys
>>> Durdles down in the crypt and among
the graves. His dinner bundle.

(Mystery of Edwin Drood. —— Nº I.)

Chapter I.

~~Prologue~~   The Dawn

change title to The Dawn

opium smoking and Jasper
Lead up to Cathedral

Chapter II.

a Dean and a Chapter also

Cathedral and Cathedral town   / Mr Crisparkle
and the Dean.   Uncle and Nephew.
Murder very far off
Edwin's story and Pussy

Chapter III.

The Nuns' House

Still picturesque suggestions of Cathedral Town
The Nuns' House and the young couple's first love scene

Chapter IV.

Mr Sapsea

Connect Jasper with him.   (He will want a solemn donkey
bye and bye.)

Epitaph brings them together, and
brings Durdles with them.
The keys.   Stony Durdles

Bring in the other young couple.   <u>Yes</u>

or

Neville and Olympia Heyridge ——_∧ Heyfort?

> Philanthropy in Minor Canon Corner

<u>Neville and Helena Landless</u>

Mixture of Oriental blood – or imperceptibly acquired mixture in them.   <u>Yes</u>

<u>No</u>

(Mystery of Edwin Drood. —— Nº II.)

Chapter V.

The Blustrous Philanthropist
Mr Honeythunder

Old Mrs Crisparkle
China Shepherdess

Minor Canon Corner

Chapter VI.

More Confidences than One

Neville's to Mr Crisparkle,
    Rosa's to Helena

/ Piano scene with
    Jasper. She singing,
    he following her lips.

Chapter VII.

Daggers Drawn

quarrel

(Fomented by Jasper)   Goblet.   And then
                    confession to Mr Crisparkle
        Jasper lays his ground

Chapter VIII.

Mr Durdles and friend

Deputy engaged to stone Durdles nightly
Carry through the woman of the 1st chapter

Carry through Durdles's calling – and the
bundle & the keys
    John Jasper looks at Edwin asleep

Pursue Edwin Drood and Rosa?

    Lead on to final scene between them in N? V?   IV?

                                            Yes

    How many more scenes between them?

    Way to be paved for their marriage —

              ————and parting ~~fore~~ instead. Yes

      Miss Twinkleton's? No. Next N?

      Rosa's guardian? <u>Done in N? II.</u>

      Mr Sapsea?   Yes. last chapter

      Neville Landless at Mr Crisparkle's

                    And Helena? | <u>Yes</u>

       Neville admires Rosa. That comes out

      from himself.

(Mystery of Edwin Drood. —— N° III.)

Chapter ~~IX~~

Smoothing the Way

——That is, for Jasper's plan, through Mr Crisparkle;
who takes new ground on Neville's new
confidence.

Minor Canon Corner. The closet I
remember there as a child.

Edwin's appointment for Xmas Eve.

Chapter XI

A Picture and a Ring

P.

J.   T.

1747

Dinner in chambers.

The two waiters

Bazzard the clerk

Mr Grewgious's past story.

'A ring of diamonds and rubies delicately set in gold.'

Edwin takes it

Chapter XII.

A Night with Durdles

Lay the ground for the manner of the murder, to
come out at last.

Keep the boy suspended.
Night picture of the Cathedral.

Once more carry through Edwin and Rosa?
> or, Last time?   <u>Last time</u>

~~Last scene but one between them.~~
Then   outside
Last meeting of Rosa and Edwin ~~in~~ the Cathedral?
> <u>Yes</u>

> Kiss at parting.
> 'Jack.'

Edwin goes to the dinner.
> The Windy night.
> The Surprise and Alarm.
> Jasper's failure in the one great
object made known by Mr Grewgious.

> Jasper's Diary?   <u>Yes</u>

(Mystery of Edwin Drood. ——— N⁰ IV.)

Chapter XIII.

Both at their Best

The Last Interview

And Parting

Chapter XIV.

When shall these three meet again?

How each passes the day.

	Neville	
Watch and shirt pin all Edwin's jewellery	Edwin	Watch to the jeweller
	Jasper	

'And so <u>he</u> goes up the Postern stair'   Storms of Wind

Chapter XV.

Impeached

Neville away early.

Pursued and brought back.

Mr Grewgious's communication:

And his scene with Jasper

Chapter XVI.

Devoted

Jasper's artful use of the communication on his recovery.
  Cloisterham Weir, Mr Crisparkle, and the Watch and pin.
  Jasper's artful turn
  <u>The Dean.</u>   Neville cast out.

Jasper's Diary. 'I devote myself to his destruction.'

Edwin and Rosa for the last time?   <u>Done already.</u>

Kinfrederel

Edwin Disappears

<u>Done already</u>

<u>The mystery</u>

(Mystery of Edwin Drood. —— N⁰ V.)

Chapter XVII.

professional and

Philanthropy ~~in divers places~~ unprofessional

Chapter XVIII.

~~Shadow on the Sun Dial~~

A Settler in Cloisterham

Chapter XIX.

~~A Settler in Cloisterham~~

Shadow on the Sun Dial

Chapter XX.

~~'Let's Talk.'~~

~~Various Flights~~ Divers Flights

[Dickens made no notes for the sixth monthly part . . .

(Mystery of Edwin Drood. —— Nº VI.)

Chapter XXI.

A Gritty State of Things comes on

Chapter XXII.

The Dawn again

Chapter XXIII.

. . . Nor for any of the three chapters he planned for it.]

The Illustrations

The twelve illustrations and the carefully designed wrapper accompanying the six published parts of the projected twelve instalments of *The Mystery of Edwin Drood* follow Dickens's practice. Beginning with *The Pickwick Papers*, each of his monthly serials made its appearance in instalments of thirty-two pages with two plates per number printed on heavy stock paper and bound into the front of each part. Advertising before and after the plates and the text and a coloured paper wrapper (green in most instances) completed the monthly 'package'.

Of all the covers drawn by Dickens's illustrators none has been more closely scrutinized than Charles Collins's design for *Edwin Drood*. Reference to the purpose of the monthly wrappers helps explain this interest. At one level, of course, the front cover was simply utilitarian. It supplied the work's title, author, instalment number, date and price, together with information about the publisher, printer and bookseller. Throughout the run of the serial the cover remained unchanged save for the details of the part number and date.

This last point merits further attention when we take into account the second and more important objective of the cover. For each of his novels published in monthly instalments cover designs were executed by artists acting on instructions from Dickens. Invariably he issued his commands weeks before he began writing and many months in advance of the completion of the particular work. Consider moreover the implications of the injunction under which the illustrators worked. Their mission, they were told, was to shadow forth the trajectory of the story by hinting at the book's themes and contents. Working from information supplied by Dickens, sometimes by letter but often orally, the artists were challenged to find ways to render in visual terms a book's substance without revealing too many details of its plot.

The original artist Dickens chose to illustrate his last novel had talent but lacked experience as a book illustrator. Fortunately Dickens knew what he wanted. He insisted that Charles Collins, his son-in-law, receive a fair price for his work. He also asked his publishers to send Collins any copies of the old green covers for *The Pickwick Papers* designed by Hablot K. Browne that were available. That Collins studied Browne's work and schooled himself in the ways of Dickens's long-time illustrator we can infer from the wrapper design he created. By December 1869 he had produced the design for the cover and six preliminary sketches of scenes relating to the opening chapters of the novel. These included two drawings of figures in the opium den, two tentative illustrations of the Crisparkle dinner party, one showing guests at the table, the other with guests gathered round the piano, and a pair of drawings of figures with the Cathedral in the background.

It is to the wrapper we must turn for hints about the novel's overall design. Working to the novelist's specifications and with iconographic conventions and devices inherited from Browne and from Robert Seymour and George Cruikshank, Dickens's first illustrators, what did Collins convey in visual terms of Dickens's intentions? What pleased the novelist so much to move him to pronounce the completed cover 'excellent'?[1]

The wrapper plays skilfully on the Wheel-of-Fortune design Browne had exploited on several previous occasions. This convention integrates verbal information with a movement that tracks a rise up the left-hand margin and a fall that descends on the right. In this instance, branches of roses in bud and in bloom entwine the letterpress on the left while bare branches and thorns predominate on the opposite side. An allegorical figure in the right upper corner holds back the curtain of the design; dagger drawn, she conveys a preoccupation with hatred, suspicion and retribution. The left-hand figure, representing Love, overlooks the novel's romantic scenes. Working both against and with this circular paradigm, the figures of Edwin and Rosa walk down from the Cathedral on the left, while pursuers (policemen in Collins's version, plainclothes men when revised by Fildes) rush up a circular staircase on the right. At the top right, Jasper, detached from members of the choir, casts a lingering glance at the couple to his right, while the figure leading the chase points urgently at Jasper's left. Might this represent Jasper pointing deliberately to himself? Or could

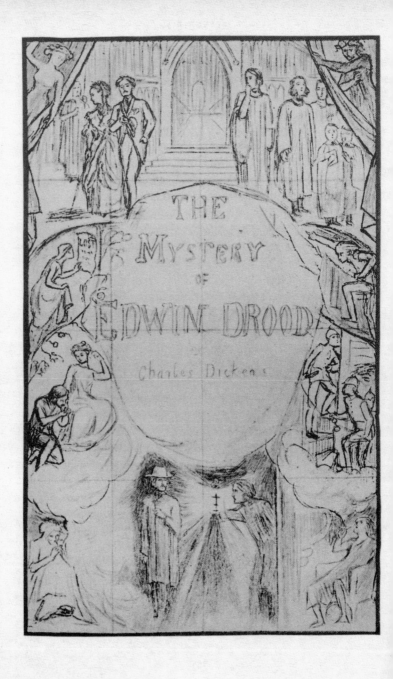

THE
Mystery
OF
EDWIN DROOD

Charles Dickens

it be Neville Landless or some other pursuer? Perhaps most crucial – and certainly most enigmatic – the eye is drawn to the scene at the bottom centre. In a dark passage, possibly suggestive of a crypt, a figure with a light confronts a second in the act of retrieving or concealing something in his coat pocket. Figures exhaling clouds of smoke in each bottom corner underpin the importance of the opium scenes in the novel.

The withdrawal of Collins from the project on account of his health led to some small changes when Luke Fildes took over. Presumably acting on instructions from Dickens, Fildes sharpened the design. The opium smoker at the bottom right became unambiguously male, Collins's three ascending policemen were reduced to two men in plainclothes, and the branch of roses and thorns received greater definition, as did all the other figures. The other change constituted an addition. In the cover by Fildes, a spade, key and 'dinner bundle' appear above the two mysterious figures in the lower portion of the design. All three objects belong to Durdles and may indicate the stonemason's role in the plot's resolution. But beyond this addition, nothing essential is changed, thereby ensuring for Collins, as Jane R. Cohen notes, a 'peculiar kind of immortality' attained by virtue of his association with the novel.[2]

The twelve illustrations contributed by his talented successor have had a less dramatic impact. The first six certainly pleased Dickens, who praised them for their photographic realism. In this respect, Fildes's illustrations, with fewer figures, drawn from real life models and grounded in unobtrusive backgrounds, reflect developments evident in both the fiction and the graphic art of the time. The remaining six have been judged uneven, perhaps on account of Fildes's being deprived of Dickens's inspiration and supervision. The younger man nevertheless earned Dickens's friendship and his respect. Requested by Dickens to show Jasper mounting his postern staircase with a murderous expression on his face and a neckerchief wound twice round his neck, Fildes hesitated. Why abandon Jasper's usual small black tie? When Dickens explained the purpose of the long black scarf, Fildes tactfully suggested that it would provide too obvious a clue, an opinion the novelist accepted. In a further display of trust, Dickens talked with

No. II.] **MAY, 1870.** [Price One Shilling.

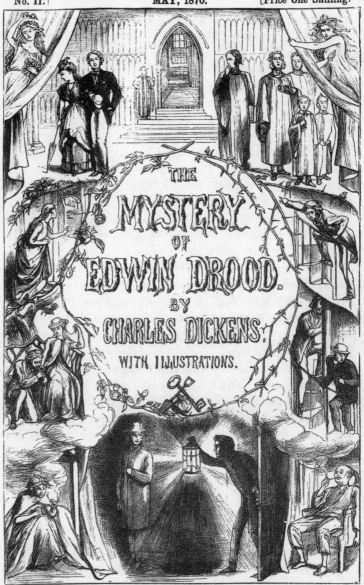

THE
MYSTERY
OF
EDWIN DROOD.
BY
CHARLES DICKENS.
WITH ILLUSTRATIONS.

LONDON: CHAPMAN & HALL, 193, PICCADILLY.

Advertisements to be sent to the Publishers, and ADAMS & FRANCIS, 59, Fleet Street, E.C.
[*The right of Translation is reserved.*]

him about the final scene he projected in the condemned cell and invited Fildes to Gad's Hill for a weekend early in June 1870 to visit Maidstone jail.

Dickens's death prevented this expedition and cut short any further collaboration between the two. Of the remaining three numbers to be published, Fildes, it appears, selected the scenes to be illustrated, executed the work and devised titles for the illustrations himself.[3]

Rochester as Cloisterham

Dickens makes use of Rochester and Chatham at both ends of his career. The 'ancient little city of Rochester' and the adjacent naval dockyard town of Chatham appear in *The Pickwick Papers* (1836–7); Rochester in *The Mystery of Edwin Drood* (1870) serves, with London, as one of the two centres of the unfinished novel. The hold of both Medway towns remained imprinted on his memory, testimony to the sense of place present in everything Dickens wrote. Novels, short stories, essays and letters all attest to the visual way his imagination worked as he recorded pictures of what he saw in his mind's eye and stored for future use. So distinctive is this trait, and topographical specificity so much a hallmark of his fiction, we might usefully recall John Forster's comment. While Dickens habitually copied from nature, Forster wrote, he was always careful 'not to overstep her modesty by copying too closely'.[1]

The portrait of Rochester that emerges in *Edwin Drood* illustrates Forster's point about the necessary 'reserves' Dickens employed in his fiction. For full details about that city we must turn to Victorian guides and to later historical studies.[2] Yet the fact remains that the portrait of Cloisterham stays close enough to its original to allow readers to distinguish many of Rochester's landmarks. Take the three identifying features of the city: the mile-long narrow High Street by which you get into Rochester and out of it, the Castle and the Cathedral. The first opens to quiet courts, closes and 'yards with pumps in them and no thoroughfare' (ch. 3), while the Castle and Cathedral, twin sentinels facing the Medway, guard the entrance to the city from the north-east. Each features in the novel, appropriately adapted to Dickens's fictional agenda.

The importance of John Jasper inevitably heightens our interest in Rochester's cathedral church of St Andrew and in the monastic remains on its southern flank. Their long history (the Cathedral was consecrated

Cloisterham: An Ancient English Cathedral Town

in AD 604; the Benedictine priory dates from the 1080s) and subsequent vicissitudes occupy little of the narrator's sustained attention. But repeated references to the Cathedral's 'ancient' character and to the 'earthy' nature of its Norman crypt (one of the older surviving parts of the building), juxtaposed with pieces of historical information, provide verifiable details that point to Rochester and to nowhere else. In Chapter 3, for example, Dickens comments on the succession of names history has given to 'the old Cathedral town' on which he bestows 'a fictitious name'. To the Celts who occupied a clearing there in the first century AD it was Durobrivae ('stronghold at the bridges'), a name which continued in use with the Romans, who transformed their bridgehead settlement overlooking the river into a permanent military camp in the last quarter of the second century.[3] Eventually a walled and moated city with four gates and a main street running from east to west, this Roman stronghold became known as Hrofceastre, or the camp of Hrof, a former Saxon chieftain, before evolving into Rochester, its present form.[4]

Situated on the Medway where the river could be crossed and on the main road connecting Dover and London, the Cathedral's geographical position increased both its importance and its vulnerability to attack. 'The early history of the city is of constant destruction: in 676 by Ethelred, King of Mercia, in 839 by the Danes, who again laid siege to it 50 years later', when they were repulsed by Alfred. In 998, the Danes sacked the city for a third time. Fires caused further destruction in 1130, 1137 and 1177. And so on, into the thirteenth century and beyond.[5] The Norman castle on a hill overlooking the right bank of the river suffered a comparable fate. Constructed in the eleventh century, the castle and massive keep were besieged by King John in 1215, by Simon de Montfort intent on wresting the castle from Henry III in 1264, and in 1381 by the followers of Wat Tyler, the rebel who led a revolt against an unpopular poll-tax and who died after he marched on London.

A glancing reference to Rochester's turbulent past occurs in Chapter 6. Within 'the sound of the Cathedral bell, or the roll of the Cathedral organ', the absolute silence of nearby Minor Canon Corner contrasts dramatically with events long past. 'Swaggering fighting men had had their centuries of ramping and raving about Minor Canon Corner', the narrator comments, the site where beaten serfs drudged and died and where 'powerful monks had had their centuries of being sometimes useful and sometimes harmful there'.

References to specific architectural features of the Cathedral extend further the sense of local colouring and indebtedness to place. Singled out by the narrator are 'the low arched Cathedral door', belonging to the imposing Norman western front, the 'massive grey square tower', some 156 feet high, from a later period, and 'the rugged steps' which lead down to the spacious crypt. Similarly, on the night of Jasper's expedition there, accompanied by Durdles, the narrator describes the crypt's 'groined windows, bare of glass', and the 'heavy pillars which support the roof [and] engender masses of black shade' (ch. 12). Heightened by Jasper's 'curious' behaviour and Durdles's recollection of a 'terrific shriek' he heard almost a year before, the passage evokes the Norman and Gothic structure of this part of the Cathedral.

Connections between the real and the fictive are equally compelling when we move outside. Within the precincts of the Cathedral live two of the novel's most important characters, each persuasively linked with existing buildings. An 'original' customarily proposed for the home of the Reverend Septimus Crisparkle has the fewest complications. Housing for the three minor canons attached to the Cathedral in 1860[6] existed in what Dickens calls 'Minor Canon Corner'. This was a row of six Georgian houses to the south of the Cathedral, built between 1721 and 1723. A seventh was added to the terrace in 1735. Described in Chapter 6 as a quiet place within the shadow of the Cathedral, its red-brick walls 'harmoniously toned down in color by time' and by 'stone-walled gardens' where fruit ripens every year, the terrace imparts an atmosphere of serenity and peace.

So definitively is the fictional Minor Canon Corner linked with the real place that on one occasion Dickens uses the true name 'Minor Canon Row' in the text (ch. 16). Further evidence of the linking between an imaginative picture Dickens created in his mind's eye and something that actually existed occurs in the working notes to the novel. In the scene in which the Minor Canon and his mother differ over their views about Neville's recent behaviour, Dickens describes a closet to which the China Shepherdess repaired whenever she detected that her son 'wanted support' (ch. 10). This 'most wonderful closet, worthy of Cloisterham and of Minor Canon Corner' – 'this rare closet . . . [with] a lock in mid-air' – is the repository of home-made biscuits, sweet Constantia wine and an array of delicacies comparable to those Porphyro assembles for Madeline in Keats's 'The Eve of St Agnes' (1819). Dickens's description of 'this closet of closets' clearly derives from the memory of a visit to one of the terraced houses in Minor Canon Row. 'Minor Canon Corner', reads one of the memoranda recorded for use in Chapter 10, 'Smoothing the Way', 'The closet I remember there as a child.'

If harmony and good health define the quarters of Crisparkle and his mother, darkness, shadow and solitude predominate in the case of the Cathedral's lay precentor. The lack of light in Jasper's rooms has a real source. Pendant masses of 'ivy and creeper' cover the front of 'the old stone gatehouse' (ch. 2), thereby imparting a gloomy aura to quarters which are narrow, enclosed and secretive. His two windows look out in opposite directions: one into the Cathedral close and the other down into the High Street. Dickens's later description of Jasper's dwelling in Chapter 14 as a 'lighthouse on the margin of the tide of busy life' precisely captures its location midway between the sound and hum of traffic on the High Street and the peace of the lonely Precincts, dark because they 'are never particularly well lighted'. Known locally as College Gate, this particular structure, one of three leading to the Priory Precincts, corresponds closely with the description given in the novel.

To be sure, the choirmaster's dwelling bows to the demands of fiction. Jasper gains access to his rooms by a postern stair off the arched gateway. While this description corresponds more or less with the actual architecture of the Gatehouse, a subsequent development in the plot calls for adjustments. These occur when Dickens invents something 'Cathedraly' for Dick Datchery, the single old gentleman who arrives in 'the picturesque old city for a month or two, with a view of settling down there altogether' (ch. 18). In search of lodgings, Datchery is directed to the Verger, whose wife has long attempted to let two chambers 'to an unappreciative city'.

The 'official dwelling' of the Verger, Dickens explains, communicates by an upper stair with Mr Jasper's '(hence Mrs Tope's attendance on that gentleman)'. Both this 'upper stair' and the two modest rooms in question with 'ancient walls' and 'a groined roof' represent departures from Dickens's model. Most importantly, Datchery quickly understood that by sitting with the main door open, 'he would enjoy the passing society of all comers to and fro by the gateway', thus giving him a perfect place from which to keep his eye on the choirmaster (ch. 18). This reworking of the existing Gatehouse is purely fictional too.

Other distinctive local buildings required fewer alterations to fit the needs of the novel. Easily recognizable from their given location (in the High Street, the one 'over against' the other) and from their various descriptions are Eastgate House and the gabled, half-timbered building both with modern shop fronts. Eastgate House was erected in 1590–91 and supplies details Dickens incorporates into his presentation of the Nuns' House, 'a venerable brick edifice' with a trim gate 'enclosing its old courtyard' and 'its quaint old garden' opening to the west (ch. 19). Used during Dickens's time as a school for girls, the same building appears as 'Westgate House' in *The Pickwick Papers*, transposed from Rochester to Bury St Edmunds (ch. 16). Opposite stands the residence of Mr Sapsea. This building dates from *c.* 1684, most likely a single mansion. His premises, writes Dickens, 'are of about the period of the Nuns' House, irregularly modernized here and there, as steadily deteriorating generations found, more and more, that they preferred air and light to Fever and the Plague' (ch. 4). The wooden effigy of Mr Sapsea's father 'in a curly wig and toga', however, is one of those small rearrangements Dickens frequently makes. The carving formerly adorned another building further down the High Street towards Chatham.[7]

Dickens adapts local residences to the needs of minor characters as well. The Dean, for example, lives in a 'snug old red-brick house' nearby (ch. 2), in fact an elegant Georgian building just south of the Cathedral and the former Priory of St Andrew and chapter house. Also within a short distance is Durdles's dwelling, a 'crazy wooden house of two low stories', with 'scant remains of a lattice-work porch

over the door, and also of a rustic fence before its stamped-out garden'
(ch. 5). Fictionalized as 'The Travellers' Twopenny', this 'house all
warped and distorted' was recognizable to Dickens's contemporaries
as Kit's Lodging House. With a brick first floor and with wood-framed
lath and plaster for the two upper floors, the building was distinctive.
In fact, it had three not two storeys and was always known as
the Fourpenny, not the Twopenny, Lodging House. Another small
instance of artistic licence is apparent in the way the House announced
its prices. The 'inscribed paper lantern over the door setting forth the
purport of the house' was in reality a gas street lamp on which was
painted information about the beds.[8] To reach the house from the
Cathedral one had to cross a piece of land formerly a vineyard
belonging to the monastery. It is still known locally as The Vines;
Dickens alters the name to 'the Monks Vineyard' and refers to it on
several occasions (chs. 5, 14 and 23).

Two remaining features of Rochester alluded to in the novel deserve
mention. The city's location on the Medway serves as a setting against
which significant scenes take place. The Landless twins, for example,
enjoy walks along the exposed shore where the wind blows and where
the river at Cloisterham, being sufficiently near the sea, frequently
throws up 'a quantity of seaweed' with the tide. The athletic Minor
Canon also trots off in this direction to scale 'his favorite fragment of
ruin' (ch. 10), another local landmark based, presumably, on the Castle
ruins, unlike the swimming spot near the Cloisterham weir, for which
there is no obvious local counterpart. On the last night Edwin and
Neville are seen together, they leave Jasper's Gatehouse to go down
to the river to 'see the action of the wind there' (ch. 15). And the work
on the river the following day, done at Jasper's insistence, as men
search for a body using drags and poles along the muddy and rushy
shore, evokes the local terrain. 'Now, in barge and boat; and now
ashore among the osiers, or tramping amidst mud and stakes and
jagged stones in low-lying places, where solitary watermarks and
signals of strange shapes showed like spectres', men and dogs search,
to no avail (ch. 15). In such inlets Rochester's well-established oyster
trade flourished. This fact earns no place in the narrative, but Dickens
does allude to the local appetite for oysters on one occasion. In a

passage commenting on how all things in the city 'are of the past', the narrator notes that 'The most abundant and the most agreeable evidences of progressing life in Cloisterham are the evidences of vegetable life in its many gardens'. So prolific are these that even the city's 'drooping and despondent little theatre' has its 'poor strip of garden', where 'scarlet beans or oyster-shells' predominate according to the season of the year (ch. 3).

The final matter of topographical relevance is Rochester's relationship with the metropolis. By 1851 London was accessible to most important Kentish towns by rail. This development occurred as competing companies extended their lines to the coast, thereby reducing dramatically the time between London and Rochester. Earlier in the century horse-drawn coaches had covered the thirty-two miles between the two cities in five or six hours. By the mid-1840s, trains cut the time sufficiently to make it possible to leave either city in the morning and to return home the same day. Dickens himself took advantage of these new rail services. Two decades later and removed to Gad's Hill, he frequently used this option, a convenience he extends to his characters, with modifications.

On several occasions different individuals travel between Cloisterham and London by train. Jasper uses the railway when he goes back and forth on his opium-smoking expeditions. Trains also transport Mr Honeythunder, Mr Grewgious and Septimus Crisparkle on matters of business. Rosa uses the train when she takes flight following Jasper's unwelcome advances in the walled garden of the Nuns' House. Together, these journeys impart little beyond establishing London as the novel's second centre and the metropolis's accessibility by rail from north-east Kent. Specific details in the text, however, convey a less obvious point: the way Dickens backdates the novel's action by separating the sequence of events in the story from the narrator's telling of time.

The extent to which the action is set back can be inferred from the narrator's response to Mr Sapsea's contention that 'In those days' there was no railway to Cloisterham and that 'there never would be'. 'Marvellous to consider', responds the narrator, 'it has come to pass, in these days, that Express Trains don't think Cloisterham worth stopping at, but yell and whirl through it on their larger errands casting the dust off their wheels as a testimony against its insignificance' (ch. 6). Their destination was Dover, some eighty-two miles from Victoria station, a distance which trains owned by the London, Chatham and Dover Company completed in approximately two hours and ten minutes. Known as 'The Chatham Line', this service opened in 1861.

We can date the narrator's 'these days' with no precision beyond saying that at least fifteen years have passed since the events narrated in the novel occurred.[9] Details in the text about the rail journeys undertaken by the characters confirm this point, when we learn how travel to and from London required a coach journey to Maidstone, eight miles to the west, and then passage by the South East Kent Railway from Maidstone to London Bridge station. This route, available from 1844, was not without inconvenience, requiring the services of Joe, the fictional local omnibus driver, who collected and delivered passengers between Rochester and Maidstone. It was, however, much faster than any stagecoach service from Rochester to London and it was the mode of train travel to the metropolis that prevailed until 1849. On 30 July of that year, North Kent trains began a through service between London and Strood with a ferry link to the cathedral city from their station at the canal basin.[10] This option, however, was unavailable to any of the characters in the novel, for whom Strood, on the opposite bank of the river, would have been the obvious station for journeys to and from London. Instead, they had to leave or enter Rochester via the Maidstone Road in 'a short squat omnibus'. Once within the city walls, the driver deposited them in the High Street near Eastgate House. From there, they made their way on foot to their various destinations.

'Everyone in writing', Dickens commented on one occasion, 'must speak from his own experience.'[11] The Cloisterham setting in this novel illustrates the extent to which he stood by his own pronouncement. The provincial city of Rochester was one Dickens knew and one whose buildings and streets he transformed for use on the page. This much is clear, fragmentary though the novel remains.

APPENDIX 5

Opium Use in Nineteenth-century England

Historians trace the use of opium to Sumerian ideograms dating from *c.* 4000 BC. The white poppy – *Papaver somniferum* – earned the description 'the plant of joy' on account of its ability to relieve pain and effect a change of mood. Knowledge of these two properties subsequently spread through successive civilizations. By the sixteenth century medical usage of opium was established in western Europe among a limited group of physicians and apothecaries. Among them was Dr George Turner of Bishop-gate Street, London, who, in 1601, sold a compound called laudanum. Advertised as being 'good for alleviating pain', laudanum (one of several opiate preparations dissolved in alcohol) moved steadily into the mainstream of medical practice. By the late eighteenth century its usage had become no more remarkable than that of aspirin and other analgesics today.[1]

Dr Jonathan Pereira, writing in 1853, summarizes the prevailing view of opium's status among members of the medical profession in the first half of the century:

Opium is undoubtedly the most important and valuable remedy of the whole Materia Medica. For other medicines we have one or more substitutes; for opium, none, – at least in the large majority of cases in which its peculiar and beneficial influence is required. Its good effects are not ... remote and contingent, but they are immediate, direct, and obvious; and its operation is not attended with pain or discomfort. Furthermore, it is applied, and with the greatest success, to the relief of maladies of every day's occurrence, some of which are attended with the most acute human suffering.[2]

Approximately 80 to 90 per cent of England's supply came from Turkey, a country noted for producing opium of high quality and strength. The drug was traded on the London market where it was examined and tested by medical personnel before passing into circulation, just like any other commodity, via wholesalers and local dealers.

No restrictions hampered its sale before 1868. It was available from pharmacists, apothecaries, grocers and general dealers, all of whom dispensed raw opium and laudanum.

While little was known about how the drug worked, its anaesthetic properties could hardly be disputed. Its power against neuralgia, toothache, menstrual cramps, severe discomfort arising from broken limbs, from childbirth or from almost any other known cause provided testimony to the drug's effectiveness. The availability of opium-based preparations other than laudanum corroborates this point. Among the numerous compounds for purchase without prescription were: Paregoric Elixir, a 'soothing' or 'consoling' camphorated tincture of opium; Dover's Powder, a compound of opium, saltpetre, tartar, liquorice and ipecacuanha widely used in hospitals; Godfrey's Cordial, 'a children's opiate' administered to colicky infants; and chlorodyne, a later compound of chloroform, morphia and tincture of Indian hemp. As Virginia Berridge and Griffith Edwards conclude, at all levels of Victorian society, 'opium and laudanum were commonly and unselfconsciously bought and used'. Few taking the drug regularly would bother to analyse the reasons behind their consumption.[3]

The shift in attitude towards opium which *Edwin Drood* documents needs to be set against this background of prevailing medical practice. To smoke opium as opposed to taking it orally in some form of tincture was indeed less common. For those who smoked opium a single, non-medical motive sufficed: a pleasurable relief to which, in some degree, they were addicted. As the Princess Puffer comments, noting her surprise at Jasper's absence of six months or more: '"I didn't suppose you could have kept away, alive, so long, from the poor old soul with the real receipt for mixing it! . . . Why didn't you come and have a pipe or two of comfort?"' Noting Jasper's irritability, she adds: '"We've got the all-overs, haven't us, deary? But this is the place to cure 'em in; this is the place where the all-overs is smoked off"' (ch. 23).

The side-effects of self-administered opium – taken initially for pain – did not go unnoticed. Thomas De Quincey's *Confessions of an English Opium Eater* (1821–2) provides perhaps the most eloquent and best-known testimony of the drug's ability to create what he termed 'an artificial state of pleasurable excitement'. The inducement of such had not been his motive for taking it in the first place, nor had he known such effects were indeed possible. Like many users who eventually succumbed to the slavery of opium in the nineteenth century, De Quincey's habit began innocently as an anodyne. 'It was not for the purpose of creating pleasure, but of mitigating pain in the severest degree, that I first began to use opium as an article of daily diet. In the twenty-eighth year of my age, a most painful affection of the stomach . . . attacked me with a violence that yielded to no remedies but opium.'[4]

By coincidence, John Jasper and Thomas De Quincey are almost exactly the same age. Had Dickens completed the second half of the novel, further resemblance between the two might have emerged. We might have learned, for example, about the origin of Jasper's habit and about a possible link between events in his early childhood and recurring elements in his dreams, a connection in the case of De Quincey made clear in his *Confessions*. Handsome, outstandingly gifted and conscious of his abilities, De Quincey, not unlike Dickens's 'dark man of some six-and-twenty', nevertheless felt frustrated, curtailed and thwarted owing to a combination of early sorrows and the inter-ference of unsympathetic guardians to whom the young orphan was left.[5] Before reaching his seventeenth birthday, the brilliant young scholar resolved to leave school and go immediately to college, sup-ported by 'a small patrimonial property' sufficient to supply his needs. 'I made earnest representations on the subject to my guardians,' he recollects. But to no avail. One guardian responded positively, but two resigned their authority to a fourth, who, though a worthy man, would brook no opposition to his wishes. Letters and personal interviews failed to move him, leaving De Quincey, in his own words, with 'nothing to hope for, not even a compromise of the matter . . . unconditional submission was what he demanded'.[6] Rather than comply, De Quincey ran away, an action that led, ultimately, to severe hardship and near starvation in the streets of London. Two years later he first tasted opium and indelibly altered his life.

A similar sense of resentment and constriction defines the emotional boundaries of John Jasper and constitutes the skeleton he keeps hidden in his house. Even 'a poor monotonous chorister and grinder of music', he confesses to his nephew, 'may be troubled with some stray sort of ambition, aspiration, restlessness, dissatisfaction, what shall we call it?' (ch. 2). The absence of further evidence renders impossible a more extended comparison between De Quincey and Jasper. But Jasper's confession about hating the cramped monotony of his existence and the broad hint that his only relief consists in carving demons out of his own heart provide a plausible motivation for his turning, at some point in his life, to opium dreams as an escape from a reality he hates.

We are on firmer ground when we consider the facts behind what Berridge and Griffith misleadingly call Dickens's 'melodramatic presentation' of the subject of opium and the way in which he links opium usage with mystery and evil by dwelling on the degrading and demoralizing effects of the drug on users.[7] In matters of detail, Dickens was very much a facts man, an investigator and observer with a journalist's eye for veracity. Sustained and intermittent references to opium smoking and its consequences throughout the twenty-three chapters of the novel support this contention.

Lacking clinical norms for opium use of that time means that we must employ caution before labelling Jasper's behaviour. Information provided by Dickens in the novel, however, clarifies his habit. On a continuous curve from never, escalating to daily usage, Jasper clearly belongs at neither extreme. Approximately seven or eight months after his first visit to the opium den, the focus of the novel's opening chapter, Jasper returns to get 'relief'. On that second occasion, we learn from his principal supplier that at some recent, unspecified time he 'was quite new to it'. But now, past the stage of a novice, he can take his pipe 'with the best of 'em', according to the Princess Puffer. Familiar with Jasper's habits, she expresses surprise that he has kept away from having 'a pipe or two of comfort' for over half a year. It would seem that Jasper, like De Quincey in his early stage of dependency, could ration his pleasures and indulge on his own terms rather than compulsively, a slave to an appetite that had mastered him. Jasper in fact says as much in response to the old woman's questions. ' "I have been taking it now and then in my own way," ' he admits (ch. 23). We see one instance of this in Chapter 5. Having established a credible reason in front of the city's pompous mayor to visit the Cathedral crypt one night in the company of Durdles, Jasper later retires to bed. The scene is both calm and implicitly menacing. Before passing into his own room, with 'a peculiar-looking pipe' in hand whose bowl has been carefully adjusted and filled – 'but not with tobacco' – he looks at his sleeping nephew only to retire, light the pipe and deliver himself 'to the Spectres it invokes at midnight'.

Periodic references to Jasper's health provide additional information about his degree of subordination to the drug. After a heavy bout in which he has taken several pipes, such as the one we witness in Chapter 1, Jasper rises slowly from the bed he has occupied and withdraws to 'a lean arm-chair by the hearth', placed there, the narrator notes, perhaps 'for such emergencies'. Leaving the den on the second occasion, he is accurately described as chilled and shaking as he disappears from the court 'with a wavering step' (ch. 23). Made weak and dizzy by their indulgence, practised opium smokers return unsteadily to the world they have left as they attempt to reintegrate themselves with their daily lives. Smoking also renders users short of breath, prone to coughs and momentarily disabling fits, leaving them with 'a strange film' over their eyes. Such are the symptoms in Jasper some twelve or so hours later when he entertains his nephew at dinner. So obviously overcome he is forced to offer an explanation: ' "I have been taking opium for a pain – an agony – that sometimes overcomes me. The effects of the medicine steal over me like a blight or a cloud, and pass" ' (ch. 2). Common to all users, the symptoms are easily recognized. Hands shake, drops of perspiration accumulate on foreheads, eyes stare blindly covered with a curious film while lungs wheeze and rattle. ' "Good Heaven!" ' Edwin thinks to himself, encountering similar signs in the infirm old woman with a cough he meets in the streets of Cloisterham on Christmas Eve. ' "Like Jack that night!" ' (ch. 14). Hers is an acute case, a sufferer prematurely aged and one whose dependency rests at the extreme of the continuum.

A similar quest for accuracy informs the description of the London location to which Jasper repairs for his serious sessions. In an evident wish to get things right Dickens planned and executed at least two trips to Shadwell in 1869 and 1870.[8] This was an East London suburb whose narrow lanes and dark alleys housed opium dens of ill repute, frequented largely by foreign seamen. One area in particular, known as Bluegate Fields, corresponds closely in detail to the setting evoked on the occasion of Jasper's second visit, in Chapter 23. In the words of one contemporary journalist, Bluegate Fields 'is a narrow lane opening on to High Street, Shadwell, at one end, and St George's Street at the other. To the left and right of the narrow lane are many villainous courts and alleys, consisting of one-storey high hovels'. Inside one of these was the home of Chi Ki, a celebrated Chinese, 'the renowned opium master', whose public smoking-room drew a mixed collection of patrons. 'It was an extremely mean and miserable little room,' according to the author of the same account. Sparsely furnished with three wooden chairs, a narrow fireplace and a small round table, a large four-poster bed served as the principal piece. The mattress was bare 'except for a large mat of Chinese grass' and the linen rolled up like a bolster. On occasions, the house was full when two or three ships came in. 'We've had as many as fourteen smoking in this room at one time and them that couldn't find room on the bed lay all about the floor.'[9]

A second contemporary account of a similar den in Whitechapel at no great distance from Shadwell corroborates the authenticity of Dickens's portrait. The room was small, dark and dirty, its patrons Chinese, Lascars and 'a few British blackguards'.[10] In both articles women featured as assistants. In the first, 'a youngish [English] woman, very thin and pale-looking' helped Chi Ki; in the second, the writer investigating came across an old woman in an upstairs room accessible via a ladder. She had dishevelled white hair, a thin face, 'and dull-looking eyes'. Exhaling a cloud of smoke, she coughed intermittently, 'like a person in the last stage of consumption'.[11]

For those who see melodrama rather than truth in the opium scenes of the novel, sceptical questions arise. Perhaps reasonably they might ask: since the drug was so widely available and since 'Everyone had laudanum at home',[12] why does Dickens set two chapters in a notorious East London opium den other than for reasons of sensation? The answer, I believe, has two components. First, Jasper travels 'Eastward and still eastward through the stale streets' of London in pursuit of his destination, an upstairs room in 'a miserable court' accessible by 'a broken staircase', because he wants to *smoke* opium, not ingest it orally in liquid form. And second, to do so with maximum satisfaction required assistance from an expert. True, he can – and does – take it now and then 'in his own way' (ch. 23). But sustained, drawn-out pleasure required several pipes and help from someone who 'has the true secret of mixing it' (ch. 2). The Princess Puffer is well-named: not only is she indelibly addicted, Her Royal Highness is a true princess of her art, a point she makes twice to her loyal subject, Jasper.

The journalist writing for *London Society* in 1868 supplements what we can infer from the novel about the role of 'opium masters', of whom there were few in the metropolis. To the novice, smoking afforded little pleasure, for 'to be enjoyed, the opium must be prepared by a competent hand. It is this secret that constitutes the rarity of the luxury'.[13] Once discovered, experts drew visitors to their rooms, no matter how 'vile or villainous' their actual location. And there, divested of their shoes, coat and any weapons they carried, customers prepared themselves, according to their means, for a prolonged bout of pleasure afforded by a succession of pipes. Included in the cost, which ranged from fourpence to one shilling for the largest cups, were the loan of the pipe, the bed or mattress to lie on, a cigarette or two for consumption afterwards, and, most important, 'the trouble of frizzling and preparing the drug'.

Masters of the trade were those who had acquired the art of careful preparation. This process began with taking the raw opium purchased from a supplier, shredding it into little pieces and laying these on a stout piece of canvas suspended in a small iron pot partly filled with water and positioned above a small oil lamp. 'In the process of boiling the essence of the opium drains through the canvas and forms a sediment at the bottom of the pot, leaving on the canvas the refuse, not unlike tea-leaves.'[14] Then, using an iron bodkin or needle, the master dipped the tip into the treacle-like residue, withdrew it, held it in the flame of a lamp until it partially hardened, dipped it into the pot and continued to repeat the process of 'cooking' until he had accumulated a piece the size of a large pea.

Once properly toasted, the opium was placed in a wooden or clay cup attached to a bamboo pipe approximately eighteen inches long, with the cup itself about three inches from the end. Thereupon 'the hungry customer sprang up on to the bed to enjoy it'. As he sucked at the pipe, which emitted a gurgling sound, 'the spirits of ten thousand previously smoked pipe-loads stirred to life'. Hearing this sound, the smoker sucked harder, swallowing all the black smoke 'as the lids of his elongated eyes quivered in ecstasy'. The witness on this occasion expressed surprise at the short time it took to consume the contents of the pipe – not much longer than ninety seconds. The gurgling sound in the stem of the pipe indicated that the smoke was all over, terminating 'in a brief rattle'.[15] Following that, customers might smoke a tobacco cigarette for five minutes or so and then depart. Those who could afford it, stayed on and enjoyed a succession of pipes.

The details we can gather about opium smoking from the novel corroborate to a remarkable degree those available from contemporary written accounts. The subject, however, also afforded fictional opportunities which Dickens was not slow to exploit. The dens carried an undeniable combination of the exotic and the dangerous as did the existing lore about the kind of dreams opium was thought to inspire. On this subject De Quincey is perhaps our best authority. True, the drug evidently worked as a stimulus to exotic, grandiose dreams, replete with spectacles of theatrical splendour and vast processions of 'mournful pomp'. But, as De Quincey also notes, what one dreamed tended to reflect one's preoccupations. That is to say, if smoking opium furnished dreams of 'tremendous scenery', one needs to look to the dreamer and not to the substance. In De Quincey's memorable assertion: 'If a man "whose talk is of oxen", should become an opium-eater, the probability is, that (if he is not too dull to dream at all) – he will dream about oxen.'[16] Thus it is Jasper's mind or psyche we must probe when we examine the extraordinary sequence of the opening, a rich combination of colourful images juxtaposing dancing girls and several acts of violence. 'What visions can *she* have?' exclaims Jasper, confident in the superiority of his imaginary world. Those of the old crone, he speculates, confine themselves to mundane phantoms derived from 'butchers' shops, and public-houses, and much credit' (ch. 1). His, by contrast, draw on exotic and indeed erotic material.

Victorian medical texts support the connection between opium smoking and the stimulation of the male libidinal impulse. According to one authority, 'Opium has long been celebrated as an aphrodisiac', the likely effect of which was 'a heightened condition of venereal feelings, in consequence of an increased determination of blood to that part of the brain supposed devoted to the sexual function', the cerebellum, according to phrenologists. 'Moreover, it is said to produce erection,' wrote Pereira. No slave to medical discourse, however, Dickens shows Jasper pouncing 'on the Chinaman' (ch. 2), an act of violence which reverses received wisdom. It was the common 'scientific' hypothesis among physicians like Pereira that aggression was less likely among Caucasians owing to the greater development of their brains. The operation of opium on the different races was 'not uniform', it was thought. 'On the Negro, the Malay, the Javanese, it more frequently acts as an excitement, causing furious madness, or delirium and convulsions.'[17]

A final point deserves mention. By linking opium smoking with danger and perhaps with violence, by suggesting how submission to the drug degraded and unleashed tendencies that could end up destroying the user, Dickens's portrait evidently signals a changed response to opium that evolved during the course of the century. Several strands in the spectrum of public opinion account for this shift. Members of the medical profession, for example, had understood for some time that the drug could easily prove fatal. 'Everybody knows that a large dose of laudanum will kill,' noted George Young in his *Treatise on Opium, Founded Upon Practical Observations* published in 1753.[18] A century later, Alfred Taylor, writing in 1849 in the third edition of his *Medical Jurisprudence*, warned that three to five grams of opium powder could easily kill a young child, while much smaller quantities contained in the various cordials and syrups commonly given to infants had similarly fatal potential. The absence of controls or the means of imposing strict pharmaceutical standards on the preparation of drugs meant that the strength of the opium content varied greatly. The absence of controls over the sale of opium also meant that a drug with fatal capabilities could easily be purchased and administered to unsuspecting victims whose deaths from opium were not always easy to detect. 'There are no means of detecting opium itself, either in the solid or liquid state,' wrote Taylor, 'except by its smell and other physical properties.'[19] Physicians, however, concluded that the gains from opium outweighed the risks and so its widespread medicinal application continued.

A growing awareness of the need to combat fraudulent adulteration practices, widespread in food, in drinks and in 'substances then loosely referred to as drugs', eventually challenged prevailing assumptions about opium.[20] Parliamentary inquiries, begun in 1852, documented the imperfections of existing legislation and the fact that the sale of dangerous drugs and poisons was possible by 'even the lowest class of shopkeeper'.[21] Attempts to restrict the sale of drugs and poisons to qualified personnel resulted in the Pharmacy Act of 1868. The Act listed opium and all preparations of opium or of poppies on its schedule of poisons. But despite attempts to restrict the sale of opium, the abuse of narcotics continued since the 1868 Act failed to implement the degree of stringency effective curtailment required.

Other factors lent increased urgency to those aware of the dangers posed by the widespread availability of opium. Medical professionals, for example, expressed a wish to limit the dispensing of opium solely 'to medical use'. Typical are the comments of Sir Benjamin Brodie, a distinguished surgeon held in high esteem, whose views were later cited by members of the Anglo-Oriental Society for the Suppression of the Opium Trade in the sketch they prepared in 1880 for the use of Members of, and candidates for, Parliament. While conceding the value of opium employed solely as 'an article of medicine', it is impossible, Brodie noted, to doubt that the habitual use of it is productive of 'the most pernicious consequences'. These Brodie listed as the destruction of the digestive organs, the weakening of both the body and the mind, and the reduction of those who indulged in opium, either eating it or smoking it, to a 'worse than useless member of society ... I cannot but regard those who promote the use of opium as an article of luxury as inflicting a most serious injury on the human race.'[22]

Brodie's reference to the use of opium as a 'luxury' carried a dual resonance to Victorian readers. By the second half of the century, those who took opium for pleasure, either eating it or smoking it, came under increasingly censorious scrutiny. This shift in attitude seems to derive from two principal sources. First, more people understood what the critics of opium termed 'the terribly fascinating power of the drug, whereby from small beginnings it soon held its victim in a grip', that of an adamant, coercive power from which it was almost impossible to escape. Speaking on behalf of the Anglo-Oriental Society for the Suppression of the Opium Trade, the author of an earlier publication wrote:

At first the opium pipe was no more than a pleasant companion to while away an idle hour; at last it becomes an imperative necessity, more indispensable than food or clothing. Attempts to discontinue its use rack the victim's frame with a hundred tortures, which speedily drive him to seek relief by yielding to the imperious craving. Absolute deprivation in the case of confirmed smokers in a few days terminates in death.[23]

Second, a growing number of missionaries, Members of Parliament and individuals with a conscience criticized the British government's policy of forcing on the Chinese, against their wishes, the importation of opium almost solely for consumption by increasing numbers of addicts. The custom of smoking opium in China dates from the mid-eighteenth century and the trade in opium, conducted first by the East India Company and then, after the company lost its monopoly in 1833, principally by British merchants, did much to augment a lucrative practice. Thus when the Chinese attempted to retaliate in late 1839 by interdicting the sale of opium and seizing a British merchant vessel in Chinese waters loaded with two million pounds worth of opium, England went to war, initiating the first of two so-called Opium wars. The Treaty of Tientsin in 1858 concluded hostilities between the two countries, but in such a way as to leave the British government open to its critics.[24] Opponents of the treaty quickly pointed to two 'facts' unacceptable to them. 'The first is, that the use of opium is fearfully injurious to the Chinese. The second is, that we are compelling them to admit opium against their will.'[25] Such immoral profiteering, opponents of the trade warned, would bring a day of retribution.

None came. But the public will against the use of opium purely for pleasure hardened.[26] Increasing numbers rallied to the cause as members of the Anglo-Oriental Society for the Suppression of the Opium Trade did their best to overcome the indifference evident among 'the English people and the Christian churches'. Evoking the spirit associated with an earlier cause, on the occasion of the society's first meeting in London on 13 November 1874, the chairman expressed his view that the traffic in opium could be put down 'as we have put down the slave trade'.[27]

Opposition from this energetic pressure-group gradually broadened public support for the suppression of the opium trade. An investigation by the government, conducted over two years, yielded a thorough report in 1895. But no decisive action was taken until World War I concentrated people's attention. In 1916 cocaine and opium were classified as 'dangerous' drugs under regulation 40B of the Defence of the Realm Act. Four years later, the Dangerous Drugs Act followed, implementing stringent controls for opium and other drugs, thereby forcing them underground into the problematic and difficult status they continue to occupy today.

These notes rely extensively on the research of Wendy S. Jacobson, to whom I am much indebted. Her *Companion to 'The Mystery of Edwin Drood'* (London, 1986) provides an indispensable and comprehensively annotated resource detailing the novel's social, historical, literary and topographical backgrounds. Readers interested in Dickens's use of Rochester as the setting for the fictional Cloisterham and his knowledge of opium smoking in Victorian England will find pertinent information in Appendices 4 and 5 respectively. I have also included several textual notes provided by A. J. Cox for his Penguin edition of the novel in 1974; these appear in their respective places as 'Cox'.

The following editions and abbreviations are used below:

AYR	*All the Year Round.*
BCP	The Book of Common Prayer.
Book of Memoranda	*Charles Dickens' Book of Memoranda*, ed. Fred Kaplan (New York, 1981).
Cardwell	*The Mystery of Edwin Drood*, Clarendon Edition, ed. Margaret Cardwell (Oxford, 1972).
Confessions	Thomas De Quincey, *Confessions of an English Opium Eater*, ed. Alethea Hayter (Harmondsworth, 1971). The work originally appeared anonymously in two parts in the *London Magazine* (1821) and as a single volume the following year. All references are to the 1821 text, on which Hayter based her Penguin edition.
Forster	John Forster, *The Life of Charles Dickens*, 2 vols. (1872–4); London, 1969.
HW	*Household Words.*
Jacobson	(See above.)
Letters	*The Letters of Charles Dickens*, Pilgrim Edition, ed. Madeline House, Graham Storey, Kathleen Tillotson et al. (in progress; 10 vols. to date, Oxford, 1965–).
Nonesuch	*The Letters of Charles Dickens*, Nonesuch Dickens, 3 vols., ed. Walter Dexter (London, 1938).
OED	*Oxford English Dictionary.*

Pascoe   *Charles Dickens: Selected Journalism, 1850–1870*, ed.
                          David Pascoe (Harmondsworth, 1997).

References to the text of this novel are to chapter; references to other works
by Dickens are to chapter, or to book and chapter. Biblical references are to
the King James version of the Bible, and for Shakespeare *The Complete Pelican
Shakespeare*, edited by Alfred Harbage (1969), has been used. Where the
symbols < and > are used, this indicates words deleted in the MS.

TITLE-PAGE

This is taken from the first book edition, published in August 1870.

The vignette by Luke Fildes of the Medway with the Castle and Cathedral
towers rising behind trees comes from the same edition.

CHAPTER I

The Dawn

1. *The Dawn*: The MS title reads 'The Prologue'.
2. *Cathedral town? . . . Cathedral town*: All texts published from 1870 onwards
erroneously read 'Tower' and 'tower' for 'town', until Cardwell restored the
MS reading in 1972. Resemblances between the 'ancient English Cathedral
town' of the novel and the city of Rochester are discussed in Appendix 4.
3. *by the Sultan's orders*: The description of sultans, processions, dancing-girls
and attendants evokes *The Arabian Nights Entertainments*. No one tale supplies
the details; rather, Dickens draws freely on his knowledge of the work, one
of 'a small collection of books' he devoured as a child (*David Copperfield*,
ch. 4).
4. *no writhing figure is on the grim spike*: A variant of this image occurs in *Little
Dorrit*. The old bedstead in Arthur Clennam's room has 'four bare atomies of
posts, each terminating in a spike, as if for the dismal accommodation of
lodgers who might prefer to impale themselves' (1.3).
5. *scattered consciousness*: The portrayal of Jasper's mind as being in a continuous flux in which a succession of states blend into each other anticipates
subsequent modernist trends. See, for example, Henri Bergson's examination
of the mind's fluid psychological processes in *Matter and Memory* (1896), and
attempts by T. S. Eliot and James Joyce to represent the mind in action

(Harry Stone, 'Dickens and the Interior Monologue', *Philological Quarterly* 38 (1959), pp. 52–65).

6. *a Lascar*: An Indian sailor from the Bombay region, a cheap source of maritime labour.

7. *the true secret of mixing it*: For the preparation of opium for smoking, its impact on one's health and details relating to its sale and popularity among foreign seamen in the east end of London, see Appendix 5.

8. *this unclean spirit of imitation*: That is, Jasper's hostess, whom the narrator links with the devil, as in Mark 1:25–6, 'And Jesus rebuked him, saying, Hold thy peace, and come out of him. And when the unclean spirit had torn him, and cried with a loud voice, he came out of him.'

9. *That same afternoon*: A line opened in 1844 by the South East Kent Railway Company between London Bridge Station and Maidstone speeded communication between the metropolis and most important Kentish towns. For further details relating to rail travel, see Appendix 4.

10. *gets on his own robe*: Jasper's assumption of outward respectability resembles the way in which Bradley Headstone puts on his formal attire after a night wandering the streets. 'Up came the sun to find him washed and brushed, methodically dressed in decent black coat and waistcoat, decent formal black tie, and pepper-and-salt pantaloons' (*Our Mutual Friend*, 3.11).

11. '*WHEN THE WICKED MAN* –': Compare 'the wicked man turneth away from his wickedness that he hath committed, and doeth that which is lawful and right, he shall save his soul alive' (Ezekiel 18:27). Thereafter follows, 'I acknowledge my transgressions: and my sin is ever before me' (Psalms 51:3). Both are among the sentences the Minister can read 'with a loud voice' at the beginning of Morning or Evening Prayer (*BCP*). The omission of the reference to repentance and salvation has been taken as a suggestion that Jasper is beyond hope (Henry Jackson, *About Edwin Drood*, Cambridge, 1911).

CHAPTER 2

A Dean, and a Chapter Also

1. *A Dean, and a Chapter Also*: 'Dean', originally the title for a monk who supervised ten novices, is now used to designate administrators of cathedrals or collegiate churches. Deans assume responsibility for church property and serve their bishop in numerous ways. The 'Chapter' refers to the members of the corporate body responsible for the spiritual and temporal concerns of the Cathedral.

2. *the rook*: A traditional image for the clergy. Dickens had originally written 'crow' in the MS.

3. *wings his way homeward towards nightfall*: A variant of this image occurs in *Bleak House*: 'a crow, who is out late, skim[s] westward over the leaden slice of sky' (ch. 10). Compare also *Macbeth*: 'Light thickens, and the crow / Makes wing to th' rooky wood' (III.ii.50–51).

4. *mere men*: A poeticism, as in *Paradise Regained*, 'To th' utmost of meer man both wise and good' (4.535).

5. *Not only is the day waning, but the year*: The events of the twenty-three completed chapters closely follow the seasons. The novel opens in the late autumn as Edwin visits Cloisterham shortly after Rosa's eighteenth birthday; several weeks pass after they quarrel, when the couple meet again in December and jointly agree to cancel their engagement. Edwin disappears on Christmas Eve. A full half year comes and goes before the plot moves forward again (ch. 17), bringing on Jasper's violent declaration of love to Rosa and her subsequent flight from Cloisterham, as the city basks in the sun 'so bright and sunny in these summer days'. Bright summer weather continues during the remaining scenes in both London and Cloisterham until the story breaks off.

6. *fallen leaves lie strewn thickly about*: Compare *Paradise Lost* (1.300–303):

> he stood and call'd
> His Legions, Angel Forms, who lay intrancs't
> Thick as Autumnal Leaves that strow the Brooks
> In Vallombrosa.

7. *seek sanctuary*: The phrase also plays on the Church's former authority to offer criminals sanctuary. See Chapter 16, note 13.

8. *and cast them forth*: Biblical phraseology, as in 'He casteth forth his ice like morsels: who can stand before his cold?' (Psalms 147:17).

9. *Mr Jasper*: Southey's ballad 'Jaspar' (1798; 1799) recounts the tale of a gruesome murder which inspired Thomas Hood's *Dream of Eugene Aram, the Murderer* (1829; 1831). Further similarities between the ballad and the novel are explored by Susan Shatto, 'Dickens's *Edwin Drood* and Southey's "Jaspar"', *Notes and Queries*, NS 32 (1985), pp. 359–60.

10. *Tope*: In the MS the name appears as 'Peptune' through to the end of Chapter 4.

11. *Mr Crisparkle*: The name connects him with Muscular Christianity. See note 16 below.

12. *that breathed*: Shortness of breath.

13. *Mr Jasper's heart may not be too much set upon his nephew*: Compare 'What

is man, that thou shouldest magnify him? and that thou shouldest set thine heart upon him?' (Job 7:17).

14. *is at present 'in residence'*: The Ecclesiastical Commissioner's Act of 1841 required deans to reside in their cathedrals for eight months out of the year.

15. *Minor Canon*: A canon is a diocesan priest attached to a cathedral; 'minor' designates one whose ministerial order is below the order of bishops, priests and deacons, who all belong to 'major orders'. Other 'minors' include lectors, cantors and subdeacons.

16. *pitching himself . . . deep running water*: Crisparkle's vigorous athleticism and his profession of Christianity align him with 'Muscular Christianity', a term current from about 1857 to describe the ideal of religious character championed by Charles Kingsley (1819–75) and Thomas Hughes (1822–96). In his original formulation, Hughes stressed the need for intellectual and spiritual fortitude rather than physical courage or prowess. 'The conscience of every man recognizes courage as the foundation of manliness, and manliness as the perfection of human character.' The route to this state, he suggested, was through moral effort, honed by 'constant contact and conflict with evil of all kinds . . . for without such conflict with evil there can be no perfection of character, the end for which Christ says we were sent into this world'. The struggle, furthermore, extended into one's domestic life, 'For we are born into a state of war, with falsehood, and disease, and wrong, and misery in a thousand forms, lying all around us, and the voice within calling on us to take a stand as men in the eternal battle against these' (*The Manliness of Christ*, 1879, 6–7, 34). Proposing a toast on 12 April 1864 at a dinner for the University College Hospital, Dickens revealed a humorous sympathy for Muscular Christianity, 'holding, as I do, that muscular development of anything that is good is strong presumptive proof of soundness of condition' (*Speeches of Charles Dickens*, ed. K. J. Fielding, 1960, p. 326).

17. *his early tea*: The different kinds of evening meals reflect the habits of various classes. Edwin and Jasper have dinner (ch. 3), while 'the Dean withdraws to his dinner, [and] Mr Tope to his tea' (ch. 12).

18. *doctors' stuff*: Opium, as the only effective anodyne, was, in fact, the medicinal drug of choice.

19. *schoolgirl*: The epithet conveys imprecision; in the MS Dickens had written 'schoolgirl of sixteen at the utmost'.

20. *'Tell me, shep-herds, te-e-ell me'*: A fragment from the chorus of 'The Wreath', a pastoral glee for three voices by J. Mazzinghi (1765–1844).

21. *Septimus*: Latinate names signifying a child's position in a family by birth occurred both in Victorian life and in fiction (see ch. 6). Elizabeth Barrett

Browning's two younger brothers were named Septimus (Sette) and Octavius (Occy). Initially, Dickens used the name 'Joe' up to Chapter 6.

22. *Edwin*: The name was fashionable in High Church circles; Jacobson (p. 40) also detects an allusion to the name in the ballad recounted in Goldsmith's *Vicar of Wakefield* (1766). He is loved by the fickle Angelina, who drives her admirer away, only to regret her folly.

23. *Don't moddley-coddley*: Edwin's wish is not to be treated as an invalid in need of special care. The *OED* cites this as the first recorded instance of the phrase.

24. *a look of intentness and intensity*: The first of several allusions to Jasper's mesmeric powers (see Fred Kaplan, *Dickens and Mesmerism: The Hidden Springs of Fiction*, New Jersey, 1975).

25. *'What a jolly old Jack it is!'*: Compare 'The Sailor's Consolation' (1791) by Charles Dibdin:

> Spanking Jack was so comely, so pleasant, so jolly.
> Though winds blew great guns, still he'd whistle and sing;
> Jack lov'd his friend, and was true to his Molly,
> And if honour gives greatness, was great as a king.

26. *Pussy's*: The epithet has several meanings. Here, it signifies a playfully familiar term of endearment.

27. *Marseillaise-wise*: The French national anthem, written in 1792 by Rouget de Lisle, later adopted by the Parisians and renamed 'La Marseillaise'.

28. *Begone dull care*: John Playford's popular song, published in 1667. Near the end of the chapter, Edwin quotes the last lines of the second verse: 'My wife shall dance / And I will sing, / So merrily pass the day.'

29. *includes the portrait*: A slip; the portrait hangs in the other room.

30. *My dead and gone father and Pussy's . . . must needs marry us together by anticipation*: Allusions to this Eastern custom were current in various fictional sources; see 'The Betrothed Children', a story in *HW* 10 (23 September 1854, pp. 124–9) about two children bound by their parents at birth, and Tennyson's *Maud* (1855), whose heroine is bound to the narrator before her birth (1.7.289–92). Bella Wilfer is engaged to marry John Harmon under the provisions of old Harmon's will (*Our Mutual Friend*). The story of two young people engaged to be married also appears in Dickens's *Book of Memoranda*. But there he notes that the interest is to arise out of 'the tracing of their separate ways' as they grow up and apart from each other (entry 72). Dickens used this same notebook, begun in January 1855 and maintained until almost the end of his life, to record fragments of conversations, ideas for plots, peculiar characters or characteristics and names for future characters. Other entries taken from the *Book of Memoranda* are duly noted where relevant. See also Introduction.

31. '*I have been taking opium for a pain*': Continuing to 'addresses him', this is a revised passage, written in the MS on paper pasted over the first draft. Subsequent removal of the slip reveals that Dickens had originally written:

'I have been taking opium for a pain – an agony – [I] sometimes have. Its effects steal over me like a blight or a cloud, and pass. <There is no cause for alarm> You see them in the act of passing. Put those knives out at the door – both of them!'

'My dear Jack, why?'

'It's going to lighten; they may attract the lightning; put them <away> in the dark.'

With a scared and confounded face, the younger man complies. No <lightning> flash ensues, nor was there, for a moment, any passing likelihood of a thunder storm. He gently and assiduously tends his kinsman who by slow degrees recovers and clears away that cloud or blight. When he, (Jasper) – is quite himself and is as it were once more all resolved into that concentrated look, he lays a tender hand upon his nephew's shoulder and thus addresses him (Cardwell, pp. 10–11).

32. *Lay Precentor, or Lay Clerk*: One who leads or directs the singing of a choir or congregation. In cathedrals, the office was often held by one of the minor canons, but lay persons could also perform the duties. The prefix in both cases indicates Jasper's unordained status.

33. '*I hate it. The cramped monotony of my existence grinds me away*': Philip Collins notes that Jasper's confession of a sense of alienation between himself and the institution he serves extends one of the motifs in *Our Mutual Friend*. By day, Bradley Headstone presents himself as a respectable schoolmaster; by night, he prowls the streets of London as a wild animal (see Collins, *Dickens and Crime*, 1962). A second possible stimulus to Dickens's thinking may well have been the visit he made to Canterbury Cathedral in the summer of 1869. Reportedly, 'The seeming indifference of the officiating clergy jarred most acutely' on Dickens's feelings, prompting him to wonder how any persons accepting an office, 'or a trust so important as the proper rendering of our beautiful Cathedral Service', could go through their duties 'in this mechanical and slip-shod fashion' (Charles George Dolby, *Dickens as I Knew Him: The Story of the Reading Tours*, London, 1885, p. 426). James T. Field, also present on the same occasion, records how Dickens noted the 'sleepy and inane' expressions on the faces of many of the choristers, to whom the evensong was 'but a sickening monotony of repetition' (*In and Out of Doors with Charles Dickens*, Boston, 1876, p. 131). For an earlier expression of similar sentiments by Dickens, see 'The Doom of English Wills', *HW* 2, 28 September 1850, pp. 1–4.

34. *quite devilish*: De Quincey commented that music might oppress the opium eater as being 'too sensual and gross. He naturally seeks solitude and silence' ('The Pleasures of Opium', *Confessions*, p. 81).

35. *I shall then go engineering into the East*: Opportunities for European engineers in Egypt occurred throughout the century, initiated first by the expulsion of the Turkish pashas in the 1820s and later by work on the Suez Canal. Travelling up the Nile to Cairo in 1844, William Makepeace Thackeray noted when he neared his destination that besides the 'majestical, mystical' pyramids, 'tall factory chimneys also rise here; there are foundries and steam-engine manufactories'. In addition, canals, embankments, and an improved system of agriculture spread 'at an almost feverish rate of speed' (*Notes of a Journey from Cornhill to Grand Cairo*, vol. IX, p. 228). Several hundreds of miles of railway were completed and in operation by the mid-century; and telegraph wires intersected every part of the country (Preface, *A Handbook for Travellers in Egypt*, London, John Murray, 1873, p. v). A decade later, Ferdinand de Lesseps, the French engineer, visited England in 1855 to win support for the Canal project. His campaign, together with the opening of the Canal on 17 November 1869 and the recognition of its strategic importance to British interests in the Far East, created additional professional opportunities for trained engineers.

36. *Only gloves for Pussy*: 'Nothing was more commonly in the way of present-making than gloves' ('Gloves', *AYR* 9, 27 June 1863, pp. 425–30).

37. *'Nothing half so sweet in life'*: From the first stanza of Thomas Moore's 'Love's Young Dream' (*Irish Melodies*, 1807–35):

> But there's nothing half so sweet in life
> As love's young dream:
> No, there's nothing half so sweet in life
> As love's young dream.

CHAPTER 3

The Nuns' House

1. *a fictitious name must be bestowed . . . Let it stand in these pages as Cloisterham*: For Rochester as Cloisterham, see Appendix 4.

2. *the Cloisterham children grow small salad in the dust . . .*: This passage about our eventual fate as dust echoes the Bible and Shakespeare. Compare 'for dust thou art, and unto dust shalt thou return' (Genesis 3.19) and *Hamlet* (V. i.200–203),

> Imperious Caesar, dead and turned to clay,
> Might stop a hole to keep the wind away.
> O, that that earth which kept the world in awe
> Should patch a wall t' expel the winter's flaw!

3. *the Ogre . . . grinds their bones to make his bread*: The threat made by the ogre in 'Jack and the Beanstalk', 'Be he alive, or be he dead, / I'll grind his bones to make my bread.'

4. *sun-browned tramps*: 'Tramps' (*AYR* 3, 16 June 1860, pp. 230–34) categorizes the various itinerants who belonged to 'that numerous fraternity' whom Dickens saw 'on all the summer roads' travelling between Dover and London.

5. *a paved Quaker settlement*: Evidently a fictional detail, perhaps suggested by the prevailing quietness and sobriety of the Cathedral close, since no such settlement by Quakers occurs in the history of Rochester.

6. *Seminary for Young Ladies*: In the earlier half of the century the phrase commonly designated a private school for girls. Such establishments typically taught arithmetic, reading, writing and either French or Italian. Dancing, music and other forms of refinement lightened the curriculum on the assumption that social skills prepared young ladies for marriage more successfully than rigorous intellectual training.

7. *Miss Twinkleton*: John Beer notes that the name recalls Miss Pinkerton, the head of the school Becky and Amelia attend in *Vanity Fair* (see '*Edwin Drood* and the Mystery of Apartness' (*Dickens Studies Annual* 13, 1984, p. 188)).

8. *a battered old beau with a large modern eye-glass stuck in his blind eye*: The image suggests excessive, even ludicrous attention to appearances in one who, presumably aged, is nevertheless vain enough to wear a single corrective lens in his blind eye.

9. *a stiff-necked generation*: 'Ye are a stiffnecked people' (Exodus 33:5).

10. *walled up alive*: The traditional fate of nuns who broke their vow of chastity. Reference to the practice occurs in Matthew G. Lewis, *The Monk* (1796), Sir Walter Scott, *Marmion* (1808) and Charlotte Brontë, *Villette* (1853).

11. *As, in . . . drunkenness, and . . . animal magnetism, there are two states of consciousness which never clash*: Animal magnetism was so called by the Austrian Franz Anton Mesmer (1734–1815), who, knowing that physicians often employed magnets as a remedy for various conditions, claimed to have 'cured himself by magnetic plates of a severe cardialgia'. Taking his theory further, Mesmer 'began to imagine the existence of an universal magnetic power, distinct from that of the common magnet, depending upon a fluid pervading all living and animate matter, and the source of all in art and nature'. Under the magnetic influence, induced by a repetitive movement of the hand, patients

typically experienced what Dr John Elliotson called 'double consciousness': 'In their ecstatic delirium, they know nothing of what has occurred in their natural state: they know not who they are, nor their ages, nor any thing which they learned in their healthy state: and in their natural state they are perfectly ignorant of all that has passed in their delirium' (*Human Physiology*, 1840, pp. 662, 1165).

12. *thus, if I hide my watch when I am drunk, I must be drunk again before I can remember where*: The reference is to the case of an Irish porter whom Elliotson cites as dubious proof of the existence of two states of consciousness. On one occasion, the porter, being drunk, 'lost a parcel of some value, and in his sober moments could give no account of it. Next time he was intoxicated, he recollected that he had left the parcel at a certain house, and there being no address on it, it had remained there safely, and was got on his calling for it' (*Human Physiology*, p. 646). Dickens's interest in mesmerism is examined by Fred Kaplan (*Dickens and Mesmerism*).

13. *Tunbridge Wells*: A market town in Kent, once famous as an inland watering-place on account of its chalybeate springs, approximately twenty-six miles west of Rochester and thirty-five south-east of London.

14. *a certain finished gentleman*: 'Finished' in the sense of accomplished.

15. *she has seen better days*: Compare Shakespeare, 'True is it that we have seen better days, / And have with holy bell been knolled to church' (*As You Like It*, II.vii.120–21).

16. *transported*: Sent overseas, a common fate for felons from the early seventeenth century onwards. The shipping of convicts to the North American colonies ended with the Declaration of Independence in 1776. Thereafter, prisoners were temporarily housed in hulks on the Thames until the government developed Botany Bay as a penal colony in 1790. Transportation to New South Wales ended in 1840, but the system continued elsewhere intermittently until it was totally abolished in 1867.

17. *the Mark goes round*: A demerit badge passed from one pupil to another on a culprit's being detected of committing the same offence, in this case, looking out of the window.

18. *Wandering Jewess*: The Wandering Jew, a legendary figure condemned to wander until the second coming of Christ for taunting Jesus on his way to the crucifixion.

19. *like mice in the wainscot*: Compare Tennyson's 'the mouse / Behind the mouldering wainscot shrieked, / Or from the crevice peered about' ('Mariana', 1830; lines 63–5).

20. '*And how did you pass your birthday, Pussy?*': The passage beginning with this sentence and continuing to 'He checks the look, and asks' is not in the

MS. Dickens inserted the dialogue in order to bring the first instalment up to its full complement of thirty-two pages.

21. *the legendary ghost of a Dowager*: Unidentified, although the reference might not be specific.

22. *'Ah! you should hear Miss Twinkleton'*: Several factors accounted for England's growing interest in Egypt, as the country's past was exposed to scrutiny following Napoleon's defeat by British forces in 1801 during the revolutionary wars against France. In 1809 William Bullock opened the so-called 'Egyptian Hall' in Piccadilly, which became the centre for interest in Egypt. Major archaeological discoveries by Giovanni Belzoni (see note 24 below) created further excitement, as he and others organized exhibitions of Egyptian artifacts, pictures and statuary, all beautifully mounted and carefully displayed. In the ensuing years, increasing numbers of travellers and professionals (see Chapter 2, note 35) extended the public's awareness of the country. Until then knowledge about Egypt had been acquired primarily from the Bible. Equally significant, especially by the mid-century, was the country's geographical location: 'The geographical position of Egypt – standing midway between England and her Indian possessions – the great highway of a constantly increasing communication – must have a political importance of the highest order' (Sir John Bowring, *Autobiographical Recollections*, 1877, p. 174).

23. *Tiresome old burying-grounds! Isises, and Ibises, and Cheopses*: Respectively, the Valley of the Kings at Luxor, the ancient burial ground of Egypt's pharaohs; the goddess and wife of Osiris, one of the chief gods of Egypt; the sacred bird venerated by the Egyptians; and Cheops, the king who built the Great Pyramid.

24. *Belzoni . . . half choked with bats and dust*: Giovanni Battista Belzoni (1778–1823), Italian-born hydraulics engineer and renowned explorer. His account of his excavations of tombs, pyramids and temples in Egypt and the Nile valley aroused archaeological curiosity about the Ancient World early in the nineteenth century. Setting foot in galleries filled with mummies and various treasures, he recounts: 'A vast quantity of dust rises, so fine that it enters into the throat and nostrils, and chokes the nose and mouth to such a degree, that it requires great power of lungs to resist it and the strong effluvia of the mummies' (*Narrative of the Operations and Recent Discoveries . . . in Egypt and Nubia*, 2 vols., 1820, 1.242–3).

25. *you Egyptian boys could look into a hand and see all sorts of phantoms*: Egyptian magic, according to an article in *HW*, worked 'by putting a blot of thick black fluid into the palm of a boy's hand, and commanding him to see various people and things' ('The Magic Crystal', *HW* 2, 14 December 1850, pp. 284–8).

CHAPTER 4

Mr Sapsea

1. *Sapsea*: The name appears among the list of 'Available Names' recorded in the *Book of Memoranda* (entry 109). The 'sap' in Sapsea possibly refers to his foolishness.

2. *'dresses at' the Dean*: 'To dress at a person, is to dress and adorn in order to enamour or gain the affection of a person' (*OED*, dress, v. 7c).

3. *Fever and the Plague*: Epidemic diseases associated with England's rapid urban growth in the nineteenth century flourished in crowded and ill-planned cities. Among the most common were typhus, smallpox, and cholera, a water-borne bacterial infection prevalent from the 1830s. Cholera proved especially dangerous until the discovery of the link between the disease and contaminated water later in the century.

4. *eight-day clock*: One that requires winding once a week, as opposed to those that required winding after only thirty hours. Eight-day clocks were common from the mid-eighteenth century.

5. *'Ethelinda'*: The name appears in the *Book of Memoranda*, where it is spelled 'Ethlynida' (entry 110); it had also been used by Charlotte Smith in her novel *Ethelinde: or, The Recluse of the Lake* (1790), and by Elizabeth Gaskell in her short story 'Morton Hall', published in *HW* 8 (19 November 1853, pp. 265–72).

6. *'When the French come over, / May we meet them at Dover!'*: A toast taunting the army assembled in 1804 at Boulogne by Napoleon Bonaparte (1769–1821) to invade England.

7. *'If I have not gone to foreign countries . . . foreign countries have come to me'*: A play on the proverb 'If the Mountain will not come to Mahomet, Mahomet will go to the mountain'.

8. *a French clock*: French manufacturers set the pace for the production of clocks from the seventeenth century onwards. It is likely that the reference is to the French travelling or carriage clock, a model introduced early in the nineteenth century and exported in large numbers. Such clocks stood from three to twelve inches high, had a carrying handle and were usually encased in plain brass.

9. *'Pekin, Nankin, and Canton.' . . . bamboo and sandal-wood*: All three cities were among the many early sites in China with kilns capable of achieving the controlled high temperatures necessary to vitrify clay and so produce distinctive ceramic wares for both useful and decorative purposes. Imported bamboo was used for basket-making, furniture, umbrella handles and walking sticks;

sandalwood from India and the Pacific islands supplied the material for boxes, fans and other ornamental objects.

10. *now dead three quarters of a year*: The autumnal opening (see Chapter 2, note 5) would suggest that Mrs Sapsea died in January, nine months before.

11. *it is not good for man to be alone*: Compare 'And the Lord God said, It is not good that the man should be alone; I will make him an help meet for him' (Genesis 2:18).

12. *Miss Brobity*: Entry 116 in the *Book of Memoranda* reads, '"Then I'll give up snuff." / Brobity / An Alarming Sacrifice / Mr Brobity's Snuff box. / The pawnbroker's account of it.' Forster notes that since Brobity 'is the name of one of the people in his unfinished story . . . the suggestion may have been meant for some incident in it' (Forster, 2.311).

13. *the dictation-exercises of Miss Brobity's pupils*: A common pedagogical practice used to improve spelling and handwriting while imparting knowledge.

14. *the finger of scorn*: See Shakespeare, *Othello*, 'But, alas, to make me / A fixèd figure for the time of scorn / To point his slow unmoving finger at!' (IV.ii.53–5).

15. *wasting my evening conversation on the desert air*: From Thomas Gray, 'Elegy Written in a Country Churchyard' (1751): 'Full many a flower is born to blush unseen. / And waste its sweetness on the desert air' (lines 55–6).

16. *Man proposes, Heaven disposes*: Thomas à Kempis (1380–1471), *Imitatio Christi*, ch. 1. section xix.

17. Such 'vulgar extravagancies' as Sapsea's epitaph for his wife occurred in real life. For one such example, see 'Curious Epitaph' published in *HW* 1 (11 May 1850, p. 168). Immoderate tombstone inscriptions drew critical attention in the 1840s. The reaction against inflated sentiments was led by reformers such as A. W. Pugin, J. C. Loudon, J. H. Markland and George Blair, all of whom advocated a return to simplicity and to plain epitaphs. Dickens practised what he advocated. In his will he directed that his name be inscribed 'in plain English letters on my tomb without the addition of "Mr" or "Esquire"' (Forster, 2. Appendix). *AUCTIONEER, VALUER, ESTATE AGENT*: Advocates of plain language argued that the survivor's profession or trade should be stated simply; Sapsea's flourishes inevitably draw attention to him rather than to his deceased wife. *STRANGER PAUSE*: An adaptation of the Roman inscription, 'Siste, Viator' ('Stop, Traveller'). 'We depart from Nature when we imitate the Romans, and so miss all due effect altogether' (*HW*, see above). *WITH A BLUSH RETIRE*: In *Tristram Shandy* (1760–67), Sterne had written: 'Ten times a day has Yorick's ghost the consolation to hear his monumental inscription read over with such a variety of plaintive tones, as denote a general pity and esteem for him . . . not a passenger goes by without stopping to cast a look upon it, – and sighing he walks on, Alas, poor YORICK!' (vol. 1, ch. 12).

18. *Durdles*: See *Book of Memoranda* which lists 'Duddle' (entry 109).

19. *He is the chartered libertine of the place*: See Shakespeare, *Henry V*, 'when he speaks, / The air, a charter'd libertine, is still' (I.i.48). In Chapter 23, Dickens refers to Sapsea as 'the chartered bore' of the city.

20. *a wonderful sot*: Sextons and gravediggers were commonly regarded as drunkards on account of the nature of their work. In particular, Edwin Chadwick's *Supplementary Report on the Results of a Special Inquiry into the Practice of Interment in Towns* (1843) drew attention to their behaviour, as did reviews of Chadwick's *Report*. See especially an article in the *Quarterly Review* 73 (1844), pp. 458–9.

21. *turned to powder*: Accounts by several nineteenth-century writers perpetrate the fanciful notion of bodies turning instantly to dust on exposure to air. See Tennyson ('Alymer's Field', 1864), Mrs Hamilton Gray (*Tour of Etruria*, 1840), R. C. Trench (*The Etrurian King*, 1842) and Edmund Ollier ('Eternal Lamps', *HW* 8, 22 October 1853, pp. 185–8). Dickens refers to the phenomenon in *Bleak House* (ch. 29), *A Tale of Two Cities* (1.3) and *Great Expectations* (ch. 29), and appears to accept such exaggerated descriptions as fact.

22. *sounding and tapping*: Belzoni and other antiquarians employed this same method to discover by sound hollow spaces between seemingly solid walls. See Belzoni, *Narrative of the Operations and Recent Discoveries*, 1.280.

23. *mechanical figures emblematical of Time and Death*: Exhibitions in London since the eighteenth century commonly featured wooden or wax models moved by clockwork. The figures varied in size and represented different allegorical, historical and fictional characters.

24. *as the Catechism says, a walking in the same all the days of your life*: In answer to the third question, about the promises made by godparents on his behalf, the catechumen vows 'to keep God's holy will . . . and walk in the same all the days' of his life (*BCP*, 'A Catechism').

25. *as he idly examines the keys*: Jasper's casual demeanour signals an intense interest in the keys, and points to the expedition with Durdles described in Chapter 12. In the Number Plan Dickens had noted: 'Jasper and the keys', while the phrase 'The keys' is repeated in the plan for Chapter 4. Tulkinghorn, anxious to learn about the copyist Nemo in *Bleak House*, assumes a similar strategy of unconcern (chs. 10 and 11).

26. *an Ostrich, and liked to dine off cold iron*: The ostrich's liking for hard substances, which it swallows to assist the gizzard in its functions, accounts for the traditional belief that it liked to eat iron.

27. *deigning no word of answer*: To smooth the transposition of the next chapter from the second to the first number, Dickens rewrote and added the paragraph which ends here. In the MS the chapter ends: 'and finally he gets out of the room with the sulky retort: "How does the fact stand, Mr Jasper? The fact stands six on one side to half a dozen on t'other. So far as Durdles sees the fact with *his* eyes, it has took up about that position as near as may be." '

CHAPTER 5

Mr Durdles and Friend

1. *Mr Durdles and Friend*: This was originally Chapter 8 but was moved forward to make up the length of number 1. To fill out the second number, Dickens wrote a new chapter, 'Birds in the Bush'.

2. *John Jasper, on his way home through the Close*: The transfer of the chapter (see note above) inadvertently creates a conflict with the actual topography. The direct route home from Mr Sapsea's would have been down the High Street rather than the detour required to arrive at the Gate House by crossing the Close, which accords with Jasper's leaving Minor Canon Corner, as Dickens had originally planned in Chapter 7. See map of Cloisterham.

3. *'Mulled agin!'*: An athletics term meaning to fail, as in mulling a catch in cricket.

4. *cock-shy*: Live cocks, later replaced by models, served as targets at Shrove-tide fairs. Boys who displaced the bird or the toy with a well-aimed stone kept their prize. By 1865 the custom was virtually extinct.

5. *chants, like a little savage, half stumbling and half dancing*: Jacobson (p. 70) speculates that entry 100 in the *Book of Memoranda* may relate to this scene: 'The father and boy, as I dramatically see them. Opening with a wild dance, I have in my mind.' Kaplan records this entry as 'untraced'.

6. *'Widdy widdy wen!'*: A challenge or caution delivered from behind a line when playing 'Widdy' or 'Warning'. The player then runs out after the dare to touch the first person she can; these two return to the line, repeat the provocation and then try to catch others in the group.

7. *a poetical note of preparation*: See Shakespeare, *Henry V* (IV. Chorus. 10–14):

> Steed threatens steed, in high and boastful neighs
> Piercing the night's dull ear; and from the tents
> The armorers, accomplishing the knights,
> With busy hammers closing rivets up,
> Give dreadful note of preparation.

8. *'Do you know this thing, this child?'*: Deputy resembles the boy in *The Haunted Man* (one of Dickens's Christmas books, 1848) who troubles the conscience of Redlaw. 'A baby savage, a young monster, a child who had never been a child, a creature who might live to take the outward form of man, but who, within, would live and perish a mere beast' (ch. 1).

9. *Travellers' Twopenny*: A cheap lodging place providing shelter for a few pence. Such houses were characteristically crowded, unsanitary, afflicted with rats and without adequate washing facilities.

10. *Garding*: Garden.

11. *'All us man-servants at Travellers' Lodgings is named Deputy'*: A common practice. See 'On Duty with Inspector Field', when Dickens, accompanied by a police escort, makes the rounds of some of London's roughest lodging houses (*HW* 3, 14 June 1851, pp. 265–70; Pascoe, pp. 306–17).

12. *Your own brother-in-law*: Presumably the importance of this fact, together with other details of Jasper's family, would have been developed in the second half of the novel.

13. *devoted wife*: The MS reads 'with inscription finished'. The transposition of the chapter made it necessary to cancel this phrase.

14. *broken column . . . a vase and towel, standing on what might represent the cake of soap*: The reformers of ecclesiastical art objected to emblems derived from classical models, arguing that they disfigured both burial grounds and 'the interior of the sacred building itself'. Instead, they preferred recumbent effigies, angels, crosses and other 'emblems of mercy and redemption' rather than 'pagan abominations' like urns, broken pillars, extinguished lamps and inverted torches. See A. Welby Pugin, *An Apology for the Revival of Christian Architecture in England*, 1843, p. 37.

15. *the common folk that is merely bundled up in turf and brambles*: The portion of a cemetery set apart as unconsecrated ground for the bodies of paupers, unbaptized infants and suicides. See the description of a pauper's burial in *Oliver Twist* (ch. 5).

16. *Peter the Wild Boy*: One of a number of 'wild' children found abandoned throughout Europe between 1500 and 1700. Retrieved from woods, where they had lived isolated and like animals, they were taken in by doctors and others who sought to educate them. This particular boy, discovered in 1725 near Hamlin, Germany, was brought to England as the protégé of George I and placed under the care of Dr Arbuthnot (1667–1735), who named him Peter. After failing to respond to treatment, he was later entrusted to a farmer in Hertfordshire and lived with him but died shortly after the farmer's death in 1785.

17. *a sort of a – scheme of a – National Education*: Until the Education Act of 1870 introduced secular rate-supported elementary schools, England and

Wales lacked a national system of education, the development of which had been slowed by religious conflicts over the state's role. Schooling depended instead on voluntary efforts organized principally by religious, philanthropic and private bodies. The Act of 1870, however, opened the way to free and compulsory education and to increasingly interventionist policies by governments willing to recognize the importance of schooling to a modern, democratic society.

18. *a rear rank of one, taking open order*: Military terminology for men at the back and for the formation in which individuals are set three or more yards apart ('open order').

19. *than in mine*: A paragraph describing Durdles follows 'mine' in the MS: 'As the mental state of Durdles, and of all his sodden tribe, is one hardly susceptible of any astonishment in itself, so it is one hardly susceptible of any reasonable interpretation by other minds. But it happens to fall out tonight – just as it might have happened to fall out quite the other way – that Durdles rather likes his position in the dialogue, and chuckles over it.'

20. *hanged by the neck . . . until they are dead*: The words of the former death sentence: 'The sentence of the Court upon you is, that you be taken from this place to a lawful prison and thence to a place of execution and that you be hanged by the neck until you be dead.' The Labour Government abolished hanging in 1965 following a sequence of controversial judgments and miscarriages of justice.

21. *Say Mrs Sapsea*: This hypothetical case of Durdles perhaps hints at how the body of Edwin would eventually be discovered.

22. *feeble lights of rush or cotton dip*: Rush lights were made from the pith of a rush dipped in tallow or other grease; a dip candle was made by repeatedly dipping a wick into melted tallow. Both were cheap forms of lighting and provided far less illumination than wax candles.

23. *come near*: The passage cancelled from the MS reads:

As Durdles and Jasper come near, a woman is seen crouching and smoking in the cold night air on a seat just outside the door, which stands ajar.

Of a sudden, Jasper stops, and looks at this woman – the lighter-colored figure of Durdles being between himself and her – very keenly.

'Is that Deputy?' she croaks out in a whimpering and feeble way; 'where have you been, you young good for nothing wretch?'

'Out for my 'elth,' returns the hideous sprite.

'I'll claw you,' retorts the woman, 'when I can lay my fingers on you. I'll be bad for your 'elth! (O me, o me, my breath is very short!) I wanted my pipe and my little spoon, and ye'd been and put 'em on a shelf I couldn't find.'

'Wot did yer go to bed for then?' retorts Deputy, quite unabashed. 'Who ha' thought yer wos going to get up agin?'

'You. You might ha' known I was like to do it.'

'Yer lie!' says Deputy, in his only form of contradiction.

Jasper, touching Durdles on the shoulder, and laying his finger on his lips when that worthy looks round, leads the way onward gingerly enough. He more than once or twice looks back, but utters no word until they have reached the corner of the lane; then he casually remarks in a subdued voice that he is well out of any unseemly quarrel or discussion in such a place, and glances back again. All is still.

The revision appears to represent a consequence of bringing forward Chapter 8. In his notes for that chapter as originally planned, Dickens had written: 'Carry through the woman of the 1st chapter'. Then in the left margin appears the notation 'No', which suggests that the revised position was too early to indicate the link between Jasper and the opium-woman.

24. *according to a custom of late years comfortably established among the police . . . where Christians are stoned on all sides . . . days of Saint Stephen were revived*: The comment is ironic. In 'The Ruffian', Dickens blamed a combination of leniency on the part of the magistracy and a tendency to contemplation rather than swift, punitive action by the police for increasingly uncivil behaviour among young ruffians. 'The throwing of stones in the streets has become a dangerous and destructive offence, which surely could have got to no greater height though we had had no Police.' Similarly, 'The throwing of stones at the windows of railway carriages in motion . . . [has] become a crying evil' (*AYR* 20, 10 October 1868, pp. 421–6). Stephen, accused of blasphemy, was the first Christian martyr to die: 'And thou shalt stone him with stones, that he die; because he hath sought to thrust thee away from the Lord thy God' (Deuteronomy 13:10).

25. *John Jasper stands looking down upon him*: Compare the officer who confesses to the murder of his nephew, who would occasionally steal upstairs to watch the boy as he slept, thinking 'how easily it might be done' ('The Clock-Case. A confession Found in a Prison in the Time of Charles the Second', *Master Humphrey's Clock*, 1842).

CHAPTER 6

Philanthropy in Minor Canon Corner

1. *boxing-gloves*: Jack Broughton (1705–89), a well-known Regency figure and England's greatest teacher of boxing, introduced padded gloves for sparring and so helped separate the sport from bare-fisted pugilism.

2. *Here's wind*: A sporting expression for regular or easy breathing.

3. *into Chancery*: A boxing term for pummelling one's opponent by holding his head under one arm and beating him with the other. The expression derives from the reputation the Court of Chancery gained for holding cases for a long time and exacting high costs from the property in question.

4. *the Lord's Prayer*: 'Our Father', the Lord's Prayer, was the prayer Jesus taught his disciples in answer to their request, 'Lord, teach us to pray' (Matthew 6:9–13 and Luke 11:2–4).

5. *the dress of a china shepherdess: so dainty in its colors*: The allusion, as the reference to Mrs Crisparkle's sister as 'another piece of Dresden china' later in the chapter makes clear, is to the porcelain figures first manufactured in Meissen near Dresden. Production began in 1710 when Frederick Augustus, Elector of Saxony, established the Royal Saxon Porcelain Factory. Pastoral figures with pink flesh tones wearing gaily coloured costumes, with pale blue predominating, found a ready market throughout Europe as decorations for the dining table.

6. *Swaggering fighting men . . .* : For Minor Canon Corner and Rochester's turbulent past, see Appendix 4.

7. *that serenely romantic state of the mind . . . a pathetic play that is played out*: In Chapter 6 of his fragmentary prose treatise *Poetics* (*c.* 330 BC), Aristotle argues that tragedy, by imitating a significant action in enhanced language, evokes pity and fear and thereby brings about a purgation ('catharsis') of such feelings in the minds of the spectators.

8. *Haven of Philanthropy*: The target of Dickens's satire is Exeter Hall in the Strand, London, a purpose-built convention centre which opened in 1831. This 'temple' of philanthropy with its 'votaries' and 'priesthood' seated 4,000 delegates, and from May to June it served as the venue for the annual meetings of England's many charitable organizations. While Dickens himself worked energetically on behalf of various good causes, philanthropy combined with arrogance and hypocrisy angered him. 'It might be laid down as a very good general rule of social and political guidance, that whatever Exeter Hall champions, is the thing by no means to be done' ('The Niger Expedition',

Examiner, 19 August 1848). See also, 'The Ladies' Societies', *Evening Chronicle*, 20 August 1835 (in *Sketches by Boz*, 1836) and 'A Handful of Humbugs', *AYR* 10, 12 September 1863, pp. 55–8.

9. *Helena Landless*: The MS shows two rejected surnames – 'Heyridge' and 'Heyfort' – and 'Olympia' as Helena's first name.

10. *the paths of peace*: 'Her ways are ways of pleasantness, and all her paths are peace' (Proverbs 3:17).

11. *Your affectionate brother (In Philanthropy)*: A parody of the signature used by the clergy, 'brother in Christ'.

12. *his voice is so much larger*: Compare Mr Jarndyce's remark, 'there were two classes of charitable people: one, the people who did a little and made a great deal of noise; the other, the people who did a great deal and made no noise at all' (*Bleak House*, ch. 8).

13. *Superior Family Souchong*: A good quality black tea from China. An article in *HW* 3 (14 June 1851, p. 283) explains that 'Souchong' means 'small or scarce sort' and that it is 'the best black tea of the second crop'.

14. *Corporation preferment in London City*: That is, he occupies a living bestowed on him by the Lord Mayor and Aldermen of the City of London, the corporation in whose hands such preferments lay. Recipients of such patronage typically received endowment income, tithes and other sources of revenue attached to the living.

15. *a public occasion of a philanthropic nature . . . glutted with plum buns*: Teas, the distribution of toys and the organization of other festivities were among the many charitable activities undertaken by women throughout the century.

16. *the fairy bride that is to be*: From 'The Mistletoe Bough'. This old English song tells of a young bride who hides in an oak chest while playing games at Christmas. Years later, her skeleton is discovered.

17. *to ruin the Money Market if it failed, and Church and State if it succeeded*: The reference is to the prospect of a collapse in the stock market if shareholders in the new railway companies panicked and withdrew their money at the first sign of failure, and also to the fears of the Sabbatarians, for whom the prospect of success and Sunday rail travel was thought to herald the end of worship and church-going in the country.

18. *omnibus*: Omnibuses were introduced in London in 1829 and quickly spread to other cities.

19. *like a little Elephant with infinitely too much Castle*: The sign of an inn on the south bank of the Thames. The name has also been transferred to its location, St George's Circus, the meeting-point of roads from Westminster, Waterloo and Blackfriars bridges.

20. *outside passenger seated on the box*: Coaches accommodated passengers

both 'inside' and 'outside'. Up to eight of the latter sat in two rows, one of whom took the place next to the driver. This 'box' seat contained tools and equipment for the coach and horses.

21. *The worm will, when –*: Shakespeare, *3 Henry VI* (II.ii.17), 'The smallest worm will turn, being trodden on'.

22. *Then they came to Minor Canon Corner*: This sentence does not appear in previous editions of *The Mystery of Edwin Drood*. It is written on the back of MS page 6 of the second number, and Cox conjectures that it was meant to open the crowded first paragraph at the top of the page, which begins, a trifle abruptly: 'Mrs Crisparkle had need of her own share of philanthropy . . .' Cox further speculates that the sentence was either overlooked by the printers or that they omitted it not knowing what to do with it. And since Dickens himself did not habitually consult his MS when correcting proofs, he, too, could just as easily have overlooked it.

23. *this very large and very loud excrescence*: John Bright (1811–89), the radical Quaker politician, is the accepted 'original' on account of his rude and brusque manner. Bright was a prominent member of the Peace Society and notorious for denouncing war in a pugnacious manner (see K. J. Fielding, 'Edwin Drood and Governor Eyre', *Listener* 48, 25 December 1952, pp. 1083–4).

24. *You were to abolish military force . . . trial by court martial*: Dickens refers to the unsuccessful efforts of the Jamaica Committee formed in 1866 to prosecute Edward John Eyre (1815–1901) for murder. In October 1865, Eyre, the English governor of Jamaica, suppressed a rising against British rule in Morant Bay. He imposed martial law and ordered numerous floggings and executions. An outcry in England prompted his recall and an official inquiry. Eyre was criticized for his severity yet praised for the rapidity with which he had quelled the rebellion.

25. *the apple of their eye*: Psalms 17:8 and Proverbs 7:2; *the face of the earth*: 'upon the face of the deep', Genesis 1:2; *to love your brother as yourself*: 'love thy neighbour as thyself', Leviticus 19:18 and Matthew 19:19.

26. *to do nothing in private . . . evermore to live upon a platform*: Loud posturing before the court of public opinion and inattention to the efforts of all who discharged their immediate obligations were among the persistent objections Dickens raised to philanthropists associated with Exeter Hall.

CHAPTER 7

More Confidences than One

1. *Ceylon*: Dickens sets the youthful hardships of the Landless twins against an appropriately difficult and unstable background. British rule in Ceylon began in 1796 following an earlier period of colonization characterized by savage wars waged by the natives against first the Portuguese and then the Dutch. A period of stability followed as the commercial development of crops (cinnamon, coconut, coffee and tea) attracted European speculators. Success, however, tempted the island's officials, judges and clergy from their duties, promoting tension which resulted in the Sinhalese rising of 1848. Dickens's knowledge of Ceylon came mainly from his close friend Sir James Emerson Tennent (1804–69), former civil secretary to the colonial government of Ceylon (1845–8) and author of *Ceylon: An Account of the Island, Physical, Historical, and Topographical*, 2 vols. (1859).

2. *brought up among abject and servile dependents, of an inferior race*: The MS reads: 'an inferior and servile eastern race, abjectly devoted to my step-father's title' (not in Cardwell). Political disruptions within the empire (the Sepoy rebellion in India in 1857, the Jamaican insurrection in 1867, and continuing troubles in Ireland) adversely affected British public opinion about native peoples united by common morphology and culture. The division of the races by skin colour – begun by Carl von Linnaeus (1707–78) – led to an increasing acceptance of the idea of a racial hierarchy, explicit in Neville's judgement, but modified by Mr Crisparkle's inward thought. Impatience and anger inform Dickens's own reaction to the Indian Mutiny, expressed on one occasion as a wish to raze the Oriental race 'off the face of the earth'. This extravagant statement was made to Miss Burdett Coutts, munificent philanthropist and close friend of Dickens, on 4 October 1857, and may have been informed by his anxiety for his sixteen-year-old son Walter, whose arrival in India as a cadet in the East India Company coincided with the start of the Mutiny (*Letters*, 8.459).

3. *dressed as a boy*: This detail serves as the basis for those who argue that Datchery is really Helena in disguise. This idea was first proposed by J. Cuming Walters (*Clues to Dickens's Mystery of Edwin Drood*, London, 1905) and received much attention in the pages of the *Dickensian*. Interest in the issue did not abate until late in the 1930s.

4. *a complete understanding . . . between my sister and me*: This unexplained bond – possibly some type of mesmerism – clears Neville of suspicion

since his sister is unequivocally convinced of his innocence in Drood's disappearance.

5. *he followed her lips most attentively*: Compare Dickens's Number Plan for Chapter 6: 'Piano scene with Jasper. She singing, he following her lips.'

6. *the future wives and mothers of England*: Sarah Stickney Ellis was the author of popular conduct manuals on 'women's duty', *The Mothers of England* (1843), *The Wives of England* (1845) and *The Daughters of England* (1845).

7. *as if he could pass in through the wall*: Mesmerists claimed that neither walls nor distance were obstacles to their experiments.

CHAPTER 8

Daggers Drawn

1. *to wake up Egypt a little*: That is, to bring Egypt into the modern industrial world. See Chapter 2, note 35.

2. *among Heathens*: Buddhism predominated among the native inhabitants since Christian missionaries, according to Sir James Emerson Tennent, had not met with great success (*Ceylon: An Account of the Island*, 1.11).

3. *mulled wine at the fire*: The recipe in Dickens's day typically called for the addition of sugar, spices, and a beaten egg-yolk to thicken the mixture by heating it in the fire.

4. *Juno, Minerva, Diana, and Venus*: The classical deities of beauty, wisdom, power and love.

5. *The world is all before him where to choose*: See the description of the expulsion of Adam and Eve from Paradise in Milton's *Paradise Lost* (12.646–9):

> The World was all before them, where to choose
> Thir place of rest, and Providence thir guide:
> They hand in hand with wandering steps and slow
> Through Eden took their solitarie way.

6. *pluck the golden fruit that hangs ripe on the tree*: The golden apples of the Hesperides, given to Jupiter by Juno on their wedding day.

7. *his dark skin*: Dark because the Landlesses have either gypsy or native blood.

8. *a blood-red whirl, waiting to be struggled with, and to struggle to the death*: The toxic effects of the drug resemble those experienced by John Harmon. On drinking some coffee, he finds himself in a whirling state as he drops

down on the ground with a sense of flames flashing before his eyes (*Our Mutual Friend*, 2.13).

9. *his steam-hammer beating head and heart*: Steam-hammers were capable of a wide range of adjustments from pounding piles to producing light taps. A drawing by James Nasmyth in 1839 is usually cited as the first practical model; it was patented in 1842.

10. *The south wind that goes where it lists*: Compare 'The wind bloweth where it listeth, and thou hearest the sound thereof, but canst not tell whence it cometh, and whither it goeth: so is every one that is born of the Spirit' (John 3:8).

11. *a dangerous charge*: The MS continues, 'You must sometime – no doubt, often – have to put yourself in opposition to this fierce nature and suppress it. After what I have seen tonight, I am fearful even for you.'

CHAPTER 9

Birds in the Bush

1. *Birds in the Bush*: Transferring this chapter to the second number (see Chapter 5, note 1) required the removal of several lines to bring the instalment to thirty-two pages. The deletions, mainly from the peripatetic conversation between Mr Grewgious and Jasper, are given below.

2. *Every fold and color in the pretty summer dress, and even the long wet hair, with scattered petals of ruined flowers still clinging to it*: Compare the image of 'Ophelia' in the painting by Sir John Everett Millais (1852).

3. *By what means the news . . . got into Miss Twinkleton's establishment*: The spreading of the news resembles the passage in Sterne's *Life and Opinions of Tristram Shandy* when Susannah 'instantly imparted' the family secret 'by signs to Jonathan': 'and Jonathan by tokens to the cook, as she was basting a loin of mutton; the cook sold it with some kitchen-fat to the postillion for a groat, who trucked it with the dairy maid for something of about the same value – and though whispered in the hay-loft, FAME caught the notes with her brazen trumpet, and sounded them upon the house-top – In a word, not an old woman in the village or five miles around, who did not understand the difficulties of my uncle Toby's siege, and what were the secret articles which had delayed the surrender' (vol. 9, ch. 32).

4. *the adulteration of his milk*: The reference is also literal; the addition of water to milk to thin it and then starch to thicken it was not uncommon. See 'Milk' in *AYR* 13 (4 March 1865, pp. 126–31). Research by Dr Arthur Hill

Hassall, published first in a series of articles in the *Lancet* from 1851 to 1854 and then in book form as *Food and Its Adulterations* (1855) brought public attention to this widespread abuse.

5. *the Graces*: Aglaia, Thalia and Euphrosyne, the three Greek deities personifying grace, charm and beauty.

6. *Peter Piper*: A familiar tongue-twister, beginning 'Peter Piper picked a peck of pickled pepper; / A peck of pickled pepper Peter Piper picked' (*Peter Piper's Practical Principles of Plain and Perfect Pronunciation*, 1819).

7. *Queen Elizabeth's first historical female friend at Tilbury Fort*: On 8 August 1588, Elizabeth I reviewed the army and navy at Tilbury Fort on the Thames after the defeat of the Spanish Armada. No female friend was present on the occasion; but Miss Twinkleton, in the person of the queen, is given an historical friend in the form of Mrs Tisher, her second in command at the Nuns' House. Dickens describes the occasion of the review of the troops in his *A Child's History of England* (1851–4; ch. 31).

8. *the bard of Avon . . . the immortal SHAKESPEARE . . . the Swan of his native river*: Familiar epithets for Shakespeare. Ben Jonson coined 'Sweet Swan of Avon' in his poem 'To the Memory of my Beloved, the Author, Mr William Shakespeare'; Dr Johnson and Pope both spoke of the poet as 'Immortal'.

9. *Rumor, Ladies, had been represented by that bard . . . as painted full of tongues*: See the stage direction for the Induction in Shakespeare, *2 Henry IV*: 'Enter RUMOR, *painted full of tongues*. Open your ears, for which of you will stop / The vent of hearing when loud Rumor speaks?' (Induction.1–2, 15–16, 39–40). Compare also Virgil's Fama, who has many eyes, tongues and ears (*Aeneid*, 4.181–90).

10. *'who drew / The celebrated Jew'*: 'This is the Jew / That Shakespeare drew' – the lines are ascribed to both Pope and Dr Johnson on seeing the actor Charles Macklin (1697?–1797), who made his reputation playing Shylock in *The Merchant of Venice*.

11. *the great limner's portrait of Rumor elsewhere*: See also Warwick referring to the size of the rebel army, 'Rumor doth double, like the voice and echo, / The numbers of the feared' (*2 Henry IV*, III.i.97–8), Portia in *Julius Caesar*, 'I heard a bustling rumor like a fray, / And the wind brings it from the Capitol' (II.iv.18–19) and *Macbeth*, 'when we hold rumor / From what we fear, yet know not what we fear / But float upon a wild and violent sea' (IV.ii.19–21).

12. *Monsieur La Fontaine*: Jean de La Fontaine (1621–95), whose poetical versions of Aesop's *Fables* served as texts for learning French.

13. *'airy nothings'*: From *A Midsummer Night's Dream* (V.i.14–17),

> And as imagination bodies forth
> The forms of things unknown, the poet's pen
> Turns them to shapes, and gives to airy nothing
> A local habitation and a name.

14. *date of birth*: According to tradition, Shakespeare was born on 23 April 1564.

15. *clapping on a paper moustache*: Edwin wears a moustache in Charles Collins's sketch for the monthly wrapper, but he appears clean shaven when drawn by Luke Fildes.

16. *near sight*: A slip. In Chapter 17, Grewgious watches from his window in Staple Inn, from which location he can see over to 'yonder house' where he recognizes Jasper lurking.

17. *'My visits . . . are, like those of the angels'*: From Robert Blair, 'The Grave' (1743; lines 586–9),

> The good he scorn'd
> Stalk'd off reluctant, like an ill-us'd ghost,
> Not to return; or, if it did, its visits,
> Like those of angels, short, and far between.

18. *the Celestial Nine*: The nine daughters of memory, goddesses of the arts, known as the Muses. Post-classical writers assigned a particular art to each one: Calliope, epic poetry; Clio, history; Euterpe, the flute; Melpomene, tragedy; Terpsichore, dance; Erato, the lyre; Polyhymnia, sacred song; Urania, astronomy; Thalia, comedy.

19. *'Pounds, shillings, and pence'*: The pound sterling, Britain's central unit of money, prior to decimalization in 1971, was divided into twenty shillings, and each shilling, in turn, divided into twelve pennies or pence. With an annuity of £250 and savings on that annuity amounting to £1,700, Rosa had a comfortable inheritance to look forward to.

20. *a bear . . . in a youthful Cotillon*: Dancing bears led by itinerant performers were a common sight well into the eighteenth century. The cotillon, or cotillion, is a dance of French origin, in which four or eight dancers advance or retire performing a variety of steps and figures.

21. *I was the only offspring of parents far advanced in life, and I half believe I was born advanced in life myself*: Compare 'The old child. That is to say, born of parents advanced in life, and observing the parents of other children to be young. Taking an old tone accordingly', *Book of Memoranda* (entry 114).

22. *a Norfolk farmer*: The East Anglian county noted for producing turkeys.

23. *when a distinguished visitor . . . goes to a school . . . he asks for a holiday, or* *some sort of grace*: Requests by visiting dignitaries (religious or secular) for the suspension of ordinary occupations as a favour were not uncommon. The practice extended beyond schools and is difficult to trace with exactness.

24. *pen-and-ink-ubus*: Dickens recorded this well-known pun in the *Book of Memoranda*: 'Such a bore with his pen. "Not merely an Incubus, but a pen-and-inkubus"' (entry 81).

25. *coming out*: The MS reads, 'Among the dirty linen that was already being unbuttoned behind with all the expedition compatible with a feint of following Mr Tope and his mace in procession round the corner was the robe of Mr Jasper. He threw it to a boy (who sadly wanted "getting up" by some laundress) and he and Mr Grewgious walked out of the Cathedral, talking as they went.'

26. *my own accord*: The MS reads, '"I have had it in my mind to come down, off and on, this long time. But more off than on, I am ashamed to say." / "Are you going to –?"'

27. *bound again*: The MS reads, '"I felt that I ought in politeness to report myself to you before I went." / "Thank you."'

28. *nephew*: The MS reads, '"Duty in the abstract must be done, even if it did; but it did not, and it does not. I like your nephew very much. I hope you are satisfied."'

29. *'I mean us'*: The MS reads, 'Jasper looked at him steadily, smiled, and said nothing. Mr Grewgious had an impression that he was shaking his head; but stopping to look at him steadily in return, found that he was not shaking his head. / "Therefore", said Mr Grewgious in a cosily arranging manner, "let . . ."'

30. *observed Jasper*: The MS reads,

'Eh?' said the other, expressionlessly innocent. But not without adding internally: 'This is a very quick watch-dog!'

'So you settled with her that you would come back at Christmas,' repeated Jasper.

'At Christmas? Certainly. O dear yes, I settled with her that I would come back at Christmas,' replied Mr Grewgious, as if the question had previously lain between Lady Day, Midsummer Day, and Michaelmas.

By this time, sometimes walking very slowly and sometimes standing still, they had reached the Gate House.

'Will you not walk up,' said Jasper, 'and refresh?'

'Thank you, no. I have a horse and a chaise here, and have not too much time to get across and catch the new railroad yonder.'

Jasper pressed his hand.

'Mr Grewgious, as you quite fairly said just now, my affection for my dear boy makes me quick to feel in his behalf, and I cannot allow any approach to a slight to be put upon him. There is such an exceptional attachment between him and me that . . .'

CHAPTER 10

Smoothing the Way

1. *It has been often enough remarked . . .*: The opinions expressed in the opening paragraph seem to reflect a personal view, shared by many of Dickens's contemporaries, that women differed fundamentally from men in their psychological and emotional make-up. Commonly remarked was the belief in 'feminine intuition', the claim that women 'instinctively' apprehended emotional truths about other people and their relationships. Commending Madame De la Rue's perspicacity on one occasion, Dickens wrote to her husband: 'I am slow to come to the conclusion' that Miss Holdscamp does not love her lover, 'but in such a case a woman's observation is invariably right – hardly seems to possess the faculty of being wrong; Nature having ordered it otherwise' (*Letters*, 4.324). Susceptibility to appearances, especially where gentlemen were concerned, was widely regarded as one of the weaknesses of this apparent gift, to which the narrator adds the less commonly voiced generalization about women's inability to revise opinions arrived at solely by intuition.

2. *Constantia*: A sweet red wine from the Constantia farms near Cape Town known for its curative powers. 'There are many varieties of it. And, oh, how seductive that same Constantia is!' ('"Cape" Sketches', *HW* 1, 14 September 1850, pp. 588–91).

3. *a portrait of Handel in a flowing wig*: George Frideric Handel (1685–1759), composer and musician. Thomas Hudson (1701–79), whose frequently reproduced portrait of Handel hangs in the National Portrait Gallery, represents the musician as a dignified man seated and wearing a large wig.

4. *led, like the highly-popular lamb . . . led to the slaughter*: 'He was oppressed, and he was afflicted, yet he opened not his mouth: he is brought as a lamb to the slaughter, and as a sheep before her shearers is dumb, so he openeth not his mouth' (Isaiah 53:7).

5. *as Lady Macbeth was hopeless of those of all the seas that roll*: See Macbeth, 'Will all great Neptune's ocean wash this blood / Clean from my hand?', and Lady Macbeth, 'All the perfumes of Arabia will not sweeten this little hand' (II.ii.59–60 and V.i.47–8).

6. *not breathed*: Not short of breath.

7. *the Searcher of all hearts*: Compare 'And he that searcheth the hearts knoweth what is in the mind of the Spirit, because he maketh intercession for the saints according to the will of God' (Romans 8:27).

8. '*What is the matter? Who did it?*': Compare Macbeth's cry when he sees the ghost of Banquo: 'Which of you have done this?' (III.iv.49).

9. '*I was dreaming at a great rate*': Victorian writers on dreams commonly associated restlessness and agitation with a guilty conscience: 'If we remember right, it was Bishop Newton, who remarked that the sleep of innocence differed essentially from the sleep of guilt' (Thomas Stone, 'Dreams', *HW* 2, 8 March 1851, pp. 566–72).

CHAPTER 11

A Picture and a Ring

1. *A Picture and a Ring*: One folio of the MS, comprising the first five paragraphs of this chapter, is missing (Cardwell, p. 88).

2. *Holborn, London, where certain gabled houses . . . stand . . . looking for the Old Bourne*: Holborn, the name of an area north of the Strand, in which are situated Lincoln's Inn and Gray's Inn, and also the name of a main thoroughfare running east to west from Holborn Circus to New Oxford Street. The name possibly derives from the Holebourne, a tributary of the Fleet river, or from the 'old-bourne' or brook which used to run down the middle of the street before flowing underground to join the Thames near Blackfriars Bridge (Henry B. Wheatley, *London Past and Present*, 3 vols. (1891), 2.219).

3. *two irregular quadrangles, called Staple Inn*: Staple Inn, formerly one of ten Inns of Chancery, houses or sets of collegiate buildings in London which began as places of residence for students and apprentices of the law. Many resembled Oxford colleges with a hall, chapel, library and rooms occupied by attorneys, solicitors and law clerks. The houses, built about an open quadrangle, are situated behind a row of sixteenth-century timber buildings on the south side of Holborn, facing the southern end of Gray's Inn Road.

4. *one of those nooks . . . imparts to the relieved pedestrian the sensation of having put cotton in his ears*: Nathaniel Hawthorne noted a similar effect. Visiting Staple Inn one 'beautiful summer afternoon', he described it as 'this little island of quiet' unswept by the roaring tide of London. 'There was not a quieter spot in England than this; and it was very strange to have drifted into it so suddenly out of the bustle and rumble of Holborn' (*The English Notebooks, 1853–1856*, Centenary Edition of the Works of Nathaniel Hawthorne, 23 vols., vol. 21 (1997), p. 312).

5. *smoky trees*: Smoky on account of the smoke from coal, the fuel of choice in the nineteenth century.

6. *a little Hall, with a little lantern in its roof*: The Hall, which dates from 1581, had an open timber roof into which was set a windowed and domed louvre or lantern.

7. *in those days no neighbouring architecture of lofty proportions had arisen*: Evidently a reference to new buildings further along the terrace erected in 1843 for the Taxing Masters but occupied later in the century by the Patent Office and the Land Registry Office.

8. *the mysterious inscription*: The initials over the portal belonged to Principal John Thompson, President of Staple Inn in 1747.

9. *He had been bred to the Bar*: Once qualified as a barrister, Mr Grewgious follows a legal career that leads via 'Conveyancing' (a major branch of law that deals with creating, transferring and extinguishing rights in property, particularly in or over land) and 'Arbitration' (the settling of disputes submitted to a qualified individual rather than to a court of competent jurisdiction) to 'Receivership'. In this latter capacity, he does well. Receivers, appointed by the courts, receive money on behalf of others, often from a deceased estate or a bankruptcy, and are charged with the protection or preservation of property for the benefit of persons who have an interest in it.

10. *'convey the wise it call,' as Pistol says*: Shakespeare, *The Merry Wives of Windsor* (I.iii.25–6):

NYM: The good humor is to steal at a minim-rest.
PISTOL: 'Convey,' the wise call it. 'Steal?' foh, a fico for the phrase!

11. *blown towards him by some unaccountable wind*: Shakespeare, *2 Henry IV* (V.iii.83–4):

FALSTAFF: What wind blew you hither, Pistol?
PISTOL: Not the ill wind which blows no man to good.

12. *under the dry vine and fig-tree*: Compare 'But they shall sit every man under his vine and under his fig tree; and none shall make them afraid: for the mouth of the Lord of hosts hath spoken it' (Micah 4:4; also 1 Kings 4:25).

13. *the hotel in Furnival's Inn*: Formerly an Inn of Chancery on the north side of Holborn and situated between Leather Lane to the east and Brooke Street to the west. When the Inn was rebuilt in 1818 many of its chambers were let and a portion of the property was reconstructed as Wood's Hotel. Grewgious lodges Rosa here in Chapter 20. The hotel was demolished in 1895 and the rest of Furnival's Inn in 1897.

14. *like a fabulous Familiar*: The genie, in the tale of Aladdin, in the *Arabian Nights*.

15. *that baleful tree of Java which has given shelter to more lies*: The Javanese tree *Antiaris toxicari*, whose poisonous vapour allegedly destroyed any form of life within a vicinity of fifteen or sixteen miles. Knowledge of this harmful property was subsequently embroidered by English Romantic poets following the introduction of the tree to Europe in the seventeenth century.

16. *Bazzard*: The name appears as the author of a play performed in Brussels in a piece Dickens and others contributed to *HW* I ('Foreigners' Portraits of England', 21 September 1850, pp. 601–4).

17. *it makes my eyes smart*: London's fogs, the vapour laden with carbon particles from furnaces and private coal-fires, adversely affected people's health. Respiratory discomfort and burning eyes were common symptoms.

18. *collected his skirts*: That is, the skirts of his frock-coat, to prevent scorching them in the fire.

19. *My Lords of the Circumlocutional Department*: A slight variant of 'Circumlocution Office', the phrase Dickens coined in *Little Dorrit* (I.10) to describe the political heads of governmental departments such as the Colonial, Home or Treasury Offices. The phrase Circumlocution Office is now synonymous with almost any kind of bureaucratic malfeasance or inefficiency.

20. *the National Gallery*: The permanent building in Trafalgar Square, designed by William Wilkins and constructed in 1832–8, to house the nation's collection of paintings.

21. *a zest far surpassing Doctor Kitchener's*: William Kitchener (1775?–1827), an epicure convinced that one's health depended on the proper preparation of food; author of *The Cook's Oracle* (1817), *The Art of Invigorating and Prolonging Life* (1821) and *The Housekeeper's Ledger* (1825).

22. *Harvey*: Harvey's sauce, called after Peter Harvey, an innkeeper, who developed the condiment for travellers eating at his inn. In 1776 he gave the recipe to his sister, who married into a firm of London grocers. On the death of her husband, she devoted her time to sauces and pickles. Eventually the concern was acquired by Crosse & Blackwell.

23. *like Macbeth's leg when accompanying him off the stage*: A piece of stage business developed by W. C. Macready (1793–1873) to convey his hesitation before murdering Duncan. Crossing the stage to Duncan's chamber in the part of Macbeth, he hears the signal bell sound twice before delivering the lines: 'Hear it not, Duncan, for it is a knell / That summons thee to heaven, or to hell' (II.i.63–4). Thereupon, with an elaborate show of pause, his body moved off the stage while his left foot and leg remained 'trembling in sight, it seemed, fully half a minute' (John Coleman, 'Facts and Fancies about *Macbeth*', *Gentleman's Magazine* 226, 1889, p. 223).

24. *the thorn of anxiety*: Bazzard's play. See Chapter 20.

25. *much as a charity boy . . . might get his catechism said*: The recipient of a

free education, often provided by a denominational school, hence the emphasis on religious instruction.

26. *the Book of Proverbs*: A teaching compendium in the Bible consisting in part of short sayings in pithy form and insights into human affairs, especially of a social and religious nature.

27. *some queer Joss*: The pidgin English name given to deities and idols worshipped in the East Indies.

28. *ashes among ashes, and dust among dust*: From the Burial Service: 'we therefore commit his body to the ground; earth to earth, ashes to ashes, dust to dust; in sure and certain hope of the Resurrection to eternal life' (*BCP*).

CHAPTER 12

A Night with Durdles

1. *the whole framework of society*: The first recorded figurative use of the phrase is 1816. 'That the frame-work of a nation may be strong, each of its divisions must be let closely into others' (John Scott, *A Visit to Paris*), *OED*.

2. *Mayors have been knighted for 'going up' with addresses*: That is, merely for delivering speeches, mayors have been knighted, during which ceremony they kneel before the monarch who commands them to 'Rise, Sir —'.

3. *Of such is the salt of the earth*: A conflation of Mark 10:14, 'of such is the kingdom of God', and Matthew 5:13, 'Ye are the salt of the earth'.

4. *no kickshaw ditties, favorites with national enemies, but gave him the genuine George the Third home-brewed*: 'Kickshaw' (from *quelque chose*) was used contemptuously to describe something 'frivolous' or 'trifling', including French cookery, as opposed to familiar and substantial English fare. George III (1738–1820), King of Great Britain and Ireland (1760–1820), was the first of the Hanoverian kings to be born and bred in England. Publications such as William Chappell's *Collection of English National Airs* (2 vols., 1838-40) and Charles Dibdin's *Songs, Naval and National* (1841) contained many anti-French and patriotic songs exhorting English sailors with 'Hearts of Oak' to stand to their guns and similar calls to duty.

5. *continents . . . promontories, and other geographical forms of land*: The list is a parody of the kind of 'Question and Answer' text used in schools to teach definitions.

6. *far more ecclesiastical than any Archbishop of York, or Canterbury*: In the Church of England there are two archbishops: Canterbury, styled Primate of All England and Metropolitan, and York, styled Primate of England. Each superintends the ordinary diocesan bishops within his province, and within his own diocese exercises episcopal jurisdiction.

7. *Fetch*: The apparition, double or wraith of a living person.

8. *as a lover of the picturesque*: Jasper's definition of the term to include 'tombs, vaults, towers, and ruins' conventionally defines the sources of 'melancholy' inspiration familiar to Thomas Warton, Thomas Gray and other eighteenth-century poets of the 'Graveyard School'.

9. *It'll grow upon you*: The MS reads, 'You'll be boasting, before long, that His Reverence the Dean is your friend. And if you don't check yourself we shall have you, next, claiming the bishop.'

10. *The lamplighter ... his little ladder ... aghast at the idea of abolishing*: Local authorities frequently opposed the replacement of the traditional oil lamps with gas. Both required lighting by hand, the job of the lamplighter, who carried a ladder to rest on a projecting arm of the lamp-post and a small oil-lamp whose flame was protected by a perforated cylinder. Gas lighting was introduced to the streets of London from 1820 onwards and gradually spread to towns and cities throughout England.

11. *two skeleton journeymen out of the Dance of Death*: A series of drawings by Hans Holbein (1497?–1543), representing death as a skeleton following people from various orders of society. The *Danse macabre* appears to have originated in France and expressed in different media the ubiquity of Death the Leveller.

12. *ardent*: Used here in the original chemical meaning of combustible, thus with a fiery taste.

13. *Surely an unaccountable sort of expedition!*: The phrase, interjected and repeated four times by the narrator, seems to underline Dickens's own statement of purpose for this chapter in the Number Plan: 'Lay the ground for the manner of the Murder, to come out at last.' Comments elsewhere by the narrator heighten our sense of a sinister dimension to Jasper's behaviour. Even Durdles, whose observational powers are dimmed by alcohol, registers the 'destructive power' in Jasper's face as he regards Neville talking with Crisparkle. Throughout the 'expedition' he experiences an uncomfortable sense of being watched, despite successive draughts of 'the good stuff' bought on purpose by Jasper and 'filled with something stiffer' than either of them supposed.

14. *quick-lime*: Quicklime (CaO), lime which has been burned but not yet slaked with water – erroneously believed to have the ability to promote the rapid decomposition of corpses – is in fact a preservative which promotes saponification: the production by hydrolysis and hydrogenation of adipocere, a waxy substance that resists insects and retards putrefaction. Forster's account of Dickens's intentions suggests that Dickens shared the common misapprehension of the lime's corrosive ability. See Introduction.

15. *Chairs to mend*: The cry of one of the many itinerant street-sellers who called out their services and wares.

16. *This time last year, only a few days later*: The significance of this strange incident, carefully dated to correspond presumably with the murder of Edwin, remains unexplained.

17. *As aëronauts lighten the load they carry*: Enthusiasm for ballooning followed the first successful manned flight in France in 1783. Balloon ascents remained a popular form of outdoor entertainment into the nineteenth century.

18. *A mild fit of calenture*: A type of heat-stroke afflicting sailors within the tropics. Victims characteristically turn delirious, imagining the sea as a green field into which they want to jump.

19. *'Durdles wouldn't go home till morning'*: A parody version of 'Billy Taylor', a song by John Baldwin Buckstone (1802–79). The tune of 'We Won't Go Home till the Morning' is founded on an air which originated during the Duke of Marlborough's campaign, and is known as 'Malbrough', or 'Malbrook'.

> On such an occasion as this,
> All time and nonsense scorning,
> Nothing shall come amiss,
> And we won't go home till morning.

20. *'bellows me!'*: 'Bellows away!' or 'Bellows him well!', boxing slang encouraging one's favourite not to spare his opponent but to force him to pant for wind.

21. *as everything comes to an end*: 'Everything has an end', proverbial.

CHAPTER 13

Both at their Best

1. *'the half'; but what was now called . . . 'the term'*: The old school year of thirty-eight weeks used to be divided in two, each of which, colloquially, was spoken of as 'the half'. The reorganization of the school year after the recommendations of the Taunton Commission in 1867–8 into four periods saw the introduction of the calendar traditionally employed by the law courts and universities. Thus it was considered genteel to speak of 'terms' and to refer to Michaelmas, Hilary, Easter and Trinity.

2. *cowslip wine*: A drink made from honey, water, lemons and cowslips. Yeast and sweetbriar were also added to that mixture, which was left for three or four days before it was strained and casked for six months. The alcoholic content was minimal.

3. *little Rickitts . . . took her steel drops daily*: Iron chloride (steel drops) was widely prescribed to counter the ill-effects of rickets. The disease was common among children of the poor, victims of a diet deficient in vitamin D. Adverse effects included emaciation, and spinal and other deformities of the bones.

4. *until suffocated in her own pillow by two flowing-haired executioners*: Dickens records the traditional story of 'the two hardened ruffians' hired to murder Richard III's nephews in his *Child's History of England* (ch. 25). The young boys were shut up in the Tower of London and later 'smothered with the bed and pillows' on which they slept. Historians have recently questioned Richard's role in the murder on the grounds that the survival of the princes posed more of a threat to his successor, Henry VII.

5. *'at home'*: The phrase, written on a card, invites guests to an intimate gathering either in the afternoon or evening.

6. *held a Drawing-Room in her own apartment*: That is, she emulated the monarch by holding a levee or formal reception and treated her drawing room as if it were a court at which ladies could be 'presented'.

7. *revolving year*: A poetic cliché.

8. *the opening words of Mr Addison's impressive tragedy*: See Joseph Addison, *Cato* (1713), which opens with Portius speaking these lines.

9. *couleur de rose*: The first recorded use of this French phrase, meaning 'rose-coloured' or 'roseate', occurs in 1783 in one of Horace Walpole's letters (*OED*).

10. *the Spartan General . . . at the battle it were superfluous to specify*: At the battle of Thermopylae (480 BC) Leonidus and a force of 300 Spartans held off the Persian army. Before the engagement, Leonidus exhorted his troops saying, 'Come, my fellow soldiers . . . let us dine cheerfully here, for to-night we shall sup with Pluto.'

11. *next friend at law*: Legal terminology, common since the late sixteenth century, meaning nearest friend or relative or next of kin.

12. *the bill*: Fees at such establishments at that time typically came to between eleven and twenty pounds, covering board, instruction and supplies.

13. *of sly faces carved on spout and gable peeping at her*: Compare 'The silent High-street of Rochester is full of gables, with old beams and timbers carved into strange faces' in Dickens's 'The Seven Poor Travellers' (*Christmas Stories*, 1854).

14. *the effigy of Mr Sapsea's father*: This wooden figure is described fully in Chapter 6; see also Appendix 4.

15. *If Rosebud in her bower*: The allusion is to the 'Fair Rosamond', Rosamond

Clifford (d. 1176?), daughter of Walter de Clifford, whose story Dickens tells in *A Child's History of England*. The legendary beauty of 'all the world' attracted the attention of Henry II, who 'had a beautiful Bower built for her in a Park at Woodstock'. According to legend, she fell dead in her bower, poisoned by Henry's wife; Dickens, however, denies the bower and the choice between poison and a dagger forced on her by Queen Eleanor; he claims that this beauty died peaceably in a nunnery near Oxford (ch. 12).

16. *'sister Rosa, what do you see from the turret?'*: An echo of the urgent question put by the wife of Blue Beard as she stalls for time knowing her husband intends to kill her. Pleading for the opportunity to say her prayers, she sends her sister Anne to the top of the castle tower and repeatedly asks her what she sees. Eventually her brothers arrive; they kill Blue Beard and save their sister.

17. *Among the mighty store of wonderful chains . . . forged in the moment of that small conclusion*: Compare Pip's reflection on returning home after his first 'memorable' day at Satis House, 'Pause you who read this, and think for a moment of the long chain of iron or gold, of thorn or flowers, that would never have bound you, but for the formation of the first link on one memorable day' (*Great Expectations*, ch. 9).

18. *he vanished from her view*: The MS records several attempts to write this final sentence. Among the legible deletions are: '<and never looked upon him> <and never thought [that he was to?] vanish from her view>'.

CHAPTER 14

When Shall These Three Meet Again?

1. *When Shall These Three Meet Again?*: From the opening lines of *Macbeth*, 'When shall we three meet again / In thunder, lightning, or in rain?'

2. *the faces of men and women who . . . find the city wonderfully shrunken in size*: Dickens remarks on his changed perception of Rochester in 'Dullborough Town': returning to the city in later life, he found the High Street 'little better than a lane' (Pascoe, p. 67).

3. *in their dying hours afar off, that they have imagined their chamber floor to be strewn with the autumnal leaves*: The description carried a personal resonance. A day or so before Dickens's sister Fanny Dickens Burnett died, she told him that in the night 'the smell of the fallen leaves in the woods where we had habitually walked as very young children, had come upon her with such strength of reality, that she had moved her weak head to look for strewn leaves on the floor of her bedside' ('New Year's Day', *HW* 19, 1 January 1859, pp. 97–102).

4. *Twelfth Cake*: A large cake frosted or ornamented with a bean or coin traditionally featured among the festivities held on 6 January, the feast of the Epiphany, the last day of the Christmas period.

5. *The Wax-Work which made so deep an impression on the reflective mind of the Emperor of China*: Possibly an allusion to an incident Oliver Goldsmith attributes to the Chinese philosopher Lien Chi Altangi, whose impressions of his visit to London are recorded in Goldsmith's *Letters from a Citizen of the World to His Friends in the East* (1760). Commenting on Londoners' fondness for 'sights and monsters', the visitor reports how he had heard of one man adept at exploiting people's curiosity who made money by exhibiting himself 'as a wax-work figure from behind a glass door at a puppet show' (Letter 45).

6. *Christmas pantomime*: English pantomime as an exclusively Christmas-time entertainment dates from the early eighteenth century. The impetus derived from French fairground performers, who put on 'night scenes' using *commedia dell'arte* characters. Pantomime subsequently developed through several forms before arriving at what had become by the mid-nineteenth century a traditional English version. This included 'dame roles' played by men, 'principal boys' played by women in tights, various stage tricks and instantaneous transformations. Pantomime, Dickens wrote, was 'a mirror of life' ('The Pantomime of Life', *Bentley's Miscellany*, 1 March 1837).

7. *Signor Jacksonini*: Dickens mocks the convention of taking foreign-sounding pseudonyms in 'Private Theatres' (*Sketches by Boz*).

8. *a few score miles together. I should leave you nowhere now*: Dickens remained a strenuous walker throughout his career, putting in seven or eight miles at a fast pace, occasionally performing 'an insane march against time' of eighteen miles in four and a half hours or clocking some fifteen or twenty miles about the streets of London at night 'when all the sober folks had gone to bed' (*Letters*, 3.547 and 4.2). Even later in life, his pedestrian excursions intimidated younger men whom he easily outpaced (see, for example, Edmund Yates, *Recollections and Experiences*, 1884).

9. *'Do you come back before dinner?'*: Compare Macbeth to Banquo, 'To-night we hold a solemn supper, sir, / And I'll request your presence' (III.i.14–15).

10. *sound mind in his own sound body*: Juvenal, 'mens sana in corpore sano' (*Satires*, 10.356).

11. *Poor youth! Poor youth!*: MS cancellations suggest Dickens hesitated about the degree of explicitness regarding Edwin's fate. '<He> Poor Youth! <He little, little knows how near a cause he has for thinking so.> Poor youth!'

12. *'Come from London', deary*: The words of the opium woman in Chapter

23 – 'I'll not miss ye twice' – make it clear that when she followed Jasper home from London, she missed him, and instead met up with Edwin.

13. '*The proverb says that threatened men live long*': An English proverb dating from the sixteenth century.

14. *He says that his complexion is 'Un-English*': Sapsea's expression and tendency to dismiss all that he dislikes as 'Un-English' resemble Mr Podsnap's outlook (*Our Mutual Friend*, 1.11).

15. *the bottomless pit*: 'And I saw an angel come down from heaven, having the key of the bottomless pit and a great chain in his hand' (Revelation 20:1).

16. *the pathetic supplication to have his heart inclined to keep this law*: 'Lord, have mercy upon us, and incline our hearts to keep this law' is the response made by the people kneeling, while the priest rehearses all the ten commandments at the beginning of Holy Communion (*BCP*).

17. *a large black scarf of strong close-woven silk*: Noting that he had previously drawn Jasper wearing a black tie, Luke Fildes, the novel's illustrator, questioned Dickens about the importance of wearing the long black scarf. Disconcerted for a moment, Dickens confirmed that the scarf was necessary, 'for Jasper strangles Edwin Drood with it' (letter to *The Times Literary Supplement*, 3 November 1905, p. 373).

18. *Chimneys topple in the streets*: Compare the description of the night when Duncan is murdered, 'Our chimneys were blown down; and, as they say, / Lamentings heard i' th' air, strange screams of death' (*Macbeth*, II.iii. 51–2).

CHAPTER 15

Impeached

1. *The Tilted Wagon*: 'Tilted', that is, covered with a tilt or awning. Cox notes that Dickens initially considered 'The Fox and Goose' and then 'The Hare and Hounds'.

2. '*If eight men, or four men, or two men, set upon one*': Compare Falstaff's exaggerated account of the robbery on Gad's Hill to Prince Hal, 'If there were not two or three and fifty upon poor old Jack, then am I no two-legged creature' (*1 Henry IV*, II.iv.176–8).

3. *to set his mark upon some of them*: Compare 'And the Lord set a mark upon Cain, lest any finding him should kill him' (Genesis 4:15). This is the first of four other biblical references which link Neville and Cain. See next note and Chapter 16, note 16 and Chapter 17, notes 8 and 21.

4. *'Where is your nephew? . . . Why do you ask me?'*: Compare 'And the Lord said unto Cain, Where is Abel thy brother? And he said, I know not: Am I my brother's keeper?' (Genesis 4:9).

5. *He washed his hands as clean as he could*: Compare Pilate, who, when he 'saw that he could prevail nothing, but that rather a tumult was made . . . took water, and washed his hands before the multitude, saying, I am innocent of the blood of this just person: see ye to it' (Matthew 27:24).

6. *a heap of torn and miry clothes upon the floor*: Edwin accurately forecasts that Jasper would be 'struck all of a heap' when he and Rosa discuss the consequences of informing him of their decision not to marry (ch. 13). The image of a man reduced suddenly to a bundle of clothes haunts Fagin as he contemplates his imminent death (*Oliver Twist*, ch. 52). Compare also Dickens's description of the dismal spectacle he witnessed at Horsemonger Jail on 13 November 1849. Writing of the execution of George and Maria Manning for the murder of their lodger, he notes in 'Lying Awake' that the body of the dead man was like 'a limp, loose loose suit of clothes as if the man had gone out of them' (*HW* 6, 30 October 1852, pp. 145–8; Pascoe, p. 27).

CHAPTER 16

Devoted

1. *Devoted*: The title of the chapter points to the last sentence in Jasper's diary in which he declares, 'And that I devote myself to his destruction'. See also *Book of Memoranda*: 'Devoted to the destruction of a man. Revenge built up, on love' (entry 37).

2. *'Do you know'*: Writing to James T. Field on 14 January 1870, Dickens said, 'There is a curious interest steadily working up to No. 5, which requires a great deal of art and self-denial. I think also, apart from character and picturesqueness, that the young people are placed in a very novel position. So I hope – at Nos. 5 and 6 the story will turn upon an interest suspended until the end' (Nonesuch, 3.760). Possibly the 'curious interest' refers to the manner of 'Jasper's artful use of the communication on his recovery' (see Appendix 2), which commences here, and is 'suspended until the end' as he considers how best to shelter himself from suspicion.

3. *a seven days' wonder*: The phrase conflates the Seven Wonders of the World with a 'nine days' wonder'.

4. *'How did I come here!'* . . .: The passage continuing through to 'as if it were tangible' is not in the MS.

5. *airy tongues that syllable men's names*: See Milton, *Comus*, lines 205–9:

> What might this be: A thousand fantasies
>
> Begin to throng into my memory
>
> Of calling shapes, and beckning shadows dire,
>
> And airy tongues, that syllable mens names
>
> On sands and shoars and desert wildernesses.

6. *a gold watch*: The use of a gold watch found in the river to identify the victim occurred in the case of Dr George Parkman, who had been murdered by John White Webster, a Harvard chemistry professor. An account of the crime, 'The Killing of Dr Parkman', appeared in *AYR* 18 (14 December 1867, pp. 9–16); Dickens visited the scene while in Cambridge in 1867–8 (Nonesuch, 3.591). The implications of this murder have been examined by Jim Garner, 'Harvard's Clue to the Mystery of Edwin Drood', *Harvard Magazine* 83 (1983), pp. 44–8, and more recently by Robert Tracy, 'Disappearances: George Parkman and Edwin Drood', *Dickensian* 96 (2000), pp. 101–17.

7. *he had caused to be whipped to death sundry 'Natives'* . . . *vaguely supposed* . . . *to be always black, always of great virtue* . . . *always reading tracts*: The boisterous opponents of Governor Eyre calling loudly for his trial made much of his use of corporal punishment in putting down the rebellion in Morant Bay (see Chapter 6, note 24). Equally misguided supporters of Britain's colonial subjects, in Dickens's view, were individuals who patronized 'natives' by exaggerating their virtues, and those Evangelical missionaries and philanthropists who sought to convert heathens to Christianity through the distribution of 'reading tracts'.

8. *Mrs Crisparkle's grey hairs with sorrow to the grave*: Compare 'if mischief befall him by the way in the which ye go, then shall ye bring down my gray hairs with sorrow to the grave' (Genesis 42:38).

9. *in the words of* BENTHAM, *where he is the cause of the greatest danger to the smallest number*: A parody of the formula of Jeremy Bentham (1748–1842), philosopher and legal reformer. 'The greatest happiness of the greatest number is the foundation of morals and legislation' (*Introduction to the Principles of Morals and Legislation*, 1780; 1789).

10. *dropping shots from the blunderbusses* . . . *a trained and well-directed fire of arms of precision*: Rifling gun barrels (patented in 1868) substantially improved the precision of firearms and led to the eclipse of old-fashioned, inaccurate weapons like blunderbusses.

11. *The more his case was looked into, the weaker it became in every point*:

Resisting suspicion arising from circumstantial evidence is one of the professional challenges those investigating crimes customarily face. Dickens 'burrowed' for information on this point when he met with several members of the Detective Force in 1850. 'Whether in the case of robberies in houses, where servants are necessarily exposed to doubt, innocence under suspicion ever becomes so like guilt in appearance, that a good officer need be cautious how he judges it? Undoubtedly. Nothing is so common or deceptive as such appearances at first' ('A Detective Police Party', part 1, *HW* 1, 27 July 1850, pp. 409–14; 'Detective Police', Pascoe, p. 249).

12. *Jasper labored night and day*: Compare 'For ye remember, brethren, our labour and travail: for labouring night and day, because we would not be chargeable unto any of you, we preached unto you the gospel of God' (1 Thessalonians 2:9).

13. *The days of taking sanctuary are past*: The Church's former practice of protecting criminals and fugitives dates from the fourth century. The privilege lingered on beyond the Reformation and also spread to civil processes in certain districts before legislation in 1623 and 1723 finally abolished the practice. Affording criminals such protection was based on an ancient right of privilege founded on the primitive and universal belief that it was sacrilegious to remove anyone who had gained the holy precincts of a consecrated building.

14. *'It is very lamentable, sir,'* . . .: The passage continuing to 'returned the Dean' is not in the MS.

15. *'we clergy need do nothing emphatically'*: Cautiousness among churchmen has been identified as a topical issue. Margaret Cardwell (*The Mystery of Edwin Drood*, ed. World's Classics, Oxford, 1982, p. 238) cites an article in the *Spectator* 42 (9 October 1869) which criticizes *The Times* for encouraging the appointment of men with safe, inoffensive views ('The Duty of Keeping the Church Insignificant').

16. *with a blight upon his name and fame*: Compare the plight of Cain, 'And Cain said unto the Lord, My punishment is greater than I can bear. Behold, thou hast driven me out this day from the face of the earth; and from thy face shall I be hid; and I shall be a fugitive and a vagabond in the earth; and it shall come to pass, that every one that findeth me shall slay me. And the Lord said unto him, Therefore whosoever slayeth Cain, vengeance shall be taken on him sevenfold. And the Lord set a mark upon Cain, lest any finding him should kill him' (Genesis 4:13–15).

17. *That I will fasten the crime . . . upon the murderer*: The significance of Jasper's diary entries has been variously interpreted. To Edmund Wilson, they are sober expressions of Jasper's 'ecclesiastical side', free from the

intoxicating effects of opium and expressive of the choirmaster's double consciousness ('Dickens: The Two Scrooges', in *The Wound and the Bow*, 1941, p. 93); to Philip Collins, they project 'a less interesting irony', an instance of miscalculation or over-reaching that Dickens ascribed to criminals. It was a pet theory of his that even the most clever criminals 'were constantly detected through some small defect in their calculations' (Katey Dickens, quoted by Collins in *Dickens and Crime*, 1962, p. 355n.).

CHAPTER 17

Philanthropy, Professional and Unprofessional

1. *Philanthropy, Professional and Unprofessional*: The original title was '<Several Phases> Professional and Unprofessional'. This chapter opens the fifth number, which originally included Chapters 18, 19 and 20. Finding he had overwritten the instalment by 154 lines, Dickens had to cut material in order to bring the number to its prerequisite thirty-two printed pages. In this chapter he trimmed the conversation between Mr Crisparkle and Honeythunder, and removed about one half of the lines in which Crisparkle praises Helena's character to her brother. But because Dickens died before the number went into print, John Forster, his literary executor, reinstated all the excisions in order to place before readers everything Dickens had written and to round out the sixth, unfinished number by carrying over matter to it. This edition retains the excisions reinstated by Forster, as do all texts of the novel. It also follows the practice established by Forster of renaming Chapter 20 and dividing it in two, thus bringing the total number of published chapters to 23. Cox, in his edition, retained the excisions but he followed Dickens's original chapter titles and divisions.

2. *In his college-days of athletic exercises*: By the 1840s athletics had gained acceptance in several of England's leading public schools, Rugby, Eton, Harrow and Shrewsbury among them, following the introduction of athletic exercises at the Royal Military College, Sandhurst, in 1812. Sports played no significant role in university life until they were introduced at Exeter College, Oxford, in 1850; the first contest between Oxford and Cambridge occurred in 1866 when college members from the two universities met to compete in track and field events.

3. *Noble Art of fisticuffs*: The reference is to the boxing world of the Regency period when the sport gained increasing acceptance. This development owed much to the efforts of Jack Broughton (1705–89) and John Jackson (1769–

1845), who helped separate contests from bare-fisted pugilism. Aristocratic patronage conferred further respectability as boxing began to emerge as a 'manly' sport, combining an evolving sense of fair play according to rules and opportunities for the display of courage, strength and training. Rules governing prize-fights nevertheless remained minimal until the introduction of the Queensberry Rules in 1867. This code, drawn up under the supervision of Sir John Sholto Douglas (1844–1900), eighth Marquess of Queensberry, required the use of padded gloves and introduced limits to the number and length of rounds. Boxing analogies and references appear throughout the paragraph. *'pitch into'*: Pugilistic slang, to assail and attack. *a turn-up with any Novice*: Boxing slang for a contest with a beginner. *the Fancy*: A collective term for the followers of prize-fighting; included were the fighters, patrons, trainers and fans. *a moral little Mill*: A 'mill' is a pugilistic encounter and a 'Grand Mill' a major contest. *sporting publicans*: Innkeepers who placed bets on individual boxers. *Frosty-faced Fogo*: Jack Fogo, a popular sports writer and organizer of fights, so-called on account of his pock-marked face. Many fighters had colourful nicknames, a fashion now transferred to the combatants in professional wrestling. *magic circle with the ropes and stakes*: The space defined by a circle of bystanders for prize-fighters was replaced by a square marked off with ropes and stakes following the introduction of a more extensive code governing competitions. *Suet Pudding*: Pugilistic slang for body fat. *the Philanthropists had not the good temper of the Pugilists*: Pugilists were enjoined by their trainers to keep their temper. *to bore their man to the ropes*: Holding an opponent against the ropes contravened boxing rules. *to hit him when he was down*: Another infraction of the rules of the sport.

4. *the phrenological formation*: Phrenology, a quasi-respectable theory of mental faculties, was based on the assumption that 'the agitation of a man's brain by different passions, produces corresponding developments in the form of his skull' ('Our Next-Door Neighbour', *Sketches by Boz*). Phrenologists assigned behaviours to specific contours of the head, and arranged character traits hierarchically, starting with the animal propensity of Amativeness (number 1) at the lower part of the back of the head, and progressing to the perceptive and reflective faculties (numbers 22–35) located in the forehead. The organ associated with combative or quarrelsome behaviour (number 5) was located just behind the ear. Phrenology was founded by Johann Kaspar Spurzheim (1776–1832) and spread by Franz Joseph Gall (1758–1828) and George Combe (1788–1858).

5. *Resolutions might have been Rounds*: Philanthropists conducted much of their business by passing resolutions.

6. *'Now, Mr Crisparkle,' said Mr Honeythunder* . . .: Honeythunder's belligerent

rhetoric caricatures the sweeping attacks of philanthropists and others on Governor Eyre (see Chapter 6, note 24) when they sought to bring him to trial for the means he used to restore public order in Jamaica.

7. *'swept off the face of the earth'*: Compare 'And the Lord said, I will destroy man whom I have created from the face of the earth' (Genesis 6:7).

8. *'Bloodshed! Abel! Cain!'*: The opponents of Governor Eyre evoked the murder of Abel by Cain (Genesis 4:8–12) when they spoke out against the executions Eyre had ordered.

9. *'The Commandments say no murder'*: 'Thou shalt not kill' (Exodus 20:13 and Deuteronomy 5:17).

10. *'you shall bear no false witness'*: 'Thou shalt not bear false witness against thy neighbour' (Exodus 20:16 and Deuteronomy 5:20).

11. *Mr Crisparkle rose; . . .*: This passage, ending with 'by a layman', was deleted in proof.

12. *its first duty is towards those who are in necessity and tribulation*: Compare the Litany or General Supplication, which may be sung or said after Morning Prayer on Sundays, Wednesdays and Fridays: 'We beseech thee to hear us, good Lord, That it may please thee to succour, help, and comfort, all that are in danger, necessity, and tribulation' (*BCP*).

13. *keeping a wicket*: The role of the player stationed behind the wicket is to stop the ball if it passes it, catch the ball if the batsman tips it, or strike the wicket and call 'out' if the batsman steps beyond the crease.

14. *measuring people for caps*: The proverb is 'If the cap fits, wear it'.

15. *I will not bow down to a false God of your making*: 'Thou shalt have no other gods before me . . . Thou shalt not bow down thyself to them, nor serve them: for I the Lord thy God am a jealous God' (Exodus 20:3–5 and Deuteronomy 5:7–9).

16. *War is a calamity*: Philanthropists frequently pronounced against war in ringing terms.

17. *you would punish the sober for the drunken*: Dickens opposed temperance zealots who would deny alcohol to all, emphasizing instead his view that drunkenness was symptomatic of poverty, ignorance and sorrow, rather than their cause. While he held individuals responsible for their lives, he believed the government was equally at fault for failing to provide the working classes with education and opportunities to alleviate their poverty.

18. *to turn Heaven's creatures into swine and wild beasts*: Circe, the sorceress Odysseus encounters on the island of Aeaea, enchants his men and turns them into swine (*Odyssey*, Book 10).

19. *run amuck like so many mad Malays*: Malayans were thought to be particularly susceptible to opium taken for pleasure. Thomas De Quincey

notes how some known to him had run 'amuck' at him and led him 'into a world of troubles'. Accounts by Eastern travellers, he adds, bore out his own experience. Often their descriptions spoke of 'the frantic excesses committed by Malays who have taken opium, or are reduced to desperation by ill luck at gambling' ('Introduction to the Pains of Opium', *Confessions*, p. 92). See also Appendix 5.

20. *'I wish your eyes were not quite so large and not quite so bright'*: Possibly an indication of Neville's eventual death, a victim of sickness marked for demise in the tradition of Smike, Nell and Richard Carstone.

21. *I feel marked and tainted*: For the links between Neville and Cain, see Chapter 15, note 3.

22. *while the grass grows, the steed starves*: A mid-fourteenth-century proverb.

23. *the yet unfinished and undeveloped railway station*: London Bridge, terminus for the Greenwich line, which opened in 1836.

24. *my name is Tartar*: 'Tar' is slang for sailor.

25. *my garden aloft here*: Dickens expressed his belief that the love of gardening ran deeply in the human mind in a speech to the Gardeners' Benevolent Institution on 9 June 1851. 'The prisoner in his dismal cell would endeavour to raise a flower from the chinks in the floor of his dungeon; the invalid or lodger in the garret took delight in the pot of flowers on the parapet, or endeavoured to cultivate his scarlet runners in communication with the garret of his neighbour over the way' (*Speeches of Charles Dickens*, p. 133).

26. *'I was bred in the Royal Navy'*: Interest in and respect for the navy informs Dickens's response, perhaps the result of his early exposure to ships and naval men. His father worked as a civil servant employed in the navy pay office at both Plymouth and Chatham; Dickens's youngest son, Sydney, went to sea at thirteen as a naval cadet. Offering advice to Dion Boucicault on how the sailor in his play *A Long Strike* should be portrayed, Dickens wrote on 4 September 1866: 'The very notion of a sailor, whose life is not among those little courts and streets, and whose business does not lie with the monotonous machinery, but with the four wild winds, is a relief to me in the reading of the play. I am quite confident of its being an immense relief to the audience when they see the sailor before them, with an entirely different bearing, action, dress, complexion even, from the rest of the men. I would make him the freshest and airiest sailor that ever was seen' (Nonesuch, 3.482).

27. *his gaze wandered . . . to the stars, as if he would have read in them something that was hidden from him*: The recent discovery of spectral analysis by Gustav Robert Kirchoff (1824–87) renewed the old idea that the stars might contain a hidden message. Addressing persons attending the thirty-fifth meeting of the British Association for the Advancement of Science in Birmingham in

September 1865, President John Phillips said: 'What message comes to us with the light which springs from distant stars, and shoots through the depths of space to fall upon the earth after tens, or hundreds, or thousands of years? It is a message from the very birthplace of light, and tells us what are the elementary substances which have influenced the refraction of the ray. Spectral analysis . . . has been taught by our countrymen to scrutinize not only planets and stars, but even to reveal the constitution of the nebulae, those mysterious masses out of which it has been thought new suns and planets might be evolved – nursing mothers of the stars' (*Report of . . . The British Association for the Advancement of Science*, 1866, p. liv).

CHAPTER 18

A Settler in Cloisterham

1. *A Settler in Cloisterham*: The excisions from the proofs of this chapter (some thirty-four lines altogether) affect Datchery, since Dickens systematically removed every line which showed Datchery's interest in Jasper and those that indicated he had never before been in Cloisterham. The narrative sequence is thus left intact but the mystery enhanced. For the principal deletions, see below.

2. *blue surtout*: A frock-coat whose collar descended below the top of the waistcoat and with tails reaching above the knee. It was worn tightly buttoned beneath the collar to show off the figure.

3. *at the Crozier*: The ecclesiastical sign chosen for the inn possibly derives from the Mitre, an actual inn in Chatham known to Dickens. Recalling the inn in 'The Holly Tree' (*Christmas Stories*), he notes that the bar at the Mitre 'seemed to be the next best thing to a bishopric, it was so snug'.

4. *pint of sherry*: Such an amount was customarily diluted with water.

5. *as a Newfoundland dog might shake*: 'Characters. The Newfoundland-Dog man, and teazing capricious woman', *Book of Memoranda* (entry 99).

6. *buffer*: Slang for a dog, a fellow or a chief boatswain's mate, one who acts as a 'buffer' between the Commander and the upper deck.

7. *with a general impression on his mind . . .*: Deleted in proof to 'He was getting very cold indeed'.

8. *the game of hot boiled beans and very good butter*: A game in which an object is hidden; as the seeker moves towards it, the hider cries out, 'Hot boil'd beans and very good butter, / If you please to come to supper!' If he moves away, he is 'cold'.

9. *'Indeed?' said Mr Datchery, with a second look of some interest*: Deleted in proof.

10. *Mr Datchery, taking off his hat . . . had been directed*: Deleted in proof.

11. *Perhaps Mr Datchery had heard . . . last winter?*: Deleted in proof.

12. *Mr Datchery had as confused a knowledge . . . unmixed in his mind*: Deleted in proof.

13. *'Might I ask His Honor,' . . . his white hair streaming*: Deleted in proof.

14. *the end crowns the work*: A commonplace phrase; see Shakespeare, *Troilus and Cressida* (IV.v.3), and Robert Herrick, 'The End', *Hesperides* (1648).

15. *'the secrets of the prison-house'*: *Hamlet*, I.v.13–16:

> But that I am forbid
> To tell the secrets of my prison house,
> I could a tale unfold whose lightest word
> Would harrow up thy soul.

16. *like Apollo shooting down from Olympus to pick up his forgotten lyre*: Apollo, god of music and song, plays the lyre at the banquets of the gods on Mount Olympus.

17. *one of our small lions*: An expression which derives from the practice of taking visitors to the Tower of London to see lions in the menagerie. The Tower menageries were abolished in 1834.

18. *'[Mister Sapsea] is his name . . .'*: A verse commonly used by children to indicate their ownership of books. Captain Cuttle, introducing himself to Toots, uses a similar rhyme (*Dombey and Son*, ch. 32).

CHAPTER 19

Shadow on the Sun-Dial

1. *Shadow on the Sun-Dial*: This was originally Chapter 18, but Dickens decided, after he had written two MS pages of 'A Settler in Cloisterham' (which was then Chapter 19), that the positions of the two should be reversed. There were no excisions from the proofs of this chapter.

2. *city kennels*: Gutters carrying sewage either down the centre or along the margins of the road.

3. *in deep mourning*: Victorian funeral practices recognized degrees of mourning, each of which was signalled by the appropriate use of colours and trimmings. For deep mourning one dressed entirely in black; black lace,

ribbons, buttons and other useless accessories were required for women mourners.

4. *If anything could make his words more hideous*: Jacobson (pp. 156–7) notes the possible influence in this scene of the Archdeacon of Notre-Dame's declaration of passion to Esmerelda, alone and helpless in her prison cell (Victor Hugo, *The Hunchback of Notre Dame*, 1831).

5. *a rival of my lost boy*: The MS reads: 'I charge him with the murder of my lost boy. I was slow of belief at first, but the circumstances [undecipherable] aloud is against him, and I fully believed'. Noted by Cox but not in Cardwell.

6. *as certainly as night follows day*: Proverbial.

CHAPTER 20

A Flight

1. *A Flight*: The Number Plan lists three alternatives: <'let's talk.'>, <Various Flights>, and Divers Flights. Forster chose 'A Flight' when he divided the chapter in two (see below). All subsequent editions of the novel bear this title except for Cox's 1974 Penguin edition which retained Dickens's single chapter and used 'Divers Flights'.

2. *for what could she know of the criminal intellect . . . a horrible wonder apart*: Dickens frequently asserted the superiority of his knowledge of 'the criminal intellect' over that of lawyers, prison officers and policemen. Titles in his library reveal a range of books devoted to criminology; in his fiction and journalism, he repeats his belief in a species of criminal who have 'no heart'. See the description of Rigaud in *Little Dorrit* (1.11), 'The Demeanour of Murderers' (*HW* 13, 14 June 1856, pp. 505–7; Pascoe, pp. 476–81) and the Introduction.

3. *The fascination of repulsion*: A variant of Dickens's frequently used phrase, 'the attraction of repulsion'. For its origin and *locus classicus* in Dickens's work, see Rick Allen, 'John Fisher Murray, Dickens, and "The Attraction of Repulsion"', *Dickens Quarterly* 16 (1999), pp. 139–59.

4. *over the housetops*: A literal description; trains were carried into central London over a series of viaducts. Elsewhere, Dickens exploited the figurative possibilities of being whisked by rail over streets, market-gardens, dust heaps and waste ground by a train departing from the London Bridge terminus and bound for Paris via Folkestone. See 'A Flight' (*HW* 3, 30 August 1851, pp. 529–33; Pascoe, pp. 137–45).

5. *Hiram*: The name of the King of Tyre; derived from the Hebrew, it means

'my brother is high'. A popular given name in England from the seventeenth century.

6. *a cab*: A hackney cab, a two-wheeled vehicle drawn by a single horse.

7. *music playing here and there*: Mid-century London was a noisy place, beset by a variety of street musicians, whose string, percussion, wind and mechanical instruments became increasingly annoying to residents.

8. *'Confound his politics!'*: From Henry Carey's 'God Save our Gracious King', first published anonymously in his *Harmonia Anglicana* in 1742. The second stanza reads:

> O Lord our God arise,
> Scatter his Enemies,
> And make them fall;
> Confound their Politicks,
> Frustrate their Knavish Tricks,
> On him our Hopes we fix,
> God save us all.

9. *There are some other geniuses . . . who have also written tragedies*: An allusion to the Syncretic Society, a group of aspiring dramatists whose unacted dramas theatre managers, in deference to the monopoly held by the patent theatres, refused to produce. Jacobson (p. 161) notes that Bazzard's inflated idea of his own talent and his sense of injustice (as related by Grewgious) echo the aggrieved assertions of Dickens's friend R. H. Horne in his *A New Spirit of the Age* (2 vols., 1844).

10. *the hotel*: Wood's Hotel; see Chapter 11, note 13.

11. *the stairs are fire-proof*: Narrow streets and wooden buildings made London particularly vulnerable to fire, resulting in preventative measures that date back to the thirteenth century. The Great Fire of 1666 brought about a move to brick for building material, yet progress towards greater safety remained slow, with initiative left mainly to individuals. In the nineteenth century, insurance companies began to insure their premises against fire; fire offices equipped with fire fighters also became common, as privately initiated preventative measures increased. No central authority for fighting fires existed, however, until the passage of the Metropolitan Fire Brigade Act of 1865.

CHAPTER 21

A Recognition

1. *A Recognition*: Forster chose this title after he reinstated passages from the previous chapters deleted in proof in order to shorten the fifth number and make the sixth (unfinished) instalment conform approximately with the other five.

2. *I wished at the time . . .*: Deleted in proof to 'It was quite natural'.

3. *'Have you settled . . .'*: Deleted in proof to 'what must I be!'

4. *fag*: The term formerly used for junior boys in English public schools who acted as servants for seniors.

5. *'Am I agreed with generally . . .'*: Deleted in proof to 'favor us with your permission.'

6. *'I begin to understand . . .*: Deleted in proof to 'freely at your disposal.' Mr Grewgious's speech (' "There!" cried Mr Grewgious') is run on.

7. *his garden in the air*: Compare the nursery tale 'Jack and the Beanstalk', whose hero exchanges his poor mother's cow for a handful of beans which magically produce stalks reaching to the sky. Cox notes that this is one of the 'divers flights' of the original chapter 20. Before Forster split the chapter in two, it contained both this fanciful flight and Rosa's earlier entrance into London by train 'over the rooftops'.

CHAPTER 22

A Gritty State of Things comes on

1. *A Gritty State of Things comes on*: Originally Chapter 21 in the Number Plans, but changed to Chapter 22 when Forster gathered deleted material to make the new chapter, 'A Recognition'.

2. *and the neatest, the cleanest, and the best-ordered chambers*: According to Mamie Dickens, her father 'had some of the sailor element in himself': 'One always hears of sailors being so neat, handy, and tidy, and he possessed all these qualities to a wonderful extent. When a sea captain retires, his garden is always the trimmest about, the gates are painted a bright green, and of course he puts up a flag-staff. The garden at Gad's Hill was the trimmest and the neatest, green paint was on every place where it could possibly be put, and the flag-staff had an endless supply of flags' ('Charles Dickens at home', *Cornhill Magazine*, NS 4, 1885, p. 41).

3. *under the sun, moon, and stars*: Compare 'And lest thou lift up thine eyes unto heaven, and when thou seest the sun, and the moon, and the stars, even all the host of heaven' (Deuteronomy 4:19).

4. *London blacks*: Particles of soot or smut from coal fires.

5. *household gods*: Lares and Penates, the spirits who traditionally guarded the households of ancient Rome.

6. *like a seedsman's shop*: Seedsmen used small drawers to store split peas, various kinds of hulled grain, bird-seed and garden products for sale to the nurseryman or gardener.

7. *cot*: 'Hammock', derived from Hindi *khat*, meaning bedstead, couch or hammock.

8. *Mr Tartar doing the honors*: The passage beginning with these words and ending with Rosa's call to Helena, 'Helena! Helena Landless! Are you there?', is written in the MS on a slip pasted over the original. A partial reading of the latter by Cox is as follows:

There ministered to Mr Tartar . . . his servant in these chambers, a . . . with a shaggy red beard and whiskers . . . his big head . . . the conventional hair as with rays . . . appeared to be shining . . . pantaloons of canvas, with shoes of buff . . . when first seen by the visitors.

. . . Said Mr Tartar, 'He is a Triton.'

'Don't you mean a sailor?' said Mr Crisparkle . . .

'I don't indeed. He is a jack of all trades, but he was apprenticed to . . . [end of page].

9. *When a man rides an amiable hobby*: Compare Sterne, *Tristram Shandy*: 'so long as a man rides his hobby-horse peaceably and quietly along the king's Highway, and neither compels you or me to get up behind him, –, pray, Sir, what have either you or I to do with it?' (vol. 1, ch. 7).

10. *First Lady of the Admiralty*: Wife of the first Lord of the Admiralty, one of a board of seven 'Commissioners for Executing the Office of the Lord High Admiral'. Of these seven, three were usually naval officers, called 'professional' Lords, and four civilians, or 'civil' Lords. The board evolved early in the eighteenth century as a replacement for the office of the Lord High Admiral.

11. *I would sooner see you dead at his wicked feet*: Compare 'The curse never fell upon our nation till now . . . I would my daughter were dead at my foot, and the jewels in her ear! Would she were hearsed at my foot, and the ducats in her coffin!' (*The Merchant of Venice*, III.i.75–80).

12. *Southampton Street, Bloomsbury Square*: Southampton Street, named after the former Earl of Southampton and part of a site laid out in a series of squares during the Georgian reconstruction of this part of London. The street is conveniently close to Staple Inn.

13. *as I hever ham*: Not knowing whether or not to aspirate 'is simply a habit of ill-bred people everywhere throughout the three kingdoms. Nor is the plea of dialect any real excuse' (*The Habits of Good Society: A Handbook for Ladies and Gentlemen*, New York, 1860, p. 69).

14. *with gas laid on*: Use of gas for domestic lighting dates from the 1840s.

15. *The gas-fitter himself* . . . *under your jistes*: Compare entry 9 in the *Book of Memoranda*, ' "The gas fitter says Sir that he can't alter the fitting of your Gas in your bedroom without taking up almost the ole of your bedroom floor, and pulling your room to pieces. He says, of course you can have it done if you wish, and he'll do it for you and make a good job of it, but he would have to destroy your room first, and go entirely under the Jistes." ' According to Forster, this was a verbatim report from a servant at Tavistock House who, having conferred with Dickens on some proposed changes to his bedroom, 'delivered this ultimatum to her master' (Forster, 2.298).

16. *open as the day*: The simile is 'as honest as the day', or, proverbially, 'It is as clear as the day'.

17. *It is not Bond Street nor yet St James's Palace*: Bond Street, after its extension northwards to Oxford Street in the early eighteenth century, was a fine new street mostly inhabited by members of the nobility; St James's Palace is the oldest of London's royal establishments, but by the 1850s used only for ceremonial purposes.

18. *Mewses must exist*: Mews provided necessary accommodation for carriage and riding horses. Proximity to them, however, inevitably detracted from lodgings on account of the smell and sanitary problems created by a combination of manure and hot weather.

19. *Respectin' attendance; two is kep'*: Two servants to assist with the various household chores of cleaning and cooking.

20. *Words has arisen as to tradesmen* . . . *by the fire, or per the scuttle*: Mrs Billickin's practice is to take orders to tradesmen, not because she wants a commission for lodgers' purchases, but in order to preserve her freshly whitened doorstep from the boots of tradesmen who would call. Also she would either charge to keep the fire going or supply coal by the scuttle to be used at the lodger's discretion.

21. *Dogs* . . . *they gets stole*: 'Dog-buffers' made a living stealing dogs and waiting for owners to advertise and offer a reward for the recovery of their pets. If no word was received, the dogs were killed, their skins sold and their carcasses were fed to other stolen dogs.

22. *down the airy*: An obsolete form of 'area'; an enclosed, sunken yard which gave access to the basement, characteristic of Georgian and Victorian town houses.

23. *But commit myself to a solitary female statement, no, Miss!*: Prudence required that women living alone took precautions when advertising for lodgers.

24. *baronial way*: Peers sign only the name of their title.

25. *Temple Stairs*: A wharf originally used by the lawyers of Middle and Inner Temple giving them access to the Thames. The grounds of the Temple extended north from the river to Fleet Street.

26. *down by Greenhithe*: Formerly a village on the south bank of the Thames, almost seven miles short of Gravesend and approximately twenty-two miles east of London Bridge.

27. *image of the sun in old woodcuts*: Traditional representations portray the sun with a round, jolly face from which radiates beams of light.

28. *to whom shoes were a superstition and stockings slavery*: Sailors commonly went without shoes while at sea, making footgear uncomfortable to their hardened soles.

29. *its dark bridges*: Returning from their excursion upstream, the rowing party would have passed under as many as five bridges (Hammersmith suspension bridge, Vauxhall, Westminster, Hungerford suspension bridge and Waterloo) on their return trip to Temple Stairs.

30. *not Professed but Plain*: That is, a 'good plain cook', the common phrase used to advertise for cooks as opposed to professionally trained chefs familiar with foreign dishes.

31. *the Mill I have heard of, in which old single ladies could be ground up young*: An allusion both to the frequency of accidents common among women operating machinery in cotton mills and to the popular song, 'Manchester's Improving Daily':

> 'The spinning-jennies whirl along,
> Performing strange things, I've been told, sir,
> For twisting fresh and making young
> All maids who own they're grown too old, sir.'

32. *a lamb's fry*: 'The product of lambs' castration' (*OED*).

33. *killing-days*: Before refrigeration, the killing date was an important index to freshness.

CHAPTER 23

The Dawn Again

1. *a hybrid hotel . . . behind Aldersgate Street, near the General Post Office*: Aldersgate Street, formerly a main entrance to the City from the north, is the northern continuation of St Martin's-le-Grand, a wide street which extends south to Cheapside and Newgate Street. In the nineteenth century the General Post Office (built in 1829) occupied the whole east side of St Martin's-le-Grand. No single original has been verified of the several small hotels which flourished in the vicinity, a new kind of establishment offering accommodation to the increasing number of passengers who travelled by rail as trains gradually eclipsed horse-drawn coaches during the century. In 'Lively Turtle' Dickens mentions one known to him: 'I go to Mrs Skim's Private Hotel and Commercial Lodging House, near Aldersgate Street, City . . . and there I pay, "for bed and breakfast, with meat, two and ninepence per day, including servants"' (*HW* 2, 26 October 1850, pp. 97–9; Pascoe, pp. 414–15).

2. *the new Railway Advertisers*; The practice of advertising accommodation, products and services dates from 1839 when George Bradshaw introduced his first railway guide. Issued monthly from 1841 and popularly known as *Bradshaw's Railway Guide*, this and similar publications were an important resource for travellers. In addition to providing timetables of trains to all parts of Britain, *Bradshaw's* included information about locations, costs and facilities offered by numerous hotels. It ceased publication in 1961.

3. *a pint of sweet blacking*: 'Blacking', a form of liquid shoe polish; 'sweet blacking' is slang for poor quality wine or porter.

4. *many true Britons . . . except in the article of high roads, of which there will shortly be not one in England*: A common lament among those who prized their social superiority and deplored the levelling spirit of the age. Rail travel in particular, which was soon to eclipse coach travel, was thought to promote an unwelcome mixing of the classes. Scenes which register reactions to this change occur in *Great Expectations* (ch. 29) and in Disraeli's *Sybil; or The Two Nations* (2.11).

5. *cabbage-nets*: A small net used to boil cabbage which is suspended over a large pot or copper.

6. *'Died of what, lovey?'*: Initially, Jasper answered, 'Not of what we take. Death. I'm out of sorts. Get to work. Get to work.'

7. *the all-overs*: A common expression for an indefinite feeling of unease.

8. *I did it over and over again*: The phrasing resembles part of a MS passage

dropped from *Our Mutual Friend* in which Bradley Headstone repeatedly rehearses his murderous attack on Eugene Mortimer: 'But he must be up and doing. He must be ever doing the deed again and again, better and better, with more and more of precaution, though never in a swifter way' (Michael Cotsell, *The Companion to Our Mutual Friend*, 1986, p. 261).

9. *when it was really done, it seemed not worth the doing*: Compare 'If it were done when 'tis done, then 'twere well / It were done quickly' (*Macbeth*, I.vii.1–2).

10. *'Time and place are both at hand'*: Lady Macbeth (I.vii.51–4) says,

> Nor time nor place
> Did then adhere, and yet you would make both.
> They have made themselves, and that their fitness now
> Does unmake you.

11. *But she goes no further away . . .*: This and the next two paragraphs are written on a slip of paper pasted over the original MS. Legible underneath is written: ' "So far, I might a'most as well have never found out how to set you talking," is her commentary; "you are too deep to talk too plain, and you hold your secrets tight, you do!" '

12. *buy bread within a hundred yards, and milk as it is carried past her*: Street vendors in both commodities made these purchases an easy matter.

13. *grey-haired gentleman*: The first of two uncorrected slips; Datchery's hair is white.

14. *Mr Datchery . . . gives her a sudden look*: How Datchery knows of Jasper's opium habit is one of the unanswered questions of the novel.

15. *Which . . . it would be immensely difficult for the State, however Statistical, to do*: A satirical reference to the Victorian commitment to gathering economic and demographic data. In 1832 the Board of Trade created a Statistical Department to organize and publish information gathered on its behalf; two years later, the Statistical Society of London was established, committed to accumulating and arranging facts in such a way as to exclude opinion and theory and facilitate the development of general laws; in 1837, the civil registration of births, marriages and deaths commenced.

16. *Jacks. And Chaynermen. And hother Knifers*: Violence characterized London's East End and places of entertainment frequented by sailors and foreign seamen.

17. *the old tavern way of keeping scores*: The use of chalk scores by publicans to keep track of customers' accounts dates from the sixteenth century. 'On tick', or writing up with chalk a 'score', represented an account of credit given; when debts were paid the chalk score was erased.

18. *A brilliant morning shines . . .*: This paragraph and the following sentences represent the last lines Dickens wrote. Forster comments movingly in his *Life*:

On the 8 June he passed all the day writing in the Châlet. He came over for luncheon; and, much against his usual custom, returned to his desk. Of the sentences he was then writing, the last of his long life of literature . . . the reader will observe with a painful interest, not alone its evidence of minute labour at this fast-closing hour of time with him, but the direction his thoughts had taken. He imagines such a brilliant morning as had risen with that 8 June shining on the old city of Rochester. He sees in surpassing beauty, with the lusty ivy gleaming in the sun, and the rich trees waving in the balmy air, its antiquities and its ruins; its Cathedral and Castle. But his fancy, then, is not with the stern dead forms of either; but with that which makes warm the cold stone tombs of centuries, and lights them up with flecks of brightness, 'fluttering there like wings'. To him, on that sunny summer morning, the changes of glorious light from moving boughs, the songs of birds, the scents from garden, woods, and fields, have penetrated into the Cathedral, have subdued its earthy odour, and are preaching the Resurrection and the Life. (Forster, 2.414–15)

19. *the one great garden of the whole cultivated island*: Kent, traditionally known as 'the garden of England'.

20. *the Resurrection and the Life*: 'I am the resurrection and the life, saith the Lord: he that believeth in me, though he were dead, yet shall he live: and whosoever liveth and believeth in me shall never die' – the opening words of the burial service (*BCP*).

21. *Jasper leading their line*: The place of honour traditionally belongs to a choirboy.

22. *falls to with an appetite*: Below this line in the MS a flourish indicates the end of the chapter.

APPENDIX I

The 'Sapsea Fragment'

1. Forster, 2.370.
2. Cardwell, p. xxviii.
3. Charles Forsyte, 'The Sapsea Fragment – Fragment of What?', *The Dickensian* 82 (1986), pp. 12–26.

APPENDIX 2

The Number Plans

1. John Butt and Kathleen Tillotson, *Dickens at Work* (1968), p. 27.

APPENDIX 3

The Illustrations

1. Nonesuch, 3.748.
2. Jane R. Cohen, *Charles Dickens and His Original Illustrators* (1980), p. 220.
3. Further information on the illustrations may be found in the following: Cardwell, Appendix E: 'The Illustrations', pp. 238–43; Cohen, *Charles Dickens and his Original Illustrators*, pp. 210–20, 269–71; Robert Patten, 'Illustrators and book illustration', in *Oxford Reader's Companion to Dickens*, ed. Paul Schlicke (1999), pp. 288–93.

APPENDIX 4

Rochester as Cloisterham

1. Forster, 2.216.
2. Factual information in this Appendix is based on the following sources: G. Phillips Bevan, *Handbook to the County of Kent* (London, 1876); *Black's Handbook for Kent and Sussex* (Edinburgh, 1860); Colin Flight, *The Bishops and Monks of Rochester 1076–1214*, Monograph Series of Kent Archaeological Society, No. VI (Maidstone, 1997); Colin Flight, *The Earliest Recorded Bridge at Rochester* (Oxford, BAR British Series 252, 1997); Judith Glover, *The Place Names of Kent* (Rainham, 1982); Richard King, *A Handbook for Travellers in Kent and Sussex* (London, 1858 and 1868); Edwin Harris, *Local Historic Publications*, Nos. 1–23 (Rochester, [1896–1917]); R. W. Kidner, *The South Eastern and Chatham Railway* (Tarrant Hinton, Dorset, 1963); Ronald Marsh, *Rochester: The Evolution of a City and its Government* (Rochester, 1974); John Oliver, *Dickens' Rochester* (Rochester, 1978); Leslie Oppitz, *Kent Railways Remembered* (Newbury, 1988); *Rochester Cathedral*, A Pitkin Cathedral Guide

(Ditchling, 1994); Frederick Francis Smith, *A History of Rochester* (London, 1928); H. P. White, *A Regional History of the Railways of Great Britain:* vol. 2, *Southern England* (Dawlish, 1964); H. P. White, *Forgotten Railways*: vol. 6, *South East England* (2nd revd edn; Newton Abbot, 1987).

3. The city was in fact built on the lines of a Roman *castrum tertiatum*, a camp one third longer than it was wide. The area was enclosed with earthen ramparts and four gates opposite each other and nearly facing the cardinal points. The whole consisted of approximately 29 acres, the expanse required for an encampment of a Roman legion numbering, at that time, 6,500 men. It is thought that the Roman ramparts remained unchanged during the time of the Saxons and Danes until 1225, when Henry III surrounded the city with a wall built on the foundation of the Roman ramparts.

4. The evolution of Rochester's various names is more detailed than the summary above indicates. First recorded as 'Durobrivis' (with the emphasis on the first syllable) *c.* 730 and also as 'Dorobrevi' (with the accent on the second syllable) in 844, the name later changed owing to Bede's copying down the name *c.* 730 and mistaking its meaning to be 'Hrofis's fortified camp' (Old English: Hrofes caester). In this form Rochester developed from Hrofaescaestre *c.* 730 to Hrofescester in 811, to Rovescestre in 1086 and finally to Rochester in 1610 (Glover, *The Place Names of Kent*, p. 159). According to Smith, in the Roman military tables it was written 'Roibis', 'from which contracted, and with the addition of the word "ceaster" (derived from the Latin *castrum*), it was called "Rhoneceater", and by further contraction to Rochester' (*A History of Rochester*, p. 4). Compare the explanation offered by Colin Flight, who suggests that the later stages of the name reflect 'shifts in pronunciation and spelling under way during the eleventh century'. 'The "classical" tenth-century spelling was . . . *Hrofesceastre*; the usual twelfth-century spelling was *Rouecestre* . . . One possible trajectory [of many intermediate forms] would be *Hrofesceastre* > *Hrofeceastre* > *Rofesceastre* > *Rofescestre* > *Rouecestre*' (*Earliest Recorded Bridge*, pp. 15, 20).

5. *Black's Handbook for Kent and Sussex*, p. 29.

6. Ibid., p. 34.

7. Oliver, *Dickens' Rochester*, p. 113.

8. Edwin Harris, quoted in ibid., pp. 109–10.

9. In a cancelled MS passage in Chapter 9, Grewgious declines an invitation from Jasper to walk up to his rooms 'and refresh' on account of his not having enough time since he must use his horse and chaise 'to get across [to Maidstone] and catch the *new* railroad' (my italics); 'new' in this context refers to the recently inaugurated route from Maidstone to London. Among other details

in the novel which support anachronistically the later narrating time are contemporary allusions to Governor Eyre, Egypt, opium smoking, muscular Christianity, and so on. See Introduction, and the respective notes above.

10. White, *A Regional History of the Railways of Great Britain*, p. 38.

11. *Letters*, 7.460.

APPENDIX 5

Opium Use in Nineteenth-century England

1. Virginia Berridge and Griffith Edwards, *Opium and the People: Opiate Use in Nineteenth-Century England* (London, 1981), pp. xii–xiii, 63.

2. Jonathan Pereira, *The Elements of Materia Medica and Therapeutica* (3rd edn; London, 1853), 2.2122. Compare Samuel Crump writing in *An Inquiry into the Nature and Properties of Opium* (London, 1793), p. vi: 'Among the many daily articles employed in the practice of medicine, none are more frequently exhibited, none affect the human frame more powerfully, and few are oftener the subject of medical reasoning, than Opium.'

3. Berridge and Edwards, *Opium and the People*, p. 49.

4. *Confessions*, pp. 34, 35.

5. The resemblances also extend to Dickens, for whom childhood hardship and exposure to London's streets were equally defining experiences. In fact, Dickens much admired De Quincey's work and held his writings in high esteem throughout his life.

6. *Confessions*, pp. 36–7.

7. Berridge and Edwards, *Opium and the People*, p. 196. See also Virginia Berridge: the stereotype of opium dens found in Dickens's *Edwin Drood* and Oscar Wilde's *Picture of Dorian Gray* (1891) 'had little foundation in reality' ('Victorian Opium Eating: Responses to Opiate Use in Nineteenth-Century England', *Victorian Studies* 21, 1978, p. 460).

8. One expedition to the opium establishments in east London occurred on 31 May 1869 (Nonesuch, 3.727); writing to Sir John Bowring on 5 May 1870, Dickens also refers to going down to Shadwell for the same purpose 'this last autumn' (3.775). Compare James T. Fields, for whose benefit the first outing was arranged, who speaks of two expeditions 'made on two consecutive nights' under police protection. 'It was in one of the horrid opium dens that [Dickens] gathered the incidents which he has related in the opening pages of "Edwin Drood"' (*In and Out of Doors with Charles Dickens*, Boston, 1876, p. 105).

9. 'East London Opium Smokers', *London Society: An Illustrated Magazine of Light and Amusing Literature for the Hours of Relaxation* 14 (July 1868), pp. 68, 70, 72.

10. 'In An Opium Den', *The Ragged School Union Magazine* 20 (1868), p. 199.

11. 'East London Opium Smokers', p. 69; 'In An Opium Den', p. 199.

12. Berridge and Edwards, *Opium and the People*, p. 29.

13. 'East London Opium Smokers', p. 68.

14. Ibid., p. 72.

15. Ibid., p. 71.

16. *Confessions*, pp. 103, 33. De Quincey later returned to his thoughts about the dreaming faculty, originally intended as the never-finished sequel to his *Confessions*, in the first part of *Suspira de Profundis*, published in *Blackwood's Magazine* (March 1845).

17. Pereira, *The Elements of the Materia Medica*, 2.2109.

18. George Young, *A Treatise on Opium, Founded Upon Practical Observations* (1753), p. iv.

19. Alfred Swaine Taylor, *Medical Jurisprudence* (3rd edn; 1849), pp. 144, 152.

20. The adulteration of food received little attention until Friedrich Accum alerted both the public and the medical profession with the publication of his *Treatise* on *Adulterations of Food and Culinary Poisons* in 1820. Thereafter interest grew, helped, in part, by a series of mid-century articles in *The Lancet*. See Arthur Hill Hassall, *Food and its Adulterations: Comprising the Reports of the Analytical Sanitary Commission of 'The Lancet' for the Years 1851 to 1854 Inclusive* (London, 1855).

21. *Catalogue of British Parliamentary Papers, 1800–1900*: Health, General, Food and Drugs (Dublin, 1977), p. 121.

22. Benjamin Brodie, cited in *Our National Responsibility for the Opium Trade* (London, 1880), p. 11.

23. *The Friends of China; The Organ of the Anglo-Oriental Society for the Suppression of the Opium Trade* (London, 1875), p. 3.

24. *Our National Responsibility for the Opium Trade*, p. 12.

25. *The Opium Trade. Report of the Proceedings of a Conference at the City of London Tavern, London, November 13, 1874* (London, 1875), pp. 3, 5.

26. William H. Brereton offers a spirited polemic in his *The Truth About Opium* (London, 1882) against the gathering opposition to opium smoking. In particular, he dismissed claims made by members of the Anti-Opium Smoking Society as total propaganda, 'utterly preposterous, false, and artificial'. His three lectures, delivered at St James's Hall in London on 9, 16 and 23 February 1881, denied that the drug caused harm, and presented opium as a safe, relaxing drug, one that was introduced into China by the Arabs in

the ninth century and one that had been used since then without severe consequences. Smoking opium, he argued, was 'an infinitely milder indulgence' than ingesting it and far less detrimental to one's health than either alcohol or tobacco (pp. 233–4).

27. *The Opium Trade Report*, p. 3.

READ MORE IN PENGUIN

In every corner of the world, on every subject under the sun, Penguin represents quality and variety – the very best in publishing today.

For complete information about books available from Penguin – including Puffins, Penguin Classics and Arkana – and how to order them, write to us at the appropriate address below. Please note that for copyright reasons the selection of books varies from country to country.

In the United Kingdom: Please write to *Dept. EP, Penguin Books Ltd, Bath Road, Harmondsworth, West Drayton, Middlesex UB7 0DA*

In the United States: Please write to *Consumer Services, Penguin Putnam Inc., 405 Murray Hill Parkway, East Rutherford, New Jersey 07073-2136*. VISA and MasterCard holders call 1-800-631-8571 to order Penguin titles

In Canada: Please write to *Penguin Books Canada Ltd, 10 Alcorn Avenue, Suite 300, Toronto, Ontario M4V 3B2*

In Australia: Please write to *Penguin Books Australia Ltd, 487 Maroondah Highway, Ringwood, Victoria 3134*

In New Zealand: Please write to *Penguin Books (NZ) Ltd, Private Bag 102902, North Shore Mail Centre, Auckland 10*

In India: Please write to *Penguin Books India Pvt Ltd, 11 Community Centre, Panchsheel Park, New Delhi 110017*

In the Netherlands: Please write to *Penguin Books Netherlands bv, Postbus 3507, NL-1001 AH Amsterdam*

In Germany: Please write to *Penguin Books Deutschland GmbH, Metzlerstrasse 26, 60594 Frankfurt am Main*

In Spain: Please write to *Penguin Books S. A., Bravo Murillo 19, 1°B, 28015 Madrid*

In Italy: Please write to *Penguin Italia s.r.l., Via Vittorio Emanuele 45Ia, 20094 Corsico, Milano*

In France: Please write to *Penguin France, 12, Rue Prosper Ferradou, 31700 Blagnac*

In Japan: Please write to *Penguin Books Japan Ltd, Iidabashi KM-Bldg, 2-23-9 Koraku, Bunkyo-Ku, Tokyo 112-0004*

In South Africa: Please write to *Penguin Books South Africa (Pty) Ltd, P.O. Box 751093, Gardenview, 2047 Johannesburg*